Praise for *Where Dreams Descend*

"If you're looking for a spectacle of a read, look no further than *Where Dreams Descend*, which is so atmospheric you will feel like your world is sparkling." —*Bitch Media* (25 YA Novels Feminists Should Read in 2020)

"This is an intricate love song between the book and the reader, one expertly composed by a phenomenal author. Not only does Janella Angeles seamlessly weave together a fantasy where illusions seem to have more power than reality itself, but she executes each scene with the grace of a dancer gliding across the stage." —The Nerd Daily

"An absolute success . . . It met every expectation and more. This story was unbelievable and so much fun to read." —YA Books Central

"A sweeping, atmospheric debut, *Where Dreams Descend* by Janella Angeles is perfect for fans of *Caraval*." —The Young Folks

"A lush, captivating blend of *The Phantom of the Opera* and fresh, new magic . . . As the romantic tension ratchets up, so deepen the mysteries. Readers will ache for the next installment." —*Kirkus Reviews* (starred review)

"Readers will find themselves quickly immersed in this quirky, well-paced tale of danger, adventure, and magic. The enigmatic ending reassures fans that the mysteries have answers that are yet to be discovered, and that there is more to come in the second part of this Kingdom of Cards duology. Give this to those who enjoyed Cole's *Arcana Chronicles* or Powell's *Game of Triumphs* twosome." —*Booklist*

WHERE DREAMS DESCEND

KINGDOM OF CARDS, BOOK I

JANELLA ANGELES

PLAINVILLE PUBLIC LIBRARY
NEW YORK

Published in the United States by Wednesday Books,
an imprint of St. Martin's Publishing Group

WHERE DREAMS DESCEND. Copyright © 2020 by Janella Angeles.
All rights reserved. Printed in the United States of America. For information, address St. Martin's Publishing Group, 120 Broadway, New York, NY 10271.

www.wednesdaybooks.com

Map and interior illustrations by Rhys Davies

Designed by Anna Gorovoy

The Library of Congress has cataloged the hardcover edition as follows:

Names: Angeles, Janella, author.
Title: Where dreams descend / Janella Angeles.
Description: First edition. | New York : Wednesday Books, 2020.
Identifiers: LCCN 2019059154 | ISBN 9781250204356 (hardcover) |
    ISBN 9781250204363 (ebook)
Subjects: CYAC: Magic—Fiction. | Contests—Fiction. | Missing persons—
    Fiction. | Ability—Fiction. | Secrets—Fiction.
Classification: LCC PZ7.1.A566 Wh 2020 | DDC [Fic]—dc23
LC record available at https://lccn.loc.gov/2019059154

ISBN 978-1-250-20437-0 (trade paperback)

Our books may be purchased in bulk for promotional, educational,
or business use. Please contact your local bookseller or the Macmillan Corporate and Premium Sales Department at 1-800-221-7945, extension 5442,
or by email at MacmillanSpecialMarkets@macmillan.com.

First Wednesday Books Trade Paperback Edition: 2021

For the dreamers who rarely saw themselves in stories and on stages.
You belong in the spotlight. Never let anyone tell you otherwise.

DRAMATIS PERSONAE

Kallia. . . . The Star
Jack. . . . The Master
Demarco. . . . The Magician
Aaros. . . . The Assistant
Canary. . . . The Entertainer
Erasmus. . . . The Ringleader
Mayor Eilin. . . . The Judge

THE FAMILIES

The Alastors ▲
The Fravardis ▣
The Vierras ★
The Ranzas ◉

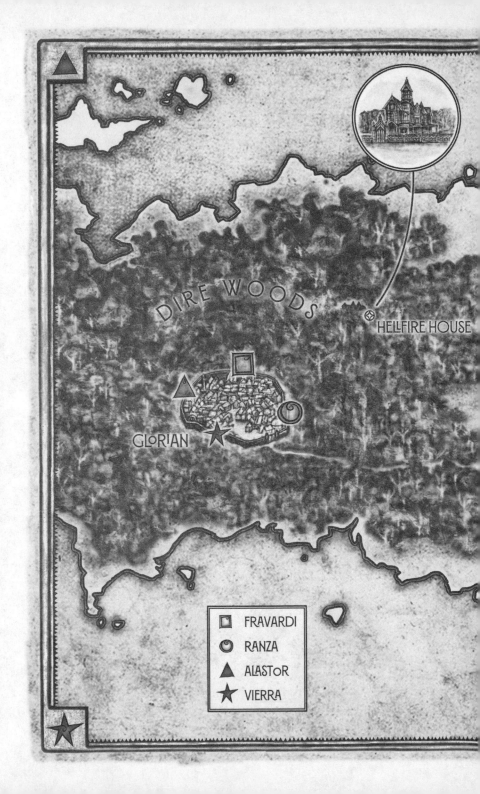

DIRE WOODS

HELLFIRE HOUSE

GLORIAN

□ FRAVARDI
◉ RANZA
▲ ALASTOR
★ VIERRA

Not all magic is good magic.

Few people can use it, even fewer are born to it. Since the closing of Zarose Gate, our world has toyed with the magic that poured into the air generations ago, turning the insignificant into the extraordinary. The human into the divine.

But even within the divine lies ugliness.

The disappearances of female magicians throughout the years is an ugliness that cannot be ignored, though others might try. Is this foul play by coincidence, or competition? The pattern is undeniable. The silence, deafening. In a world where men rule the stage of magic, it's been a public secret that any woman who dares rarely makes it into the spotlight. It's also an undeniable truth that the more others try to extinguish a flame, the greater its power must be. Why else destroy light if not envious of its radiance? Such speculation is not popular opinion, and thus, regarded as rumor. For in the world of magic, a woman's place lies in the quiet shadows of labor magic, the encouraged path. The safer one.

Because the ones who dare most often disappear.

—Lottie de la Rosa, "The Disappearing Acts,"
in issue #84 of *The Soltair Source*

Never come to Hellfire House without wearing a mask.

It was one of the rare rules in a joint without any. The only rule the master of the club did not mind following. He blended in with the sea of suits and white masks that arrived every other night, switching appearances from crowd to crowd. A bartender one moment, a dealer at the card tables the next.

Only his face remained the same, half-masked and haunting. Like a prince who relished the bloody crown on his head, and the ghosts that came with it. A face almost hardened by beauty, though glints of youth ran deep beneath soft black eyes. It always shocked new guests, to see him. The master of the House was rumored to be a dragon of a man. A monster. A magician who had no mercy for fools.

Only those who dared slur the word *boy* in his face understood how true those rumors were.

To the rest, he played the devil on all shoulders, leading patrons to his bar and game tables, guiding them toward his enchanted smoke lounge to drown in curated memories. The warmth of first love, the heady rush of triumph, the immense joy of dreams come true. The master kept a selection of sensations, and one hit of the pipes delivered magic the people came crawling to his house to taste.

They had no idea the show that was in store for them.

The master of the House sipped his short glass of scarlet whiskey in peace, tapping along the wide black strip over his brass knuckles. He'd long since manipulated his attire, sitting casually at a card table and savoring the mayhem. Raucous cheers erupted from the next table as dice rolled out across the surface. Smiling Hellfire girls in black blazers and masks of lace denied patrons begging for a dance. Loudest of all, the dealer's crisp shuffling of the black cards with teeth-white numbers before she doled out hands to players at the table.

"No, no more," one moaned. "I can't."

"Sure you can, chap." A young man in a white thorn-edged mask cheerfully pressed him back in his seat. "We can't leave. Haven't even finished your drink yet."

His drunken friend's mouth puckered under another gulp. "Think it's true, the drink? *Magician's Blood*, the menu said."

"Think you have power, now?" Thorn Mask laughed, leaning back to appraise the club. "Here, you take your magic where you can get it. You wear a mask. You flip a card, smoke a memory. Or you look up . . . at her."

The master's fingers tightened around his glass, just as the lights dimmed. Dancers cleared the floor under the hush of music, shifting from smooth, steady beats to a racing rhythm loud as thunderous applause.

Right on cue.

The band's worth of instruments he'd charmed for the night started up a wild entry tune of drums, the thick trill of trumpets. Chatter ceased and backs straightened as a beam of light speared toward the ceiling. A panel slid open over the dance floor.

And the chandelier descended.

Strings of crystals dangled along tiered rims of rose gold, cutting sharply into a jewel-set swing where a masked showgirl sat. A throne of glittering jewels, casting luminous lace across the walls and the ground and the audience taking her in. Her brown skin glowed against her corset, red as her gem-studded mask. Arms stretched out, she crossed and extended her legs in smooth lines all the way down, until her heels touched the lacquered black dance floor. With the hint of a smile, she rose from her throne and stalked forward, thrusting a hand up with a snap.

Darkness engulfed the room.

Hoots and hollers rang at the drop of the beat, before a glimmer of her form reappeared in the shadows. The room pulsed at her command, matching the spike of heartbeats the master sensed throughout the club.

The smirk on his lips mirrored the girl's as she arched her back to the raw stretch of the melody. She thrived under the attention, like a wildflower under the sun. A star finding the night.

His star.

"I'll be damned." The drunk at the card table breathed in awe, as the girl's palms began brightening with a molten glow. "Nothing like an academy girl."

"Worth the trip, right?" His friend clapped a hand on his shoulder.

"I didn't know they could be magicians like . . . *this*."

The master smothered a dark scoff under a sip of whiskey. The girl showed off good tricks—improvised and bettered from his basic crowd-pleasers. Treating the ceiling like a sky and showering comets from it, casting an elaborate shadow show of dancing shades over the floor, shifting every candlelight in the room to different colors to the beat of the music.

But always the performer, she preferred to be front and center. Teasing her power just enough to make the audience want more of her magic, more of her.

He wet his lips as flames shot from her hands, arcing over her head and around her body. The fire's melody bent to her every movement, and she gave everything to it. If she wasn't careful, she'd overexert herself like she did most nights, never knowing when to stop. How to pull back.

Careful never was her strongest suit.

Sparks fell before her, sizzling on the ground. Unafraid, she sauntered down her stage of flames with slow swaying hips and a firelit smile.

"Magicians like this are best kept a secret," Thorn Mask went on. "And besides, the work is far too scandalous for a lady. Only clubs will take them."

"What a shame. Imagine going up against the likes of her at the competition."

The master paused, drawing his gaze back to his glass.

"Not this again. That flyer was a joke." Thorn Mask slapped the table with a groaning laugh. "A prank."

The drunk sloppily patted around his coat, pulling from his breast pocket a dirty, scrunched ball of paper. "It's real. They're all over the academies, in Deque and New Crown and—"

"A *prank*," repeated Thorn Mask, unfolding the flyer anyway. "It has to be. No one's been to that city in ages, it would never open itself to such games."

"That makes it all the more interesting, don't you think?" As another roar of cheers erupted around them, the friend sipped his drink smugly. "Imagine if she entered, the city might implode."

"Right. As if that would *ever* happen." Thorn Mask leered. "Competition would eat a creature like her alive."

"Because she's . . . ?"

With an impish lift of his brow, the man in the thorny mask flicked the flyer off the table and returned to his forgotten spread of cards. "Let's get on with the game, shall we?"

Before he could gesture at the dealer, the master suddenly appeared behind their chairs, snatching the young man's wrist in a biting grip. The man yelped as the force knocked over his drink and sent a stream of hidden cards spilling out from his sleeves.

"What's this?" The master bent toward the ground and picked up a couple, entirely too calm. "Cheating in *my* house?"

The man froze, recognition dawning at the brass knuckles alone. "Where did you— I-I mean," he sputtered, patting frantically at his sleeve. "That's impossible. Those aren't mine, I swear."

"Then where did they come from?"

Sweat dripped from his temple, his face paler than the white of his mask. "I emptied my pockets at the door. Honest."

Honest. That was the best he could do? The master almost laughed.

"You want to know the price cheaters pay in my joint?" His question offered no mercy. Only deliverance, served on ice. "Memories."

"No, please!" The man's lip trembled. "I didn't, I-I'll do whatever you want!"

"This *is* what I want." The master rose from the table with the jerk of his wrist. The cheat flew to the ground in a gasp as he gripped at the invisible chain-like weight around his neck. Sharp, staccato breaths followed the master as he dragged his prisoner toward the smoke dens.

The man screamed, but no one heard him. No one saw, no one cared. All eyes fell on the star of the show as she searched for a dance partner to join her. The drunken friend, noticing nothing amiss, raised his half-full glass of Magician's Blood to his lips before waving his hand high like the others. The man thrashed harder, only to feel his cries smothered deeper in his throat. His form, invisible at the sweep of the master's hand.

With a disdainful glance, the master chuckled. "You're only making this more difficult for yourself. One memory won't kill you."

At once, the lights blinked around them and he paused. The air had grown still. Dim and hazy, as though locked in a dream.

He thought nothing of it until he caught the movements of the patrons—their arms raised and waving slowly, increment by increment. Their cheers dulled and stretched into low, gravelly roars, as if the sound were wading through heavier air. Against time itself.

"Where do you think *you're* going?"

The sound of her voice slithered around him, stopping the master in his tracks. The man quieted. Sweat soaked his pale face, his chest heaving. The showgirl stood in their path, every stare in the room still locked on the spotlit floor where she'd been. As though she'd never left.

Impressive.

Her red corset glinted as she cocked her hip and pointed at the man on the floor. "I choose him."

She could never let things be easy.

"Kallia," he growled, warning.

She smiled. "Jack."

"Pick another. He's a cheater."

Her lips pursed into a dubious line. "Then let me teach him a lesson. He'll no doubt prefer it more." She swung a leg over the man's prone form so she stood directly above him. Invitation dripped from the crook of her fingers. "The music calls, darling. Let's have ourselves a grand time."

The man's terror turned swiftly into awe, and he looked at her as if ready to kiss the ground she walked on. As soon as he took her beckoning hand, the room resumed its lively rhythm—a song snapped back in full swing. The cheers and hollers returned to their normal speed, exploding in delight as patrons found their lovely entertainer in their midst, her chosen dance partner in tow.

She bypassed the master, pressing a casual hand on his chest to move him. It lingered, he noticed. Unafraid, unlike most. Their gazes locked for a moment, their masked faces inches apart.

No one ever dared to get this close. To him, to her.

Only each other.

At the next round of cheers and whistles, she pushed him away, smug as a cat. Tugging the man close behind her, she sent fires onto the ground that illuminated her path and warned others from trying to follow them to the stage. Never once looking back at the master, even as he watched on after her.

His fist tightened, full of the cards from his earlier trick. They disappeared into mist, having served their purpose. Along with the flyer he managed to grab.

He didn't even bother giving it a read. It died in the fire caged by his palm. Tendrils of smoke rose between his brass knuckles, and when he opened his fingers, nothing but ash fell to the ground.

ACT I

ENTER THE MAGICIAN:
A PRINCESS WITH CLAWS WHO
WISHES FOR WINGS

The nightmare had returned, in flashes thick as flesh.

It began with gray-white skies above. Fell to fingers digging into rocky damp soil. *Kallia's* fingers. Her shallow breaths cut like glass as she crawled desperately back on her hands, away from something rising above her.

A monster.

Its looming shadow cast over her, coming for her.

No.

It rushed from her lips without sound, useless. Powerless. She reached within herself to summon fire and lightning and whatever unholy element she could to ward off the beast. But like always, she couldn't. Her powers abandoned her.

The shadow easily pursued, until the dark consumed her.

Kallia jolted awake, clawing at her blankets. The fabric singed beneath her fingertips, still smoking. Blackened by the drag of nails.

Her maids never said anything when they discovered the scorched bed. She had long stopped trying to hide it, simply left for her greenhouse as they did away with the evidence. No questions asked. The one good thing about being left alone in the House.

Her nerves relaxed as she pushed past the creaky glass door into a room bursting with color. Sweet, humid air clung to her. The morning light gleamed overhead, through the murky teal glass carved into translucent scales casing the walls and ceiling. She winced at the brightness, wishing she could crawl back to sleep. On mornings after a club night, the ache in her bones and muscles was fierce, an exhaustion she welcomed like a badge of honor. Some days were worse than others, demanding rest and recovery, but she couldn't go back to bed. Not when the creature in the dark waited.

In the brightness of the greenhouse, nightmares could not touch her.

Water trickled from her palm as she passed the plump orange roses with purple edges, speckled orchids standing tall as trees, deep blue moonflowers that glowed at night. Every time Kallia mastered a trick, Jack would present her with a small pouch of seeds. *Potential,* he'd called them. No hint of what each would grow to be, but they all earned a place in her proud collection once they bloomed.

The bushes of red roses big as heads for the first time she summoned fire.

A spread of peach tulip buds small as fingertips for pulling melodies from instruments.

Golden sirenias with jade hearts for manipulating metal and wood like clay.

It calmed Kallia to walk down the crowded path of her greenhouse, the one place in the House that belonged to her alone. The sight of every vibrant, living flower proved she wasn't powerless. That even dreams lied.

Sometimes it was enough.

The sun was still climbing the sky's dusky walls when Kallia finished watering. She scaled the vine-wrapped side of the greenhouse, muscles shaking even harder when she perched on the black rusted edge. The wind washed the rest of the dream off her. It whispered through her hair and her nightgown, around her bare legs that dangled more than twenty feet in the air.

It felt good to be as far from the ground as possible. It gave her a perfect view of the thick spread of treetops, dark spires under the sun's slow rise and the morning mist between. The Dire Woods went on for mile after mile in every direction, wrapping around a wall enclosure just beyond. Even from this distance, the imposing black gates of rectangular shapes jutted up clearly from the rimmed enclosure. A few vast silhouettes peeked from behind. Buildings like mountains that could've been manors. Proud, jutting towers like the tops of palaces. Every hint, merely puzzle pieces in the distance.

The city, Kallia knew, as Glorian.

She could've spent hours staring. The Dire Woods extended like a vast ocean between them, yet it was the closest city on Soltair to Hellfire House. The only one, it sometimes seemed, in their lonely half of the island. Jack had spoken of other cities in the far east, and a sea surrounding them. Kallia wished one day to see it for herself. But every time she'd mentioned Glorian, Jack's easy smile faded. "Glorian is not the sort of place for people like you and me," he'd said.

"And why not?" Kallia bristled at his lie. He thought he carried a good poker face, but the playful glint in his eyes had iced over.

"They're not exactly welcoming to show magicians."

"What about labor magicians? I could pass as one, then work my way up. I mean honestly, *all* the customers—"

"Trust me, firecrown, that place isn't worth it." Jack leaned in close, tucking a fallen strand of hair behind her ear. "Besides, what more could you want that isn't already here?"

More.

More than a stage she owned only for a night. More than a mask without a name.

Jack knew all of this, of course. And unsurprisingly, his refusals and warnings only heightened her curiosity. She'd asked so many times about the faraway city, even went to one of her private tutors after Jack demanded she never bring it up again. But even Sanja—who'd memorized encyclopedias and contained an endless well of knowledge at the ready—had sputtered out nonanswers.

When Sanja left her tutoring position soon after—for no one lasted long at the House—Kallia's questions simply sat inside with her desires. Unspoken, unheard, but alive.

The breeze picked up, tickling the hem of her nightgown until it rippled against her legs. She nearly shivered from the sudden cold, but the sight of Glorian stilled her. Forbidden fruit to her eyes. She imagined dropping from the roof and walking through the Dire Woods barefoot just to reach it. She craved to know more. Something. *Anything.* For whatever waited in the unknown, it called to her.

As though it wouldn't stop until she called back.

Kallia finally tore her gaze away, stretching her arms in a languid arch above her head. The morning chill dissolving into warmth over her skin from the rising sun.

She didn't have much time left before Jack sent someone to fetch her.

Gripping one of the large roof shingles fitted slightly askew in the layout, Kallia loosened the stiff plaque from its place. There wasn't much space underneath, only enough for a few pretty leaves, a lone tattered ribbon that had come to her in the wind, and her most guarded treasure: the thin, soiled cloth of a stitched burgundy rose in full bloom. From far away, it was an insignificant thing, hardly big enough to fill her palm. But up close, it was no ordinary stitching. The threaded petals moved and curled to a subtle breeze.

She'd stolen it back from Jack after his father died. The former master of the House. It was her only proof of a life before this, a small scrap tacked onto the lining of her bassinet when she'd been left in the Woods. From where and by whom, she had no answers. She'd been too young to question, until eventually, whenever questions rose, they were met with Jack's silence.

Kallia pressed at the rose's outline—a garden's heart, forever in full bloom. As always, she held it close before placing it back in its safely hidden grave in favor of another.

The last of her collection: a crumpled piece of paper she'd folded thin enough to slide in. For its own good, and hers.

She unfolded the tattered flyer: a black top hat was inked at the center of the page, with words printed below in lettering bold and curved like a petal. Most of the message was mangled. A dream broken up into pieces, longing to be chased.

The Conquering Circus presents . . .

Competition

Magicians

Glorian

To Kallia, the cold of the wooden dance floors had always been the best place for plotting.

A magician's competition.

In Glorian.

It's all she'd wanted for so long, she must've willed it into existence. And if she couldn't resist the chance to win the game, neither could Jack.

"Would you *stop* looking at yourself in the mirror already?" Mari lay flat on the polished turquoise floor. She lifted a small leg, stretching it back as far as it could go and switched to the next. "Your face will still be there, no matter how long you stare at it."

Kallia jostled the other girl. "I'm thinking," she said, still fixed on the walled mirror across. "Mistress Verónn always said those in search of answers would be one step closer to finding them after an honest look in the mirror."

"Well Mistress Verónn is long gone. Thank Zarose, my legs would've probably split apart from any more of her high-kick practice regimes." Mari shuddered, turning over onto her belly. "What sort of answers *are* you looking for?"

Kallia looked away, picked at the strap over her shoulder. She had to be careful with Mari. The two had become fast friends in the few months since she'd arrived to join the Hellfire girls, but Kallia never pushed into personal territory. It was safer. She'd learned the hard way with Sanja, who'd trained her to fight for the last word and wage war with wit. And Mistress Verónn, who'd first taught her to dance, to seize a spotlight in the dark and raise roaring applause where there was silence.

They'd both left so suddenly for other pursuits. No good-byes, no promises of visiting. Her heart couldn't bear that ache again.

If one friend could stay, that would be enough.

"Nothing important." Kallia splayed out her legs on either side of her. "Keep stretching. You still have morning warm-ups."

"And you've got a lesson soon."

"They're not lessons. It's practice."

Lessons indicated he was her teacher, levels above her in every way when he was only showing her tricks to add to her repertoire. Even after several years, she didn't know what to call their arrangement, but teacher and student felt too small a mold for what they were together.

Mari rolled her eyes. "Whatever it is, he'll be expecting you soon."

"He thinks I'm wandering around in the greenhouse. I've got time."

The master didn't like being kept waiting, but Kallia didn't care. The flyer fluttered in her thoughts, each time she blinked. She wasn't sure what a Conquering Circus was, only that she wanted to know more. To see it for herself.

She couldn't ask Mari about it. Definitely not the House staff, all so loyal to Jack they might as well call him their god rather than their master. Even maids who'd spent years drawing baths and laying out clothes for Kallia kept the safe distance of an acquaintance. Such loyalties ran in only one direction.

How to get the master to run in hers posed the challenge.

"Actually, I'm thinking of skipping today's lesson," Kallia de- clared. Limbs loose and sufficiently stretched, she pulled her legs together and rose, agile as a cat. "The mornings *are* mine, after all. I deserve every last second."

"The rest of this place doesn't deserve his foul mood whenever you break schedule." She sighed. "I'm already dreading warm-up. It's always silent as a cemetery."

It was early enough that the other Hellfire girls had yet to join them in the practice room. Mari, the youngest of the dancers, craved conversation and could hardly stand their quiet focus. Hearing four words out of them was considered a sociable practice, and more than Kallia ever achieved. Aside from Mari, none of them talked to her, and Kallia repaid them in kind. There was only room for one dancer on that descending chandelier, and Mistress Verónn had always told her to never be ashamed of it. Of her power, and the place it earned her in the House. With Jack.

Kallia glanced at the instruments laid out along the mirrored walls. The practice room possessed a smaller collection than what was played at the club. Different types of stringed instruments, some drums, flutes varying in shapes and metals. She grinned at them, old friends. "What shall we play today?"

"Save your energy," Mari deadpanned, though her slight press forward betrayed her interest. "Go to your lesson."

Without turning, Kallia aimed the first tune to pop into her head at the instruments—a light birdlike jig infused into the flutes. An easy task that hardly tugged at her insides. Magicians like her and Jack, powerful as they were, did not possess an endless well of magic as others might believe. Jack always nagged at her to slow down, for some tricks packed more muscle than others, but ultimately they all succumbed to her. And there was no greater satisfaction.

"Show-off," muttered Mari, despite her toes tapping along to the beat.

Kallia bit back her smile as cheery music filled the morning air.

"I'm *proud* of my talents." She gave a full body twirl. Her hair floated off her shoulders, sweeping close to her neck. "No shame in—"

"Starting without me, firecrown?"

The music hitched.

Kallia halted, eyes on the mirror. Behind her, leaning against the door, Jack managed to make even crossing his arms look regal. His gaze wandered lazily over the scene, before finally landing on her.

Firecrown.

She recalled the first time he called her that.

"Have you ever seen a firecrown?" he'd asked, amused at the disappointed shake of her head. "They're rare night birds, red as rubies, and they don't let you forget it."

And so the nickname stayed, glinting in her ears brighter than any jewelry on her neck each time he spoke it. Sometimes the way he said the name was like a caress, a hot breath. Even now, from across the room, the words brushed over her skin.

Mari immediately rose to her feet. "Oh, sorry . . . I-I'll just," she stammered, a common reaction in Jack's presence. "The other girls will be here soon. For practice."

"It'll be best if you all meet in the clubhouse today instead."

At the dismissal in his reply, Mari scampered out of the room. Not without a quick, cautioning glance over her shoulder. *Be good.*

Kallia rarely heeded warnings around Jack. It was why he enjoyed her company so much. She wasn't one to jump at the sound of the door closing behind her. Nor did she stiffen at the swift *click* of the lock pushing into place.

She sighed. "You didn't have to scare her off."

"I merely gave a suggestion. Not my fault if she took it."

She turned, and the smaller room suddenly stretched into a sea of cold space between them. Empty, distracting. "We never take our lessons here."

Jack's fingers traced the door frame. "A change in scenery never hurts."

"Well, you're early." She yawned to cover the thudding of her heart. "Noon bell hasn't even rung. You may have kicked my friend out but I have a few more moments to myself."

The trill of music leapt to a different chord. Jack stalked forward, slowly, holding her gaze in the mirror. "Are you . . . angry with me?"

Good. If he believed that, perhaps he would be in a mood to please her.

He came up behind her, his chest pressing at her back. The heat of him worked into the thin fabric of her leotard as his chin touched her ear. "What's bothering you?"

Her lips raised at the corners, while his fingers wrapped around her arm. His signature black brass knuckles he kept on both hands brought a coolness to his touch. She fought the rise in her chest, focusing on the staggering tune of the flutes. It was all but impossible the moment the pads of his fingers turned hot, like small bites of fire running down her skin until his hand fell into hers.

"Tell me." Jack nudged her, his grip warmer. "So I can fix it."

Kallia turned, lifting her chin for a good look at him. Proud nose set between bold eyes, gleaming with charm at his best. Shadows at his worst. There was something naturally disarming about his face. Unlike his father. Sire, the staff had called him. A reclusive benefactor who took pity on a child left in the Woods. A girl who knew nothing of him, only the walls and silence of his domain. So much silence, she'd talk to her reflection just to speak sometimes. Not like Sire ever tried, always keeping to his rooms, sick with missing his son who lived on the other side of Soltair. All her life, it was like competing with a ghost, some rare creature others spoke of but had yet to be sighted. Based on her rare glimpses of Sire, she'd often imagined Jack's face to be all cruel edges or wrinkled with age, too. A stranger's face. A monster's.

She had waited so many years to punch it—had slipped on all her sharpest rings just for the occasion on the night Sire had finally passed away. She'd felt no grief for the stranger who'd taken her in.

But when it was announced his prodigal son would be returning, she armed herself. Prepared.

Her chance to finally leave, once and for all.

When she saw him waiting at the bottom of the stairs, he was not at all how she'd pictured him. Nothing like his father. More a young man than a master, built tall and sharp-muscled by the fit of his suit. A jaw that could cut glass defined his face, handsome even in its frozen expression as he studied her just the same.

Rather than take his gentle, outstretched palm, she balled her fist and aimed straight for his smooth brow.

He'd caught it with a smile, brass knuckles poised over hers. "Kallia."

"Bastard." A seething breath burst from her. No matter how hard she pushed or pulled, his touch stilled hers. "*Who* are you?"

And how had he stopped her? None of her tutors had been able to. Her rage burned past the skin. Smoke rose from beneath his brass knuckles covering her hand, fire bottled in her palm. The blood in her veins.

Unflinching, his gaze met hers through the smoke. "We're not so different, you and I," he mused. "Such power."

"And I'll use it," Kallia growled. "Those basic tutors all but ran the moment I mastered their tricks. Easily."

"I've heard." The edge of his lips curled, as if he knew this song all too well. "What a privilege it is, to be capable of what we can do. To be taught—"

"To be trapped."

She scoffed hard, but he only assessed her more intently. "Then why haven't you left? You never once came at Sire with your fists, or was that honor for me alone?"

What a strange way to talk about his father, whose corpse was not even in the ground yet. "How do you know I didn't?" she bit out, a lie. Sire rarely left his rooms enough for her to even hiss in his direction so much as fling a punch. "How do you know I wasn't biding my time, learning all that I could to destroy this place when it finally suited me?"

Like tonight. She flared warning fire across her fist, so suddenly that Jack's grip wavered. Still, he didn't let go. "How would you like to know more?"

Abruptly the room blushed deep scarlet.

Their shadows, dark as blood on the walls.

With the flick of his free hand, the world was no longer red. The candles flared to a royal purple, shifting from cold blue to warm hues at the twirl of his finger. Begrudgingly, Kallia glanced around, her skin chilling and rising in wonder. How different the world became under all manner of colors. Full and alight.

Alive.

"That's why you're still here, isn't it?" he said, restoring the candles' natural light. Watching her. "Somehow, you knew there was more to magic than having it. There's always more, and you look like you want it."

Kallia said nothing. Only glared in the way she'd practiced so often in the mirror, to ensure nothing about her faltered. But the force of his gaze stole her fire. Stripped her entirely, until even her heartbeats whispered pain throughout her chest. *Yes, yes, yes.*

He loosened his grip, stepping back. "The House is mine now, and I'll give you a choice. You can leave, but you'd soon see there's not much out there for female magicians. Your power's not what Queen Casine's Academy is used to, but they'd take you. Mold your magic for a life of quiet work."

Kallia cringed. "How do I know you're not lying?"

"I wish I were. The world's become a bleak, unfair place, especially to those with the most power," he said, eyes narrowing. "The most potential."

The truth gnawed at Kallia. All her tutors had hesitated at her aptitude for learning. For her power. They'd gather small cloths for her to embroider delicately with magic, and she'd send the spools of thread ribboning in the air, weaving each colorful strand into a braid that filled the room. They'd give her lessons to levitate ingredients into stews and bread, and she'd come out of the kitchen with dishes that danced and flew off their plates like birds.

Kallia couldn't bear a life of quiet work. "What's the other choice?"

That had been a few short years ago, enough time to change how she thought of the House. Of Jack and his presence, which held a power that called to her. A likeness that drew them together.

The kind that pulled at the strings between them, now guiding her to his chest until their bodies pressed. Heartbeats met.

Hers ran rapidly.

His, slow and taunting.

The low noon bells tolled heavily through the thick walls of the practice room. Kallia could barely hear them as her music changed. The air dipped under the new weight of a slow, dark melody—heavier stringed instruments, shrouding the room in nighttime even as daylight brightened the windows.

"Morning's over, Kallia." Jack spoke just above her ear.

She steadied her breath, stared at her palm now within his. Her fingers slender and bare; his, armored as if ready for war. It was unfair, the way he slid her hand to his neck, already leading her in a dance before they'd even moved.

Sometimes he'd join her in the practice room, just like this. Sweeping her into a dip, their chests flush and rumbling with surprised laughter. Raising her in a full lift easily as water holding her to the surface. She enjoyed when dance became a spontaneous language between them. But she hated how he would always lead, finding an upper hand wherever he could.

This time, it would be hers.

Kallia cocked her head. "Show me something new, then."

It was unclear who moved first. Their steps never belonged to a formal dance of rules and manners. Theirs were born from the rhythm, impossible not to follow. To feel a thread pulling, pulling,

pulling until there was hardly space in between. No room for compromise.

Jack's eyes lit with purpose as he pressed forward. "Look in the mirror." He nudged his chin to the closest panel. "What do you see?"

She saw the two of them in the practice room, close. Entwined. "Just us."

"Are you so sure?"

Kallia blinked at her reflection.

Smoke filled the room. Gradual and sheer as a gray veil, until it swarmed and blackened the entire space. An omen spreading its wings. Bright orange flames splintered through the darkness. A flicker, before the smell. The heat.

Fire.

The blaze crackled in her ears, drowning out her thundering heart.

Get out. The warning sliced through her and she tried pulling away, but the flames encircled them. Trapped them—

The mirror cracked in veins across the panel surface.

"Enough, Kallia."

Her breath hissed as she pulled back. Jack lifted her left palm up, thumb pressed to her wrist. "Your pulse is racing. You believed it."

Kallia's panic dropped cold. She turned from the broken mirror to the rest of the room—finding it unharmed, the air clear.

An illusion.

She swallowed down a hard knot. "You messed with my mind?"

"With the mirror," he reassured. "What I see in the mirror is what you see, to a point. The objective pieces of the picture—the background, the floor, something as simple as a book in your hand—are easier to change than the mind. A basic illusion," Jack clarified. "Prey on trivial details that don't matter, and then *make* them matter for the viewer."

"You could've warned me," Kallia snapped. She could stand the teasing and taunting, for she fought back with her own tools every time. But actual tampering of the mind crossed a line. There was no honor in a power that snuck into heads and told them how to think. "I thought we weren't doing those sorts of tricks."

Jack's smile fell. "Every trick is a manipulation, Kallia. Mirrors are merely another plane for it," he said. "What you see in any reflection is a world unto itself, one you can believe in because what you see aligns with what you know surrounds you."

"And it's not?"

"Some mirrors are like windows designed to be more convincing than others. You should always approach them with care. Always think first before trusting your reflection."

Kallia cocked her head. "If you haven't noticed, we have no shortage of mirrors."

He rubbed his thumb slyly beneath her palm as he guided them back to the center of the room. "Don't worry, firecrown, *my* mirrors are harmless."

His voice softened under a pleased laugh, but Kallia couldn't find it in her to join him. What was the point of giving her a glimmer of the dangers outside the House if she would never encounter them? To keep sharpening the blades, but never use them to fight?

"Now, I've held up my end," Jack said, the teacher gone. The master returned. "What's upsetting you?"

Glorian. The Conquering Circus. The competition.

The words threaded back into her thoughts, but the unease of his illusion sat in her like stone. "Don't do that." Her throat tightened. "You don't get to play with my mind and just . . ."

Kallia looked down—safe, away from her reflection—but Jack tipped a finger beneath her chin. "I'm sorry," he said softly, penitent. "Mirrors are those rare creatures that straddle the lines between mind, magic, and reality. There are tricks that require far more twisting, but they're very tedious. And I would *never* test them on you."

"Then what do you call this?"

The question hung around them, in the space between their lips.

Jack's brows pinched. Most times he held himself as if he'd lived a thousand years, but only rarely did he look his age. Only a little older than Kallia, she knew, though he'd never given her the specific number. Only looks, lessons, and dances.

And most important of all, knowledge.

"Are you going to teach me how, then?" Kallia stared back at their forms in the mirrors, the smooth panels shining whole before reaching the veined surface that broke them in pieces.

At the sudden squeal of strings, Jack lowered her into a dip, guiding her back up. "Something tells me your mind is still elsewhere."

Glorian.

The whole dance had been a charade to get there. He could've simply invaded her mind for answers, influenced her to spill her own guarded secrets. But not once, Jack always promised, had he ever used his magic on others in such a way. He dealt in memories, fleeting things often forgotten that were won and lost at his game tables, but not the actual puppeteering of one's mind and actions. He wasn't one for empty-eyed dolls; he preferred those who came to him to be very much alive and aware of their choices.

Even after the mirror illusion, she believed him.

"Kallia," Jack prompted.

She blinked. Over the years, it hadn't taken long to find ways of seizing back the game, using whatever wiles necessary. "You're leaving soon. Like you do every year."

Reluctant, he played along. "To settle vendor accounts, yes?"

Not too fast, let it build. When they were face-to-face, Kallia dropped her hands before Jack could seize them—letting her fingers travel slowly, palms grazing the taut planes of his abdomen through his shirt, his chest.

"What if you didn't have to go alone?" she drawled, feeling his muscles stiffen on her way up. "You spend too much time by yourself, working. Even on your free days, you're off in your workroom packing smoking leaves and memories into pipes."

His eyes darkened. "What are you suggesting?"

Kallia hooked her leg around his waist, tilting her head with a sweet minx's smile. "I'll go with you."

"It's dry business, Kallia. You'd find it boring."

"We'll make it fun," she said slyly. "There's got to be more than just business beyond these woods. I hear there's a show happening in town."

The music spiked louder for a second.

Jack paused, and for a brilliant moment, Kallia thought she'd won. Heart racing and flushed, she waited, thumbing the edge of his shirt collar. His pulse jumped beneath it, before he pushed away her tight-clad thigh from his waist. "What town?"

"Glorian."

The room fell silent. His steps slowed, and Kallia nearly jerked at the hardness of the wall that met her back. Jack didn't press her into it, just lowered his head enough by hers that she shifted back on her own.

"Kallia." He breathed out like a warning. "You know very well we can't do that."

Most people would never dare be so close to the master of Hellfire House. It was like encountering a starving wolf in the woods. He fixated on the curve of her shoulder, her neck, her mouth—roving with a freedom, a hunger, as if each glance were a taste.

Channeling the wolf herself, her lips curled. "Why not? There's a circus in Glorian hosting a magician's competition. Are we not magicians?"

The words before were a spark to the flint; now, a douse of cold water. Jack withdrew the hands he'd caged over her head, tension roiling over him. "Where did you hear about this?"

"Some of the servants were gabbing about it in the kitchens." The lie flew easily from her. She'd grown adept at training lies into truths, fixing her expressions and the tone of her voice. But it was the skip in her heart she couldn't fix, and the corner of Jack's mouth turned as if he heard that loudest of all.

"They lied."

The flyer flashed in her head. "I know what I heard."

"Oh really?" His posture eased a fraction. "You heard, or you saw the message on the rooftop of your hideaway?"

An uncomfortable flush crept over Kallia's skin, little bumps bursting across her arms. Jack stared, as if admiring his handiwork. "The secrets you hold are louder than you think, firecrown. There's little anyone can hide from me in my own house."

Kallia had thought the same about her greenhouse—Jack had made her believe it.

But he knew her tucked-away secrets, and the betrayal for something so seemingly small stung harsher than she dared admit. "Then I guess you know what I want," she said. "To go to Glorian and have a look at the competition. Show magicians have a place there now, and you know I'm good enough." There was no chance he could doubt skills forged under his tutelage.

Yet quiet anger poured from his tight expression. "How many times must I tell you—"

"That Glorian is not the sort of place for you or me?" Kallia sneered. "That excuse is getting old, Jack."

"You can't lay out your powers on the show floor and just expect they'll take you." His eyes simmered. "Your audience here will not be the same as the one you'll find there. Out there, it'll be harder to protect yourself, and your powers will be vulnerable."

"Against what?" she seethed and pushed at him, breaking their hold. "I am *not* powerless."

"There are other ways to be powerless." Jack frowned, as if the possibility disgusted him. "You still have much to learn. You're not ready."

All of it came at her like a blow to her chest. "You think I'm any better off staying here, performing for drunks and learning tricks I'll never use?" One by one, dagger by dagger, she'd felt doubt before, but none like this. She wasn't going to just accept them. "If you won't throw me to the wolves, I'll find them eventually."

"You *want* danger?"

"I want more than this." It was like a breath releasing. A scream. "And I can't get that if I stay here." It was all he'd ever done, keeping her in place like a dance set to a song with no end.

"Don't forget. You chose this, firecrown." His voice curled over with a snarl. "You honestly believe you could walk into that barred city and come out with them bowing before you? You're too ambitious for your own good, Kallia."

"And what's so terrible about that? What do I have to be ambitious about *here*?"

"Here, I give you everything—knowledge every magician on this cursed land would kill to know." His eyes flashed. "Is that not enough?"

No.

It stilled on Kallia's tongue. The moment it was released, it could not be unsaid. But like her beating heart, Jack heard it in the silence, and it pulled a cruel laugh from him as he backed away. "Stay away from Glorian. Trust me. Only fools find their way there."

At the sight of his back, her throat tightened into a metal coil, cutting her inside.

"Better a fool than nothing," she bit out.

The instruments halted their song and crashed to the ground. Jack paused at the door. The muscles of his back shifted and tensed, but something stopped him from turning.

"You're *not* nothing . . . you're just not ready. And neither are they," he whispered, looking down at his brass knuckles. "Don't mention this again. I beg you."

3

I beg you.

Others begged, but not Jack.

The sound of it haunted Kallia into the next afternoon, a couple of hours away from Hellfire House's opening. Jack had not called on her again, not even to go over tonight's performance or warm up with exercises. He hadn't left his workroom all day, and even the House was beginning to notice.

"He's always got too much on his mind," said one of the kitchen ladies. Kallia crept by the archway, hidden in the shadows. Wherever she strutted, silence followed. The only way she could ever hear anything of truth was to hide.

"I'll say," a man interjected. From the slur of his voice, it was the groundskeeper. Always drinking well into the day. "You've heard what's happening in Glorian, haven't you?"

"Difficult not to," another tsked. "Some of the gents who visit won't shut up about it."

"You all better shut up as well, if you like your memories where they are." An older woman grunted, and they spoke no more. Kallia paused like the rest of them. Careful, even with Jack flights and rooms away.

She hated feeling just as delicate. Her fights with Jack never lasted long, but this one was different. It wasn't over an accident or bruised ego; this was something she wasn't sure could be fixed with mere words.

Kallia wasn't sorry, but the hardness inside her chipped away when she ventured to his workroom, only to find it unexpectedly empty.

Frustration reeled through her. It wasn't like them to not speak, especially when he was about to depart for his trip. It wouldn't be for long, yet Kallia couldn't let him leave like this.

The door to his bedroom was the most beautiful of the House. Each one was carved and crafted like portals to different worlds. Wooden frames and panelings all soaked in a burgundy wine shade, designed with dramatic shapes that told stories across the archway. A forest of blooming trees over one door, scrolls of sheet music with sprawling notes over another. Kallia's door possessed an archway of wooden birds in flight studded with gems across their wings.

Jack's door frame rose tall, cased in black glass.

The farthest she'd ever gone. Each time she'd ever reached for the doorknob, he'd somehow been the first to open it. She'd had no problem avoiding it before when the room had been occupied by Sire, who'd hardly ever left his bed. At first Kallia had found it strange how Jack had settled into the room his father had withered away in, but she never questioned him. Having never known grief, Kallia couldn't judge how it manifested.

For the first time, Kallia raised her fist over the surface and no one answered. Before she could knock, muffled noises burst from the other side. A gruff, heated curse on someone's lips.

"I won't be blamed for this. I've done my part *every* damn year."

Jack. With someone, though Kallia was certain no guest had

passed through the entrance today. She couldn't quite hear the response, but Jack's scoff was clear.

"That won't happen. Of course she's not going."

Her. They were talking about her. Kallia's heart thudded as she
leaned closer against the door, worried the slightest creak would give
her away.

"I was set to depart in a few days, but I'll leave tonight."

Kallia strained to hear what the other person said, but it was a
gravelly murmur too soft to reach her.

"No, it'll be quick. Always is."

She flinched back at the sound of his feet, suddenly pacing, and
nearly turned away to the wall—

"I never stay in Glorian longer than I need to."

She froze, the air so quiet around her that it felt like a mockery.
The words echoed again and again, the nausea twisting her stomach.
Punching her heart with loud, brutal beats. Each hit against her
chest, a realization.

Every year, once a year.

Not to vendors across Soltair.

To Glorian.

Ice entered her, fury following. She had to know who else was in
that room. Her fingers trembled as she grasped the knob and shoved
the door open.

Shards of a smashed glass scattered the floor, the room warm
and barely lit except by the windows at the wall swathed in gray, a
mirror hanging in between. And there was only Jack, looking at his
reflection before whirling around at the interruption.

Kallia's eyes were fixed on the mirror. Only it didn't show Jack or
his turned back, but something else, dark and shadowed.

A monstrous face.

"Kallia." Jaw clenched, Jack began striding toward her, enraged.
Or stricken. She suddenly couldn't tell the difference as she backed
out of the room, realizing she was shaking.

That face. The harshness of it branded the back of her eyelids each time she blinked. Whoever it was—whatever it was—it was too much. A million voices inside her suddenly screamed all at once to go. Run.

And one: *stay.*

"Kallia—*wait.*"

Jack's voice ran circles in her head, over and over.

Glorian is not the sort of place for people like you or me.

Glorian had never been a horrible, forbidden place. Jack's business trips led him there. No one but him, doing Zarose knew what.

All this time.

Hearing Jack's feet pick up after her, Kallia took off down the hall. Stumbling, her vision wavering. It was instinct to run as far and fast as possible, but Jack didn't need to in order to catch her. He could close the walls in around her, raise the floors until they blocked every path imaginable. Trap her, without so much as taking a step.

Panic hammering at her chest, she glanced over her shoulder and threw a slap to the wall. The force reverberated down the hall behind her, rippling the sides until every hanging portrait and candle and ornate table came crashing down in a wave.

"Kallia!"

Mild annoyance, at best. At her back, he stomped over glass and debris, each step shaking the ground. Her muscles tremored in tune with the loss and surge of energy, running high and low as her eyes darted everywhere until landing on the stairs ahead.

Kallia cried out as the long hallway rug yanked violently, tripping her. Dragging her back in the opposite direction from where she came.

"Please, firecrown. Stop running."

The nickname sounded wrong, all wrong. Rage that had been simmering, that had been buried so deep she'd forgotten its name, seared through her. She gritted her teeth and thrashed to the side off the moving fabric. Kallia could barely hear what he said next as she ran for the stairs, only her heart thundering. The roar in her ears, deafening.

Flying down the grand wooden stairs, she clawed the air at her back. With each step down, the one behind her collapsed. One by one, the levels cracked and caved after contact with her heel until the thick bannister snapped. The entire structure, fallen by force.

Kallia couldn't even tell if he was still following her. She expected staff to come running at her from all directions, but the entire first floor was chillingly empty. The main door at the entrance, unguarded.

The quiet around her broke under a voice, calling her name from behind. A muffled echo. It could've been Jack's. It could've been anyone.

Kallia ignored it and wrenched her gaze away from the broken staircase. Ears ringing, breath held, she headed straight for the door.

To the forest that had held her prisoner for as long as she'd known.

The voice persisted.

Kallia, stop.

Kallia, wait.

Her feet plodded through the lawn's damp grass, her focus shooting straight ahead yet acutely aware of each marker in the corners of her gaze.

Through the twisted metal archway.

Over the cement pathway that ended in grass.

Past the groundskeeper's shed on the left, the horse stables to the right.

Inside the House, she'd been restless. Stirred by the storm beating inside her skin, looking for a way out. Now that she'd found one, the storm took hold. Guiding her.

"Kallia, *wait!*"

Mari. Kallia paused long enough for her friend to catch up, out of breath and red-faced. "I've called your name dozens of times, what happened?"

There were no words, nothing but fragments. A hand closed over hers, slowing her but not enough to stop her. Kallia didn't have the luxury of stopping.

"You look like you ran through hell." Mari shook. "Wh-where are you going?"

The chilling sound of a chuckle finally burst from Kallia. "I'm going into the woods no one dares enter, to the city nobody speaks of."

"*What?*" The girl stumbled with a shriek. "That's not funny, Kallia."

"I'm not joking, Mari. I can't go back."

Kallia had thought about the people who'd left the House over the years. Who had formed such holes in her heart. She could've gone with them. Should've. If she had known, if they had said good-bye, she would've begged them to take her along.

"Well, you can't go *out there,*" Mari pleaded. "It's dangerous."

"I'll manage. I know people on the other side."

Her intuition teased at the possibility that her old tutor and dance teacher had made their way to Glorian. Unless they had the fortunes to pay their way to the eastern cities, which Kallia doubted, it was a natural next step after Hellfire House.

Kallia clung to that hope fiercer than anything, imagining their faces when she strolled into town. Sanja would berate her for forgoing a horse in these Woods to journey on foot. Mistress Verónn would be even more horrified, for the sake of her feet.

Mari hurried after her. "I meant the Dire Woods. You know it's cursed."

Kallia inhaled roughly. She'd heard the stories. People would enter the forest clearheaded and leave losing their minds. Guests of Hellfire House, especially. There were numerous accounts of those who wandered through the trees drunkenly, only to come running back sober as death. *If* they found their way out.

Maybe those were more lies Jack had planted. But even he rarely ventured into the Dire Woods, despite owning horses. Animals were far more attuned to the ever-changing rhythms of the Woods. Only customers who could afford travel by carriage would venture to the club because of it.

And yet, Kallia marched onward. "I don't care."

"You may be a magician, but not even you're immune to the Woods or the travel." Mari's panting grew more labored. "Seriously, let's go back. Please? I've never gone this close to the edge before."

Fear clung tight in her voice, and Kallia nearly faltered over how well she knew it. Had bottled it, all these years. "Come with me."

"What?"

"Come. With. Me." In a sudden rush, Kallia grabbed both of her wrists. "Mari. There's nothing more for us here. We could leave this place." The idea instantly warmed her, to find her way through a world unknown with a friend. To not have to say good-bye.

Mari couldn't have looked more slapped in the face. "Kallia, we have no supplies, no money. And we'd never survive that journey without a horse."

Kallia gave a frustrated huff. Trying to gather supplies would give Jack every opportunity to stop her. She couldn't risk it. "There's no time."

"Then I . . . I'm sorry, Kallia. I can't leave. None of us can."

In the stilted silence, Kallia felt her heart crack, and only she could hear it.

She dropped Mari's wrists and stepped away, simmering. "People leave *all* the time, why can't we?" she countered, blinking hard. "You know what? Fine. You can stay, but I won't. I can't. I—"

"Stop, Kallia."

Just before the forest edge, Kallia whipped around, breath locked in her throat. *Jack.*

Except Jack wasn't there.

And neither was Mari.

The wind howled in her ears. No way the girl could've run so fast back to the House. "Mari?" Her lips trembled. *"Mari!"*

"She's gone."

A hand brushed over her shoulder. Kallia's heart became a cold, shivering thing. She shuddered away, and instantly buckled to the ground.

Jack stepped into being and stood in her path to the Dire Woods. Rising over her, as if he'd always been there.

"What did you do to her?" she whispered. "Jack, what did you *do*?"

"You always bring them too close to the forest," he spoke, sadly. "Its power drowns out any magician's. Kills even my most well-crafted illusions, so it can raise its own."

Illusions. Her blood turned to ice. "Wh-what are you talking about?"

Where was Mari, she wished to ask, but feared the answer.

"You learn so fast." Jack raked a hand through his hair. With the blinding gray sky behind him, he was only a shadow. An omen, looming. His step forward sent Kallia crawling back on her hands, her pulse crashing with a panic both foreign and familiar—

Her nightmare.

The realization seized in her chest. How many times had she dreamed of this, of backing away from some beast while clawing through the dirt? Unable to do anything more than scream?

No. Biting back a sob, Kallia forced herself up from the ground to run. So often her own mind had given warnings she couldn't understand. For the reality was just as terrifying as the nightmare. The truth as poisonous as the lie.

"I'm sorry, firecrown." Calm iced in his voice at her back. "This part of the game is not my favorite, either."

The last thing Kallia heard was the snap of fingers as she fell back to the ground.

And the thrashing trees above her blurred everything to black.

4

"Miss Kallia?" A deep voice sounded as she came to, scattered and cloudy. "Miss Kallia, wake up . . ."

Kallia's head rang, a bit sore. Little by little, her senses returned. The cold press of the dance floor at her back, the brightness of the day reflecting off the high walls of mirrors.

Warmth radiated from the three concerned faces above her, clearing in her vision. A redheaded girl in a loud blue dress to her right, Jack standing center, bearing a troubled expression, and an older, paunchy man to her left lightly pressing beneath her jaw.

Scowling, Kallia jolted back from his touch. "What the *hell* are you doing?"

"Checking your pulse," he replied jovially, drawing back. "Seems there's no need for that anymore, though."

"Oh, thank goodness!" the girl exclaimed on a fluttering breath and kneeled closer. "*Don't* do that again, Kalls. You had us worried sick. Even the doctor."

"No, I kept telling you she'd be fine," the older man rejoined with an eye roll. "Seamstresses. Have to add flair to everything."

It took effort summoning the girl's name. A seamstress. Somehow it escaped her. "Wh-what happened?"

"Oh, nothing too serious." The doctor patted her arm. "You took a small spill, is all. Something about headstands, according to Miss Lucina."

Lucina.

Kallia searched for the name in her mind, finding it familiar. Like the feel of a new pair of shoes she'd only begun to break in. Yes, Lucina. Her closest friend. It all clicked into place—the faint taste of floral tea on her tongue from the post-show breakfast they'd shared that morning, as they did every day. Cinnamon cakes drizzled with cherry honey, and laughter over the mess. Warmth filled Kallia, and she relaxed as Lucina began combing back strands of hair from her face.

"While you were rehearsing, I was in the corner sewing up the last touches to your costume for tonight, like usual," Lucina went on, her voice as dramatic as her dress. "And all of a sudden, you had this grand idea to go vertical the wrong way, before it all came tumbling down. Literally."

Jack rubbed a hand over his face. "Thank you for the fifth recounting of that story."

"Well, *somebody* had to tell her." The girl sat back on her heels, haughtily inspecting her nails over her lap. "Not as though she'd remember on her own."

Remember.

Kallia's eyes squinted as though she were still waking up. The throbbing at the back of her head lightened, but something was missing. A lot, from the gaps in her mind. The strange void in her heart.

A palm rested on her kneecap.

"How are you doing, firecrown?" Jack's voice warmed her, an anchor reeling her back into place. "Can you remember anything?"

Remember.

"Why would you ask that?" Kallia snapped. Her brow crinkled at how the words had flown out like fire, a question that didn't quite feel like hers.

"I mean—" Heat burned her cheeks at the tense quiet that fell. *Get ahold of yourself.* "You know what happened already."

"Ah. There's nothing to be embarrassed about." The doctor rose with a wan smile. "Just be careful next time. You're lucky you weren't hurt worse."

Kallia nodded, staring off into the room as their voices played a casual melody above her. The doctor's clearance of health, Jack's gruff worry regardless. Lucina's endless interjections, more emphatic than necessary.

A peace swept over Kallia, the first calm she'd felt since waking, until she caught her eyes in the mirrored wall.

A web of jagged cracks flashed across her mind.

Just as suddenly, when she blinked, the surface remained flawlessly smooth. Unbroken.

Always think first before trusting your reflection.

Jack had taught her that.

When had he first said it?

The lesson floated to the surface of her thoughts like a small piece of the day freed from the blackness of the fall. It felt more true than what she saw, the group of people gathered around her in the scene playing against her reflection.

Some mirrors are like windows designed to be more convincing than others.

The lesson unfurled faster with a ringing pain, a fracture splitting wider, allowing more words in. Her memory, returning in little fragments. She grasped at them, names and faces blurred before, now clearing at the forefront.

Sanja. Mistress Verónn.

Mari.

A monstrous face, waiting in the dark.

"Kallia?"

She jerked her gaze back to the group, heart pounding. "I'm sorry, what?"

"Are you well enough to perform tonight?" Jack asked, walking over to her. He offered her his hands. "You don't have to if you don't want. You seem—"

"*No*, I'm fine. I . . ." She didn't want to take his hand. Didn't want to believe it, but in his face she knew so well, she saw a tenderness that didn't belong. That waiting carefulness, as though he were placing the last cards on top of a house of them, willing them to stay in place.

He was a dealer of memories, after all.

Her vision wavered in violent thrums until the room pulsed around her, shrinking. The rage so familiar, like a memory itself. And betrayal, swallowing her from the inside.

Kallia looked down at her feet, the backs of her eyes smarting. She couldn't let him see. Couldn't let anything fall. For if she was the house of cards, she couldn't let him knock everything down just to rebuild. All those delicate pieces around her needed to stay. *She* needed to stay.

The hot knot pulling in her throat cooled, her heart steeled over. Until she whittled that scream of pain inside into a harsh whisper. *Do not let it out, do not let it out.*

She composed her features, swallowing hard before taking his hands. The grooves of his brass knuckles pressed into her skin as she rose. "Of course I want to perform."

"I don't want you pushing yourself too hard."

Kallia cocked her head, her teeth clenched beneath a pout. "Sweet of you to underestimate me." Her nails bit slightly into his skin as she laced her fingers within his. She lifted their hands and gave an experimental spin. "See? I can dance just fine."

Silently, Jack twisted her back to him. He slid his right hand through her hair, to the back of her head to gauge the pain. Kallia smothered her hiss at the slight soreness, and leaned into his touch.

More ice than the fire she knew. She suppressed a shiver by moving her fingers up and down his right forearm.

Head tilted, he stared at them. "You're sure?"

The earnestness in his voice almost fooled her. She would've preferred not to notice it at all. But still, it caught at her and latched. Tugged on the part of her looking for reasons to explain *why*, why he would ever do this to her.

Do not let it out, do not let it out.

Her smile was a mask; her voice, a spell. "I'm sure."

She was back on the greenhouse roof, to Lucina's dismay.

It had taken Jack a while to finally leave them, and Lucina was far too ready to start primping and preparing for the club tonight as if they'd done so hundreds of times together.

"Get down from there, Kalls, or you'll fall. *Again.*" Lucina huffed from below, strutting and pacing like an overworked peacock. "A bath and makeup can only hide so much. Broken bones, they cannot."

Kallia observed the girl, lingering on her sure movements. Waiting for the first hint of wrongness. She fit in too well with the House, perfect as a doll built to live within it. But bone deep, Kallia *knew* Lucina was a stranger—even if there was something familiar about her, vivid flashes and images, tastes and smells from a past so convincing. So real, as if she had been trapped in the House alongside Kallia for ages.

It hadn't taken long for Kallia to play her part. She'd linked arms with the girl, nodded eagerly at every tease she gave about tonight's attire. An act, well-played. Enough that when Lucina steered them toward the club, she found nothing amiss when Kallia took them outside.

"It's a surprise," Kallia promised. "For Jack. Don't tell."

Lucina grinned at being in on a secret. She acted as the lookout while Kallia had a quick word with the groundskeeper to saddle up a horse so Jack could take her riding late in the night.

"Oh, how sweet," the seamstress gushed. "You two haven't ridden together in ages."

It unnerved Kallia how she knew. She must have a store of information about her and Jack, this newly crafted illusion with the same purpose as all the rest.

Her enthusiasm wavered, as she next guided them to the greenhouse for some fresh air.

Only when Kallia began to climb did the illusion hesitate.

She had to be quick. When she reached the top, her first moment alone since her supposed fall, she forced herself to keep going. Every emotion beating wildly inside her, she caged them all. She couldn't lose herself, couldn't cry, couldn't *stop* even for a second.

Not if she wanted to get out of here.

Calling out cheerful reassurances, Kallia slid the roof tile out of place, fingers shaking. Everything of hers in the House could burn, but not this. The cloth, still dark-smudged and wrinkled and stitched with the flower. The only thing that felt real. Swiftly she pocketed it, before pausing at the crumpled flyer. But there was no need to keep it. Glorian rose in the distance like a beckoning hand, posing a question. Promising more.

Her name was called once more, with exasperation now.

Kallia left her collection laid across the roof, hoping the wind would take back the gifts it had given.

Hellfire House was filled to the brim.

Delirious laughter and smoke poured from the dens in sprawls of mist and spent memories. The lusty beat of the music drowned the whole club, ushering in hordes of masked guests, while dancers slinked around them in sparkling corsets and suits. Drinks poured from the slender necks of green glass bottles. Cards were shuffled and folded.

The master of the House prowled his domain. He had not seen his star since the incident earlier. An easy enough cover-up for the mess he'd made. What had gone wrong with the illusion this time? She'd always been resistant to them, even more so now. And it troubled him, the direction she was always looking toward. The city she'd always been drawn to, in the way one looks for the shore after being at sea for too long.

From his usual table, glass in hand, he watched the spot where the chandelier would drop. Others around him kept shooting waiting glances skyward as well. She was a magnificent performer, and the evidence filled him with pride. But there was still so much to show her. To *tell* her.

Soon, he'd always say to himself, knowing what a lie that was.

If she found out, one thing after the other would unfold.

And ruin everything.

The master sipped at his short glass of emerald whiskey, ignoring the fluttering of cards and the gaggle of girls sauntering nearby. His stare lingered on the black sea of the ceiling, expecting the panels to open any second.

When he realized he'd started his second drink, his brow deepened.

The room's energy was off. Usually, her performance revived the air, fallen stagnant at his instruments' continuous melody.

Unease prickled through him. He clawed his armrests and rose to investigate, before the sudden start of drums halted him. The welcoming blare of trumpets followed, and finally, he relaxed.

Only a small delay.

Lowering back into his seat, he savored a slow sip of his drink. At the darkening of the lights, the entire crowd took a collective breath. The first hints of the chandelier tips gleamed, and as it descended, the cheers began to rise like a song before petering out into silence.

The master of the House stilled, fingers tight over his glass.

Nothing.

Just an empty, glittering chandelier.

The applause scattered and thinned to confused murmurs. Was this some other trick? Had the girl gone invisible? What sort of show loses its star?

Hidden among his guests, the master was grateful nobody approached him. Whatever expression hardened in his eyes could only be as icy as the sharp coiling in his gut.

Something was very, *very* wrong.

No more than a second later, his nose scrunched. He rose from his seat suddenly, knocking over his drink. For it was only then that he heard the desperate shriek from backstage, followed by the distinct smell of smoke.

5

Kallia tightened the clasp of her cloak and hiked her wide-strapped bag over her shoulder.

She had to move fast.

Music from the House pumped into the night, unwilling to let her go just yet. With enough distance, she'd never have to hear another entrance song, or be lowered from another damn chandelier. Hopefully the little surprise she'd left for Jack in her dressing room carried the message, loud and clear. Anything she could do to buy her some time. But the moment he realized she was not among the ashes, he would look for her.

And he wouldn't stop.

Kallia squeezed the old cloth secured in her pocket for strength. She soldiered on, her sturdy boots weathering the marshy, damp grounds near the stables.

Most of the horses' heads drooped out of their stalls. As Kallia passed, some were curled up in the hay, resting before they were needed to transport their masters back home. Jack kept a few, in case there was ever a rare need to ride into the forest.

Dark, solemn stares and long faces followed Kallia all the way down the stalls. A few shifted restlessly in place, as if they could feel a charge rippling off her. Eager for it themselves.

Once she reached the last stall, she smiled at the familiar pair of glassy eyes staring back. In her daydreams, she'd always picked Sun Gem to leave with her. The stunning black mare was a little older than the rest, and just like her, more than ready to leave. All saddled up.

It was the calmest she'd been all night as she reached out. "Hey there, gir—"

A scream came from outside.

Then another.

A stream of drunken protests followed, sounding more from a large gathering than a passing group.

Kallia's heart sank. Hellfire House was closing early. Once Jack realized she was gone, a search would follow. But the distraction of the club should've given her a little time, at least. He never officially closed down the club except on designated off nights.

Or on nights when his main act vanished after setting fire to her dressing room.

A curse flew off her lips. If she dashed off with Sun Gem, she'd be exposed instantly. She could try escaping in the crowd, but Jack would still find her. Always.

Pulse spiking, Kallia quickly ran through every option before a damp nose nudged her arm. Sun Gem pawed at the floor in soft, insistent strokes. All the horses stirred, rising in their pens with restless shakes of their heads.

Her elbow rested on the paint-chipped half-door, before she heard the dull metal *thunk* of the lock giving way. Her skin prickled at the sound, at the line of doors down the length of the stable, the horses' heads bobbing as if nodding. *Yes. Do it.*

With a steady call to her magic, Kallia gave a quick flick of the wrist.

A series of hard metal *clicks* followed, and a chorus of squeaky groans as the stall doors swung open. The horses did nothing at first, the stable entirely still.

The crowd of voices grew nearer outside.

With a frustrated glance toward the rusty lanterns hanging before each station, Kallia snapped her fingers until the fires inside the glass seared brighter with white, burning light—exploding in small, vicious shatters.

Neighs erupted like a discordant surge of violins as the horses, young and old, blew out of their stations. Covering her ears, Kallia sought refuge in Sun Gem's stall to avoid the violent wave rushing out. The floor shook under the force of their hooves racing across the stable. Soon, the shouts outside rose from discontent to terror. Chaos.

There was no leaving the way she came. Lifting her palm to the end wall of the stable, she pulled all traces of heat lingering under her skin, bringing it to the surface in a surge against the wood.

Any remaining horses whinnied and scurried out of their stalls from the blast. Sun Gem reared up on her legs from the shock of fiery light—which left a gaping hole at the end of the stable, straight for the Dire Woods.

Kallia's heart lifted.

"Come on!" Patting Sun Gem's neck, she ran through, the remaining horses thundering behind. Cold fresh air hit her instantly, along with the clash of screams and harsh neighs nearby.

The cacophony faded as Kallia halted at the edge of the forest, catching her breath. The horses gleefully ran straight through with the moon guiding their path, but Kallia withered before the towering, shadowy trees. Their dark silhouettes haunted her, and her nightmares.

Nothing was here to stop her now.

No monsters or illusions, nor their maker.

Kallia clutched at the cloth in her pocket and inhaled deeply, before letting go. She took a step toward the edge—

A flash of dizziness hit her.

A pull.

Jack, calling her back. Wielding whatever hold he had on her—or was it the madness? Taunting her, already? His whisper barely reached her ears before a cold nose pressed at her back. Jolting her.

Sun Gem's long face watched her, waiting.

Now.

Kallia gritted her teeth, another small spike of pain surged inside her head as she grabbed a chunk of Sun Gem's thick, black mane and the front of the saddle. Foot in the stirrup, Kallia grunted as she lifted herself over. Her arms burning, legs quaking. Sun Gem didn't even need the command of the reins to be told to go.

It was like flying. Her hair rushed behind her, her bones knocking about with each hard gallop. The shouts and hollers behind them faded as they drew deeper into the forest, until all that was left was the rustling of leaves, the steady beat of hooves, and Sun Gem's panting.

The dizziness ebbed from Kallia's skull, little by little, but her hands grasped the horse's mane tightly at every jarring turn and jolt. She barely caught herself as they navigated over serpentine tree roots that seemed to slither beneath them, rocks crawling and scuttling onto their moonlit path.

A person could go mad, imagining such things. But Sun Gem charged forward, determined and confident. As if she'd never once gotten lost and wouldn't start tonight.

It should've worried Kallia more, but she had no map. No hint of Glorian beyond the rise of trees around her. If she could place her faith in anything of these Woods, it was the restless horse searching for freedom just like her.

"Stop, Kallia."

Kallia bolted upright, nearly losing balance. Her breath grew ragged as she looked around for the source. *No.* He'd never ventured out this far without—

"Here, I give you everything."

Memories of his voice blew in like a breeze that kissed roughly against her jaw. Wrapped around her neck, and tightened.

"Is that not enough?"

A sob ripped from her. Sun Gem huffed out sharply at the falter in her grip of the reins, the limpness of her legs. Irritated. They must've been nearing the border wall of Glorian from her impatience, or were nowhere close. It was hard to tell, as Jack's words teased her. Forcing her to listen, willing her to stop.

Inhaling deeply, Kallia gave a hearty pat to Sun Gem before continuing on. Another harsh breeze swept through, carrying more of Jack.

"Glorian is not the kind of place for people like you or me."

She leaned forward as they picked up speed, a sheen of sweat coating the back of her neck. Her legs burning, heart thundering.

"You're too ambitious for your own good, Kallia."

Her eyes shut at the pull in her throat.

"You're not ready."

In the dark underbelly of the Dire Woods, the madness found her. It knifed inside, twisted and wrestled to weaken her. The forest never played fairly, for there were no rules once you entered. No direction, no time. What seemed like a mile could've only been mere steps. A minute, a handful of hours. Torment that stretched beyond reality wanted you to feel it, until even the strongest couldn't survive. Kallia felt her resolve cracking, signaled for Sun Gem to gallop faster, as if she could outrun sound itself. But her head was full of Jack's voice, her bleary gaze catching hints of his form following her between the shadows of the trees encompassing her.

Were the Woods just humoring her with the guise of escape?

Would she find him at the end of her path, waiting?

She shivered, the possibility haunting. Their steps, feeling numbered. Until the horse soon shuddered to a lighter canter, then a stop.

The motion sent Kallia reeling as she looked to the sky to anchor her—finding the tree branches lacing the sky. And in between them, tall walls with gated tops.

The Glorian border. It looked so different from how she'd viewed it from her greenhouse. Always a fixture in the distance, not one she would ever meet.

Everything fell silent. The howling of the wind in the trees, Jack's voice. The world around her fell still in the face of the immense stone wall curving to the iron-wrought gates.

Larger than Kallia imagined it would be. On the roof, it looked more like the brimstone rim of a teacup. Here, it was an impenetrable fortress. So tall and imposing that, after always looking at it from afar, it didn't seem real.

Glorian.

Impatiently, Kallia dismounted. She almost twisted her ankle in her intense yet graceless battle to reach the ground, but Sun Gem stayed firmly in place, ears perked and alert. Kallia could hear her following behind toward the gates, the gaping archway that interrupted the stone expanse.

Kallia stroked the horse's neck sadly. "I'm sorry girl, I can't take you with me."

Sun Gem blinked as Kallia's fingers smoothed back the spot between her ears. She found the fastenings of the saddle and unbuckled them one by one, letting them drop to the ground and kicking them aside. In this city, Sun Gem would only be tied down again, to a carriage or another stable. It was not fair to escape one prison only to fall back into another.

The horse gave a soft huff before backing into the forest. In no time, Kallia heard her hooves galloping away, running farther and farther from the wall. The retreating sound, both comforting and cold.

Kallia was alone.

Light peeked from behind, grazing the tops of the wall in a smattering of sunrise. She could barely feel the exhaustion seeping in, not when she was just breaths away from Glorian, of feeling the sun she'd always known on a different side of the Dire Woods.

With each step, more of the city's music filled her ears—birds chirping and wings flapping, hammers hitting away in the clamor of construction. Kallia soaked in these new sounds. They were no different from those she'd heard around the House on a busy morning, but there was something exhilarating in the rise of an entire city rather than a household.

A smile touched her lips as she finally faced the entrance.

She'd imagined it a thousand times over.

The black gates were flung wide open, welcoming and sleek in the morning light. The stacked stones of the walls shone dark gray, but the gates that completed it were smooth and just as striking. When her eyes worked around them, the designs and the intricacy, Kallia laughed. From afar, they'd only appeared like odd wired forms. Up close, she devoured each circle and block, star and triangle, all twined in the corners. Symbols steeped in mystery. A new hand ready to be dealt.

Kallia walked through the gates, entering the city of cards.

ACT II

ENTER THE DEVILS:
THE BEASTS THAT HUNT, AND THE
GHOSTS WHO HAUNT

The master of the House had not left his room all day. The entire night before, he had searched the Dire Woods on horseback, her voice teasing his ear, whispering that she'd returned. That she would never leave, happy and satisfied right where she was.

Only a fool believed the forest and its lies. When he'd found her dressing room drowning in flames but no sign of her, he'd taken to the Woods. It was a risk to venture out that far, for that long. He'd spent hours calling her name, resisting the forest answering in return. But he'd already known.

Gone.

With all the curtains drawn tight, barring all light, he sat on his leather couch facing the fireplace that roared too hot for the day. He was a mess of disheveled hair, in a white shirt he didn't bother to button, and a drink his maids tsked at permanently attached to his right hand.

A knock came at the door, and still, he didn't move.

"It's nearing sunset," a servant called. "I've got another tray out here if you—"

"Leave it." He barely raised his voice, but the message was

received from the sudden clink outside, the sound of feet scurrying away. The noise reminded him of the chaos of the night before, the horses storming the House grounds, the screams of his patrons. No one had been hurt too seriously, but then, everyone had avoided his path.

Until he wiped their memories clean to rid the night from their minds.

He wished he could do the same to himself. He threw back another swig, nostrils flaring from the burn. The fire spiked higher as he refocused on the flames.

She was gone.

To where, he didn't need to guess.

He turned his glance to the mirror on the wall. Glaring at it, even though the shadowed, sneering face no longer dominated the surface.

Every year, you play your games with them. One day, you might lose.

Remembering that monstrous voice, the master's fist curled tighter, close to shattering the mirror. It had been a mistake to answer the old devil's call. He hadn't bothered in years, the glass darkened and dead as glass ought to be.

How much had she heard?

Not like it mattered. She'd heard enough.

Snarling, he knocked his empty glass over and rose to look out the window. His joints cracked under the prowling movement, eyes fixed to where he ripped open the curtains. Light hit his chest as he watched the sun set. In the distance, the hint of gated walls and shadowed buildings peeked over the dark wave of trees.

Damned city, and the monsters that waited there.

THE CONQUERING CIRCUS PRESENTS...

SPECTACULORE

WHERE THE STAGE TELLS A STORY, AND LEGENDS ARE BORN!

Join our competition to find the magician among magicians:
a man among men who'll rise as the next star of the Conquering Circus.

Open auditions in Glorian held at the Alastor Place.
Born or acquired magic welcome. Stage assistants optional.

It could've been hours that Kallia had spent shivering by the public bulletin. *It is so much colder here,* she thought. The unfamiliar ice gripped at her bones, her cloak staving off the worst of it. Her eyes took in the board, studded with papers like the flyer on Kallia's roof—the half-torn page, in full.

Magician among magicians.

A man among men.

She dug her hand into her pocket for the cloth, fingers running over the stitched rose to relieve the tight pressure in her chest. She wanted to blame the succinctness for the sake of catchiness, but it lay plain in the message staring her in the face.

You can leave, but you'd soon see there's not much out there for female magicians.

So Jack hadn't lied. The idea was so small-minded, so limiting and presumptuous. Her stomach soured as the words repeated in her head, an angry rhythm forming. She hadn't run away only to be stopped before the games had begun.

She would show them.

With the raise of her chin, Kallia clutched her cloak tighter and turned her back on the posters. She blew out a stream of mist, the kind she'd only seen on winter mornings after cracking open her window at the House. Except this mist was even finer, colder. Just like everything else about the city.

For so long she'd envisioned streets bustling with people. The air warm with the sounds of laughter. Bright buildings built with broad windows, rooftops glittering beneath the break of daylight.

Not streets paved in frost. Or dull windows webbed with ice. The towering buildings lining the street were all capped with white, snowy patches, the fingerprints of a long winter leaving its mark. Even the birds darting from streetlamps to rooftops carried a chilling look to them. Kallia squinted, certain snow fell from their wings from the fine powder dusting the air in their wake.

It was a cold world. Colder than anything Kallia had ever known. A city frozen in place, quiet and lonesome even as people passed her on the street. Men and women were dressed in coats buttoned to their chins, with neat, proper hairstyles for the women and crisp top hats for the men. All in bland, neutral palettes.

Kallia had never felt more out of her element, conspicuous in her billowing emerald-green cloak. With her dark hair worn down and wild in the wind, her burgundy boots peeking out with each step, she was honestly more grateful for how much her cloak covered than its warmth. If people saw what she wore beneath or the clothes in her bag, she'd probably have a mob chasing her out the gates. From the offended stares and whispers following her, it was still a possibility.

What have I gotten myself into?

The question beat mercilessly inside with no answer. No other choice but to move forward, because what else was there, looking back?

Nothing.

No one.

Kallia lifted her head high and strutted down the street, combating all the side eyes and the hopelessly lost feeling that pricked at her inside. Beneath the ice, Glorian was carved with rough redrock roads and serpentine paths as confusing as the Dire Woods. The buildings were not at all like the mountainous manors that had welcomed her from afar, but tall, austere masses. Discordant architecture without signs or labels, and it only infuriated Kallia more. As if she were wearing a blindfold in an already pitch-black room, all while an audience watched.

The Alastor Place. Finding it would be the first step. When Kallia had looked closer at the flyer, her chest nearly caved with relief at the fine print promising accommodations and a stipend to the contestants, for as long as they kept their spots in the game.

And yet no one would offer her even the grace of a direction when she asked. They grunted out hurried responses, rushing away each time she tried approaching.

On a sharp breath, Kallia crossed her arms, above caring if she was in someone's way. Growing more frustrated as she—

"Oh, excuse me, I'm sorry!"

Someone had collided into her. She nearly toppled over, were it not for the warm grip latched tightly on her elbow. Suppressing a scowl, she looked up at a young, long-limbed stranger in a dusty beige coat. Finely made, with the top brass buttons missing.

"Apologies, miss, I'm not usually so clumsy." The young man grinned sheepishly, struck with surprise. But the face peeking out from the shadow of his hat spoke a different story, a hint of wickedness that would not be masked.

In the silence that lingered, the man drew his fingers away from her elbow. "I was only on my way to the post, are you all right? Can I get you anything?"

Brows arched, Kallia never broke eye contact. Not even as she grabbed the hand that had begun sliding stealthily into her pocket. "Over-politeness is an obvious tell, you know."

The man paused under her hold. "A tell?"

"Same with your whole getup." Kallia looked him over. "It's almost *too* obvious. You don a fine coat, but the top buttons are missing. Your shoes are clean, but haven't been buffed in some time. There are a few stray threads off the rim of your hat you probably pilfered." She considered him closer, tapping on her lip. "The smudge beneath your chin was a nice clue, as well."

The young man didn't stiffen like a caught deer. Instead, he tilted his head, curious as a bird. "Pitfalls of being taller than a lamppost. Still, you've listed lots of details but not the sum of them."

"Fine, you want specifics? You're a thief."

At this, he smiled. "Am I, now?"

"Don't act proud—you're clearly not that good at it." Kallia looked down, inspecting the nails of her free hand. Tightening the grip of her other. "Kindly let go of what you were trying to take, or I'll twist until something snaps."

The thief complied, and her viselike grip loosened. But when she released him, he didn't run. Just stood there, blinking. "Zarose, where did you come from?"

"Nowhere remarkable," she said without missing a beat, shifting her glance over her shoulder. "Now, if you would be so kind, could you point me in the direction of the Alastor Place?"

"Ah, I knew it. Lots of people from the outside have been popping into town." The thief's brow quirked. "Here to audition for the competition? Are you an assistant?"

"I most certainly am *not*." Kallia's jaw worked when he only snickered. "Point me in the direction of the Alastor Place, and we'll be even."

"For what?"

"You did try to steal from me." With a casual shrug, she cocked her head in the direction where a gathering of people crossed the street. "And I'm guessing the uniformed man over there with the odd hat and pleasant-looking club will not simply run away if I scream."

"But I didn't even nab anything off you! All you had was a hanky, for Zarose sake."

"Shall we test your word against mine?"

Admittedly, it was a gamble. For all she knew, the guardsman would regard her with no more than a sneer. She had yet to experience any semblance of kindness from anyone here. Except for the thief. His brand of kindness was exactly what she'd been looking for, and somehow, Glorian had delivered.

He held Kallia's gaze long and hard, before amusement reared its head beneath his veneer of defeat. "Somehow, I hear you working in more than one favor in that threat. Though it does make me wonder if you're truly as wily as you seem if you're asking for *my* help."

"Favors are not a matter of lifelong trust, only guaranteed delivery," Kallia remarked. "You seem like the kind who delivers very quickly."

"I can even perform miracles, too." The thief lifted his palms with a flourish. "I can make things disappear and reappear."

"Stealing is not magic."

"I'd say it is if your only working props are quick hands and a disarming smile." He winked, almost pulling a laugh from Kallia. Her sparring partner had always been Jack. But with the thief, it was easy and light, as if they could go on for hours like this without injury.

Oh yes, the thief would do very nicely.

"Want to see some real magic, thief?"

When that flicker of mischief in his eyes flared, mirroring her own, a deal had been struck in the exchange. Intrigue started it, and curiosity sealed it.

The air in Glorian was less chilly against Kallia's skin when the man tipped his hat. "The name's Aaros. And yours, miss?"

He'd know soon enough.

This whole city would, by the time she was through with it.

The Alastor Place was built like a tomb. Cold and forgotten.

Spacious, more importantly.

The perfect venue to house this brand of foolish chaos, Daron thought as he rubbed his hands for warmth, knuckles whitening beneath tawny brown skin. Paling without the constant graze of sun he was used to back home.

This city was not a place for sunlight.

Biting back a shiver, he settled deeper into his seat at the long table before the stage, the chairs beside him occupied by the rest of the judge's row. An assortment of elderly former show magicians: Sydney Bouquet, a pale, reedy man who always appeared utterly unimpressed by his surroundings; Ricard Armandos, a sleepy-eyed gentleman donning a long silvery beard that he constantly stroked as if petting a cat; and Victor Silu, a stout man with the tallest top hat who kept sneaking sips from the flask hidden in his coat jacket.

Daron had not even been born when they'd graced the stage. Then again, with so many stage magicians, it was impossible for each one to remain memorable past their prime.

At only eighteen, Daron was by far the youngest present. His seat at the very end made that abundantly clear.

"I cannot believe it's come to this," bemoaned the mayor of Glorian, Andre Eilin, tugging at the collar buttoned up to his chin. "I wanted more business, not some mad talent show."

Daron's first impression of the mayor was that he was clueless, but too proud to admit it. Whether or not he willfully kept his ears plugged here in Glorian, it was as though the man knew nothing beyond the confines of his city. He'd had no idea who Daron or any of the other magicians were, suspiciously eyeing them until provided with an extensive list of their feats and performances. All Daron had to assert was his aunt's name.

"Wasn't it by *your* word that this whole event was allowed to occur in the first place?" Daron pointed out, rubbing the skin beneath his eyes. He'd long avoided mirrors of any kind, but could all too clearly imagine the mess. Dark hair in disarray, exhaustion scoring his face. He really should've put more effort into his appearance to fit in here. Dragged a comb through his hair, shaved his jaw smooth. A look in the mirror would inspire him to clean up, he was sure. Yet his resolve shattered each morning without fail. Only dread.

One could only run from their reflection for so long.

"Being mayor means making sacrifices," Mayor Eilin grumbled. "I wouldn't expect you to understand, Demarco. You're still young."

He wasn't sure what that was supposed to imply, but opportunity was the last thing on Daron's mind when he reassessed the Alastor Place—more a cemetery of dreams than the stage to make them come alive.

"Young is right," Judge Bouquet muttered. It was difficult to believe someone as scowl-mouthed as him had once had enough charisma to entertain a crowd. "Doesn't perform anymore, but counts himself an expert. *Hmph.* The youths believe they know everything."

"Funny," Daron bit out drily. "I was just thinking the same about the elderly."

Judge Bouquet's face remained flat as paper. "*Why* did you invite the boy, again, Andre?"

Boy. Daron grinded his teeth.

"Didn't even have to ask him," Mayor Eilin chortled. "Rayne handled the invitations. Sent them to the topmost gentlemen still on the circuit, and somehow, Demarco answered instead."

The other judge sneered suspiciously. Daron remained unfazed. "Magicians talk."

"No complaints here, young blood. Like I could ever turn a Patron away."

He'd meant it as a compliment, but Daron cringed. Family privilege served on a platter comes with its own brand of grease, his sister would say. He could barely swallow it.

"Though from what I heard, I am shocked you came." Mayor Eilin paled, awkward and apologetic as Daron's face darkened before turning back to the stage. "Of course people know who you come from, and they say you weren't in retirement for that long, after all."

Another *hmph,* from Judge Silu this time. "Retirement, after *one* bad act. You have your whole life ahead of you. It does you no favors to be so sensitive."

It took everything in Daron to not knock off the man's top hat and crush it beneath his shoe before putting a fist in his face.

Two years ago, Daron had left the stage and everything that came with it. Packed audiences and parties, front-page stories after festive nights of revelry. Young performers had no need for retirement, and those older than he was never failed to tell him. As if it were their duty to shame him for taking a break from what had nearly broken him.

Two years.

And then one day, when Daron happened to glance at the morning newspaper boasting a flashy flyer with a top hat, he woke up.

Glorian.

The city lost in the Woods—opening its gates to a show, and its participants.

And his sister's words began trickling back in like an old song.

"I had the dream again." Eva had said during one of their card games, only a few nights before his last performance. "I'd made it through the Woods, to Glorian."

"You're *obsessed*. That's why you keep dreaming of it." Daron picked up a card from the center deck. Five golden petals branded the card he tucked into his hand. "It's just Glorian. I'm surprised the Woods haven't devoured it like a snake yet."

"You're no fun anymore." Eva flicked a forgotten speck of glitter from her gown off her elbow. "Maybe some of the rumors are true."

"Name one." Everyone loved to speculate and exaggerate over the unknown. They made for amusing tales in the papers—mysterious horned beasts stampeding through the city once a month, inexplicable storms of blood rain, an abundance of cats prowling the streets—but none that could be proven. The Dire Woods made sure of it, like a serpent holding court over a garden. A treacherous ocean between lands that no one dared navigate.

Only Eva would, given a chance.

"You have to admit, the cats theory does not seem *completely* outlandish." Eva shrugged. "Lottie stands by it."

"She stands by anything that'll sell papers."

She ticked her tongue defensively before pressing her rouge-painted lips to the side. "I have a theory."

He rapped his fingers across the table. "Surprise, surprise."

Ignoring him, she let her thumb dance across the tops of her cards. "At Casine's, they never taught us much about it, only that the Woods make it hard as hell to find. And no one should go looking in the first place."

"They *prefer* isolation." Daron snorted. "To avoid being overrun by certain fanatics and outsiders curious about its insides."

Her deep brown eyes remained undeterred. "What if they're . . . hiding something?"

"Hiding what?"

"I don't know. Something powerful."

Her tone teased at something more. More than nonsense, more than conspiracy theories. "Like weapons?"

"No, if they wanted war they would've come for the rest of Soltair already. It must be something else, something valuable." She bit her lip in consideration. "The ability to travel back in time, to make memories and erase feelings like they never existed, to bring people back from the dead or elsewhere!" she exclaimed. "Even magicians have limits. If there was a source of magic, a different kind . . . well, that's something worth hiding."

"Magic is not a treasure to be buried somewhere. You're talking in tales."

It's what their aunt had said years ago, every time Eva had asked questions only a child with magic could. Is Zarose Gate really a gate? Does magic truly come from below? Do the trickster devils who live there come above to play?

"And besides, it's impossible," he continued. "Magicians have their limits. Thank Zarose magic like that doesn't exist."

"Not here, not yet. Maybe it depends on where you are."

Daron shook his head, counting his cards. "If that were even a little true, Aunt Cata would never allow it. She'd have the place swarming with Patrons."

"Not if she doesn't know," Eva posed. "*No one* knows what's happening in there."

He sighed. "See, this is what happens when you hang out with the press."

"Don't insult my friends. What's the harm in a little possibility? Where's your sense of imagination, Dare?" She kicked him lightly under the table. "Or does the spotlight suck that from your soul, too?" She always teased about the spotlight going to his head, both joking that if it ever found her, she'd be on a relentless ego trip.

"There's no such thing as hidden magic," he said. "And besides, that's all impossible. Contradictory."

"Most stories are. It's like the difference between a good trick and a great trick." A knowing gleam twinkled in her tired, kohl-lined eyes. "A good trick amazes, leaves everyone breathless in that moment. But a great trick truly deceives, keeps the audience wondering what happened, long after the performance. Like the Vanishment."

Daron snorted. "All right, but the Vanishment is a showstopper. You can't even equate it to Glorian, Eva. That's like comparing a raindrop to the sea." He threw down a card, smiling despite himself. "It's just a dead city."

"What if that's what they want you to think?"

As soon as Daron had seen the flyer, it hadn't taken him long to find an invitation to Spectaculore, a map leading straight to Glorian. He was far too established to be a competitor—thank Zarose for that—so he needed a spot on the judges' panel. Determining which notable magicians might possess actual invitations proved easy. Astor and Atlas, the infamous Alexandros twins of New Crown always knee-deep in gambling debt, all but bowed out at the sight of Daron's envelope of money. His old partying friend, Griff Kaysim, oh so conveniently had no care for the competition with all his other engagements lined up. And the rest, former friends and rivals alike, backed away from the event as soon as Daron appeared at their doors like a ghost come to settle a score after years without a word.

Certain he'd closed the playing field, Daron packed his bags and stack of invitations—hand-delivering them to the mayor as soon as he landed in Glorian. The white shock on the man's face had been laughable, a precursor to the displeasure from the rest of the judges: older, esteemed magicians long retired before Daron ever took the stage, and they seemed to resent him more for the distinction.

The Daring Demarco. A name once cheered in theaters packed to the doors, now a joke to the weathered-faced judges who regarded him as a pet still learning tricks. But with the formidable Cataline Edgard, the current head of the Patrons of Great, for an aunt, no one could say no to Daron. As much as he detested playing the family card, he'd needed that extra leg up to earn a place here as an esteemed judge.

In the city.

Right where he wanted to be.

Daron's jaw ticked as he leaned back in his seat. His gaze darted up to the proscenium arch of the stage, tracing the broken, rusted squares bent out of place. Like ugly cards thrown above, stuck in midair and forgotten by the dealer below.

The rest of the stage was no better, more a cold barren platform than the backdrop of a grand show. Much like the city itself. Still, he hoped today's audition would end soon so he could explore more of Glorian. Eva had always framed it as an abandoned puzzle of lost pieces, one he refused to leave without solving.

For his sister.

Wherever she was.

He pinched the bridge of his nose. He needed to focus. Play the part: a judge in a competition held by the Conquering Circus, led by a ringleader who fancied himself a king of show business.

"Next in line—number twenty-four!" called the short, broad-chested man in glaring red from the other side of the table. Erasmus Rayne, the only person Daron might've disliked more than the mayor of Glorian. A showman to the core, the man beamed brighter than diamonds at the sight of Daron arriving as a judge. No questions asked, just praise, flattery, and the keys to one of the finest rooms in his traveling hotel. Anything to keep his youngest judge in his good graces.

But the rest of the men had made clear his voice was not welcome amongst theirs. Not that Daron cared to give it. The first few days of watching magicians audition had hurt more than he'd expected. His chest twinged, remembering what it was like stepping onto a new stage for the first time. Power sparking at your fingertips to deliver a trick, delight a crowd.

The pain was only fleeting. It didn't take long to shove it away, sit back and observe, unimpressed. Some magicians possessed skill, but many more lacked it. And amongst the judges, more arguments arose than agreement over who deserved a place in Spectaculore. Most people with power were destined to be labor magicians, an honorable path to be sure, but rare were the ones meant for the stage. The glory of packed houses and endless applause.

The next contestant swaggered onto the stage in a starchy brown suit and a wide casual top hat. There was an air about him similar to the others, as if he had all the magic in the world at his fingertips. It wasn't until he heard a second set of clicking steps that Daron realized why.

An assistant sauntered behind him in a gaudy rose-colored dress studded with sequins that caught the morning light beaming in from the windows. She was by far the most colorful figure in the room, no doubt freezing in her getup like the others who'd strutted in before her. Most candidates were accompanied by a charming assistant to wink and giggle at the audience. An accessory to the performance, and a scapegoat if anything went wrong.

Daron's pulse stilled, his heart quiet. A sudden flash of mask sequins glinted like dark fires in his memory, but this girl wore no mask. His gaze drew to her face. Lovely, as they always were. The other judges thought the same from the way they stole peeks of the assistant's legs stalking out from under the rosy pink feathers and tassels of her skirt.

Erasmus's face lit up as the assistant and the magician made their way to the raised prop box in the center. "Welcome to the stage!" His voice boomed, at its most charming. "Acquired or born?"

"Pardon?"

"Your magic," Erasmus clarified. "Is it acquired, or born?"

Daron waited, head tilted. The distinctions came right from the Patrons, as part of their mission to define the known from the unknown. Magic was an unpredictable element, both controlled yet volatile depending on the magician, and his aunt and her team did their best to monitor its dangers and anomalies, to ensure no magician abused their power on anybody or anything throughout Soltair.

Aunt Cata would likely have words about this entire competition. *Magic and show business are dangerous enough games alone,* she'd tsk whenever the Patrons were called in to shut down a few stage events in New Crown for spiraling out of control. So far Daron had seen no cause for alarm in Glorian. The magicians who'd auditioned had all claimed acquired magic, displaying mostly tame tricks and boasting how the prestigious Valmont Brothers Academy had groomed them. Their powers were not inherently in their blood, but pulled from the air. Unlike born magic: raw natural talent within.

Daron raised his brow as the magician looked nervously at his assistant, who shrugged. Both of them, clueless.

"I . . . uh," the man on stage stuttered. "Acquired?"

If he'd said *born,* Daron would've been the first to chew him out. Of the entire judges' row, he was the only born magician among them. The trait skipped generations in families, so rare that when he and Eva were born, it was something of a city-wide celebration. Born magicians, amongst the Patrons again! Probably the only reason his first audiences were drawn to his shows when he was still so fresh to the stage, fascinated by what a servant of a Great could pull off.

Even Erasmus appeared dubious, but continued. "As you see, we've provided a prop. Simple, no tricks to it. At least, until you're done with it."

The last sentence ended on a flirtatious note, and Daron rolled his eyes when the sparkly assistant giggled in reply. Especially when the man on stage tripped over his own feet.

"Oh, terribly sorry!" He was even clumsier in his process of straightening back up. "It's . . . all part of the illusion, you see."

Daron sighed, waiting for the man to do more than let his assistant guide him. He had inspected the prop box himself, to make sure no tricks had been planted in the basic medium-sized wooden crate. Some contestants had attempted to pull out objects and animals from within as if they'd been in there the whole time. Predictable, but with a few mystifying results. A feather preceding a flock of birds taking flight, a stack of hats taller than the box itself. Several tried inserting themselves or their assistants inside to make them disappear. All but a few failing to impress.

"No, *I'm* the one who's terribly sorry."

Ice brushed up Daron's spine at a bold new drawl—the assistant, taking center stage. Seizing it, like it was her right. She curled her satin gloved fingers, and the lights around them began to dim.

"My assistant is not what he used to be, it seems."

All part of the illusion. Daron's mouth fell as the man tore off his hat and gave a flourishing bow toward the girl. The dusty old curtains of the high windows around them lowered into place until all hints of the bleak morning vanished. The darkness sent the other judges stirring in their seats, and even Daron felt a reel of unease and excitement tightening his core.

Looking down at them, the girl smiled. Satisfied.

"I won't be needing this, either." With a snap of her fingers, all sides of the wooden box broke apart with a slam. Mayor Eilin jumped back, but Daron leaned forward. His ears perked at the slow click of her heels on stage, deliberate and unhurried.

Shadows bathed the room entirely, until a bright glow revealed itself in the palm of her hands, illuminating her face. The amused purse of her lips, hiding a secret.

Without warning, she raised the fire in her hands until the flames stood like globes, which she tossed into the air. They hovered above her head as she conjured two more orbs, and another—tossing them up in a row of spiraling flames.

Daron watched as she sent the fire spinning fast, traveling around her assistant in all manner of patterns. Not once did the assistant flinch, but he bore a raw look of awe as the flames circled him like sparrows dancing in flight. His fellow judges were just as mesmerized by the display.

Zarose. This girl had power.

And yet, Daron could tell she was holding back. As if she held all the cards in her hands, and had only decided to indulge them with a brief flash of one. She narrowed her eyes on each judge all the way to the end, and met Daron's stare with a wink.

He recoiled and looked away, jaw tense. With a sudden intensity, he focused back on the spinning fires. They spiraled and speared out of pattern as they dipped and made way for the table.

Judges Bouquet, Armandos, and Silu all cowered back. The mayor edged lower in his seat. Only Erasmus's excited yowl sounded when a flame brushed too close. Daron felt the heat by his cheeks, and the hairs on his arm stood on end. It truly *was* fire. Not merely an illusion, but actual flames she'd pulled out of thin air.

A true show magician, at last.

After circling the judges' table, the fire arched high above the girl's head where the flames collided and burst in a shower of sparks over the stage. They fizzled fast, leaving nothing but the dark. Light gradually filtered in as the curtains of the high windows were slowly drawn open.

The silence afterward stretched on, long enough that the performer crossed her arms with a relaxed smirk that appeared more wicked than it had any right to be.

Mayor Eilin stood from his seat first, his hands balled into fists against the table. "Young miss, just who do you think you are?"

"Number twenty-four."

"Absolutely *not*! After a display like that?" Judge Silu shot straight up from a few seats down, staggering a bit. "Is that what they're teaching the ladies at Queen Casine's nowadays?"

A few men chortled, but the magician's brow rose. "I'm relieved you all know how to laugh. I wasn't so sure when you were cowering in your seats."

The men abruptly stopped. She certainly was *not* from Queen Casine's Academy. From what he remembered of Eva's heated complaints, the sister school to Valmont Brothers would never be able to contain a magician quite like this one.

"You attacked us," Judge Bouquet countered, red-faced and unamused. "You disregarded your one object. And on top of that, you cannot simply use a man for a prop."

"Well, why not?" The girl paced in her showgirl's outfit with all the might of wearing steel-forged armor. "You have your assistants in sparkly attire like this, yes? I don't know about them, but *my* assistant entered into this arrangement willingly. And decently dressed, at least."

The man next to her nodded rather smugly, while the judge's nostrils flared as he sat back down. The whole room was drenched in the same frigid uneasiness across all the men. With the exception of a beaming Erasmus.

"Wonderful, my dear! And *so* very curious," he praised, clapping slowly. "After days of all these dreadful auditions, you finally give me light. You give me a show—"

"Rayne, you're not seriously considering this." Mayor Eilin sighed heavily. "I thought we had an understanding. Remember that odd girl we turned away the other day? At *your* insistence?"

Daron cringed at the memory. A dark-skinned girl with ruby-red hair had taken to the stage, determined and hungry-eyed. But before she could deliver a trick, Erasmus had ordered her away without delay. No explanation, only a cruel dismissal.

"She was one of my circus girls, and according to their contracts, they have a job," Erasmus said flatly, before gesturing to the magician on stage. As though she were a new toy. A weapon. "But *she* is something else. What we've been missing!"

"She cannot be permitted to enter." Mayor Eilin's voice tightened. "Female magicians are not meant for the stage, it's unorthodox—"

"All the more reason to have her!"

"You don't get it. Magic like *this*—" He waved a hand at her, grimacing. "—doesn't belong in Glorian. It's too risky. And indecent."

"What, *me*? Indecent?" The girl gasped, a trembling hand over her heart. Daron nearly choked as she chuckled and twirled the skirt of deceptively sweet pink sequins about her, flashing even more of her legs. "Your flyer never specifically stated anything about women or anyone else *not* being allowed to enter, so I really don't see what you're concerned about."

"How about how you clearly don't listen to the rules?" The mayor pointed to the dismantled box abandoned on the stage. "Besides, acts like yours would be far too dangerous for the audience size we're expecting."

"Trust me, that was only for today. I guess I was wrong to think you would be up for some real magic." She shrugged. "Apologies if you were intimidated."

The men grumbled in reply, echoing vague agreements on why her performance posed a threat to Spectaculore. Funny how they couldn't keep their eyes off her when she entered the room—only to now regard her as a sort of demon sent to haunt them.

Nevertheless, the girl appeared unfazed. Not shivering in her dress even a little.

"You fools, this is *my* show!" Erasmus cried out.

"Well, this is my city, Rayne," Mayor Eilin countered in a low growl. "I don't care how different things are on the outside nowadays, but a show can't go on without a venue."

"Please. My investment and this show are the only things that could save your city from disappearing into ice altogether," Erasmus scoffed. "Don't forget that you need me a lot more than I need you. I have no problems finding business elsewhere."

The mayor blanched. There could only be one reason why such a straitlaced place would open itself up to a spider like Erasmus Rayne. Daron had read enough on the proprietor to know that each time he and his circus preyed on a new location, they left their mark. The city of New Crown had been a mere labor town before the Conquering Circus blew through its gates and turned it into a show magician's paradise. Now it seemed Erasmus had found his next target: Glorian, the lost city in the cursed Woods. The appeal of such a stage was undeniable. Though it was clear who between the two held all the cards in this game.

"Apologies, my dear, for dragging out this nonsense," Erasmus said, fighting to get his most charming word in. "Merely a spat between old dogs. Suffice to say, I'm not investing anything into this madness if you're not in it."

When the girl didn't giggle at his attentions this time, the proprietor gazed impatiently at the judges. "Why don't we hear out every opinion amongst this esteemed group . . . ah, *Demarco*! How about you?"

Daron's face flamed instantly when all eyes drew to him like spotlights. The girl's, in particular, were beams of fire scorching his skin.

"Aside from myself, you out of everyone here can see the potential and worth of a true performer. Care to weigh in?"

Nope. Absolutely not.

He'd become so accustomed to shutting himself off in private since he'd stopped performing. If only Eva could see him now, she'd be cackling. The hard worry lines of his brow always amused her, and they carved around his head as he tried reviving the parts of the Daring Demarco in him that everyone else sought.

No, he did not take part in Erasmus's avid enthusiasm, nor the mayor's disapproval. No doubt she would bring in crowds and raise them to their feet, but she also favored chaos with her magic. Danger. One wrong move, and she'd probably hail the attention of the Patrons.

And yet, she was the most interesting person to walk through those doors. No one could deny that, least of all him.

"Your magic." He finally lifted his gaze, delivering the same question they asked everyone who crossed the stage. "Born or acquired?"

Her gaze boldly met his for a lingering moment. "What do you think?"

Daron ignored the thump of his pulse, the smattering of laughs and ticking tongues around him. Whether it was doubt or denial, the answer was obvious. Not even the strongest acquired magician who'd crossed the stage performed with a fraction of what she'd displayed. A great trick instead of a good one.

The jeweled tassels of her skirt slowly clinked as she cocked her hip, waiting.

"You'll have no problems filling the seats with this one, that's for sure." Daron finally nodded his assent. "But I can see why you're all wary."

"And why is that?"

When Daron looked up, sure enough, she was watching him. A sharp scowl paired with viper eyes, still studying him. Unable to properly pin him down, as she had all the others in the room, which gave him a small bit of satisfaction.

"Read the room, twenty-four," he said, clasping his hands on the table. Mask on, voice cooled. "And there's your answer."

"Zarose, they *really* did not like you," Aaros remarked as they walked down the steps of the Alastor Place. The hotel key ring Kallia twirled between her fingers halted with more aggression than necessary. Easily threatened men always acted like fools. From the older, stuffier top hats, the reaction was to be expected. But even the youngest of them had come off like a stiff sod who hadn't seen daylight in years.

Demarco, they called him.

And Erasmus Rayne, the overeager ringleader of the circus.

Together, they made up the dubious force whose favor kept her in the competition, and she could not have asked for a more uncertain pair of supporters.

Especially Demarco, with his uneasy praise. Seemingly kind eyes, narrowed in doubt. He certainly didn't act like a strong show magician, yet must've been highly regarded to be invited as a judge. So young and already in such an esteemed position.

Glowering, Kallia tightened her coat around her. "Who is he, anyway?"

"Daron Demarco?" Aaros supplied. "Some young, big-time stage magician, but I heard he stopped performing a few years back. Stopped using magic altogether."

A shocked grimace sharpened her lips. "Why?"

"No clue. Hadn't heard of him until today. Soltair news and gossip don't usually circulate to these parts of the island." Aaros popped up his coat collar at the next brush of wind. "A few magicians backstage were fawning about him. Apparently he's no ordinary performer, his family runs the Patrons of Great. As in Keepers of the Gate, Patrons of Great." His face lit up in wonder.

Kallia groaned inwardly. "Of course."

The first time she'd heard about Zarose Gate was through her lessons with Sanja. Even if her tutor hadn't been real, the facts were true. The history behind Zarose Gate had rooted through time, and grown into something of a legend. That magic came from the earth. The life it bred in the beautiful trees, plants, and flowers could not have been possible without a strange power from below. But when the magic tore open the earth, like a gate loosed open, a terrible flood of power unleashed.

While others grew mad, Erik Zarose grew powerful. A magician. One of the rare few affected so, to forever be revered as a Great when he alone closed the gate. Zarose Gate, as it was known today. A miracle remembered as the greatest feat in magician history, guarded by those he'd trained and trusted. A tradition passed down, from generation to generation.

"No wonder he retired so early," Kallia grumbled. "If you have the right blood, why even work at *all*?"

"Have some respect, for Zarose sake," Aaros said, grinning. "His aunt is practically the iron fist of magicians. If you mess up, she'll find out. No doubt from her dear nephew."

As if she needed more obstacles. "I don't give a damn who he's related to. Besides, he liked me enough to get me through to the next stage."

"You keep sending him dagger eyes like earlier, and it'll be enough to send you right back." He sighed. "But at least you won't be forgotten."

"Exactly. Attention is attention." She gestured down the folds of her clasped cloak, hiding the showgirl outfit she wore beneath. "Clearly it worked."

Demarco aside, there was no way the judges could've turned her away. They wanted a show, and that's what she gave them.

Aaros reared his head back with a bemused, curious look. "All right, I *have* to know what your story is. The mystery is killing me. You're not some rogue runaway from Casine's, are you?"

Kallia nearly tripped, but righted herself before he noticed. He no doubt had been forming illusions of grandeur since the audition. What would he think if he knew she was no worldly traveler, no great name on the stage unless the one at a neighboring nightclub in the Woods counted?

She steadied her strides, voice even. "I got us a place in the competition, with food, lodging, and amenities included. That's all that matters."

If only Jack could see her, he'd swallow back every doubt he ever had.

For she was a contender, here to stay.

Here to win.

It had only ever been a daydream. Surely she would jerk awake at any moment and find herself back in the House. Yet somehow, she was still walking down an unpaved path with a stranger beside her, and a key to a new home.

The realization filled her with a bubbling giddiness, her insides like shaken champagne, nearly bursting with light. Unable to help herself, Kallia spun into her next step when Aaros wasn't looking, composing herself the instant he did.

The Prima Hotel was not too far from the shadowy, unkempt city corner where the Alastor Place resided. The sight became more of a curiosity to Kallia. Neglect and ruin ran rampant in the air of

Glorian, but the Alastor Place appeared trapped in its most forgotten parts, only now slowly emerging from the rubble.

They passed the quiet caravan of circus tents parked around the vicinity, lying like the empty, silken skin shed from a snake. Stretched tall and striped in warm white and purple so dark it almost seemed black, the tents stood motionless, betraying no movement inside. As they reached the end of one tent, Kallia paused and peered closer. A symbol was embedded among the closed folds: three swords side by side with their blades tipped toward the middle, as if piercing through the two letter *C*s forged at the center.

Kallia's heart gave another leap as the circus tent rustled.

"For Zarose sake," someone cursed as a hand shot out to pull back the fabric. "How can you rats even muster the urge to spy on us when it's so damn cold?"

The slit was drawn wide open, and Kallia met a pair of gold cat-like eyes belonging to the most beautiful face she was certain she'd ever seen. Metallic serpentine markings emblazoned the girl's round cheeks and soft chin, clasping around her throat before disappearing to the back of her neck. The snake marking might've caught Kallia's attention first, but it wasn't the girl's only tattoo. A collection of other shapes and scripts branded her skin.

And they were all moving.

The girl's mouth fell open in shock. "Sorry! I thought you were one of those nasty boys from before." She laughed, batting a tattooed hand against her chest, before marveling at Kallia's green cloak with delight. "Oh, I just *adore* that shade—"

"Juno, who the hell are you talking to?" a shrill voice drawled harshly from within the tent. "Get away from there. We're getting cold."

"Relax, thought it was another creeper," she called over her shoulder before dropping her voice. "You may be like us, but I'd scram if I were you. Ringleader's in a mood." The girl cocked her head back at the tent.

Kallia's pulse fluttered. She had so many questions, like how the girl's marks seemed to be moving. Or how Erasmus could possibly be inside the tent when she could've sworn she'd heard a female voice call out. One question among them all won out: "What do you mean I'm like you?"

"I can spot a fellow performer a mile away." Juno winked. "Runaways, too."

With that, the tattooed girl strutted back into the tent, swinging her large hips all the way. The tent flap swung closed, leaving Kallia slightly stunned. When she rounded the corner, Aaros doubled back with a worried expression. "Oh no, did they threaten to sic their stage animals on you, too?"

"What? *Who?*"

"The Conquerors, of the Conquering Circus." Aaros lifted his hands around him as they resumed walking. "Don't know much about them, but this is their territory now. One of the lads I used to run with tried taking a peek inside for fun. No one's ever seen a circus before, much less an all-lady gang. Next thing I knew, he's running for the hills with his coattails singed, muttering about birds and lions eating his brains."

"Sounds like he got off easy." Kallia laughed, with a quick glance back at the tents. As soon as they drifted onto the sidewalk toward the city center, the Alastor Place, and the circus, disappeared from view. Everything except the knowing gleam in the tattooed girl's stare.

Runaways, too.

She'd whispered it like a gleeful secret only they were in on, thus Kallia felt no urge to worry. She had no energy for it. The surge of adrenaline from the audition, on top of the fatigue from it, had numbed her to exhaustion.

Enough that she was about ready to happily collapse on the spot.

She could've cried when they finally reached the Prima Hotel at the corner of the main intersection, built tall and round with deep wine-red bricks and rows of black circular windows closed against iron-laced shutter gates. For a traveling hotel right out of Erasmus's pocket, it looked as if it had stood for years—a sparkling, established fixture in the city. A jewel in the rough.

Kallia forced Aaros through the grand entrance, for his wonderment would've kept him cemented in place. Not even she, used to the extravagance of Hellfire House, was immune. Here, every flower vase draped with crystals as if dusted with frost. Scents of bread and cinnamon and freshly poured coffee wafted warmly from the little café with open seating.

They reached the marble front desk, where the old concierge turned instantly in Aaros's direction for instructions—before Kallia slapped her key on the desk.

"My room is already taken care of." She slid it forward with a slow snakelike smile. "Would you kindly point my assistant and me in the right direction?"

The man's eyes bulged out of their sockets. He nodded and scurried out from behind the desk to guide them past the hotel's quaint café and up the majestic spiraling staircase.

Kallia immediately adored the brightness of the hotel, how it contrasted with the shadowed Hellfire House in all ways but one. Both buildings had been built with beauty in mind, but the Prima's appealed to the senses a touch more. A fresh new flavor she'd never tasted before. Airy and fragrant, like rose champagne. As they ascended, she could've looked out the windows along the walls forever. Their gleaming frames bore sunlight, glimmers of the quiet streets down below. Not rows upon rows of imposing trees or leaves rustling against the glass. Nothing of the Dire Woods anywhere near her.

The lump in her throat tightened. She wasn't alone in her awe. Beside her, Aaros gaped at just about everything. The luxury of the sweeping, painted ceilings, the lush carpeting, swirling candelabras tall as coatracks standing at each corner. Each new piece of the hotel was a discovery. A marvel.

"I've . . . never been in a hotel before." Aaros's face softened, vulnerable in a way Kallia hadn't expected from someone like him. "Are they all like this?"

"Some." She never had, either, but the lie rolled off her tongue more like a wish. She found comfort in pretending she'd frequented palaces and castles and hotels such as this. Better that than to show even a sliver of the emotion that stripped away the hardness of the wily thief she'd met hours earlier.

The concierge was smart enough not to question their living arrangement as he stopped in front of their door at the end of the second-floor hall; though if people made such assumptions of her and Aaros, so be it. Let people think what they will. The longer she stayed in their minds, in any capacity, the better.

After the concierge unlocked the suite's door, he gestured for both to enter as he gathered Kallia's bag. Aaros staggered in, stopping dead center in the common room. *"Zarose."*

Small chandelier lights hung from above, matching the dark golden furniture and thick curved metal of the glass side tables and stools. Even the walls were lined with patterned gold, delicate filigree designs embroidered all over like gilded borders of playing cards. Kallia devoured each detail, breath held. She'd grown up in the luxury of Jack's estate, but there was something much more precious to this space. Even more than her greenhouse.

This suite at the Prima, she had earned. It was *hers*.

"I hope this room will do," the concierge said before bowing out, swinging the door quietly behind him.

"Will this do?" Aaros parroted, slack-jawed. "Hell, this suite alone is bigger than all the places I've ever been in my entire life put together."

"Start getting used to it." Kallia clapped a hand over his shoulder. "Stick with me, and we'll be richer than kings and queens."

Aaros couldn't even muster a witty reply, only an amazed shake of his head. "You're truly willing to share this with *me*? Why? . . . I don't even know your name."

Kallia had withheld her name, waiting to see how the audition would unfold. She hadn't realized how valuable an asset Aaros would be, or how soon she'd grow to like him so much.

Another lie stood at the edge of her tongue, another life. She could take a new name and banish everything from before. But the idea of erasing herself, her name, pulled at her. Her name wasn't owned by the House or by Jack—it belonged to her, and no one else.

"If this arrangement is going to work between us, start by closing your jaw before it falls to the floor," she ordered, crossing her arms loosely. "And please, call me Kallia."

The night was cold, but young. The club, alive and well.

The master watched on as masked patron after patron entered the doors, foolishly hoping she'd be among them. But she would never come back like this—in a flood of people looking to lose themselves and revel in the loss. More than usual lined up outside the door that night, but the master instantly knew which top hats to stalk.

The boisterous group swaggered into Hellfire House, eyes devouring every inch of the club. A few pointed and gaped as though they'd entered an impressive dream; the majority regarded their surroundings as if it were a sumptuous gift for the taking. Even beneath their white masks, newcomers always made themselves known.

This group all but hooted and hollered their way to the bar. Other guests parted a path for them.

Frowning, the master followed. He vanished into the crowd before swiftly reappearing behind the bar, in a new slick suit and a mask to match. Like he'd been there all this time, cleaning glasses with a small rag. "What'll it be, gentlemen?"

"Champagne," the blond man among them crowed over the music. "As many bottles as you can spare!"

The master procured only one from the bed of ice below, setting it on the black marble counter to unwrap the jade-green foil. Without warning, the entire top popped off, but the master had already conjured a flute to catch the fizz spilling over.

Laughter instantly roared around him.

"Good reflexes," the same man said smugly, foil crumpled in one hand and cork in the other. "Sorry, couldn't help myself."

The master gritted his teeth, but continued filling glasses. "You're a magician?"

"We all are," another one in the group stated with a grin. "We're competing in a grand magician's show. *Spectaculore.*"

As he disposed of the empty bottle, the master hid his sneer. "Sounds *very* exciting."

"Oh, it will be." The man with the tallest top hat reached for a flute. "And it'll be over terribly quick when I wipe these gents across the stage."

Someone knocked his top hat off, spurring another round of raucous laughter and shoving of shoulders. They began regaling their skills and repertoire of tricks, as though the best magician could be proven by boasts alone.

"Let's have a toast." The blond man lifted his glass, eyeing the others. "To knocking you boys out of the ring. Cheers."

The magicians booed and cackled, drinks sloshing as they punched the blond man in the back. The master wiped down the surface, counting the rungs of his brass knuckles as he counted his breaths, close to throwing them out of the club altogether.

"Don't forget the girl."

The master paused, head tilted.

"You going to knock her out, too, Ives?"

"Zarose, Robere. That was only a rumor." The magician next to him scoffed. "The judges would never allow it."

"I saw her waltz through the Prima myself, strutting like she owned the place," Robere insisted. "And she has a *male* assistant, can you believe that?"

The master pressed closer, ignoring the taps on empty glasses around him aiming for refills.

The girl.

Only a few days and already she was stirring up trouble.

"Well, is she at least something nice to look at?" the one with the tall top hat asked with a large belch.

Cackling laughter exploded, off-putting as broken glass. It took everything in the master not to drag them by the necks to the memory den, but he was curious what more would spill from their lips. News from the outside was like cards, and each patron came in with a different hand.

It was the reason Hellfire House existed, after all.

"Either way, she's not here to stay," a redheaded man spoke up. "Girls never last in these games. Never have."

The others nodded and tipped their glasses in assent.

Though he detested the band of magicians, the master hoped they were right. If she were no longer in the game, he might have a chance to fix this. Wipe the game board clean, and start over again. Leaving all else in the dark, except him.

The only one in his way, now, was her.

And *them.*

The thought dropped cold in his stomach, the fear creeping back in.

"To us." Ives raised his glass once more, and the others followed. The master's fist tightened until his metal bands dug into bone. Silent, he listened as he always did, to the conversations webbing around him all over the club. To the series of clinks pouring into the air.

"May the best magician win."

Days later, an invitation arrived at Kallia's door. No matter how she'd adored wandering through the Prima, ordering teas and sampling desserts of all kinds down in the café, she'd been restless for news of what would come next. Part of her wondered if it had all been an elaborate joke, the other half fearing she would wake up one day only to be escorted from the premises for they'd changed their minds.

To her delight, a dinner party would be held the following night. The judges had finally whittled down their choices to ten competitors. Nine men Kallia would have to best if she wanted to stay in the game, and she was determined to remain the front-runner.

"Don't you want to be in the middle?" Aaros asked, combing back his swath of black hair in the mirror. "Play it safe until it really matters?"

"I don't know how to play it safe." Kallia's mouth parted as she applied kohl against her eyelids in a smooth line. She'd missed this, the process of pampering as much as preparing. For the first party she'd be attending where she wouldn't have to wear a mask, she wanted to look her best. Unforgettable. This was the first time all the contestants would be in the same room, and she needed to dress and act like a winner. No hesitation. Only confidence.

Aaros made for a good subject to practice on, though it was only a matter of time before he started asking more questions. Until she ran out of easy lies.

Kallia's fingers paused over her brush. She hoped it would never come to that, losing his trust. He'd already become the strangest sort of anchor. In the early mornings, she'd trudge out of her private room, more than a little disoriented to be surrounded by golden hues and city sunlight, and find Aaros awake and staggering around just as floored. Even more so. The streets he roamed had little luxury to them. It was one thing stealing bits of it to get by, and a whole other suddenly drowning in it for a living.

They grew used to their surroundings together, and though she'd never admit it out loud, there was comfort in not having to face this newness alone. The unfamiliarity. Worse were the days when Kallia found herself unconsciously looking for Jack. The routine of seeing him every day left her with an odd hollowness, a longing for the House. Applying makeup as she would before a performance at the club, Kallia felt that same old thrill sparking beneath her skin. Putting on the gown to perform, descending on that chandelier to a sea of faces looking up, finding his.

With a deep breath, Kallia rose from her vanity seat. She smoothed her fingers over the long black satin gloves stretching to her elbows, along the fit of the evening gown that wrapped around her hips like liquid before spilling at her feet.

The invitation had simply said to dress well. Kallia had only snagged a few dresses from her wardrobe at the House. Decidedly not in the Glorian style, they were bold statements, each one of them. She would have to find a dress shop soon to add to her selection, but tonight, she aimed to be memorable.

She admired her handiwork in the large, shell-shaped mirror, leaning closer to inspect for smudges of red at the corners of her lips.

A shadow fell across her, the room around her dimming.

Her skin chilled. When she looked up, her entire surroundings were cast in utter darkness. No furniture, no Prima suite, no Aaros. *Cold*. Her bare arms shook, her back tremoring under a shiver.

For when she looked into the mirror, darkness stared back.

Slowly, tendrils of white fogged the surface, like whispers from behind. Kallia jerked away when someone steadied her by the elbows. "Careful, or you'll ruin the suit," Aaros chuckled, before his gaze sharpened. "What's wrong?"

The next time she turned to her reflection, she saw her room. Herself. Aaros beside her, watching with concern.

"Nothing." She swallowed, hand clutched at her collarbone.

Always think first before trusting your reflection.

Jack's words slithered, coiling around her. Kallia hated how naturally they came to her. As if he were right at her ear, in the mirror.

"Nothing," Kallia repeated, keeping her back to the vanity. Cool, composed. "I rarely keep mirrors around me. Bad luck."

Aaros inspected the surface. "Really? You were just—"

"Remembering why I don't look at them in the first place." Hopefully he wouldn't notice later when she covered it for the remainder of their stay. "Performance superstition."

Raising his hands in a small, placating way, he chuckled. "Fine, whatever makes you tick. Regardless, that dress looks and fits you like sin. Hope you know that." Aaros gave an approving nod. "Now be nice and say something grand about me."

"I don't need to be nice to say you look good." The nerves had already begun to leave her as she straightened the collar of his new suit. Aaros was good at changing the subject. He'd even made no complaint when she dragged him out to buy a proper suit. Tonight, he looked a far cry from the thief who'd tried to steal from her. More dashing than devious, though the latter lurked beneath.

They made a striking duo as they exited the suite arm in arm, descending the stairs like a dark pair of devils. Any guest ascending instinctively stepped back. The attention made Kallia's lips curl with satisfaction.

The chill of the late hour hit instantly as they stepped out of the Prima and onto the street. Night hung over the city in a black velvet curtain offset by the frostbitten lampposts. Even under the trembling lights, she devoured the scene she was a part of, joining the sea of strangers. Kallia could barely contain her giddiness, occasionally lifting up onto the balls of her feet to take in as much as she could. Aaros merely snorted.

At the faint beat of drums, she dropped back on both feet. The noise persisted, cutting through the night. The rhythmic clang of metal. The sly blow of a trumpet ringing over the beats.

Music.

It called to Kallia like a hunger. A memory she'd been missing.

Her skin rose in bumps that had little to do with the cold. Aaros had set them on the path to the mayor's mansion, but Kallia turned them toward the music.

"Taking us back toward the Alastor Fold will make for quite a roundabout way," Aaros muttered, following. "You sure you want to be late?"

"Lateness makes for grander entrances," she stated. "Don't you hear the music?"

Years of music day and night gave her a natural sense for wherever it pulsed. The dancer in her craved to match the melody, and meet it.

As they passed familiar silhouettes of darkened buildings, Kallia realized they were walking toward the Alastor Place, where the sidewalks quieted even as the air did the opposite. Music had a way of raising flames from the shadows, and Kallia breathed in the smoke, following it.

The trail of sound led to the Conquering Circus tents, no longer still as a snake's old skin, but alive and sinuous in the night breeze. Lit lanterns were strung across the length of the main tent, hanging over the

heads of a raucous gathering of girls. A silver-white bonfire writhed in
the center, which seemed to provide more than enough warmth for the
musicians handling the instruments bare-handed, and those wearing
a variety of odd, flashy coats. Many wore skin-tight body suits that
reminded Kallia of her dance leotards. She recognized Juno among
them, strutting around in a formfitting outfit that stretched over the
wide flare of her hips, sheer enough to showcase all of her glimmering
tattoos. She took a sip from a bottle and raised it over her head like a
scepter, before doubling over in hysterical laughter.

Kallia watched the scene, wordless. Transfixed. Laughter min-
gling with music was a sound that made her ache, conjuring memories of joking in the practice room with Mari, Sanja, even Mistress
Verónn when Kallia had failed in teaching her a routine.

None of it had been real. Not really.

"What's the matter, boss?"

Aaros stared at her in concern. Kallia sighed shakily. "Nothing.
It's cold, is all—"

"Don't you have anything better to do than stalk us?"

Kallia turned at the spiteful voice, finding a dark-skinned girl
around her age a few steps away. Her hair gleamed ruby red under
the hazy glow of the lamp above, but that wasn't what struck Kallia
first. A light scar snaked across her face, curling down to emphasize
her fierce scowl—the face of a starving tiger before it attacked.

"Just enjoying your music." Kallia tilted her glance back at the
hub of performers. "I haven't heard any since I got here. Unfortunately, this city has a severe lack in taste."

"An outsider, too? Part of the show, then?" the girl demanded
brusquely. "Let me guess, you're the flashy sidepiece for this magician bloke."

Most of the ladies Kallia had encountered on the street barely met
her gaze. But this one talked like how a snake would bite, and it only
made Kallia like her more. "Actually, the bloke is *my* flashy sidepiece,"
she said, enjoying the other girl's reaction. "Pretty, isn't he?"

With a dramatic breath, Aaros threw back his head. "You flatter me."

"I'll be damned." The girl's scowl dropped. "I didn't know female magicians could be allowed in . . . Rayne turned me away."

"Wait, that was *you*?" Kallia briefly remembered the judges' account of a girl who'd tried auditioning.

"Oh, they mentioned me?" She coolly inspected her nails before running them through her red hair. "Wonder what colorful adjectives they used. You must've had one spectacular audition if they couldn't say no."

A sliver of envy sharpened her tone, but not the nasty kind. Impressed, almost. At least Kallia thought so. "They didn't have much choice, and neither did I. It was either I earn my spot, or I was on the streets."

A snicker came from Aaros at the mere idea, while the circus performer coolly lifted a shoulder. "These streets aren't too bad," she said. "If you ever decide to shed your fancies for a bit, you should come back. The girls would be keen to meet you."

Kallia tamped down her rush of excitement. "I'll take you up on that." She bobbed her head, ears perked at the sounds of instruments she wasn't sure she'd ever heard.

The stranger observed with a knowing tilt of her head. "You're a performer, I can smell it on you. What sort of shows could a female magician possibly put on before all this?"

Kallia stilled. The question came as no surprise, but hearing it out loud was like having the skin peeled off her bones. Everything, bared. What other secrets did she wear that others could all too easily see?

The girl's face softened suddenly, her brow drawn. "Sorry. I . . . I shouldn't have asked."

"Wait, what do you know?" Aaros exclaimed, eyes wide.

Kallia's pulse thundered even more. There was no way she could've met this circus performer, unless she frequented Hellfire

House, which was unlikely. She wouldn't forget hair that red. Still, the girl didn't seem to recognize Kallia, either.

"Calm down, pretty boy. It's nothing you could understand." The circus performer scowled at him. "Not unless you're a magician like us trying to make it anywhere."

Both girls looked at each other, as though a secret were shared between them. *I know,* they seemed to say to each other. This stranger knew where Kallia had come from without needing an answer—the shows she was allowed to put on rather than the ones she wanted—just as Kallia knew her. No words needed. No judgment, no pity.

"Looking forward to seeing you around when you do decide to stop by again." The girl backed away, a small grin curving her scar over her cheek. "You *and* your pretty assistant."

With a parting nod, Kallia headed back on their original path, Aaros following alongside. Fortunately, there was no way of getting lost with his knowledge of Glorian's shortcuts, expertly cutting them right across the street with a bemused expression. "Do you always make friends everywhere you go?"

"Friends, no," she answered, imagining a glimmer of herself among the Conquering Circus, enjoying a drink and laughing by the fire. Confiding in the red-haired girl everything she could never say to Aaros, even Jack for that matter. It took all of Kallia's will not to abandon the dinner party altogether so she could turn back. But she had a place to hold. That came first. "Allies, when I can."

"*Allies?* For what, exactly?"

"Don't you know the basics of show business? Everything is war on a stage many people want to claim. So yes, I'd like to gather my allies before the bloodshed begins."

"Zarose." It was not the first time Aaros simply stared at her, unsure what sort of world he was entering at her lead. "War, bloodshed, allies." He shook his head. "Whatever showman's war you're anticipating, let's eat first. To dinner, we finally go."

As expected, they all stared. It's exactly what Kallia wanted, and she couldn't have picked a better time to arrive at the mayor's mansion than if she'd planned it.

"Darling!" Erasmus Rayne rose to his feet like an overeager spectator, flaunting his burnt-orange suit in all its proud glory. "I was afraid you'd lost your invitation. You're just in time for the second course!"

From the look of Mayor Eilin at the head of the table, he'd probably been hoping she had lost her way altogether—especially when he caught full sight of her. A beastly monster frothing at the mouth could've stomped into the room, and his look of horror would've been no different.

The other dinner guests bore similar expressions. Shock, discomfort, a bit of disgust, especially from the scowling young woman sitting beside the mayor. Her golden hair had been spun into a tight bun, and her dress had a sleek champagne hue to its fabric that covered her arms and went all the way up to her neck.

Kallia's dress, in contrast, left little to the imagination. She ought to feel more shame, she knew, for such a deliberately un-Glorian choice. Mostly, she was relieved to have gone with a strapless dress. The room's air had grown uncomfortably warm under the candles lining the mirror-paneled walls, with more than a dozen bodies packed inside. Two more, now.

"Apologies." A thrill coursed through Kallia as she tugged Aaros toward the two empty seats at the end of the table. "We were a little caught up in some business of our own."

Judge Silu choked on his drink, while some gazes fluttered away. Others peered even closer. As Aaros pulled back her chair, she couldn't miss his slightly amused smirk.

"What business could you possibly have already?" The mayor scoffed. "The competition has not even begun."

"Mayor Eilin, the competition began the moment you let those flyers run to print and studded your whole city with them." Kallia relaxed into the thick velvet of her chair. "And besides, I'm not one to rest or toast in celebration of something I haven't won yet. Surely everyone who's earned their place has been practicing?"

"Practicing how, exactly?" a red-haired man a few seats away asked after a long sip of wine. "This is no talent show, sweetheart. Each round revolves around a prompt and props. You can't practice spontaneity when all you need is a sharp mind."

The rest of the party murmured in agreement. Kallia drummed her fingers delicately over the table. "Then I hope for your sake you've been doing all you can to keep *your* mind sharp as a knife. Sweetheart."

He'd raised his empty glass for a refill, and lowered it with a glower. "Cheeky."

"Settle down, Josev. Kallia. Save your bite for the stage. The crowd will love it." Erasmus aimed his gaze toward the other end of the table. "Demarco was *just* about to give us an update on the Patrons of Great. Fascinating work, they're doing."

From the look of Demarco's grimace, he was clearly not as in awe. He shifted in his seat next to the mayor, sparing a cursory glance across the table. "Yes, I've received a letter saying they're currently investigating a few . . . odd cases cropping up across Soltair's eastern side."

He spoke delicately, Kallia noted. Sparingly. As though he were used to the way all the guests clung to his words, uninterested in entertaining them a moment more.

"Anything serious?"

"Is it that case of labor magicians?" one of the contestants piped up. "It was in the papers last week. A few woke up unable to do a day's work, while others accomplished the work of ten men."

"You read gossip rags, Robere?" Josev chuckled.

"The Patrons pay attention to the press," Robere snapped. "Isn't that right, Demarco?"

"They only come when they're called upon, and that alone keeps them busy enough," said Demarco. "If they followed up on *every* story to make headlines, they'd be hunting more lies than truths."

"So say we make more than a few headlines . . ." Erasmus suggested with a wily glint in his eyes. "They won't come banging down our doors?"

"Don't get any ideas, Rayne. We're already pushing it." The mayor pointedly avoided looking in Kallia's direction. "This competition is supposed to save us, not scandalize us."

"Can't it do both?" Erasmus laughed into the next sip from his glass, and the others joined. Each threw short glances Kallia's way as the dinner party resumed, as if looking any longer would incur her wrath. Or her smile.

It was an effort to remember the names of these men when they all bore the same scowls and proud sneers. Only the places on Soltair they hailed from set them apart. The unpleasant drinker, Josev, went on loudly about the latest crop of magicians he'd taught at Valmonts. Aaros had to remind her that the guests nearest to them went by Farris, Constantin, Robere, and Eduar—all trained labor magicians hailing from the southern region of Deque, bonding over their high hopes to leave their workstations for the stage.

The Conquering Circus provided that exact opportunity. For any of the outsiders, Kallia realized, not only her.

But no one could've possibly wanted it more. She had nowhere to return to, if she lost. No work to fall back on, should she fail.

Aaros kept the mood light when the others hardly acknowledged her. A kind effort, but she'd expected the shunning. She was no stranger to it. Some petty alliance had already formed against her, and nobody bothered to hide it.

Wait for it, she thought, stroking at the handle of her dinner knife. When the competition really started, they'd all be at each other's throats.

Just when Kallia thought the night couldn't get any better, her glass tipped forward with a clatter. Not knocked over by her hands or anyone else's. Kallia immediately threw her napkin over the tablecloth to absorb the dark stream of wine running toward her.

"Oh my, it seems you've made a bit of a mess," Mayor Eilin called out, not missing a beat. "Now everyone, I told you this was to be a civil dinner. We're all good sports here."

The room rang with laughter. Seemingly good-natured but reeking of mocking. Aaros's expression hardened instantly, but Kallia patted his arm as a server came over to help clean the mess. "This little spill? Accidents happen. This can barely be considered a mess by my definition."

"You must have a lot of experience." The blond girl next to the mayor hardly hid her snicker, flicking at the tassels hanging off the candelabra in front of her.

Kallia only grinned back wider. Not that she expected the only other female in the room to side with her, but against the malicious barricade, it wouldn't have hurt. Sadly, in this room, Aaros was her only friend.

A high-pitched scream erupted, followed by a *thunk.* Every head whipped toward the mayor's end of the table, where the candelabra had fallen over onto the place setting of the girl who'd startled right off her chair.

Demarco immediately crouched to help her from the floor, but she only shrieked *"Fire!"* at the small flame eating away at her abandoned napkin.

Mayor Eilin jerked back as if it were a snake. The magician to his right, Josev, calmly pushed past him. "Allow me."

He could've easily smothered the tiny fire with his sleeve, but the magician smoothed his fingers through his hair before holding them out.

The fire grew, the more seconds ticked. Temple sweating in concentration, Josev whispered something under his breath that sent a stream of water traveling slow as molasses from a nearby glass. It floated above the flame, and with another long burst of words from Josev, extinguished the fire completely.

Light applause rang across the table as the magician dropped his hands. "Please, please, I'm no hero."

Kallia's mouth fell open at the ridiculousness of it all. *That* was acquired magic at work?

"Thank you for that display." Mayor Eilin cheerily patted Josev on the shoulder. "And for saving my table."

Unbelievable.

The mayor leaned over to set the fallen candelabra back up, giving a hopeless sigh at the girl. "No more playing with the centerpieces, Janette."

"I *wasn't*, Father." Pink-cheeked, she returned to her seat with the assistance of Demarco. He shot Kallia a look across the table, his jaw set. Always so serious.

Unable to help herself, she gave him a delicate wave of her fingers.

"Down, girl." Aaros nudged her. "I know you wanted to light up the party a bit, but that was—"

"As if I would be so petty. That wasn't me. *Honest.*" Kallia sipped at her newly replenished wine, meeting Demarco's intense gaze with another playful wave. "I'm saving all my claws for show night."

Twenty-four was a troublemaker.

Daron knew it the moment she entered the room. Not because of what she wore, but in her look of pleasure upon earning everyone's shock. She and her partner swapped sly grins throughout the night, thinking nobody would notice. But Daron had an eye for instigators, having been one himself in his show days. He knew exactly what sort of trouble arrogance could bring to the table.

"Mister Demarco, tell me about your plans after the show."

Next to him, Janette was still massaging her wrist, though no harm had come to it. Her coy blue eyes looked up at him from beneath thick lashes. As the mayor's daughter, she exuded poise and grace, even after a fall from her chair. Not a golden hair out of place, no stains marring the soft silk of her dress.

Kallia, on the other hand, looked like she'd arrived from an entirely different realm. Hair worn down and wild, red lips, and a bold dress that bordered on irreverent. It was hard to look away. And still, Daron sensed something reserved about her. A wall. He'd known a thing or two about putting up bold fronts, how well they could hide what you wished others not to see.

"Mister Demarco?" Janette repeated through a sweet smile.

Daron cleared his throat with an apology. "No plans, really."

"You're not thinking of working with the Patrons?" she asked. "With your aunt at the helm, sounds like something of a family business. It's all so, so interesting."

Her avid curiosity was on brand with Erasmus's, and it made Daron's skin itch. Somehow it was the people without magic who were most fascinated by the systems for monitoring those in possession of it. They perked up whenever they heard of the Patrons taking in corrupt magicians who abused their power, or destroying items infused with magic in unnatural ways.

Eva always said Aunt Cata tended to monitor Soltair with a tighter fist, which Daron found ironic as Aunt Cata had looked to Eva as her successor. Even he couldn't deny she was a more obvious choice; more naturally talented and quick-thinking, strategic and powerful.

Without her, the pressure was on him, and his aunt's weekly letters had burned a hole in his courier case every time one arrived. Opened, but unanswered.

"It's definitely an option." Daron's gaze dropped to where she'd folded back her cuffs to expose the delicate white skin beneath. "How's your wrist?"

"Oh, much better!" Janette's spark of delight soured almost instantly. "No apology from her, of course."

He resisted looking at Kallia. The challenge of the night for him, it seemed. "For what?"

"The candle." With a huff, she smoothed out her dress's skirt. "Squandering magic on such pettiness. Can you believe it?"

She spoke of magic like it was hers to speak of. He bit the inside of his cheek. "No, I can't."

In a curious flash, Janette's demeanor went from sweet to assessing as a spider. "You know what the judges say about you? That despite your past and your family, you're something of a monk magician now."

Heat abruptly raced up his neck. He glanced at the others, holding back a glare.

Petty gossips.

"They say you don't use magic anymore. Wastefully, at least."

"They don't know me." He spoke tersely, just as her fingers trailed over his wrist.

"Well, if it were true," she said, humoring him, "I'd find it admirable. Magic could be used for so much more than tricks on a stage. Father told me all about her gaudy audition—imagine how fire like that could warm a home, burn waste, *anything*!"

"We have labor magicians who choose that sort of work." Daron withdrew his hand to reach for his drink. Her talk was out of touch, like the beliefs of those long ago who didn't understand that magicians were more than just chattel to put to work. That their magic was not simply there to be used for those without.

Soltair had moved forward from that thinking. Except for Glorian, apparently.

"Sure, but why waste power for some vanity show?" Janette growled as she unfolded her wrist cuffs. "This town has not seen magic for ages, and we've survived. It's nothing but a mistake to start again."

He almost pressed her for more on what she'd meant, but she'd already begun talking up the other magician near her. The moment, lost.

Glumly, Daron turned back to his plate. He wasn't very good at this. After years of interacting with only his house staff, with his butler, Gastav, he'd grown rusty in the ways of cunning conversation. Not that he was an expert in the first place. But here, he came off even more graceless than usual. The Patrons might've gotten him this far, but it did not guarantee smoothness.

This pointless dinner had ended up being more of a trial than he'd imagined. Daron only attended in hopes of hearing more about Glorian. Unfortunately, it turned into a night of meaningless talk about places *outside* of the city. As well as prying into his showman's past and family, which he artfully dodged. A skill he'd acquired through no grace at all, but necessity.

If Daron had taken a drink for every time someone dropped his stage name or the Patrons, they'd have to cart him back to his room.

"Got any plans after this, Daring?" Ives nudged his shoulder with a hushed whisper. "Some of the gents and I were thinking of having some fun. Come out with us tonight."

His brow jutted up high. "In Glorian? Doesn't seem like there's much of a nightlife here at all." Not much of a day life, either.

"No, not *in* the city." Ives winked, with a warning nod the mayor's way. His voice dropped lower. "There's a club out in the Woods. Best kept secret in town."

Daron couldn't think of a more unappealing idea. "Sorry, don't think I'll be able to join."

"Oh, come on," Ives drawled. "You need to let loose a little!"

Monk magician. He wouldn't be surprised if this contestant threw the term around behind his back with everyone else. As if he gave a damn about it. Or some nightclub in a cursed forest. He wasn't that kind of magician anymore.

Without a second thought, Daron placed his napkin over his plate.

"Turning in so soon, Demarco?" the mayor observed, red-cheeked and rather loudly, enough to rouse the whole table's attention.

Daron only continued buttoning up his jacket. "Thank you for the meal, Mayor Eilin, but I'm not sure I have room for much more."

"Nonsense! We were just about to run through the layout of the competition. Can't imagine you'd want to miss that, for how eager you've been to judge and all."

Eager. A generous word.

"Oh, if the pup wants to go, let him," Judge Bouquet muttered, dabbing at his mouth with a napkin. "Not everything can be fun and games. We've got important business to discuss here."

Daron's fingers paused. Rather than stalk back to his room, he very deliberately unbuttoned his jacket and lowered back into his seat. "I would hate to miss it, then."

The bite in his reply irked the old judge all the same. The rest of the table saw nothing of it, pressing closer as the mayor began to rise.

Erasmus triumphantly shot up first.

"Congratulations, contestants," he said, beaming. "You ten have made it here from all corners of Soltair to be a part of something truly spectacular. Over the years, I've put on grand caravans of side acts, large-scale theatricals, and all manner of shows to entertain and amaze, but never one like this. A competitive audition, live to the public, to reveal who will be crowned as the next headlining act in my Conquering Circus."

A small chill ran down Daron's spine at the ringleader's words, and a quick glance across the table was proof the effect was not lost on anyone. Especially Kallia, who bore the hungriest expression from her eyes alone, burning with a hope that charged the room.

"Over the next month, our competition will consist of three acts. The remaining contestants, determined by voters' choice and judges' scores—with the first round shaving off three of the weakest showmen. After the second, another three," Erasmus continued. "And the last performance, the mentor round, will be overseen by the audience who'll then choose my future headliner."

Daron stiffened. "Mentor round?"

"We can't have the judges sitting behind a table the whole time, can we?" chortled Erasmus. "The mayor and myself aside, you four will pair up with the final four competitors to craft their grand finale. Imagine how fun it will be, to see you take the stage once more!"

Fun. Just imagining the last time he'd been on stage almost sent him fleeing. The other three judges, retired much longer than he, appeared just as displeased. No one hung up their top hats for good only to don them again.

"We'll discuss it more later." The mayor eyed them all in reassurance. "Since it's still a ways off, we're open to change. *Right,* Rayne?"

A long pause stretched in the air before Erasmus straightened his gaudy orange bow tie, tight-lipped. "Of course," he said. "Though, before we move forward, I do have one simple request that I'm afraid cannot be negotiated."

The proprietor slid from his coat pocket a narrow scroll of purple-tinted paper that unrolled all the way to the floor. "The Conquerors Contract."

The length made Daron's stomach drop. From where he sat, the lighting only bore glimmers of the fine print and text blocks spanning the scroll. At the bottom, by his feet, he found a row of blank lines. One for each participant.

"Excuse me?" Mayor Eilin snatched the paper from Erasmus's hand, squinting hard at the text. "Y-you said nothing of a contract."

"Really, have you fallen that out of touch with the world that you've forgotten the basic principles of business? Contracts exist for a reason. For records and protection. Reassurance," Erasmus listed, nonchalant. "I never start a venture without one. All my performers had to sign as soon as they entered my troupe. It's standard procedure."

"Yes, but what's the catch?" The mayor frantically skimmed. "I'll have to take time going over this—"

"Honestly, Eilin, it only says our party here agrees to play and *will* stay for the duration of the game. Forgive me if I'd rather not take your word for it."

"Then why is the contract so bloody long?"

"After much experience, I am very thorough with every scenario. Cheaters I can stand, because they make things interesting. But nothing ruins a good show more than deserters who think running is a better fate than losing." Erasmus scoffed. "That, I think, we can all agree on."

Every muscle in Daron tensed. He hadn't planned on staying in Glorian longer than he needed to. "And if we don't sign?"

Silence hardened the air, before a long, expectant sigh.

"I'm sparing no expense for this. The least you can do is spare a signature." Erasmus, a businessman to the core, tilted his shrewd gaze at the mayor. "Or the show won't go on. And you'll have to explain to your people why they'll no longer have a city when it's reduced to nothing but a block of ice in a cursed forest."

Mayor Eilin appeared more stricken than before. Face pale, frozen in thought. Daron almost felt bad for the man carrying the deadweight of Glorian on his shoulders, trying in vain to revive it.

The candles flickered, as if moved by the sweeping chill, when the mayor finally exhaled and thrust an open palm toward Erasmus. "I assume you brought a pen?"

11

Kallia had only ever signed her name in journals. She'd filled every line, every space and corner, until the strokes and loops of her name drowned all the pages within stacks of diaries. All practice for the hurried autographs for her crowded audiences one day.

She'd perfected her signature so many times that the moment she needed to sign for her place in the game, it didn't feel real.

"I'm all about doing whatever's necessary, boss," Aaros whispered. "But even you have to admit this seems horribly—"

"I know." Her fingertip traced the the scrawls of contestants and judges already lining the bottom of the contract. "But if I don't sign, there is no show."

And no show meant no home, no money, no future.

Nothing.

Jaw tight, she penned her name on the next empty line. The finality of it pricked at her with a heavy, sinking weight. Still, the sight of her looped letters gave way to an odd surge of glee that pierced through it all.

No turning back now.

"Now that the boring business part is taken care of . . ." Erasmus rolled up the scroll once all names were signed. He slid it back into his pocket with a clap. "No one enjoys a silent meal. Eilin, you're up."

"Oh, is it finally my turn to host?" The mayor's question bit with sarcasm.

"Yes," Erasmus said, oblivious. "Entertain us with a story."

"I have no stories."

"Oh, sure you do. We're living right in the heart of it!" The proprietor gestured around him before steepling his fingers. "Not even my best sources have been able to dig up much on this place, which only increased my curiosity. If I'm going to save a city from ruin, it'd be nice to know more than its name."

Murmurs rippled across the room, a shift that swept the previous uneasiness away. All her life, the only thing Kallia had known about Glorian was that it was forbidden. Like a whole other world rather than the next city over. Hushing it all up, pretending it wasn't there, only gave it more life.

All eyes focused on the mayor. Even Demarco looked rapt, barely touching his dessert.

"This is ludicrous," Janette huffed, resting a hand on her father's arm. "We are not fodder for your gossip vine."

"Fear the pesky journalists, then," Erasmus advised. "I'm not looking for gossip. Just answers. *Anything*, really."

"The world does seem to have a sick fascination with us, don't they?" The mayor gently pushed his daughter's hand away. After taking a generous sip of his wine, he reached into his coat pocket, holding out a card that, when fanned out, became four. "Upon entering Glorian, you must've noticed our gates. We were once a city built around four suits of cards. Four suits for four families, each with their own corner of Glorian," he said. "The Ranzas, the Vierras, the Fravardis, and the Alastors."

At each name, he dropped a card. One with the symbol of a triangle at its corner, then a star, a square, and a circle. The black-rusted gates flashed in Kallia's mind, their shapes cast from the cards on the table.

"Allegedly, my family's blood has some Fravardi in it. They were the noble guards of Glorian. No natural magic in their blood, but they did possess the magician's touch. A duty to the community." Pride shone in his eyes. "They became one of the first teachers of acquired magic."

"So you practice magic, Mayor Eilin?" Demarco asked.

"Oh goodness, no. I don't have the skill, or the desire." The mayor shrugged. "Magic doesn't exist in everyone. The born, on the other hand, have it right in their blood." He glanced at Demarco, briefly toward Kallia. "In Glorian, the families of born magic were the Vierras, whose gift was terrifying and rare—clairvoyance, mostly. And the Ranzas, who believed magic was a skill to be shared with the common people. Performers to the public, the lot of them."

"And the Alastors?" asked another magician.

"Those devils believed magic could be stolen." The mayor grimaced in distaste. "They acquired magic, but in all manner of vices: gambling, betting, bartering. They were more powerful in numbers. Conmen and showmen alike. Their gangs became the rot of this town."

"*Gangs?* In quiet, little Glorian?" Erasmus's face lit up in delight. "Fascinating."

Janette shot him a glare. Mayor Eilin's brow furrowed deeply, his mask of confusion so exaggerated it had to be fake. "I don't know more than that. This was a time long, long before. Most of our records no longer exist."

"On purpose?"

"Not everything needs to scandalized, Mister Rayne." Janette dragged her fork over the remains on her plate, the sound of claws over glass. "We don't need you spreading tall tales about us to fill your seats."

"Pardon my curiosity." Not even his charm could soften her. "But I can assure you, the rumors I've heard about Glorian are far more sensationalized than anything I could ever dream up."

"What rumors?"

Demarco asked the very question Kallia had been thinking. The question everyone seemed keen to know.

Erasmus smiled knowingly. "That this place is cursed."

Daron's breath almost shuddered out in satisfaction. He'd been prepared to leave after the contract nonsense, and now he was glad he hadn't.

With each casual, waiting sip from his glass, his pulse raced. *This* was what he'd come for.

"Don't act so surprised—you're quite literally surrounded by a cursed wood. It's natural deduction. I've heard stories of this place ranging from being a dead city of haunting ghosts to a lurid den of glitz and sin," Erasmus went on, chuckling. "You keep your mysterious, little town under such a lid, it's inevitable that people's imaginations run wild."

"Do people really have nothing better to do than speculate over small towns?" the mayor grumbled.

"You say it like it's a bad thing," Erasmus said. "Fascination will work in our favor. It's easier to rope in a crowd from the outside when they're already itching for a peek within."

"I've heard talk of hidden magic," Daron cut in.

Everyone turned toward him, and the acute attention made his face grow hot.

"Or something strange and powerful, at least," he added quickly, coughing over his words. "Concealed."

That had everyone's eyebrows rising.

"Thank you for adding that theory to the pile, but this isn't Zarose Gate." Janette let out a peal of laughter. "I can assure you, we've spent far too long keeping most forms of magic out. The last thing we would want is to hide any."

"Then why open Glorian up to magic now?" Daron pushed harder than he should've. There could've been secrets she and the mayor were keeping, something they *knew*. And yet their manner screamed the opposite. At each theory, their expressions shifted from lost to downright insulted, especially at Daron's.

Nothing frightened him more: the possibility of finding out Eva had been wrong all along. Or finding nothing that could lead him to her.

"Mister Demarco, you're as bad as the circus man." Janette shook her head, almost pitiably. "Like I said, wasteful stage shenanigans were never our priority. But unfortunately, they have become our last resort."

"And the only thing that could save your city." Kallia's voice rang out. She rested her chin against her palm. "Not that it really matters, or anything."

"Enough crackpot rumors." Mayor Eilin swatted his hand dismissively. "What matters is we're looking to move forward and rebuild. The renovations in Glorian have been an ongoing project, and it's time to finish fixing what's been broken. We can all agree that the Alastor Place has seen better days, am I right?"

That elicited a few chuckles, but Daron controlled his. The time for stories was over, and he knew to keep quiet. Too much interest led to scrutiny. And he already had enough eyes following him.

Daron sat back with a sigh. He didn't even attempt to participate in the discussion about the Alastor Place. There was something sad about the Alastor Fold compared to the rest of Glorian. The architecture carried itself beautifully, in the way an old iron sword worn from war would. All sharp angles and grim edges. But having spent the auditions in that broken mess of a show hall, Daron wondered how such repairs could even be completed in time for the first performance night.

"The Conquering Circus can conquer anything," Erasmus boasted in response, pink-cheeked. Daron was surprised he'd spoken aloud.

"We have over a week, plenty of time to transform. I've hired only the best workers and labor magicians for this project."

"And how will they be compensated for the rush work?"

All eyes shifted to Kallia, idly tracing her finger over the rim of her glass.

"Very generously." The man cleared his throat, though it was clear he hadn't given it any thought until now. "As you know, you will all be receiving a rather nice stipend for the work you'll be doing. Well, the ones who make the first cut." With a reassuring wink, he added, "It's in the contract."

Some contestants lifted their glasses in assent, but Kallia's deliberating finger stilled over hers. "I find it curious that you've chosen the most neglected building in which to host this grand event. It sounds like an awful lot more work for the people who have to get their hands dirty," she drawled. "And don't forget the circus workers who have to make camp there. In this cold weather, especially."

Daron was ashamed to not have even considered the circus. Aside from that one performer who'd tried auditioning, the women of the Conquering Circus didn't occupy as much attention as its leader. For a circus, they were peculiarly quiet, practically invisible except when boasted about by name.

An air of unease hung over the room. Stiffly, Erasmus loosened his tie, his color rising. "Unfortunately, the Alastor Place is the largest building in Glorian with the space we require."

Of course it was the only possibility. Glorian possessed no shows or theaters, and for the scope of what Erasmus was imagining, they needed room. They needed the universe. The gleam in the proprietor's eye brightened as he listed off proposed changes. ". . . installing new seats and more lighting!" he said. "Nothing much we can do about the hideous old bell tower; that thing hasn't been able to ring in ages. But the ruin from all else—gone. We're in the process of raising a city back from the dead, bigger and better than ever."

"But how did it die in the first place?"

Daron's brow scrunched. Kallia, not easily dazzled, had spoken the very question he'd been too wary to ask. In all their minds, seeing as how no one shot her an annoyed glare.

"There was . . . a *fire*," the mayor spoke oddly, looking down at his twiddling fingers. "A great and terrible fire, long ago. Do you remember, Janette?"

Shaking her head, she bore a similar look of alarm. "Father."

"It was so bad," he continued, tentatively, "that it forced all the families and people of Glorian to leave and—"

"No, Father, *look*!" Janette shrieked. The whole table jumped as she pointed shakily at the opposite wall. A candle had fallen to the ground. And another. Like dominos, all of the candles toppled from their holders—smoke rising in columns, flames quickly devouring the carpet as if oil had soaked into the ground.

The fires rose rampant, unnatural.

Every guest shot from their seat, trapped in the sudden ring of fire. The mirrored walls reflected the flames, illuminating the room in blinding pieces of light before a sea of smoke drowned them in gray. Amid the coughing and shouting, Daron tossed his full water glass over his napkin and shoved it against his nose and mouth. Janette was plastered to her father's side, screaming into his lapel while he hollered at his butlers to grab blankets. Throw water. Open the windows.

"No—don't open the windows!"

Daron's eyes began tearing from the smoke, but he saw Kallia taking the helm at the other side of the table, ripping her black gloves off. "Everyone, hold your breath!"

She wanted them to do what?

Daron pressed the damp cloth to his mouth, trying to think. None of the other magicians could do anything but panic. He could hardly look around, for the mirrors were everywhere. His fist clenched, frustration deep in his veins. In his performing days, he'd been able to shower water from whatever sky he chose. Now, trapped in a room of fire, his mind blanked. Useless.

Not Kallia. Through the curtain of smoke between them he observed her stance, like that of a fighter, learning her opponent. She spread her arms out wide and raised them higher, and as if some spirit entered her body, her shoulders to her chest lifted in one upward yank that straightened her spine.

All of a sudden, the air in the room turned void.

There was no sound, no smell.

No heat, no breath.

Daron resisted the impulse to inhale. That fool Josev tried, and fell over the table. Daron heard the crash of glass and utensils, but the pressure building in his ears clogged the sounds into dull little thuds.

It could've been seconds or hours—time passed slowly without air. Daron's chest grew tight, but out of the corner of his eye, the hazy flicker of flames rapidly diminished, shrinking back until all that was left was smoke thickening the air. Like a conductor, Kallia flicked her palms outward. The windows flew open.

Her whole torso collapsed, chest heaving.

The guests gathered their bearings, coughing and gasping in the fresh air from the outside. One of the magicians checked on Josev, still slumped over the table, his lips trembling at the influx of oxygen.

"Zarose," the mayor swore, mouth hanging. "What did you do?"

"More importantly," Erasmus cut in. "Who taught you that trick?"

"Show's over," Kallia's assistant snapped. "Be grateful she saved your lives."

Like everyone else, Daron wanted answers. But as Kallia straightened back her shoulders, mouth twisted in a ready retort, she swayed and slumped over before getting a single word out.

The room exploded once more into action. Daron all but rushed toward the other end as the current of panic thrummed wildly within him. He kicked aside fallen chairs in his path, shoving others out of his way before stopping himself. That strange pull.

He forced himself to stay back as her assistant began lowering her to the floor, calling her name—hissing at whoever tried laying a hand on her.

Not without noticing how Kallia looked in her long black dress spilling over the floor, joining the huge scorch marks trailing around the dinner table like a fire-burnt crown.

I'm *fine*!" Kallia barked after Aaros asked. Again. She'd only just awakened after he'd thrown some water on her face back in their suite. And still, the smoke drowned her. All she could taste and smell. Her muscles tremored and cried beneath her skin as she exhaled sharply.

Nothing had ever backfired on her like this. Her power performed well, but her? The next time she faced the group, they'd have gleeful looks of pity. How like a woman to swoon in the face of danger, they'd think. How like a *girl* to be so weak.

Her nails pressed and pulled against the frayed edges of the cloth she'd kept in her purse. Before she shredded it to pieces, she threw it on her vanity.

No one could see her like this.

"You don't seem fine." Aaros leaned against a side table, as if bracing himself for when she might collapse again. "Where are you going? It's late. Lie down for a—"

"I don't need to lie down." Fatigue trickled in. Not a show night's worth, but ridding the air had been no small trick. And she couldn't sit still. She hadn't even realized she'd started moving until she paused at the door, gripping it hard. "I just need a moment."

Alone.

She'd thought she was done being alone after the House, but it was the only safe place she could carve for herself. No eyes, no voices. No one to smile or pretend for.

Kallia slipped out without saying good-bye. Her head rang as she rested her ear on the other side of the door, listening for Aaros's footsteps. Reluctantly, they departed from the common room, into the soft close of another door farther away.

Kallia's sigh of relief left on broken breath. She leaned against the door, temple throbbing, and rubbed her hands over her face, fingers coming away with smudges of faded red and black. The water Aaros had splashed all over her makeup, but it was too late to care. Too late to be slinking around in her ruined dress, reeking of smoke and ash.

If she left soot smudges against the cream-colored surface at her back, then so be it. The cold support was the only thing keeping her standing.

That dinner party should've been a triumph. Her fingers tightened over her forehead as the chaos swept back into her mind. The fallen candles, the blaze they became, and what it left behind. While others had shot up in terror, she'd been mesmerized by what had been circling the table. A message, a warning: a crown of fire.

It couldn't be.

If Jack had followed her to Glorian, if he were here, he wouldn't waste time sending threats.

"You."

Kallia stiffened against the wall, her heart racing. *No.* Mere thought couldn't have conjured him. It couldn't—

But when she looked up, a different shadowy outline came into view. Demarco. The last person she expected to stomp toward her, which almost warranted a laugh. Hastily, Kallia raked her hair back from her face and swiped the tears off her cheeks.

"What are you doing?" He neared, faltering. "Are you . . ."

"Mister Demarco," she greeted briskly, the shakiness in her voice capped with a dry, sunny edge. "Should I even ask how you found me, or should we get right into it?"

The judge's eyes flared. "Excuse me?"

"You're the one charging your way to my suite. Don't tell me you somehow stumbled here by accident."

"Before you flatter yourself even more than necessary," Demarco said, crossing his arms, "I'm in the room right across. Trust me, you weren't the first person I expected to find loitering down this hallway, either."

So she'd been a little wrong. "Disappointed?"

"What the hell happened at dinner?"

The accusation cut harsher than a blade, yet she hardly flinched. Used to it. Demarco didn't like her. Maybe he never had. His approval had earned her a place in the competition, but from him, it was only a judgment. He was a magician who knew his craft on the stage and off. And he was no fool. She should've known she'd have to deal with those sorts of men, too.

"I don't know," she said slowly, enunciating every syllable. "There were over a dozen other magicians in the room. Why not suspect any of them?"

"They weren't the ones who could've killed us all."

"You're joking, right? I *saved* your lives," Kallia scoffed. "No one had any sense to conjure even a trickle of water. What were *you* doing when the fire almost roasted us all?"

Demarco shot her a stony look. "A contestant passed out from your elaborate display."

"I did warn you beforehand." She lifted a shoulder. "Can't blame me for the one fool who didn't listen."

"Maybe not, but I can suspect the one who thinks too quickly on her feet."

Seriously. It was all too easy to imagine how any of the other magicians would be treated if in her shoes. He'd probably receive a medal of honor.

"So what, are you going to hail the Patrons and sic your aunt on me, then?"

Aaros would be wringing her neck right about now. Kallia knew she shouldn't joke. Demarco could very well do it, though his brow seemed to harden at the suggestion.

"When confronted with fire"—he spoke calmly, as if beginning a lesson—"the first instinct is to conjure water. Even the tiniest amount, if you have the strength. Instead, you chose the riskiest, most dangerous option."

"And it paid off." They should be thanking her, honestly. "I can't see why you're trying to twist this into something it's not. Everyone came out of that room intact, yet you cast me as the villain."

"Someone has to be." His gaze never wavered. "A fire like that doesn't come out of nowhere, and it sure as hell didn't feel like an accident. Either someone was hoping to shake the other competitors, or someone staged it to show off."

"You really think I would've done all of that to *show off*?"

"That was quite a trick at the end. And from what I've observed, your style is all about the showstoppers."

"Don't act like you know anything about me just because you're some big stage name with a fancy family." She scowled. "But consider this my lesson learned. I won't lend a helping hand the next time there's trouble. Not if it only brings overprivileged beasts like *you* to my doorstep."

To Demarco's credit, he stayed silent. Simmering.

"And before you criticize me any further, Mister Demarco, I hope you realize a competition like this will only get more cutthroat. That fire was just the first baring of claws." Kallia tossed him a devious smile, relishing the challenge. "And if you can't handle that, clearly you didn't think this through when you signed on to become a judge."

"There wasn't much choice," Demarco muttered, anger clipping his tone. "But if I'd known I'd be stuck in a group like this, I wouldn't have left my home."

Liar. She smelled it as strongly as the smoke still clinging to his skin.

"And yet . . ." Kallia drawled, pushing off the wall to circle him. "You're still here."

He watched her, unflinching. "Because of the damn contract."

"No." Head tilted, she drew closer until she was right up against his chest. "You're about as much like those other judges as I am my competitors. But I have a prize to win. You, however—a glorified prince of magicians . . ." She stroked a finger under his chin. "I heard you withdrew from performing years ago. So what exactly is drawing you back?"

And what made you leave?

It surprised her, that she even cared to know.

His throat bobbed under a hard swallow. Tables turned. But to his credit, he didn't stay caged. Didn't even move away. He leaned in intently, letting her finger brush down his neck. Her pulse leaped as their eyes met. "It's none of your damn business."

Interesting. Kallia almost regretted having to squash the flare of curiosity inside her. "Excellent. How about you stay out of mine, then?"

She pulled away and turned swiftly to her door, slamming it shut in his face.

13

Daron rarely slept the next few nights. Not when the echo of that slammed door kept pounding in his ears, forming its own mad song. All beat without melody. It haunted him even more than the accident at dinner.

No, not an accident. Someone had toppled those candles, raising their flames higher than men. All of them would've been consumed by the blaze if Kallia hadn't—

The door slammed in his mind.

Again, and again.

Somehow she'd gotten inside his head, and the bloody show had not even begun yet.

In all their meetings afterward, the ice between them had not subsided. Kallia continued about her business with an indifferent air toward him. Daron had much more difficulty doing the same, for she was impossible not to notice. Always firing off comebacks or dressed in bold colors, a strike of paint against white canvas. Sitting at the hotel's café with her assistant, or laughing down the street with a Conquering Circus performer at her side.

Kallia was everywhere. And everywhere he saw her, he heard her suspicions tolling in his ears. Her curiosity. The absolute last thing he needed.

Someone looking at him, sharp enough to see through it all.

See *him*.

"No, no, no," Erasmus tutted a few mornings after the dinner, pacing in the Alastor Place. He cut off Daron's suggestion with a furious wag of his finger. "I don't care who you are, Demarco. You're *not* getting rid of my star. Besides, you can't—she signed my contract!"

That damned contract. Daron wished he'd torn it apart when he'd had a chance, but foolishly, he'd signed like everyone else, too panicked to refuse. He might as well have written *idiot* alongside his name. Eva would've done it for him, or simply knocked the pen from his hand before smacking the back of his head.

He was shackled to this show until its end, like everyone else. Including Kallia.

Daron raked a hand through his unkempt hair. "Come on, Rayne, you saw what happened at that dinner. She's unpredictable."

He glanced at Kallia, who forever seemed to be in his line of vision. In that moment, she was strutting by the newly glossed stage with her assistant in tow, along with a scar-faced circus performer who growled at any loitering workers who dared look at her too long.

If Kallia was seeking consultation from a member of the Conquering Circus, her act would probably make the dinner incident look like a quaint little bonfire.

"Does this mean you'll call the Patrons?" Erasmus asked carefully. "Shut this all down before it starts?"

It unnerved Daron, the way others looked at him. As an authority, like a Patron. As though he held the reins on a pack of wild dogs that could scourge the city, if he so wished.

The irony was not lost on him. To Aunt Cata's dismay, when he was performing, everyone reveled in his rebellion. Each night, he toed the line of stage magic and danger, defiance and daring.

Now he was dangerous for the opposite reason.

"Of course not." Daron bristled. "Though if any more accidents happen, I'm sure the news would have no trouble reaching them."

Not even he could halt the spread of gossip, but he would try. They had no clue he was just as desperate to avoid a visit from Aunt Cata. She'd done well enough to give him the space he needed, and one look at him would be all it took for her to see why.

He needed more time. To fix everything, before the others figured it out.

"But accidents *happen*. And why are you all set on blaming Kallia? Do any of you even have proof she started it?" Erasmus huffed, and the questions tightened in Daron's gut. He hated being grouped with his fellow peers and the oafish majority of magicians in the show. Truly some of the worst people he'd ever encountered, and he'd met his share of ugliness in this business.

Erasmus snapped his fingers. "Ah, you're jealous."

"Jealous?" Daron's brow crinkled. "Are you joking—jealous of what?"

"Her power," the proprietor said in one gleeful breath. "I can tell the judges and other contestants feel the same, and unfortunately, such attitudes develop from ugly complexes. Insecurities. Your behavior is not unusual—"

"This is not jealousy," Daron said a little too hotly, the words raw against his throat. "I'm concerned. She could harm someone if we don't take the necessary precautions."

Like *him*. In the hallway, she'd already begun trying to read him with those viper eyes, seeking his weaknesses so he couldn't see hers. If Kallia uncovered enough about him, there was absolutely no telling what she'd do.

And Daron wasn't done with Glorian yet. Not even close.

The tense pause broke under the faint sounds of chatter across the spacious show hall, interrupted by the constant patters and hammering of construction. Workers and labor magicians alike had been milling in and out over the past week, breaking up the stage to re-place it with new boards and lights along the edges. Daron gladly fell into the drowning rhythm of hammers on nails before he noticed Erasmus assessing him, pushing his purple-tinted glasses down the bridge of his nose.

"I must say, Demarco, you shift like the sides of a coin when it's tossed," said the proprietor. "If you're so set on kicking Kallia out, why approve her audition in the first place?"

"She's an impressive performer. Not even I can deny that." *Too* impressive, he didn't want to admit. "But if even one of her displays, or anyone else's for that matter, turn into something we can't handle, then I'd regret giving my vote to an accident in the making."

His voice dropped off as a dark cloud flooded his thoughts.

The broken mirror.

His screams.

He drowned for a moment, the first in a long time, letting the memory knife through him until it was over. He set his gaze back on Erasmus, who watched him with a new wariness.

"We don't enter this business clueless of its dangers. We embrace all that comes with this life; it's unavoidable." Erasmus pivoted away from incoming workers hauling piles of redwood planks. "The worse damage is done off-stage when you try to smother out potential. When you blow out the candle before people in the room can glean its light. And this city does not need to suffer in the dark anymore, don't you think?"

Shame coursed through him, burning under his skin. Eva would have walloped him for the very same reasons. He'd felt her prickly presence hovering around him ever since he entered the Alastor Place hours earlier, intent on removing Kallia from Spectaculore.

That morning, Daron had risen earlier than the sun, marching over to the archaic building to catch Erasmus or Mayor Eilin first, only to find one other person waiting in the show hall.

She sat in one of the dusty seats in the front row. Her back to him, observing the bare stage with the most searing brand of concentration. She never acknowledged him, though he knew she was sharp enough to hear even needles clink from the backmost rows. She simply didn't care to turn around, so focused, as though watching a show only she could see.

It was exactly what he used to do. Sit by the stage in the early hours of the day, pretending to be in the audience. Enjoying the rare peace of it.

Even as more people had filtered in, she remained. Just as Daron stood in the same place by the door. Workers and labor magicians jostled by him. Other contestants arrived, urging him to join them for a light round of warm-up exercises. He batted them all away just to continue standing there, curious.

Daron shook his head at how long it had taken him to stop. He'd been the one to instigate their argument between their rooms, after all. With help from a bit of liquor, and the residual adrenaline of surviving the dinner party.

That's no excuse, he could practically hear Eva whispering.

He snuck another glance at Kallia making her way through the show hall. Even with wooden planks, paint, and tools scattered everywhere, she all but glided around them, moving with ease in pants tucked into tall burgundy boots and a long black jacket to stave off the morning chill. They had the same effect as that tight wrap of a gown from dinner. People tensed if she got too near and watched her shamelessly when her back was turned, as though she were a flame that could spill over at any moment.

"You of all people should be more supportive of her," Erasmus interjected abruptly, as if he could hear Daron's thoughts. "I believe you see something in her that not all the judges can relate to. Perhaps her story will end differently."

Whatever regret had briefly sunk into Daron's head vanished to the cold returning. The black cloud, threatening his thoughts.

Everything about him, inside him, turned to ice.

"It's truly a real shame, what happened to that assistant of yours." The proprietor ticked his tongue sympathetically. "You two made quite a pair, and she was such a pretty girl—"

"Shut up, Rayne," Daron snarled. He edged away, into the cacophony of hammering and shouting that only brought him closer to the sound of a young woman laughing with all the confidence in the world, hours before the first performance.

The true leader of the Conquerors went by Canary.

After the scarlet canary, a songbird whose voice was lower than one would suspect for its size. Earlier in the morning, Kallia had given a sleep-rumpled Aaros instructions to find the girl as soon as he'd risen and to meet her at the Alastor Place. At such an hour, he probably would've said yes to walking stark naked all over the city.

No one but Kallia would be in their right mind to wake so early just to case the Alastor Place on the first day of the competition, hours before dress rehearsal. She'd simply watched the stage, alone, envisioning the show as the audience would behold it—the lights lit and the red curtains drawn, sliding open in answer to the applause.

The applause faded as hammering and shouting shook Kallia from the dream. Disoriented, she stole a glance around at the construction workers filing in and out. Demarco stood in the back with that inscrutable stare of his. Erasmus Rayne had only just arrived, and finally, Aaros dragged in the ruby-haired girl who appeared even more disagreeable when freshly woken. But as Kallia relayed her plans for tonight, the circus performer's scowl melted into a smirk. She'd given her name like an offering in return, and Kallia accepted with a knowing smile.

"My crew's not even allowed to watch." Canary kicked aside a broken hunk of wood by the foot of the stage. "We're supposed to hide until we're summoned for whatever Rayne wants us for. He still hasn't decided."

"But you're the Conquering Circus," Aaros declared. "The main piece of it all—he should be showcasing you ladies everywhere, not keeping you in the dark."

"Exactly, pretty boy," she remarked drily. "If the circus were *really* in my hands, we'd blow the top off this town. But alas, his money, his reins."

Kallia frowned, displeased but not at all shocked. Erasmus Rayne had a slipperiness to him, a tendency to grow easily distracted by the next great act and forget all else. He may look at Kallia like a star now, but he'd most likely looked at dozens of others the same way before. Canary, perhaps. The rest of the Conquering Circus, too.

She didn't like it, but Kallia would still give him her best. If that's what it took to stay in the game. Demarco certainly didn't approve of her anymore. They'd avoided one another since he'd accused her of being a reckless saboteur, which was fine by her. As long as she had Rayne's favor, she needed nothing else.

Except more performers.

Kallia made her last sweep of the stage with Canary and Aaros before descending the steps, going over the positions and directions she'd imagined the others coming in from. It was a smaller platform than she was used to. Nights at Hellfire House had spoiled Kallia with the luxury of her own floor, but the glossy stage was vast enough for what she had in mind. The whole place, to her amazement, was finally looking like a proper show hall for performers.

Beside her, workers paddled at the dark velvet curtains, ridding the dust and readying them for draping. The floors had been wiped, more seats repaired and installed, and the stark triangular windows and walls carried a touch of color to lift the room from its ashes. A huge improvement from the bare stage Kallia had first walked onto. In the coming weeks with more fixes here and there, the Alastor Place would properly gleam in the way it seemed to yearn to.

"I should get back." Canary nodded toward the door. "Have to call the animals to action for a decent pre-show practice."

"From what I observed last time, I'm sure you'll have no issue." Kallia gave Aaros a jostle in the gut. "Unlike my dazzling assistant here, who I swear has two left feet and the rhythm of a flightless bird."

"Look, I can lift you with one hand." He cracked his knuckles almost theatrically. "My brawn must count for something."

"Oh, it does, darling." She patted him reassuringly on the chest. "As long as you don't drop me as often as you do during practice, you'll have a place to rest those muscles of yours."

"I suppose it's a fair exchange in the place of wages." Aaros's eyes slitted at Canary's sudden snicker. "My only question is, what does the songbird get out of it?"

"I'm no bird." Canary cackled, backing away in the direction of the grand doors behind them. "My sort of songs would burn you to pieces if I sang them for you."

With that, she stalked off, sending the people in her path veering away.

"I can't help but find her a little disturbing." Aaros shuddered. "If she ends up being a serial killer out to slit our throats, I'm blaming you."

"She's not a killer." Kallia whacked him in the arm. "She's a flame-eater."

Lips pursed, Aaros let her words sink in, until finally he nodded. "Of course. And when were you planning on telling me you were incorporating a surly flame-eater into your performance?"

"A *well-connected* flame-eater, mind you," Kallia added with a slight chuckle. "One with more talents than that, and friends in high places who can—"

"You're only allowed to have your assistant on the stage with you."

Kallia and Aaros whirled around at the interruption. She tensed but tucked back her scowl. "I wasn't aware that judges had the right to eavesdrop on private conversations. Not very ethical."

"It doesn't seem very ethical to cheat, either."

How dare he? First sabotage, now *cheating*? If she were going to win this competition, it would be because she was the best. And she would earn every well-deserved moment of glory on the way. "I'm *not* a cheater."

At her ire, he edged back, his frown almost laughably penitent. "Of course not. Sorry. I . . . I actually came over to ask if we could talk in private. To apologize."

"You come over to spout the rules, accuse me of cheating—and you call this the makings of an apology?"

He scratched the back of his neck, flustered. "It was my intention."

Aaros cut in. "*Why* is there even a need for it in the first place?" Ice edged his voice as he narrowed a suspicious look at Demarco, then at Kallia.

Aaros wanted an explanation. He was long overdue one, she knew, and it pained her to observe the tentative trust between them waver. Her selective silence rankled him. And not once had he given her a reason not to trust him.

Then again, how easily had she trusted Jack at his word?

"Nothing to worry about. I can handle it." Kallia delivered a reassuring pat on his shoulder. "Would you be so kind as to run to the hotel to grab my performance dress? I'd love to get it tailored before the rehearsal."

The excuse was no lie, but the dismissal lay between them. Rather than force the issue, Aaros merely shook off her hand and strolled to the door. Not without shooting his hardest glare at Demarco, the threat clear: *I'm watching you.*

"You haven't told him about the other night?" Demarco released a breath-shaken laugh once Aaros was out of earshot. "So this is why he hasn't come at me with his fists."

"I could easily change that, if you'd like," Kallia said evenly. "But no, contrary to what everyone thinks, I don't tell my assistant everything."

Shockingly, he fired off no smug comment. Just a small, dry curl of his lips. "The trust between a magician and an assistant is a meaningful thing. He'll help you get to that spotlight, even if it means he never reaches it himself," he said. "Never take a bond like that for granted."

He was right, and she hated it. "Is this part two of your apology? Telling me things I shouldn't do?"

For a moment, Demarco looked like he wanted to snap back. Instead, his shoulders fell. "I'm quite bad at this, aren't I?"

"Quite." Skeptical, she looked him and up down. He was acting far more agreeable than she had thought him capable, even caught him almost smiling. "If you want to get it right this time, you can first start by saying *what* you're sorry for."

"All right," he said, matching her arch tone with a disarming gleam in his eye. "I'm sorry for how I approached you outside your suite that night. It was . . ." He paused, then sighed. "I was being a complete ass."

Honesty looked interesting on a man. Kallia tilted her head. "Go on."

When he lifted his gaze, her hint of a smile almost tugged one out of him. "I'm not sure if anyone has said this to you yet, but . . . thank you. If it weren't for you, a lot of people could've been seriously hurt."

"We all know that's not how the story's been spun." The other contestants and judges never said it to her face, but their silence and snide looks said well enough. "Listen, I appreciate the gesture, but what does it change? Because I have the distinct feeling I'm still not entirely cleared in your book."

Demarco let the words sink in with a tiny nod. "Glorian has not treated you fairly, but I'm a fair man. I can't ignore how the others are trying to create more odds and stack them against you. Unrightfully so."

"And what are you going to do, convince them otherwise? Save the poor, defenseless damsel from the devils?" Kallia's voice grew cold. "I already know I have to work twice as hard with all that against me. I don't need anyone fighting for me behind the scenes. Least of all you."

"I wasn't going to. This business comes with many battles, so you have to get used to fighting. For yourself. Every step of the way," Demarco said. "But the easiest way to get a rise out of those who try to tear you down is to get back up, and you're already fighting much harder than they expected."

"What makes you say that?"

"You're still here, aren't you?"

Kallia nodded, but inside, she'd become all knots. It was the first time someone had talked to her like that. Like an *actual* player. What a luxury it was to be taken seriously, and what a shame it had taken this long. For Demarco to be the first, after the way they'd fought, was unexpected.

Somehow this unseated Kallia more than the rest. She was used to angry, judgmental men. But this . . . unbalanced her. More than she liked.

"I have a question for you, Mister Demarco. One that's been lingering."

The shadow that flashed across his face disappeared so quickly, she wasn't sure it had truly been there.

"And that is?"

"To be honest, I don't know much about you, either, other than your familial ties. And that you're a notable magician." Kallia crossed her arms. "But from what I've gathered, you don't seem like a fool who becomes so consumed by panic that you're rendered absolutely useless. Why, then, was it my quick thinking that put out the fire, and not yours?"

Demarco went still. Not angry, just quiet. It frustrated Kallia, for there was nothing in it she could pick apart and read. Not even as he said, "I haven't used magic for the stage in a long time."

Kallia quelled the grimace creeping over her face, unable to imagine going a day without magic. "And why is that?"

A muscle in his jaw ticked. "You ask too many questions."

"Come on, Demarco. You can't leave it at that. My curiosity is piqued."

"Then it'll have to stay that way."

"Are we back to hissing at each other like two cats in a cage already?" Her head tilted. "And here I thought we were finally getting along."

"Consider this a temporary ceasefire." Demarco resumed his stern demeanor, and the sudden shift set Kallia at ease, the knots inside her finally starting to untangle.

Before he leaned in all of a sudden, close to her ear. "And don't forget what I said before," he said, voice low. "You're not allowed to have anyone other than your assistant lend a hand with your tricks. Not even circus performers."

The warning grazed the skin of her neck. The knots seized again, such a strange jolt to her system that she couldn't help but smile down at her crossed arms. "Don't you worry. I know the rules."

"Sure." A low chuckle escaped from him. Kallia bit back her own. "See you at rehearsal."

14

Kallia exited the Alastor Place as if she were floating. Hardly a hint of sun shone through the gloomy clouds, but her cheeks remained flushed.

She had a whole day to herself until the rehearsal preceding show night. They'd been told it was only to run through the program and tour the new stage. No practicing magic, for everything was to be done live when the seats were filled. *Good*, Kallia thought. There was no dazzling a crowd and judges if they knew what to expect, and she intended to keep her cards close.

She raised herself on the balls of her feet, about to launch into a little spin before stopping abruptly at the sound of someone clearing his throat.

"Look at you, waltzing about like an angel with new wings." Aaros matched her step, past the closed circus tents. "And here I thought you and Demarco despised each other."

Heat brushed her face. "'Despise' is rather harsh. I hardly know him," she said, smoothing her hair. Looking straight ahead. "You have the dress?"

A slight crinkle came from the long garment bag hanging off his arm. "Then what did he have to apologize for? Did he do something to you?"

"Of course not." It was the most serious he'd ever sounded, a protective side she didn't expect. "If he or anyone here ever succeeded in that, I'd make sure they were wearing their insides out."

"But he *did* do something . . . or something happened . . ." Aaros trailed off with a flicker of uncertainty. "I know you like keeping secrets, Kallia, and I respect your privacy. But being in the dark has not exactly been the greatest launch of our friendship. At least not for me."

Kallia slowed, regarding him closer. "You consider me a friend?"

Aaros laughed. "You've given me more in one week than the street rats I've been running with my whole life. And to be honest, even if I know nothing much about you . . . I'm rather attached to you at this point." He shrugged. "Nothing you can do about it, really."

She wanted to smile back, to hold on to that warmth a little longer, but she peered closer at him instead, hunting for something amiss in his manner. She'd missed it all before, countless times at the House with other companions she'd believed were true.

Anything that seemed too good to be true often was. Even a friend.

"Don't look *so* surprised," he retorted. "Your company is not too terrible."

"No, it's . . . I've never really had friends." Her pulse thrummed a disjointed beat in the awkward silence. Her skin had never been thinner, nerves pounding right beneath the surface.

Still, the confession was oddly relieving. Like it wasn't all in her head anymore.

Aaros studied her, incredulous. "I can't imagine you not being at the top of society's food chain and the talk of all the parties." He frowned when she merely shrugged. "You really had no one to whisper secrets to? To pop drinks and laugh with during the late hours of night?"

She supposed she had—tutors and teachers and friends she'd grown close to—but it couldn't count if none of them had been real. Jack had been real. The only real person in her life, perhaps. But she'd never seen him as just a friend. *Friend* always seemed too simple a word for what he was to her.

Kallia inhaled deeply, stilling her nerves. "You're right that I came from a lot, a better life than most." She looked up at the sky, the sun gone. "It was also emptier than most. I'm glad to have gotten away from it."

Saying it out loud whispered panic into her heart, as if all the world could hear her secrets, gathering like pearls tightly strung around her neck. Still, she was unwilling to give them up. Even as they choked her.

"What sort of trouble are you running from, Kallia?"

The words flashed through her mind, images of chandeliers and cold mirrors blurring into smoke. Her nightmare of the monster rising above her, joining the shadowy mass that swallowed her whole. "I simply thought it was time for me to leave, and I did."

"So there *is* trouble."

Aaros didn't glory at how he'd unreeled a confession. And Kallia, for once, wasn't racked with panic. The truth couldn't touch her here, not without her permission. "That's a conversation for another time."

He fell silent, nodding intently. He'd gotten a sliver. More than she'd intended to give, and more than he'd expected. It was strange, though, to want to give more. There was control in holding every-thing to oneself, but there was also weight. So much she couldn't be allowed to feel, for it was better to remain steel. Unbreakable.

"That Demarco fellow, though . . ." He paused, lightening his tone. "Does this mean I *don't* have to mess up his face?"

Kallia whacked him in the arm with a snort. "Don't you dare. His face looks hard as stone, you'd probably break your fists on it. And I need your hands to be in the best damn shape they can be for tonight."

The clouds above parted with sunlight, glinting off the frost-edged street curbs and corners. After she nearly slipped on a patch of ice, Aaros looped his elbow easily through hers, tugging her in another direction. "Come on, this way. You'll get us lost if you keep pretending to know where you're going."

"If this city had any damn signs, maybe it'd be easier to navigate and find a tailor."

"We do have signs." Aaros let out a smug breath. "You just don't see them yet."

"You're joking." She peered even harder at the archways and street corners, still bare as when she'd first seen them. "Is this some sort of city magic trick?"

"City knowledge, more like. Look at the architecture, the shapes of windows and gates and any other details. Four suits for four families, remember?" He gestured a hand grandly around him. "Know the suits, and you'll never get lost."

Kallia followed his line of vision across the vast spread of square-shaped buildings, their glassy windows and doors all rectangular. She'd never noticed the uniform quality, but now, it was all she could see: the signatures of squares surrounded her entirely, from the shapes of the buildings down to the details engraved upon them.

"When it comes to clothes, there's nothing really in the Fravardi Fold, that's for sure," Aaros murmured before a flash of a smile lit his face. "But I know someone in the Ranza Fold."

Not like Kallia could do much more than follow his lead. She knew nothing of the city other than what the mayor had briefly spoken of. The family names sparked a familiarity as Aaros hauled them to a grand intersection of what felt like four different versions of Glorian. The square-shaped section they'd walked from marked the Fravardi section, leading into a sector of buildings laced with rusty star-raised gates and pointed windows signifying the Vierra Fold. The Alastor Place peeked out amidst other sharp towering spires like triangles raised to the sky.

The last section, where the Prima Hotel was located, took them down the Ranza path of rounded archways and buildings. Aaros stopped in front of a shop where the circular window featured a bare, faceless mannequin. A human-shaped form of wire with its head hanging off the side, creating a nightmarish silhouette.

A little bell rang over their heads upon entering. A chill settled in Kallia's bones. The muted scent of fabrics, with a subtle undercurrent of flowery incense filled her nose. Dresses hung everywhere, some alone, others along racks of similar shades from light to dark. Soft pinks and dusty mint greens, champagne golds and creamy grays. No reds or blacks or anything particularly bold. All pure Glorian. Kallia bit back her disappointment when she heard a noise rustling from the back.

"I should probably handle this." Aaros moved subtly in front of her, rubbing his hands for warmth. "Mistress Ira is a bit of an acquired taste, but she likes me."

The noise turned into soft steps, accompanied by a steady rapping beat against the floor. From behind the racks of gowns emerged a figure effectively hidden just by her height. The older woman stooped over her polished brown cane, her squinted eyes peering through spectacles the size of saucers. First at Kallia, before darkening on Aaros. "Get out, boy, or I'll make you."

Kallia snickered, but Aaros was not the least bit deterred. "Ira, come on. I thought we had come to an understanding."

He approached her with his arms open for an embrace, and the woman scowled even more. "You put those hands away. Who knows what they'll make off with this time."

"I promise not to steal another thing. Ever again."

"You said that last time. When you stole some slip of a thing to please some lady friend, and then a skirt for the sister of that gentleman you were mooning over." She craned her head for another look at Kallia. "Ah, and you bring another. Your heart never stops finding victims, thief."

"That's *not* what this is," Kallia clarified, as Aaros bleated, "I'm not a thief!"

"No matter." Mistress Ira swatted an uncaring hand in the air. "Lovers, accomplices, whatever you two may be, you're not getting past me. I've got an endless supply of needles and pins hidden in this cane. Don't think I won't use them."

"*Ira,* no need for violence." Aaros stared warily at the cane. "Listen, I'm a changed man! I'm off the streets, and I've even got a job."

The woman barked out a laugh. "Sure. And who's the poor soul responsible for that?"

"That would be me." Kallia stepped forward, snatching the garment bag from Aaros's arm. "And we're in a bit of a hurry. I've got a dress with a small tear and some taking in that's needed before tonight, if possible—"

"I can do it," Ira muttered, tightening her shawl around her. "As long as you pay."

Erasmus had promised that the magicians who made the next round would receive a stipend after tonight's performance, but that didn't do her any good here. Noting the woman's shiver, Kallia's brow lifted curiously. "I think we can work something out."

"Right this way, then," Ira called over her shoulder without thinking twice, already hobbling away to the back. "And watch the thief, will you? His fingers might start wandering."

"You're breaking my heart, woman," Aaros lamented. "What'll it take to clear my name?"

"Just don't touch anything, and I won't stick you with a needle."

They walked between racks of full-skirted dresses before passing through a curtain into the dressing rooms. Kallia secured one to change in, moving as efficiently as she had with her costume changes at Hellfire House, before marching out in her performance gown. Aaros hooted and clapped as if the show had started, while Ira stared unblinkingly. "You won't survive this place in that sort of dress." She withdrew a needle from the top of her cane. "Where *are* you going?"

"There's a magicians competition, tonight at the Alastor Place. Surely you know of it." A small, excited flutter went through her. "You should come."

"I'll check my schedule." Ira's disinterest could not have been louder. "Figures you're here for that nonsense. You're one of the magicians performing, I take it?"

"Oh, I . . . *yes*. Yes, I am." It was the first time someone had correctly assumed she wasn't the assistant, and the recognition left her a bit breathless. "How did you know?"

"People talk, especially in this town." She circled Kallia with an eye on the dress's tear, before inserting a marking pin. "And from magician to magician, I sensed you the moment you walked in."

Kallia's lips parted as thread slithered out from the cane's top, perfectly finding the eye of the needle Ira held out. The cane must've been riddled with all sorts of tailoring gear somehow, but that levitation had all been the beholder. That ease of movement, the mastery of someone who's long practiced such work.

"Zarose." Considerably paler now, Aaros swore as the thread floated toward the needle. "Ira, you've been holding out on me. You really could've pinned me like a cushion all those times if you wanted to."

"Believe me, I came *very* close," she said, sending the needle straight into the hem of the skirt with a speed that made Aaros gulp. "But I don't waste my skill on such petty measures. Can't be too showy or loud with what we can do—the first thing they taught us, back at Queen Casine's. Were you a student there, too, miss?"

Kallia wished she could lie her way through this one, but the woman seemed like she could see through anything. "No. I was taught elsewhere."

"Hmph. Must be a different world for magicians out there, now. Hard to keep up with the outside. We always had to be careful in a place like this," Ira said. "Magicians, even old labor ones, are not really smiled upon in Glorian. Until now."

Kallia thought back to what the mayor had said at dinner, about power coursing through the founding families in different ways, and yet magic was not truly embraced by the Glorian people. None of the pieces fit together, and no one questioned it. "What happened?"

Ira's brow furrowed, and she shook her head. "Hell if I know. We don't talk much about the past around here."

"Don't talk much about anything, it seems," Kallia noted wryly, before remembering the dinner party discussion. Rumors and theories from those outside Glorian, far-fetched and curious for a city so quiet. "People say this place used to be some big show town, or there's strange magic hidden somewhere."

"Glorian?" Ira grimaced, as if she weren't sure she'd heard correctly. "A show town?"

Aaros cackled. "Please don't say you believed any of that, Kallia. If *only* we were that interesting."

"There must be a grain of truth somewhere," Kallia snapped at their twin looks of disbelief. "How else are stories born?"

Ira only tsked, staring thoughtfully at Kallia's dress without comment. Perhaps the rumors were ridiculous, but a city could not simply start anew without having a reason behind it.

"Aren't you going to turn around?"

Kallia hesitated, remembering the trifold mirrors. Ira's eyes fixed on her even more intently.

"Ah, it's a performance ritual," Aaros supplied. "She stays away from mirrors. For luck."

Kallia exhaled. Ever since she'd turned her back on her reflection, Aaros had taken her "superstition" in stride. Even covered up his own mirrors, out of respect. The gesture touched her so much, she was glad to avoid her reflection. She couldn't bear to look at herself with every deceit she played.

Ira scoffed. "That's a surprise. You seem like a vain one."

"Excuse me?"

The old woman shrugged. "If you don't care how the dress looks on you, I guess you won't mind if I make a few adjustments . . ."

Kallia's mouth parted at the feel of her skirt's hem rising. And the pair of scissors that appeared over the gathering of fabric below her knees. "Oh wait, I don't need—"

"It'll look better this way. Trust me." Ira allowed the blades to snip before Kallia could stop them, or the needle hemming its way across the newly sheared length. Kallia was only glad she wasn't too attached to the particular dress, for all the fabric pooling at her feet. The fit of the skirt, growing noticeably looser. Only when the work was done did the spell break. Ira sat back, head cocked to one side as she observed Kallia's form in silence. Satisfied.

The skirt trailed asymmetrically across her knee, slitted long enough to show only a small bare flash of her thigh. The style allowed for more mobility, and the more Kallia stared down at the finished design, the more she adored it.

"Let's talk payment before you dash off."

"What about a preview of tonight?" Aaros worked as much charm into the offer as possible. "You'd be our first audience."

The idea seemed to thrill the woman as much as dumping out bathwater.

Kallia noticed that Ira's tools did not waver as they worked, even when she burrowed her shaky hands deeper into the folds of her shawl. The chill had followed them from the front of the shop to the dressing rooms, and Kallia was glad her dress had sleeves, otherwise she'd be shivering as well. "It's a bit drafty in here. You don't have a fireplace or furnace?"

"No fire," Ira said darkly. "If even one stray ember catches on my dresses, this shop will go up like a flaming haystack."

Apparently all of Glorian took arms against fire as well. But Kallia had an alternative in mind. She carried so many memories of sitting by the fireplace, the warmth glowing against her skin. The memory tugged free with the pull of magic, sifting from her finger-tips until heat spread across the entire shop.

The warmth slithered around her neck, seeping through her

clothes until it drove the chill away. Aaros raised his brows at the change in temperature, unclenching his fingers to test the air.

The scissors thudded to the floor, the needle plinking against it. Ira's shoulders begrudgingly relaxed out of their hunched posture. "What did you do?"

"You said no fire." Kallia stepped down from the mirrored stand. "I only gave your shop the memory of it."

It was a common trick Jack had taught her for her shows, to sweep the room with a sensation. It could heighten the performance, building anticipation. For once it had a practical use, instead of just deception.

Once Kallia emerged from the curtain, back in her comfortable day clothes, she handed the dress to Ira. "Thank you for the alterations," she said, more than a little satisfied by the old woman's reaction.

Quietly, Ira took it, her hands no longer shaking. "How long will it last?"

"The heat? Maybe a few days."

The woman made a hard sound at the back of her throat. "What the hell am I supposed to do when it runs cold again?"

Kallia smiled. "Hope that I come back, it seems."

15

Daron tapped his foot anxiously underneath the judges' table. He didn't usually fall prey to nerves, but it was unavoidable as the Alastor Place ran rife with performance energy—the kind he hadn't surrounded himself with in a while. It worsened when a magician who'd arrived early to the rehearsal approached him, confessing how honored he was to perform for the Daring Demarco.

The whole exchange twisted Daron's insides. He didn't come here for that. He'd traveled to Glorian to learn more—to find Eva—and he was failing miserably.

Still, he nodded along. Smiling, as though the praise were his right.

Playing along seemed to be the only thing he could do right. Nothing in his search uncovered anything of use. No historical records dating before the last fifty or so years, no old photographs or illustrations of what Glorian might've looked like before. The only thing Daron managed to procure were the most recent journals detailing plans to rebuild and restore—proof of the fire that had swept through the town long, long ago, taking everything with it. Glorian's library couldn't even be properly called one, no more than a few shelves of books and glass-cased documentation in the mayor's mansion that were about as helpful as the mayor himself.

"We're not the kind of city that dwells on the past," Mayor Eilin had explained. "We've kept to ourselves for some time, away from the rest of Soltair. But we're embracing a new history by looking to the future."

After that, Daron stopped visiting the mayor's mansion. His research resulted only in dead ends, and he suspected he'd landed on Mayor Eilin's watch list for asking too many questions. *A new history*, she'd said. What did that make of the old one? Of the rumors that reached across Soltair?

What if that's what they want you to think?

His sister was no fool. But the puzzle kept growing the closer he looked at the pieces, searching for the strange power between them.

"What's the matter, Demarco?" asked Erasmus, observing the jittery rhythm Daron's foot set against the table. "Excited for tonight?"

The grin oozed from the proprietor's voice. Since rehearsals started, Erasmus had become all smugness, soaking in the energy of the room. Some of the judges who carried stern frowns actually perked up in their seats, watching the contestants on stage walk through the lay of the land over strewn tools and cans of paint, listening to the stage manager roll through the show's instructions.

"The repairs aren't even completed," Mayor Eilin muttered to no one in particular, taking in the theater with all the tragedy of witnessing a sinking ship before lowering into his seat. His fingers dug hard into the edges of his clipboard. "Would it be the worst thing if we pushed ba—"

"No, no, no, no." Erasmus shook a finger in the mayor's face. "The show hall doesn't have to be perfect, only passable."

"Impatience breeds mistakes, Rayne."

"And reluctance breeds *nothing*, Eilin," Erasmus spat back. "I'll be damned if I have to wait another day. Your people have had nothing to look forward to. What do you imagine they'll think if you get behind schedule?"

Erasmus had a point. The people had practically nothing except the day to wake them. Nothing to fill their nights. The show, no matter how untraditional, would ignite interest. The first night was always one of hope and anticipation, for both the audience and contestants.

Not that anyone here took it all that seriously. The magicians milling about the stage levitated a stray scrap of paper over their heads like a game of toss and catch, unbeknownst to the stage manager. Each time the paper fell a little too close, they smothered their laughter, pretending to listen.

Daron looked away, a strange sense of loss pushing in like a blade. It was so easy for them. The level of camaraderie already surprised him. He supposed when they all had one common enemy, alliances would naturally form.

The common enemy in question, however, was late. And no one waited, with all manner of details left to finalize and run through. Most importantly, the order of performances.

Unsurprisingly, everyone wanted to go first.

"Gentlemen, gentlemen, *please!*" Erasmus held his hands up, flustered by the match he'd lit amongst the group. The first performance always jump-started the night, the second would be held in direct comparison. And so on. One thing was for certain: nobody wanted that last slot—when the audience had grown so fatigued by the spectacle and ready for their beds.

The decisions were finalized right as the doors of the Alastor Place flew open. As if she'd timed it, Kallia strutted through, arm in arm with her assistant. The playful clicks of her heels stopped all chatter as she entered.

"I say," Mayor Eilin declared, his face reddening. "We have a *real* show to put on. If you're not going to take this competition seriously with a bit of punctuality, miss, you might as well turn in your keys and leave."

"Admirable effort, Mister Mayor, but I'm quite all right with where I am," Kallia called back as she and her partner continued down the aisle. A lioness stalking forward, meeting her prey more than her pride. "Besides, this rehearsal seemed more like a bit of hand-holding across the stage. It wasn't even required, yet I came anyway."

"At the expense of being placed in the last time slot."

Kallia arrived at the foot of the stage, beaming. *"Excellent."*

The corners of Daron's lips tugged up a bit. Nothing would throw her. The men who had anticipated her disappointment appeared more agitated. Nobody more frustrated than Mayor Eilin, and nobody more delighted than Erasmus, who all but shoved past Daron.

"Oh darling, I'm *so* thrilled you've made it!" He clapped his hands eagerly. "Would you like a quick run of the—"

"No." The mayor was the one wagging his finger now. "Showtime is upon us, and there's simply no time. We can't just favor a contestant with exceptions."

"But we can sure single them out with insults, apparently." Erasmus sniffed, straightening his shoulders. "Sorry, darling, I'm still fighting the stodgy old dogs for you."

"No need." Kallia gave a casual glance around. "A stage is a stage. I'll manage."

She was lying. She'd examined that stage this morning with all the intensity of an artist watching his muse before striking the canvas. She was far more focused than she let on. Maybe it was all part of her strategy: look the fool others expected, only to be three steps ahead.

When her eyes flitted over Daron, they paused.

"You be careful acting cocky so close to the show, miss," one of the magicians on stage warned, in no way genuine. "It's bad luck."

"At least I'm here at all." She threw her hands up. "I'm not the one who was so cocky he decided not to show up to rehearsal altogether."

"What are you talking about?"

"We're down a buffoon," Kallia said flatly, nodding to the stage as if counting. "Where is Josev?"

The mayor glowered. "Impossible." He studied his clipboard before him. "I could've sworn all our contestants were accounted for."

"Then count again, Mister Mayor. Because I think the one who favors too much drink must've gotten himself lost onstage."

Daron's eyes swung back to the group, counting and recounting as everyone searched amongst themselves for Josev. But Kallia was right.

One of them was missing.

16

Josev was still nowhere to be found as the hours crawled into show night. Some swore they saw him in the group on the stage, while others vowed that the last time they'd seen him was the night before, lingering by the hotel bar. The only sign of a farewell was a note inexplicably left on the chair of his dressing room, bearing the words: *Four of Flesh*.

"That's ridiculous." Juno ticked her tongue sharply as she applied blush over Kallia's cheeks. "It did *not* say that."

"I swear," Aaros said, shutting the door to her dressing room behind him. "You should've seen Rayne's face, he was spitting mad when they discovered it."

Kallia tilted her head up so the pearlescent dust on Juno's brush could find the rest of her cheekbone. "Understandable. It's odd that anyone would even think of leaving on opening night."

"Odd last words for an odd departure." Aaros shrugged. "A few of the contestants thought it sounded like some kind of club. Like the one out in the Woods. Might be others somewhere."

Kallia's gaze dropped to her lap. Her knees tensed. It was the first time she'd heard Hellfire House acknowledged in Glorian, and the mere mention had a strange power over her. Like the pull of a puppet string that refused to be cut.

No. She gritted her teeth, grinding them hard. She was stronger than string, than a place far behind her. It could not touch her here.

"That's an interesting location for a club." Juno traced the end of her brush by her chin, considering.

"If that's the case, I'm sure he's fine," Kallia deadpanned. "If he'd rather run off and be a fool in the forest, that's his choice."

She stared straight ahead as Juno stood back, observing her handiwork. "And if it wasn't?"

"You Conquerors get so dark about everything, I swear," Aaros snorted.

"Only because we know how dark the stage life can get," she countered, setting down her brush. "In games like this, it's so much more than winning and losing. There's a lot of ugliness we hide from those who fill the seats."

"Are you saying there are dirty secrets among the Conquering Circus?"

"We're not all angels, but even still, we'd *never* hurt one another. Though I'm sure Rayne would certainly love to bottle cattiness for an act, if he could." Juno tapped a finger along her blush tin. "Games between magicians always get cutthroat. You mix the primal urge to win and the ability to do the impossible, and it ends in chaos. The Patrons are always breaking up dueling magicians in New Crown because of it." Finally satisfied with Kallia's face, she clasped her tattooed hands. Tonight, they were marked like smoothly carved gems sparkling in clusters all the way to her brow. "You made a wise choice coming to me. Take a look."

Kallia had her back to the vanity mirror, but before she could protest, Juno raised a small handheld mirror before her. Like a sudden flash of the sun, Kallia winced at her reflection and quickly glanced away. "Perfect. Thank you, Juno."

It wasn't practical to flee from mirrors forever, but she would avoid them as much as possible. Tonight, especially. The circus performer had all too eagerly accepted Kallia's request to help glitter and paint her face into the fiercest mask it could be. It was a shame she couldn't admire it, but she wouldn't take any chances. Nothing would rattle her tonight.

As soon as Juno departed, the room quieted. Aaros's fingers played an absent drumbeat against his knee. "Are you *sure* you had nothing to do with it?" he asked.

"With what?"

"The missing magician."

"Not you, too." Kallia reared her head back with a glare. "How many times do I have to defend myself? *No.* I had absolutely nothing to do with it. The man obviously couldn't get his head out of the bottle. Why can't we blame the fool for his own foolishness, for once?"

"Zarose, Kallia, I wasn't trying to pin blame on you." Aaros held his hands up with a lopsided smile. "I just want to understand what's going on. You *know* I'd be miffed if you didn't include me in your showman's villainy."

"Not to worry, thief. You'll have your spotlight soon enough." Kallia twiddled with the top of a perfume bottle. "Besides, I don't play games that way. Only the threatened are desperate enough to stoop to sabotage. I'm the best. I have no reason to cheat."

"Incredible." He shook his head slowly. "Normally such ego would be incriminating. Only you could make it your saving grace."

"It's the truth. I've been taught that victories only count if they're well-deserved. The only way to win is to *truly* win."

"Whoever taught you that must've been quite an honorable game master."

Honorable. Kallia felt everything inside her grip tight as a corset, squeezing the air from her. The last thing she ever wanted to do was bring up Jack. Like if she could forget him, and all the things he'd done, he would disappear. Clearly he'd forgotten her, or he would've come after her already. But since that dinner party? Nothing. No word, no warning, no nightmares. It wasn't like him to threaten and retreat. Especially when she knew the truth, that he *could* waltz into Glorian at any moment.

So why hadn't he come?

Her paranoia dug its roots into the calm quiet. She'd vowed not to think of it tonight of all nights. But snapping on her dress and toeing on her shoes carried the weight of a costume. Once more, she was back in Hellfire House, about to be called from her dressing room any moment now to don her mask and mount the chandelier. The music would start, and she would descend.

A smattering of applause traveled through the walls and shook her awake. Every clap muffled yet still sharp as percussion.

The sound twisted something new inside her. Something painful and thrilling. *Different.*

Everything about tonight was different.

This was not the House. Not his club nor his stage, nor his show. Tonight was all hers.

Kallia allowed herself to turn to the mirror—one moment to see what the rest of Glorian would—and vain as it was, her chest swelled. Juno had done well, complimenting and heightening her features in the most effective places. Bold scarlet lips. Kohl-lined eyelids dusted with a pearlescent sheen that made her brown eyes appear almost black. Her face, without a mask to conceal it. Ever again.

Tonight was only the first step.

Into the dream she now lived, no longer a dream.

A shiver ran down her spine as her reflection shook from the force of boots stomping down the hallway outside her door. Stage hands and crew members barked out instructions in hushed voices, rushing into place. The world behind the curtain, finding its beginning.

Applause rang once more like the muffled start of a song, clearing and calling to her.

The show, at last, had begun.

"Once upon a time, a magician vanished into a world below, and found something quite . . . *Spectaculore!*" Erasmus uttered the haunting, opening words of the night to a shower of applause. It was a play on the closing of Zarose Gate, always a crowd pleaser. Some said before he closed the gate, Erik Zarose had fallen through first and found himself lost in a dream. In another world. Others spoke of the devils he met below, to spook children from misbehaving or else the monsters would see.

It was a fitting story for a competition, for just as one magician entered the world below, only one would make it back to the other side. But whichever interpretation Erasmus threaded throughout the entire competition was bound to be the most theatrical.

Daron clapped halfheartedly as the proprietor basked, an entirely different man from just a few hours earlier. After the no-show magician, Erasmus had spent the afternoon cursing up a storm of threats about Josev. But after hours of searching and showtime nearing, he'd had to accept they were down one performer.

One loss would not stop the show. If anything, the air was more charged than before, with Erasmus overcompensating in dramatics. The audience ate it up.

The prompt set the scene, broad enough for the magicians to build their act, to start the story with an amazing feat.

As the night wore on, Daron watched contestant after contestant take the stage, pulling off their tricks with as much showmanship as they could muster.

"Watch as I lift the water within this glass!" The magician now performing—Daron forgot his name, the men already blurring together in his mind—delivered a dazzling grin. Daron cringed at the man's efforts to fill the silence. Good stage acts called for light conversation and engagement, but Daron never could stomach speaking to the public at length. Then again, he was never the one in his acts doing the talking.

He'd never thought the sight of every assistant who graced the stage would hollow him so deeply. Each time, it slammed him into his seat, the familiarity. The feeling of revisiting one of his past shows as an audience member, waiting for the worst to happen.

It took at least the first five dull acts for him to settle enough to notice the energy of the room had waned into restlessness. He stole a quick glance behind, surprised to find a couple of small families bundled across rows, and some stiff men and ladies dressed in their furs and formals as if this were the opera. The majority of attendees who seized the front seats were of the younger crowd, from children to almost-adults, scrappy with the streets still on their hands, and lights shining in their eyes.

Performance magic hadn't graced Glorian in a long while, that much was clear. Even the most basic tricks were regarded with awe. An advantage for the first to go. The more applause, the better chance the magician had of staying. The more silence, the more forgotten he and his act were. The only equality in the playing field lay within the same prompt and props.

Once upon a time, a magician fell into a world below . . .

A glass of water, a black round stool, and a dusty old top hat.

The test required quick thinking, which fell to predictable performances. Pouring water into the hat and pulling out some other object, sitting the glass atop the stool and making it disappear under the hat. Levitation, especially, was an overdone feat, and by the fourth magician who dared lift all three items, only a scattering of claps trickled from the audience. The magical ability was there, but these magicians lacked imagination.

They were playing it too safe.

Not like he was one to talk. He thought up a hundred different tricks with the combination of props, not sure if he could even pull off one after such a long time away from the stage. After—

A crash on the stage made him jerk. The contestant, red-faced, glared at his assistant who had sent his glass of water rolling across the floor. She assumed a pose as if it were all part of the act. After a smattering of snickers, the man had the dignity to call it a night and stomped off.

Sighing, Daron glanced down the table at the mayor. The timekeeper of the performances. The man's head had drooped in slumber, until Judge Silu jostled him with the end of his small score paddle. Like ducklings following suit, each judge splayed out their hands across the width of the green velvet board. Fours and fives shone brightly down their row, like they had for all the performances thus far. Judging from the meager applause, Daron felt no guilt in pressing two fingers to his board and letting it shine out with the rest of the scores. A generous mark, given what he'd seen.

More applause was earned by the cleaning crew who came in to wipe the stage floor and reorder the props. They tipped their hats good-naturedly before bounding off behind the curtains.

A noticeable shift took the air at the commanding clicks of steps.

A collective breath held, Daron's included.

Kallia wasn't dressed in the sparkly getup she wore that first time she took the stage. Instead, a dark emerald dress clung to her, flaring out with an asymmetrical hem. No less bold, but tonight, she looked more like herself. In her element.

And nobody, not even Daron, could tear their stares away. The lights washed over her in a radiance he'd seen plenty of times, yet somehow it caught her differently. Like fire, or sunlight. She assessed the crowd, shrewd and closed-lipped. Giving nothing away.

Erasmus stood and beamed, his teeth as dazzling as the silky purple sheen of his vest. "Like with every performer and performance, we leave you with three props. An old top hat, a stool, and a glass of water. From there the story is yours to tell," he said. *"Once upon a time, a magician vanished into a world below . . ."*

Kallia nodded intently, circling the items with quiet, intense focus. Before long, she casually took a seat on the stool, balancing the hat and glass in both hands. Her eyes drifted teasingly across the audience, over the judges' table. At Daron.

Don't you worry. I know the rules.

Her words returned to him in the small curve of her lips as she cast her gaze forward, topping the hat over her head. After taking a long sip from the glass, she tossed the remnants in a line behind her before smashing it to the ground.

The entire room jumped from the noise. Kallia bent over the broken glass, cupping her hands as if to capture a creature born from the sound. She hurled her hands out before her, releasing a noise of smashing glass. Again and again, she repeated the action, until the sound took on a life of its own. A strange, slow beat. Steady as a heart.

With the tempo set, Kallia smiled at her confused audience before lifting a single arm. Fire rose high from the ground, in a perfect line behind her from the remnants of water she'd thrown.

In a matter of moments, she'd caged sounds in her hand and bore fire from water.

"We must stop her—she'll burn the whole place down!" Mayor Eilin wheezed from his seat, suddenly very much awake. Fire was obviously no friend to Glorian, but only the mayor reacted in fear. The rest of the judges appeared too mesmerized to even blink. Just like the audience.

Daron blinked at the glimmers of other sounds following the pattern of smashing glass: the slow rapping of a metal drum. A piano, pounding out lower chords. Robust blows of a horn that melted and melded everything together.

Music.

The floor shook at the sudden stomping of heels. At the startled gasps and exclamations, Daron craned his neck around. Women paraded down the aisles in flashy red circuswear, wielding their rusty instruments with flair. They played to the rhythm of the smashing glass, seizing the tempo with a song of their own. The bold tune of a midnight party, nowhere close to ending.

"This is *ridiculous*," Judge Bouquet half-shouted, half-seethed, the music drowning him out.

Not a soul in the room was sleeping anymore. Some had even begun standing for a better look, their mouths agape. Eyes round as moons, and grins unsure but catching as the flames before them.

The fire rose high behind Kallia like a curtain, turning her into a dancing shadow for a moment while the Conquering Circus moved like flames below the stage. Daron wasn't sure if he'd somehow fallen into a grand, chaotic dream. A world below, as the story would go.

Kallia swayed her hips, fierce triumph playing across her face. Her heels hit every beat as she kicked back the stool, taking the arm of a tall man in black pants and no shirt. Why the man needed no shirt was beyond Daron, but it was none other than the assistant, giving Kallia a playful spin before helping lift her onto the pegs of the stool.

And somehow, she kept ascending. After the first step from the base of the wood, another step formed to meet her foot. Then another, and another. The backdrop of the fire darkened her silhouette on the strange staircase of wood, bending and stretching in impossible ways to keep her standing.

Rising.

The applause intensified. From the rowdiest in the front to the quiet spectators in the back. Erasmus jumped up and stood on his seat, whistling with his fingers. None of the judges joined him, or dared show enjoyment. Only Daron, with a wry shake of his head. This would easily be his first and only five of the night.

The table banged beneath his elbow. Startled, he shot a quick glance down the line of judges and found the mayor thrusting his empty hourglass in the air. Time was up.

And nobody cared. No doubt Kallia was aware of the mayor's signals and chose to ignore them. The people had become her time keepers, and they weren't ready for the show to be over.

The floor gave another rumble beneath Daron's feet, but not from the dancers surrounding him. He braced himself against his seat as the violent motion continued—rougher—impossible to ignore or mistake as any part of the act when one of the circus performers shrieked a note out of tone from her flute before stumbling.

The crowd stirred in a flurry of wooden groans and creaks from seats gripped and patrons rising. Even the music sputtered in discordant spikes as the players fought to plant their feet firmly over the carpeted aisles, their expressions aghast at the stage.

When Daron looked back up at Kallia, his blood chilled.

The top hat tipped on her head dropped to the ground.

A high scream.

It sounded from the audience, all watching as Kallia wavered in the air—nothing to steady or balance her still—before she slipped over her next step.

And fell.

Daron shot up from his seat. A barb-like feeling burst in his chest—a strange familiar panic—before a wave of applause came roaring.

Kallia had landed in the arms of her assistant.

Safe. The word pulsed through him. It took Daron a second to catch his breath, lower back into his seat, and calm his heart. Whether it had been a trick or a mistake, Daron couldn't tell. Kallia hid her face in her assistant's chest before throwing a coy smile out with a grand sweep of her arm, a burst of victorious laughter.

As if the fall hadn't been enough, a series of lights sparkled from the stage. The top hat, which had fallen near the edge with its rim out and open to the crowd, began pouring out light. Sparks shot into the air like fireworks. And a swarm of peculiar black orbs came flying out, dissolving to glitter as they flew over the heads of those seated.

Little black birds soaring from the hat, vanishing into fireworks.

17

Kallia had never seen so many flowers in her entire life. Enough roses to fill rivers, fiery gloriosas galore, and the most curious kinds of plants with glittering scale-like petals and lights in the veins of their leaves. At Hellfire House, she'd mostly received trinkets and jewels, the occasional vase of flowers. But never this many all at once. The people of Glorian might not have had the means to attend performances before, but they sure knew how to show their appreciation.

"Marvelous act, you put on, my dear—absolutely *marvelous*!" one woman trilled, stopping Kallia with her gloved hand and a long-stemmed rose. "I don't think I've felt my heart race so fast since I was a little girl."

The whole circle that had gathered around Kallia chuckled, even Mayor Eilin. Despite the jovial manner with which he led the contestants and guests around the after party at the Prima, she couldn't ignore his tight-edged smiles. To no surprise, he and the judges had scored her a collection of ones and twos. Demarco, the only four among them. But it was the roars of the crowd that saved her, everyone standing and begging for more. Not even the experts' panel could go against the clear voters' choice. Though they'd made quite a show of it, drawing out the names of the contestants who would remain in the running, until at last, uttering Kallia's as if against their wills. Though now, they all raised their drinks. Just for tonight. Tomorrow, her success would be forgotten. And the claws would come out again, itching for another chance to knock her out.

Kallia barred those thoughts behind smiles, saving her sweetest for Aaros. He groaned underneath the weight of what looked to be his very own garden in his hands.

"Room for one more?" Kallia peered between leaves and stems and ribbons, finding a corner of a face in the mess of it.

"Don't even think about it," he warned. "I agreed to haul your spoils of war but it doesn't mean you can abuse the power."

"I just gave this city the best damn show it's ever seen. You can't expect me to be able to lift anything other than my wine." She sipped at her glass and twirled the rose in her other free hand. Aaros squared her a look. "Oh fine, I guess I can hold *one*."

"My hero." Aaros craned his head over a bright orange-and-pink bouquet as he mouthed, "How are you holding up?"

Kallia's stomach knotted. Only at the pricks at her palm did she realize how tightly she was gripping the rose. The adrenaline of performing could make her forget so much of an act, but not this one. Aaros had seen it clearly in her eyes like a fire running cold.

Fear.

Not of breaking her neck from the fall, but of something else.

That slip had rattled her; the hat only worsened it. Kallia had not been the one to make the entire show hall quake, nor had she summoned those awful birds.

It could've been anybody.

A jealous competitor. A bitter judge.

"Such promising talent across all of the gentlemen tonight, I'd say. Valmonts trained them well," Kallia overheard a man say. He looked as harsh as his tone betrayed, in his stark gray top hat and stiff coat. "That girl though . . . using circus folk? All the dancing nonsense?"

"It was far too much," his peer agreed. "A magician's stage is no place for a showgirl."

Kallia bit her tongue. She'd heard just as many whispers at her back as she had praise, post-performance, and despite how she forced herself to shake it off, it grated on her. She'd already arrived a burning fuse. It wouldn't take much more to set her off.

"From their lackluster applause, I'd say those magicians could learn a thing or two from a showgirl."

A new voice entered the gentlemen's conversation. Demarco, stone-faced as usual with a near-empty glass in his hand. The moment they realized who'd spoken, the men blanched and huffed away. Demarco lifted his glass at their backs as if to bid them good-bye, before spotting Kallia watching him.

Heat flushed to her ears. His stare was heavier than hot iron, the same as when he'd held up his score of four for everyone to see. After meager numbers across the board, she'd been pleasantly gratified, then vexed. *Four.* Out of a possible five. He'd enjoyed her act enough to grant a high score, but not enough for a perfect one. It somehow grated on her nerves more than the mayor's gleeful one.

Four. That imperfect number carved in the back of her mind.

Before she could step right up to him and demand why, he dropped his gaze, drained his glass, and turned away toward the bar.

"Look, there goes the Patron boy. What I'd give to see *him* grace the stage again."

Behind Kallia, two elderly women in gem-bright gowns—clearly outsiders—peered at the bar behind their lacy, half-moon fans. "You think he's seeing anyone?"

"What, are you asking for a friend?"

"Oh, you are *bad*. I'm just curious." Her companion swatted her with her fan. "It's been a while since he was last in the papers."

"More like since he's been in society! It's been years. He has to move on."

"Don't be so heartless, Celie." A reprimanding tsk. "It's a shame, really, his assistant. Those two were sweet on each other."

"Maybe not as sweet as we thought," the other whispered. "He sure seems fine as hell, now."

The two tittered on, venturing toward the bar as if to get a closer look at the subject of their gossip. Kallia would've followed were it not for the sudden ringing in her head, pulsing.

It was the dizziness. She'd been feeling funny ever since she stepped off the stage, especially after all the tricks she pulled. An endless tug-of-war against her body.

She teetered back when a hand caught her elbow.

"Easy there." Aaros strained to hold her up along with the flowers. "Time to turn in?"

Kallia's temple throbbed in assent, but she didn't dare show it. Not with all these people around. "Yes, it's a rather boring party, and we've had a long night."

"That we have." His shoulders relaxed. At the slight movement, a few petals fell from the bouquets in his arms. "What do you want to do with your new portable garden?"

"Just . . ." Kallia stroked at a row of soft petals, wishing she could keep them all like she had at Hellfire House. But carrying old habits from there only invited its presence. "Just drop them off at the front desk. They can toss or keep them for the hotel. It could use more color."

Aaros's brow furrowed. "I'm not entirely sure if that's how it works in hotels, but I'll give it a swing."

She didn't even have the energy to blush. She'd never been in a hotel before in her life, how was she supposed to know? She'd never had to continue entertaining guests after a night of performing, either. That, too, was new. Hours of soaking in the praises of others soon turned into a task she never thought would tire her, and Zarose, was she exhausted. Even her lips had grown stiff as bricks after hours of smiling. As the night weighed on her, she felt no guilt in abandoning her wine and slipping through the party, ignoring the calls of her name, the subtle touches at her arm to stop and chat. All she wanted was to curl up in bed alone.

"Cheater."

The hiss stopped Kallia short after one step on the stairs. Behind her, one of the younger magicians—Ives—leaned against the large marble bannister, throwing her the darkest glare.

"Excuse me?"

"You heard me." He staggered forward to stand a step above her. The sour wine on his breath reached her in full force. "First you make a contestant disappear, and next you violate the rules and saunter around like you own the place? They should've never allowed someone like you in."

Kallia bit back an enormous scoff. She shouldn't have even wasted a moment on him, but the word snapped inside her. *Cheater*.

"How astounding," she said through a grin. "I'm simply amazed."

Ives paused. "By what?"

"Your fragility." Her features hardened to ice. "I broke no rules. I outperformed you fair and square. Just because you delivered a mediocre act does not give you the right to take your frustrations out on me."

His jaw dropped. "How *dare* you speak to me like that."

"Likewise. Now get out of my way before you start to really annoy me."

And before the others noticed. She had no qualms airing him out as an ass to the whole party, but their fight was on the stage. Whatever bait he was trying to throw at her, like hell she would give him the satisfaction of taking it where everyone could see.

The young man's nostrils flared. "Funny how you act all high and mighty when you have no reason for it. I've only seen your kind at the underground clubs and bars, the only places girls like you belong."

Kallia's blood boiled. *Don't*. Her fist tightened at her side, and she kept it there. Trembling. The instant Ives noticed it, his awful leer sharpened. "But none of you make it to the top, and we all know why. You're just a spectacle, something pretty to look at—nothing more."

"And how can you be so certain I'm nothing more?" Kallia drawled, a cold calm falling over her. "When it was the crowd who cheered my name tonight, and had all but forgotten yours?"

His face reddened. "That loose mouth of yours is going to get you into trouble if you don't—"

"If she doesn't what?"

Demarco had appeared at the foot of the stairs. Leaning against the bannister, unamused. Normally Kallia would roll her eyes at his official airs, but his presence exuded a force no one wanted to go up against. Certainly not the drunken magician, who'd scrambled off instantly with nothing more than an apologetic squeak.

"An unnecessary rescue, Mister Demarco. I was handling it." Kallia inhaled, raking an exhausted hand through her hair.

"No doubt," he said, looking up the length of the stairs. "He was shaking with fear as you were practically stumbling up."

"You were watching me?"

A muscle in his jaw ticked at her suggestive tone. "You dropped something." He brought around a rose he'd kept behind his back. The poor flower had lost more of its petals, its head hanging limply over the stem.

Kallia refused to smile at the beaten rose. A small scowl twisted her lips instead. "Keep it. A rose for a rescue. Now we're even."

"What need do I have for it?" he asked, though he held onto it while gesturing up the stairs. "I was heading in the same direction, anyway. Thought it was time to call it a night."

"Not one for parties?"

"Not anymore."

It was impossible to miss the hardness in his voice, and something small within the cracks. A secret. That she wanted to know it irritated her more than anything, especially after hearing those ladies gabbing on about him earlier. "Walk with me, then. We are neighbors, after all."

Demarco cast a wary look across the sea of bodies surrounding them. "Maybe you should go first. I'll keep a few steps back."

"Embarrassed to be seen with me?"

"*No,*" he exclaimed with such earnestness, she almost laughed. "It's just . . . you know, people might think—"

"That we are going up the stairs and walking to our rooms?" Kallia held her chin high before taking the first step. "If they're inclined to spin stories, *they're* the ones with the problem. Not us."

"They'll spin stories, either way."

She continued on her way, regardless. A faction of the party already thought the worst of her, so it made no difference who she traveled up and down the stairs with. Though at the sound of him following behind her instantly, she couldn't help the flare of satisfaction working itself into a small grin. "What are you afraid they'll say? I heard you're no stranger to the gossip papers."

"No friend to them, either." His tone turned cautious. "Whatever you've heard about me, it's most likely false."

"Then you'll no doubt be thrilled to know that I haven't heard much." Some business with his assistant, she recalled. So vague, yet Kallia had turned the possibilities over in her head. She'd never admit it, never give him an inch of her interest, but she was curious.

Too curious.

Before she could act on it, she stumbled over a step. Instantly, his hand was at her back, steadying her. A quick, instinctive move on his part; a total halt of the body on hers.

"You're exhausted." He ushered her forward, sounding as concerned as Aaros. That she could endure, but not from a judge. Not Demarco.

When they finally reached the top, far from the gaze of the party, Kallia dove away from his hand. The spot remained too warm for her liking. "Don't I have a right to be? I gave the performance of a lifetime."

"At your own expense. I know the cost of tricks like that." His jaw worked as he delivered each word carefully. "When delivered in such quick succession, without control . . . it pulls a lot out of you."

"I have more up my sleeve than you think." Kallia spun on her heel down the empty candlelit hallway of doors. He followed, though the act did not bring her even a sliver of satisfaction this time. "I'm neither weak nor clueless when it comes to my magic, so if you're trying to educate me on myself, I think we're done here."

Nothing twisted Kallia's gut more than underestimation. Especially tonight, the first time she'd been able to perform as herself. *Truly* herself, and not behind a mask.

And still, the wolves came out to tear her down.

"I wasn't saying that." Demarco's breath hitched as he hastened to her side. "You just don't want to give up the best you've got so early on."

"And you assume that's the best I've got?" Near their doors, Kallia turned, her brow raised in challenge. "I know what I'm doing. I play by my own strategies, and I don't expect many to agree with them. But in the event they stop working, perhaps then I will come to you for whatever wisdom you're trying to impart."

"I'm only trying to offer some advice." He crossed his arms, matching her scowl with his own. "So many magicians have ruined their chances on the stage because of a single mistake—a flaw, a misstep, an error in thinking—"

"Excuse you, but I made no mistakes," she countered hotly. "Is that why you gave me only a four? Because I didn't perform up to *your* standards?"

She wished she could take it back as soon as she heard the crack in her voice. He'd caught it, too, from the way he cast his gaze down to his feet. "You really shouldn't be asking me that."

No, she shouldn't. His opinion should matter as little as his colleagues', yet she'd fixated on his score. That four. Why did she care so much about what he thought? "Humor me, since you're so forthright about constructive criticism," she bit out. "What about my act docked a point off for you?"

A silence fell over them, one that stretched for so long, she wondered if he'd just let the question die between them and take off for his own room.

"You almost fell," he finally said, his face unreadable. Everything about him, inscrutable. "You could've gotten seriously hurt if your assistant hadn't been there. Or was all that part of your . . . strategy?"

The last word edged with doubt. Of course he'd caught that. While everyone enjoyed the music and fanfare, he'd been watching *her*. Falling hadn't been the worst of her performance, though. Seeing those damn birds had stopped her heart more than almost breaking any bones on the stage.

"Absolutely." Kallia plastered on a smile. "Everybody loves a good damsel in distress."

"But only a fool would think you'd ever play one, which is why I gave you a four." He straightened and made a sharp swerve toward his door, before he paused, holding out the wilted rose between them. "Here, take it. You obviously didn't need the rescue in the first place. My mistake."

His tone grated against her skin—a biting blend of sarcasm and disbelief that filled her with the strangest sense of shame. He sighed and went to withdraw the rose when Kallia snatched it by the stem, his fingers closing briefly around hers. His palm coarse, warm.

Neither of them moved.

Heat pooled deep in her stomach before she moved away. Demarco withdrew just as quickly without so much as a breath. Just an abrupt turn toward his door and the sound of it closing softly behind him, as forceful as a slam.

Insufferable.

Kallia shut her door and nearly threw the rose out the window. But the worn, stubborn flower had survived this long. It did not deserve her fury.

She scoffed and thumbed the stem. As her gaze shifted up, she nearly screamed at the shadowy figure startling across the room.

Clutching at her throat, she blinked and shuddered out a breath. It was only her reflection. The heavy fabric she'd used to cover the vanity mirror had fallen and hung limply over the wooden surface.

Her pulse thrummed a panicked rhythm. She should cover the damn mirror, look away at least. But her appearance struck her like it had before her act—her performance dress so different from the glittery corsets she'd once shoved herself into, her face bared for the whole world to see.

Applause rang in her ears once more, echoing as loud as it had on stage. The delicious, warm sound washed over her. A wave of sensation she longed for even more, now that she had a taste of it.

She drew closer.

Soon, her name became its own chant, vibrating throughout the room. The audience wildly cheering in unison, until they solidified into one voice.

Kallia

Kallia

Kalli—

She halted at an icy breeze. It brushed her temple, across her collarbone. Like the unwelcome edge of a knife.

A sudden slip of a shadow flitted across the carpet, and Kallia jerked back. Frantic. Finding nothing but dark, empty corners. The wind trailed over her again. Shivering, she turned to the window that had swung open. The sheer drapes rustled against the breeze, rippling like ribbons where the moonlight hit them.

In the quiet, she swallowed and stepped back.

The shadow returned, landing at her feet. Her insides seized in a panicked grip to find it was hardly even a shadow anymore, but a bleeding black mass, spreading like ink spilled over the carpet, forcing her backward. Her calf collided with a chair in a jolt of pain.

"Wh-who's doing this?" She steadied herself. Surely this was nothing more than a prank. She swept a hand across the room, raising flames upon every candle in her suite.

Their light died almost instantly.

Kallia yelped at a hard brush of wind, her hair thrown over her shoulders. Fear caught in her lungs as the room went pitch black, but she forced herself to move. She rushed and fumbled her way to the door—only to find the handle rigid. Locked.

Kallia kept her back to the door, her chest tight. "Hiding in the dark is no way to fight," she snarled. "Show yourself!"

She risked a glance at the mirror, and everything in her froze at the answering chuckle. The sound of hands clapping. Slowly, surely.

"I'm not one to hide, Kallia. You know that."

Kallia's pulse shattered at the breath grazing the shell of her ear. The brush of fingers traveling over her shoulders to her hip. Featherlight yet burning. She shivered and whirled around to—

No one.

Absolutely no one.

"N-not real," she whispered furiously, eyes shut. Every muscle in her body shook with the need to run, but she couldn't. It was worse than her nightmare of crawling away from a monster.

This was the part when the monster took her, once and for all.

As soon as Kallia thought it, the fingers drifted away. The air quieted. She dared crack an eye open, and blinked in disbelief.

Light warmed the room. The candle flames glowed as if they'd never gone out, and the fire crackled heartily, while the moon streamed in bright as a spotlight across the furniture. Even the mirror was covered. Undisturbed.

All looked as it had before, except for the imposing figure overlooking the closed window. From where she stood, he was just a tall silhouette carved from shadow, donning a familiar dark suit. Only when he moved out of the moon's glare did the room's light touch his warm-hued skin, glinting off the black brass knuckles on his hands she knew so well. The face, she knew even better.

Her first instinct was to scream. To run. To hide. But she would not give Jack a single morsel of fear. "Took you long enough to find me."

"It wasn't that hard, firecrown. You do leave an obvious trail."

No anger in his voice. No fear, no relief. If she didn't know any better, she would've thought he'd forgotten all about the way she'd left Hellfire House from his typical, cool manner.

But his eyes were too deep and expressive to play along. And Jack's lingered on her for a long, burning moment. Like he wanted to say more, do more.

Blood thundered in her ears. She'd be lying if she said she felt nothing—she felt *everything* as she watched him in return, honing in on the familiar lines of his jaw, the set of his shoulder fitted against the black jacket. Slight shadows formed beneath his eyes, the only detail that made her believe he could be real. Here.

Until she looked down at his feet, swallowed in a mass of smoke spilling across the floor.

"You're not really here," she said evenly, still on edge. "If you're not really here, why did you bother to come at all?"

"For you," Jack said. "Because you must leave, while you still can. It's not safe."

"Safe?" She almost barked out a laugh, but her throat was already too raw. The cool mask dropped from her face, shattering in rage. "That's rich. And what makes you think I would *ever* go back, after everything?"

All of it flooded back in a heavy wave. Sanja. Mistress Verónn. Mari. Countless others she couldn't recall but was sure existed, buried deep in her thoughts. A collection of ghosts, passing through her life because of him. Memories displaced, because of *him*.

"How . . . how many illusions did you put me through?"

It shouldn't have mattered. Whatever he said would only be lies, and still, she searched for the truth in them. Anything to stop the horror of it all from clawing inside her. Filling every vein and vessel, weaving between her bones.

She kept the hurt from her voice, refusing to give it to him. But Jack knew, he always knew.

"Any person I've conjured is based on someone real. A projection of an acquaintance I've met before." He leaned against the window, releasing a soft exhale. "Kallia, it wasn't all pretend."

"That's not an answer." The ghosts danced in her mind, laughing at her. "How many times have I tried to leave, and you wouldn't let me?"

"It wasn't like that—"

"How often have you lied to me and twisted my mind?" Heat smarted behind her eyes. "How many times have you gone to Glorian, and told me that *I* shouldn't?"

At that, Jack fell still. For once, he looked like the prey, and nothing was more satisfying than to see it from the other side.

"There are things at play here that you do not understand," he said, nostrils flaring. "Though clearly you wouldn't believe me now, even if I told you."

"And who's to blame for that? You chose to lie. To deceive me again and again." Kallia bit her lip, hard enough to draw blood, just to keep it from trembling. "Until I had nothing. Only what you wanted me to see."

A cage. It was all she remembered of the House now. Not a home. A gilded place of false friends and stolen time. Any lingering fondness felt fabricated, a syrupy-sweet taste she tried ridding from her tongue, for none of it had been real. Just an act.

The worst part was, he had no remorse over it. Or if he did, he hid it well.

"I gave you all that I could." Jack drew the words out after a long, chilling pause. "To keep you away from harm. From here."

"To keep me away from anything at all," she growled. "Don't pretend like it would've stopped at Glorian, Jack. You would've done anything to keep me in that House. Just like your father."

His eyes flashed. No longer cool and collected, but burning. "I gave you far more freedom than he ever did. And you stayed."

She stayed, and she'd learn more. That was the deal set years ago. No iron and force in the arrangement. Though it was easy when her answer was yes. Had she refused, she wondered what the outcome would've been.

"You broke our deal the moment you used my mind against me." The words tore from her like a curse. "Though, in a sick way, thank Zarose you did. If you hadn't, I wouldn't be here."

"Oh, right. Because of *Spectaculore*," he said, lips thinned. "You hear a competition is in town, and suddenly it's your destiny. And for what? Fame? Glory, attention—"

"What's so wrong with wanting more? I got a taste of it tonight, and it was only the first show."

"And who do you have to thank for that?" His brow arched. "You certainly didn't learn all your tricks on your own. And you're wasting it on a ruined city, a silly circus, and people who'd rather tear you down than throw roses at your feet."

It wasn't true.

She'd received so much praise, so many flowers, enough to wreath the hotel in spring. But that was tonight. Days' worth of disdainful stares from the people of Glorian flickered back in her mind. From the judges and contestants, complete strangers who only saw what they didn't like upon her arrival. She hadn't forgotten. It wasn't as if she'd believed making it here would be easy. Then again, she'd never anticipated how many people would also crave her failure.

No, she shook her head at herself.

It wasn't true.

It wasn't true.

"Better than swinging from chandeliers at the club every other night," she muttered. "You honestly thought I would be content there for the rest of my life?"

"If you want more, I'll give you more. Far more than this place ever could." He pushed off from the windowpane, holding her gaze firmly. "Come back home. Let me show you."

His voice wrapped around her; his promise, an outstretched hand that beckoned her back to the shadows. Into the night he alone ruled, that would never let her go if she ever returned.

She refused to go back into that dark.

"Leave." She raised her empty hand to stop his next step. An oath, burning between her fingers. *"Now."*

Jack vanished in one breath.

The room went cold and quiet. Kallia looked everywhere, heart pounding as her gaze fell to her hand. Her fingertips were on fire, palm searing.

A sudden breeze raked over her arms. A presence came up close behind her, gathering like a wind, into a hard wall of muscle, before the lightest fingertips trailed along her jawline.

"Your pulse is racing," Jack whispered, the sound of it everywhere. In the room, in her mind. Right at her ear, as he palmed the side of her neck. "It's not wise to try banishing me when you're running on so little."

He was trying to unnerve her. Distract her. "You came here as nothing more than a ghost," she scoffed, tolerating the pressure and warmth of his touch, assured by the cool shadows brushing by her legs. "I'd say *you're* running on less."

The presence behind her dissolved, and Jack reemerged by the window. Her head creaked from the suddenness of the movement, and his amused smile hardened into steel. "Do you really want to put that to the test?"

He stalked slowly toward her. He could've simply appeared before her, but steps were far more menacing. Easy and certain, slow and confident. The walk of a beast closing in on its meal.

Chin raised, Kallia backed away. She would bring this entire room down on him if she could, if her powers were up to full strength. Her pulse thundered as she flicked her left wrist. The nearest objects obeyed her and shot across his path rapid as bullets.

A vase.

A pair of horned candlesticks.

A fire poker, which speared straight through him, dropping with a heavy thud.

"Come on, firecrown," he drawled, continuing his pursuit. "I *know* you can do better than that."

Heat clawed at her calves. The fireplace. With a slight flicker of fear, Kallia thought he might run her into the flames, and she wouldn't be strong enough to hold them off. She fisted both hands at her sides, hissing at the prick of thorns against her palm. The rose, clenched tight in her fist. Jack's gaze wandered down her wrist, frowning. "Who gave that to you?"

A pounding fist came at the door.

"Kallia?"

They turned toward the exit at the rough, muffled voice from the other side. Jack's eyes darkened, Kallia's widened.

Demarco?

Another round of knocks against the door, unanswered.

Panic. Sharp as glass, rising like bile. But she could hardly move, paralyzed the instant Jack turned toward the interruption.

"You don't want to be rude, firecrown. Open the door." A moment later, he was behind her. His hands traveled down her arms until he captured her wrists, guiding her forward. "Who is he?"

Kallia's ears rang with the persistent knocking. "I don't know."

"You're lying." Jack squeezed her right hand until the rose stem snapped. "Did he give this to you?"

The words seized in her throat as Demarco's fist kept pounding, pounding, pounding against the door. "Kallia, what's happening? I heard crashes," he called hoarsely from the other side. "Please, open up."

"Go on, let him see what Glorian's rising star is tangled in now." Her pulse spiked under Jack's laugh by her ear. "Let him see us, or make him leave."

Leave now, she screamed silently at the door. She needed him gone. Away from her, away from Jack.

"Let go of me." Kallia ripped her wrists from his hold. The manner in which he stood back like a spectator filled her with dread, her heart thrashing in cold, stabbing strikes. She was more than ready to cut this show short. Approaching the door, she could no longer feel anything. Only ice. "Mister Demarco, what's the matter with you? No need to break down my door, I'm fine."

The knocking stopped. "Are you really?" There was a strange surge of relief in his tone. Mixed with a trickle of doubt, and disbelief. "I heard a scream."

Swallowing, Kallia looked over her shoulder to find Jack lounging on the couch. Hands behind his neck, he grinned at her to go on.

"You were imagining things." She scowled at the door. "I was asleep."

"I don't believe for a second that you could've slept through that racket." Another wary sound came against the door, the impatient rapping of knuckles over the wood. "Is your assistant with you?"

"No." Jack's chuckle reached her. "He hasn't come back from the party yet."

She almost smacked herself as soon as she said it. Why couldn't she have lied and said Aaros was sleeping off his drunken state in his rooms? The whole conversation would've been over, with Demarco gone, and only Jack left to deal with.

"So you're alone?" The knocking halted for a breath. Two. "Can I come in, then?"

Against all reason, Kallia flushed. "Excuse me?"

"No, not for—not like that," he added quickly. "You can even just crack open the door. I only want to see if you're all right."

"What for? Nothing's wrong. And you can hear my voice now, loud and clear."

"Oh, I hear it. And something doesn't sound right."

Kallia let out an exasperated groan. She had to give the man credit—his instincts were as sharp as a hawk's. Frustratingly so. She pressed a hand to the door for stability, and somehow felt Demarco's stalwart presence instead. Like the coarse, warm feel of his palm, finding hers against the wood.

He wouldn't leave. Not until she bloody well opened the door.

Muttering a curse, Kallia cast a quick glance to the sofa, finding her audience now leaning right against the space by the door hinges with his arms crossed, waiting. Jack nodded expectantly down at her hand paused over the doorknob.

With a hard swallow, she slowly pulled the door open a crack.

Just enough for her to see a sliver of her visitor. "Look, everything is perfectly fine." Her plastered grin stiffened at his prolonged stare. "What is it?"

Of course, after putting up such a fuss, Demarco went quiet. He only looked over what little he could see of her, trying to piece something together. "Sorry, it's just . . . I could've sworn I heard a scream."

"Blame your imagination." Kallia gestured over herself in one quick sweep. "As you can see, I'm perfectly all right."

With a tight nod, his lips screwed in thought. "You said you'd been asleep, yet you're still in your performance dress."

Curse him.

"Can't a magician accidentally doze off in her dress and heels?" she snapped, her face flaming up. "What is this, a midnight interrogation?"

"I didn't mean it to sound like that." He raised his hands up in defense. "Honest."

"Good, then. You got what you wanted." Kallia gripped the door. "Have a good night, Mister—"

"Daron." He stopped a hand at the door, a few inches above hers. "Call me Daron."

A slow tide of heat rushed beneath her skin. A prick of fear. In the other corner of her vision, Jack's head tilt in observation. No longer amused.

She shivered, suddenly hesitant to meet Demarco's eye. "Why?"

"Because I think I've offended you enough times. It's only fair I give you my full name so you can spit upon it at your leisure." His tone warmed, the smile in it falling. "It didn't sit well with me, how we left things tonight. I'm here to apologize."

"Again?" Kallia groaned. The way he chased down forgiveness was so new to her that she still didn't know quite how to react. Already, something strange was happening with her pulse. She wanted him gone before Jack could sense it. "I get it, Demarco. Apology accepted—"

He gently stopped the door from closing.

"I'm the last person who should be giving performance advice. I know that." Inches from her, he pressed closer, keeping the door open. "I'm sorry for doubting you. For doing all the wrong things, it seems."

A short strand of dark hair fell past his temple, and the urge to smooth it back distracted her. "You should be focusing on other things."

"Trust me, I know."

Kallia's chest tightened. A coiled spring about to snap. Her gaze retreated to the shadows. There, she found Jack's expression focused and unsmiling, as he pressed closer to study every word. Every cadence, every sound.

Her gut tightened. Thinking fast, she channeled as much viciousness into her expression. *"Mister Demarco,"* she fired off, nostrils flared. "How many times must you apologize to me before you actually mean it?"

He faltered. "I'm . . . I do."

"Oh really?" Kallia cut out a brief cackle, shaking her head in disappointment. "You know, I've met men like you. They say one thing and mean another, weaving sugar-coated stories just to get their way. Don't tell me that's not what you're trying, using every line to get into my room at this late hour."

Demarco's face shuttered entirely.

Hot shame pricked at Kallia. Had she gone too far? She was no stranger to the scenario, but somehow she also knew that he wasn't cut from that dirty cloth. The flicker of pure disgust over his face spoke as much.

"Good night, Kallia," he said tersely, turning from her. Not back toward his room like last time, but down the hall, lost in the lights and sounds of the party still alive down below.

Good. She rubbed a hand across her face. Good for him to think the worst of her. To leave her alone, finally.

"Who is he?"

For once, Jack wasn't at her back or by her ear. Slowly closing the door, Kallia found him standing over the fireplace. A silhouette shadowed against the dying flames, a sight more threatening than if he were pressed against her.

"He's a judge." She scoffed with such disdain, she convinced even herself. "Like the rest of those top hats. I do my best to avoid him."

"He said he advised you on your performance." Jack released a harsh laugh. *"Him?"*

It had always unnerved Kallia, how easily he could intuit knowledge without having to be told. How seamlessly he could weaponize it.

"He's just a judge, Jack. Leave him alone." The slice of anger in her whisper betrayed her. It was all the answer Jack needed.

"I wonder how you'd look at him, had I not been waiting here." His entire form flickered. Eyes raw, burning. "Would you have invited him inside?"

"Go ahead and create more illusions out of nothing," she snarled, observing the rapidly fading quality of his figure with relief. The sight of a deadly storm coming to pass. "I came here for one thing, and it wasn't for distractions like him. He means nothing."

"And what about me?" Jack's voice went low, unreadable. "Am *I* nothing?"

He was talking in circles. He'd slithered into this room sly as a snake, and it took a mere moment—a delusion—to lose that lethal polish. Envy always did bring out the worst in Jack.

"I gave you power," he said quietly. "A life, a stage."

"You gave me a cage." Her breath shook. "And now you want to throw me back in it."

The sharp edges and dark planes of his face shifted under the bitterest of smiles. "That's where you're wrong, firecrown. I didn't throw you in a cage." He raised a hand by her cheek, close without touching. "You walked right inside and turned the lock. And if you're not careful, you'll lose yourself to it."

The door gave a short rustle behind them. Kallia jumped back from Jack, but he'd already vanished to the other side of the room. Right by the vanity mirror, fixing the drape that had somehow fallen again, as if he had all the time in the world. "Start by keeping this covered. There's no telling what mirrors will try to show you here."

When the lock clicked and light trickled in, Kallia whirled around, everything in her tightening as the door creaked open. Aaros poked his head inside with a droopy, drunken expression that sobered the instant he caught sight of her. "Boss? I thought you'd be passed out by now."

Brow creased, Kallia turned and paused when she found nobody behind her.

Only an open window, ushering in a dark, lingering chill.

19

Daron,

We arrived at the academies just a few days prior, answering those urgent calls out east I mentioned last time. Strange magic is afoot. It seems there might be a new development from the possible power plight among magicians in the area. Still too early to tell, but never too early to take action.

Hope you're well. Write back when you can, please.

And remember not to party too much. Especially not on an empty stomach.

—Aunt Cata

The letter had appeared in Daron's courier case that morning. Wherever he went, his letters found him. Correspondences from old friends he'd rather not hear from, the persistent press still gunning to stage interviews he'd sooner fall into a ditch than give. When he'd left

Tarcana, he'd wondered if he were better off leaving the case home altogether, but he'd always find letters from his aunt there. The only ones he read, even if he never answered them. That she still wrote meant she hadn't completely lost hope in him.

Better yet, it meant she had no idea where he was at the moment, and why.

He ran his thumb over the broken Patrons wax seal, white as bone. Eva would always rip them open excitedly, and together they'd pore over the latest adventures of their aunt leading the Patrons, along with her latest reprimand.

With Eva gone, the letters grew shorter.

Daron still read them, alone. He'd thought it might provide him a sense of ease as he sat in the café of the Prima Hotel, glittering in the cold morning light. Instead, the opposite coursed through him. He was the one dark spot amid the bustling sea of happily filled seats and tables. He couldn't relax. He overlooked his small spread of untouched bread and barely sipped coffee, his eyes constantly flitting to the staircase.

Still no sign.

His foot twitched impatiently. It was starting to hit the two-hour mark since he'd first sat down, and he wouldn't have even noticed were it not for the deep creases of his aunt's letter from all the times he'd folded and unfolded it. Or the confused waiter who kept returning for refills, only to find his coffee cup full. At this point, it would evaporate under the morning sun beaming down through the crystal glass ceiling.

Get up, you fool.

His body wouldn't obey. Whenever something did not sit right with him, it rooted inside heavy as stone. Until he found reason to move, he would simply sit with his thoughts, for the reason had not yet walked down the stairs.

Daron pressed at his forehead. She clearly wanted nothing to do with him—now more than ever, after last night's assumption. There was no denying that Kallia was beautiful. Much like a viper, and she'd accused him with all the venom of one, too.

Usually Daron was impervious to all kinds of barbs. Being in the spotlight made you the target of so many, but the one she'd speared him with stung. He owned that he wasn't a perfect gentleman, but he detested anyone who went around hunting like a foul-minded scoundrel in the night. No one deserved to be sought out like prey, to be expected to fall freely into the jaws of the beast simply because it was hungry.

He'd come to Kallia to properly apologize, and left being accused of just that.

The thought burned like acid in his throat, a wrongness searing through. The malice with which she said it, the kind that actors employed as villains on the stage.

Something wasn't right.

Daron *had* heard a scream from her room. Along with a chorus of crashes and thuds that forced him out of his door and close to knocking down hers. And when Kallia answered, cool-tongued as usual, he thought maybe he had imagined the chaos.

But there was no imagining the line of kohl smudged roughly at her eyelids. Her hand clawing at the door, prepared to shut it in his face or run from what lay on the other side.

Fear.

A secret not even her best masks could hide.

Daron jerked at a thick wooden *screech*. A young man casually pulled the other chair out across from him. Tall and lanky, he whistled and raked his fingers through his jet-black hair, which did not make his appearance any less bedraggled.

"Morning, judge." He yawned, plopping down in the seat. "Mind if I join?"

Stunned by the intrusion, Daron frantically folded the letter for the last time and slid it into his pocket. It took him a second to place the angular face with sleek, dark eyes, and the light-as-air attitude that said he didn't give a single damn about anything.

Kallia's assistant.

"Do I have a choice?" Daron countered, equally dry.

"Actually, I'm the one all out of choices. Rest of the tables are full." The assistant gestured at the café's scattered spread of tables that Daron could've sworn had not been occupied the last time he checked. Then again, much of the first floor had all but vanished for him except for the stairs.

The assistant tsked in amusement as if he could hear his thoughts, before they darted eagerly to the bread sitting between them.

"Stay, then." Daron pushed the plate forward. "Fresh bread is a poor thing to waste."

"Couldn't agree more." The assistant grinned rather triumphantly, relaxing back.

Daron lightly tapped at his chin, surprised. There was something easier about his manner today. The last few times they'd interacted were about as warm as watching two cats in a cage ignoring one another.

Now, they were each other's dining company.

The young man grabbed the slab of bread from the plate, tearing off a chunk with his teeth. Tried to, at least. His face crinkled slightly at the hard crunch. "Fresh bread, my ass. How long has this been out?"

Oh, a few hours.

"The waiter swore it was just baked." Daron coughed, averting his gaze. "If he comes over again, I'll—"

Without warning, the assistant reached over to dip a finger in Daron's cup. "Cold coffee."

The thump in Daron's pulse jumped up a beat. "Hot beverages do have the tendency to lose heat over time."

"Yes, but *how much* time, is the real question." He sat back with a glimmer of satisfaction, toying with the bread as if only getting started. "And how long have you been sitting here, judge? Waiting for somebody?"

Both men stared each other down, unblinking, while the sounds of clinking utensils and delightful chatter surrounded them in a wave of morning pleasantries. They couldn't have been more removed from it, and it was probably best to end the conversation altogether before the tension rose to more questions, and possibly fists.

Instead, Daron surrendered a hand over the table with a sigh. "Call me Demarco."

The eyes across from him widened, more at the hand itself. As if it weren't something often offered to him. "Call me surprised," he replied. "You've got notable blood and stage chops, so I've heard. You don't act like it."

It was refreshing to be in the company of those who didn't know his life as the Daring Demarco. When he could tuck it away like a secret, Daron breathed easier. "People exaggerate. I don't perform anymore, which has given me ample time to get my head out of my ass."

The assistant snorted. "Good thing. I don't think this competition could take any more egomaniacs." He leaned forward and shook his hand. "I'm Aaros."

"A pleasure to properly meet. We'll no doubt be crossing paths more with the show in full swing."

"We already have." Aaros gave a cheeky smile. "All the top hat judges spit on my boss's name, and she doesn't bat an eyelash. Yet a word from *you* drives her up the wall."

The feeling was definitely mutual. "Please. She would walk on ice like it's iron, and still reach the other side all right. I'm merely a side player in this game, nothing more."

Humming, Aaros tossed another piece of stale bread in his mouth. "Sure doesn't seem that way," he said, chewing more thoughtfully. "Now that we're chummy breakfast companions, care to tell me what exactly you are doing with my boss?"

"What am *I* doing with her?"

"Not an old flame, otherwise she'd avoid you like the plague and pretend you didn't exist," the assistant went on, head tilted. "Not a current one, otherwise you'd be . . . somewhere a little more comfortable, I imagine."

"Mind out of the gutter," Daron deadpanned.

"Nor are you spying for your aunt, I don't think. Otherwise the Patrons would've swarmed Kallia the moment she lit the stage on fire."

Daron squared him with a look of disdain. "Interesting theory. But no, I assure you, I'm no spy. And we've never met until this competition." He glanced back to the stairs, still streaming with well-dressed hotel guests. "I take it she's asleep."

"Out like a lamp thrown against the wall."

The image made Daron cringe. That's exactly what it had sounded like from his room. A scream, followed by other terrible noises. "Does she need a doctor?"

"Calm down, mate. I knocked on her door a couple of times and got a slur of profanities to not disturb her." Aaros mixed the breadcrumbs on the plate with his finger, unworried. "You magicians need your rest, right? After all she gave to last night's show, she'll no doubt stay married to her bed for the next day or two."

Daron nodded. The twisting feeling in his gut, which had him acting like some scatterbrained fool, still refused to settle. Especially when, for the first time since he arrived in Glorian, he woke not with the determination to find out the city's secrets, but worried. Far more than he had any right to be. Nowhere else would he find himself sitting at a café for hours on end, fixated on the stairs to catch a glimpse of someone who wanted absolutely nothing to do with him. No wonder Aaros had picked him out so easily in the crowd. Daron no doubt made a pathetic sight.

Space was what he needed. It's what Kallia wanted, and he'd be better off, too. What sort of judge would he look like if he was seen outside her door every time something went amiss? What would others think if they saw?

"Problem, Demarco?" Aaros cocked his head.

Daron shot up from his seat and threw his napkin on the table. "No, though I must be off." He dug through his pockets. "I have other business to take care of."

"None that involve certain contestants?"

Not anymore. Daron promptly scribbled his room number on the white card beside his plate as payment, before a vivid flash of Kallia resurfaced: her, opening the door last night. Her eyes, that fear. It all carved into him like a warning. His hand stayed clawed at the back of his chair. "Aaros, from what I've seen of you, you're a very capable assistant who's loyal to his magician."

"You flatter me, but yes, I'm quite fantastic." Aaros gave a flutter of his fingers. "So?"

"I hope you'll be discreet. I'm not sure what your boss would think of what I'm going to tell you."

"Kallia's got enough secrets to fill the sky. I'm dying for some dirt of my own."

"It's not dirt. It's *about* her, and it's something you should be aware of," Daron explained. "Something I've been concerned with ever since last night."

Intrigued, the assistant leaned forward, eager to hear. And once he did, it would be his mystery to solve. *His* worry, not Daron's. "Don't get any funny ideas about this—but I went to see Kallia last night at your suite."

Aaros's lips moved in the barest hint of a twitch. "To what end, judge?"

"Certainly not what you think." At the suggestion in his tone, Daron bristled. "I heard noises, coming from your room. Violent crashes and bangs like . . . like the room was being tossed upside down."

"Everything was fine when I arrived." Aaros shrugged. "You sure it wasn't from the party downstairs? Things got pretty rowdy."

"No, I *know* what I heard. And I heard a scream."

The assistant stilled, though his fingers had begun tapping a light, persistent rhythm on the table. "And you went to explore?" Aaros's brow arched. "I'll let you in on something: Kallia is brilliant, but strange. Half the time, I don't know if she really aims to win this competition or plan world domination. For all we know, she could've been practicing her tricks—"

"Trust me, I know." And Daron had had enough. No more tricks. No more inserting himself into situations that would only lead him down paths he didn't want to go. He'd come to Glorian for Eva. Nothing else. "Still, the whole thing left me uneasy."

"If Kallia needs help, she'll ask for it. Though I doubt she ever will. She can take care of herself."

"You didn't see her face when she opened the door." Daron quieted, her dark eyes still cutting him. Even from memory. "It was filled with a certain kind of terror—as if the worst thing that could ever happen finally did, and there was nothing she could do about it."

"And how would you know a thing like that?"

Because Daron had once seen the look before.

On his own face, in the mirror, after his last performance had taken the most important person in his life.

I t had been days since Kallia stepped outside and breathed in the frost of the Glorian air. Her numbed senses, dulled from rest, sparked alive at the cold. The scent of ice.

She wrapped her coat tighter around her as she walked from the hotel, the most activity she'd engaged in after locking herself in her room for days. Normally she knew how to stave off the drain of energy that came from casting larger magic—ice baths and sleep, with enough sweets to sugar-coat her teeth—but this fatigue had gone deeper than flesh. Fear made sure of it.

It was impossible not to imagine Jack everywhere. At every corner, within every shadow. He hadn't reappeared since that night, but he'd gotten what he wanted: her, always looking over her shoulder, unable to breathe for she felt him all around her like smoke now.

Kallia's fists tightened as she shoved them into her pockets, resolute. If he couldn't take her back to the House when she'd refused, then something was stopping him. She still had time.

Determination fired in her veins as she continued down the sidewalk. She ignored all the stares, more so than usual, though she'd worn nothing to deserve them. Her modest long brown coat itched—

the warmest she could coax out of Ira's shop—and yet it earned her more attention than when she'd first arrived on these gloomy streets in a storm of color.

A bespectacled boy with soot-smudged cheeks nearly stumbled onto Kallia's path. His eyes brightened with recognition. "Y-you're that magician lady, right?" He tipped his ratty cap in her direction. "Brilliant show you put on last week."

Before Kallia could utter a *thank you*, he was gone. The daze that hit her struck just as instantly. For so long, she'd danced with a mask, known only as the powerful showgirl who descended from the chandelier.

To pass strangers who remembered her from one night, one act, bewildered her.

She'd known she could do it, just not how it would feel. As if the world really were at her fingertips. Always there, waiting for her to reach.

Her exhaustion almost dissolved altogether in the thrilling rush. Kallia ventured on, light on her feet until the streets grew emptier, and the air more musical. Purple-striped circus tents came into view as she rounded a corner that brought her toward the Alastor Place. Nestled around the entrance of the foreboding palace, the bright campsite of the Conquering Circus was sprawled out. The tent openings flapped in the wind, exposing slivers of the whole company inside. Boisterous laughter, shrill banter, and the music of strummed strings and piano keys pounding out a melody that demanded and beckoned.

Kallia drew closer, eyes closed to savor the energy. Of all the things she missed most about Hellfire House, it was this. Music loud and lively enough to drown out all thought and transport her.

When she peeled back the tent flap and stepped in, the warm air hit her in a wave soaked sweet with gin and smoke. The wide connecting tents housed tables of all sizes, scattered and packed to the brim with card games and players on each side. Racks of costumes of all textures and colors had been pushed to corners where props of different shapes and shades stood: stacks of large metal rings studded with flowers and gems, narrow vats of water glowing with strands of seaweed and red coral, rough rope-hewn scratching posts as tall as men, and in the shape of them, too.

It was like stepping into a completely other world. One that paused, as if a storm had blown in. The musicians played on in the background, but all chairs turned in her direction. Card games stalled, and laughter hushed into curious whispers and glances.

"Look what the ice dragged in."

Canary came up behind her, arms crossed with a simmering expression. "You have a lot of nerve coming here. Finally got bored enough to spare a visit and pay your thanks?"

The bite in her tone scraped hard. "I had my reasons for not coming sooner."

"Too many adoring fans to attend to first?"

Kallia's brow hardened. "I was ill," she said, not sure why she was even admitting it. But she only had so much energy to spare, and she'd rather not waste it keeping a mask in place. Not in these tents. "You know that adrenaline you get during a performance, and the crash that hits you after? Stage magic doubles that weight. And the recovery is much longer. Being a magician yourself, surely you understand."

Canary stilled, blinking rapidly. "It's just . . . I thought you'd—"

"What, that I wouldn't feel pain like everyone else?" Kallia chuckled. "That I'm somehow indestructible?"

"No, it's . . . you're different from those other magicians, that's all. Even the ones I've seen on the road. Born, acquired," she said, running a hand through the messy ends of her hair. "It wouldn't have surprised me to see you coming out of that first show ready for another right after."

"I absolutely would've if it had to be done." Kallia cocked her hip. "Power might come naturally to some, but it's still hard work to pull off the unimaginable."

Canary absorbed the information with a chagrined tilt of her head, not uncommon from a bird listening to the song of another. "I'm sorry."

"Don't be." Kallia inhaled deeply, taking a sweeping look around her. "I truly *do* apologize for not coming sooner, though. Looks like I've been missing quite a party."

"We've been restless." The circus performer's shoulders fell. "Ever since that night."

"How did Rayne take it?" The only thing Kallia had been truly worried about was causing any problems for the girls. Who knew what *their* contracts stipulated if they detracted.

"Oh, he loved it." Bitterness cut her tone. "Went about like he'd been in on the act."

That didn't shock her in the least. "Glad to hear there was no trouble."

"Trouble doesn't scare us." Canary gave a cheeky grin that bunched the scar across her face. "He hasn't given us a shred of recognition since, though. So we've been occupying our time in other ways."

Kallia didn't quite catch her meaning, until she looked closer at the people sprawled around the game tables. Men and women, young and old, with their long coats hanging off their chairs. Glorian coats. Kallia's mouth fell open. "You invited the city into your tents?"

"It's cold in these parts. Why let a warm circus tent of curiosities go to waste? Spectaculore shouldn't be all about the top hats." Canary smugly patted at the small blue pouch hanging off her shoulder that looked near bursting. "Besides, it's not as though they come empty-handed. They pay us, we offer them a seat."

"You sure that's a good idea? The people here can be . . . critical."

"That's what Rova's for." The flame-eater gestured toward the head of a room where a severe-looking young woman in black sat on a makeshift throne of pillows and pedestals. Her pale hand rested on the head of a large, sleeping lion. "Our lead animal tamer. If anyone slights us, she'll wake Aya to restore the natural order."

Kallia snorted, almost wishing she could see a demonstration.

"Come on, Your Highness." Canary tugged on Kallia's elbow, weaving them between tables and over fallen props with her head held high—a queen passing through her kingdom. "Another reason I was hoping you'd come sooner was because you've acquired a few fans in my troupe."

"Really?"

"Yes. It's obnoxious." Canary sniffed. "Also, I don't know what sort of crowd you're used to, but none of us have a single prim and proper bone in our body. Just forewarning you."

"And to forewarn *you*," Kallia countered, lips curled, "neither do I."

They bypassed a group of girls stretching in a cramped corner without complaint, likely dancers. But when they began bending into all sorts of shapes, walking on their hands as easily as legs, Kallia's eyes widened. Her limbs suddenly felt rigid as rocks at how little she could do with them in comparison. Canary laughed, and tugged her closer to the rowdiest source of noise in the tent.

An unexpected jitter went through Kallia as a table brimming with ladies burst out in full laughter after two players slammed their cards down.

"You cheated, Cass!"

"I would never cheat family," the other girl said smugly. "It's just easy to beat someone who's shit at cards, is all."

"But I've never played with these Glorian ones before."

"Excuses, excuses . . ."

"Those are the Starling twins," Canary whispered. "Our resident acrobats. On land, it's all war between them. But in the air, nothing but harmony."

Kallia nodded, drawn to the scene. That unfamiliar ache from when she'd first seen the Conquerors returned like a bruise. Like the story in front of her was not hers to join, only as a spectator looking in from the other side of the curtain.

Juno craned her head above the group, the inked roses and thorns framing her face stretching as she smirked. "Just when I thought things around here were getting boring."

The group hushed as everyone turned in Kallia's direction. A flush broke out beneath her skin as she began to fidget in a way she never had on stage—until Juno pulled her in for a surprisingly warm hug. "You look like shit," she teased. "I can see why you've come back. Could use some more blush."

"Maybe for the next show night," Kallia replied. "If they let me back in."

The others hooted and banged the table.

All at once, it became a heart-pounding blur of shaking hands and names paired with titles too fantastic to forget. Linnet O'Lione, the animal charmer who played with beasts and laid with snakes. Camilla Falco, the fierce dagger catcher and thrower whose perfect aim made her the deadliest of the group, though her toothy smile betrayed otherwise. And along with the Starling twins, another set of sisters rounded out the group—the Cygna sisters: Silla, Sersé, Sirenna, and Sann, who had learned the graceful art of water dancing as mermaids in the sea, only to bring their talents ashore.

With a touch of awe, she shook the dancers' hands. *"Mermaids?"*

"We all have our little stories." Sann winked.

"And the public loves a good fairy tale." Canary plopped into an empty seat with a sigh. "I was tragically born in the midst of a terrible fire, the only survivor who got away with a taste for flames." She snorted. "It's a touch more epic than being a dropout from Queen Casine's who ran away to join the circus."

"Why?" Kallia cocked her head in interest at the confession. "If you have magic, you don't need the circus."

"Easy for you to say, Highness. You born magicians have power brimming from your fingernails that people would pay to see," Canary said, not unkindly. With a touch of envy. "I have magic, but no stage. Casine's sure as hell doesn't breed entertainers, so the circus became a platform. You have to chase your spotlight where you can, right?"

Kallia nodded, for she understood better than anyone.

"Now, enough talk." Canary thrust a hand out to the empty seat beside her. "You still have to earn your entry into these fine tents. Ever played before, prima donna?"

The group surrounding them *ooh*-ed and pressed closer as the dealer on the other side shuffled. "Of course she hasn't. Not with these cards, at least." Between the older woman's fingers, the cards flew from one hand to the other, effortless. "The girl is as much an outsider as your strange little gang."

Kallia knew that cranky voice and had to turn to the dealer to believe it. *"Ira?"*

The seamstress gave a minxish half-shrug without breaking her focus.

"What are you doing here? What about your shop?"

"Those *poor*, lonely dresses. How will they manage?" She blew out a scornful sigh. "It's my day off. I didn't live this long only to sew. Besides, shuffling cards is good for the mind. And it's cozy in here." Neatly weaving two sets of cards together by the edges, she folded them back together. "Are you in?"

The precision of Ira's movements captivated her. Kallia had hardly frequented the card tables back at Hellfire House. Sometimes, she'd played with Jack after they'd taken their meals. He wasn't much for card games either, though he played her with the same kind of polish and expertise with which he handled others. He paid attention, observed, and won the game before it was even over. A tough one to beat, but with other players to contend with, she might stand a chance.

She slipped into the seat next to Canary with a sweeping glance across the table. No one else sat, opting to remain an audience over their shoulders as the cards were dealt. She'd seen enough of them at Hellfire House—Jack's cards carried a simple design, black squares with spiked pearlescent white numbers—but these were foreign to her.

They appeared older, more traditional. In flashes, she spotted faded numbers along the corners of most, then more elaborate illustrations across others. All accompanied by little symbols etched alongside them. Squares, triangles, circles, and stars—the shapes scattered across the city.

"These are rare cards, ladies." Ira dealt a hand to each player facedown. "*My* special collection, passed down in my family. They stopped printing them ages ago."

"A discontinued deck," said Canary, suddenly intrigued. "What's the story there?"

Ira had passed out a small pile of cards to each player, guarding the rest of the deck under a clawed hand. "Not quite sure," she muttered, scratching her head. "Might be the way they can tell pasts and futures if you know how to read them."

That captured everyone's interests. The Starling twins whined about how they were never told they held their futures right in their hands, while Kallia merely tapped a finger on her pile, contemplating what may lay in hers. "How could simple playing cards reveal such a thing?"

"*Anything* you draw by chance tells a little about yourself. It's fate's way of making fun, if you're willing to see it." Ira leaned on her elbows, eyeing the two players. "Now, this game is called Assembly. The first person to assemble a four-card hand I call out wins. So, say I want you to assemble the nonroyals"—she flipped through her deck, and pulled out a Handmaiden's card with a star at its corner—"the fastest person to assemble a group of same-suited face cards without crowns is the winner."

Canary released a low, ready whistle. "Oh, that's easy."

"You think so, birdie? There are an awful lot of cards to go through." Ira used two fingers to push the main deck forward. "Go on. Draw one and decide if it suits your hand. Toss it in the middle if it doesn't, but remember, your opponent can always pick up whatever you drop if they decide to forgo drawing a card, so be smart. And no cheating," she growled. "You only need ten cards on hand, and I don't like those who try forcing their luck. Neither does fate."

"Why would we cheat?" Kallia scowled. "We're not playing for anything."

Canary's face lit under a small, devilish grin. "We need to play like we're fighting for something, otherwise it'll make for a boring game."

"A more dangerous one, maybe." Ira stared hard at the cards before them. "Don't joke about making deals here. It's bad luck."

"Don't worry, seamstress. I doubt we'll be resorting to any blows over wounded pride. In case my opponent is a severely sore loser."

Kallia rapped her nails against the table at the challenge. "Fine, what do you want?"

For how eager she was to stake a prize, the other girl thought long and hard, conferring with her gang in a glance. "What are *you* willing to play for?"

Kallia couldn't back down. A challenge always called to her. The game Ira described seemed easy enough to understand, and Kallia was a fast learner. She was used to mastering games she'd never played.

"Performers," she declared. "Your musicians perform with me again on the next show night, just as before."

Canary let out a small laugh. "You mean those top hats haven't demanded our exile yet for ruining their first night?"

A slow smile played on Kallia's lips. "If they haven't managed to get rid of me yet, you have nothing to worry about."

With a slow nod, Canary accepted the terms. "Fine, but if *I* win, you have to perform with us when Rayne unleashes the circus onto the streets."

Whatever chaos that picture implied, Kallia didn't bat an eyelash. "Deal."

The flame-eater perked up in her seat. "So, what are we to assemble in this round?"

"Thought you'd never ask," Ira tsked, looking between them. "I'd like to assemble a royal court. King, Queen, Crown Prince, and Crown Jewel. Dark suits all throughout."

"And the dark suits are?"

"Look at your cards."

Kallia lifted her set, fanning them out against her thumbs. She skimmed the corners of her ten cards: a Queen, King, and Servant card with black triangles by their letters; a Knight and a four set against a red square; a Prince, a five, and an eight adorned with red circles; a single star, and a black star card with a seven.

"They say the hand you start out with in any game says a lot about you." Ira watched their faces carefully, before she fished through the main deck for a card with a red circle at the corner. "For the light suits, we got circles—which stood for Coins, the suit of the Ranzas." She picked up another. "Then the square represented Shields, for the Fravardis."

"And the dark suits . . ." She shuffled both back into the deck. "The ones with the black triangles symbolized Flames for the Alastors. And stars will always mean Stars of the Vierras."

Kallia remembered the names of the families, the suits representing them all within her hand. Her selection wasn't half bad to start with. If she drew a certain pair of royals missing from her set, she could easily complete the Court of Flames. The Alastors.

Game on.

"Shall we begin?" Ira gestured to Kallia first. "Pick from the deck, and decide if you wish to keep it. If you wish for the chance to draw three, you'd have to make a consecutive set, regardless of suits. Be it one, two, three, or five, six, seven—I trust you both can count."

Both players shot her a glare before resuming their strategizing.

It was still so strange to Kallia, to be a player in the game. She wasn't glancing down in passing to see who courted a lucky hand. She held her own cards, and she carried that giddiness quietly as she reached for the first card from the choosing deck.

Crown Prince of Flames.

Kallia bit the inside of her cheeks, keeping her face steady.

This was going to be *so*, so easy.

As if a little unsure of herself, she blew out a long breath, carefully looking at all her cards one by one.

Canary yawned. "Any century now, prima donna."

"Oh, all right," Kallia sputtered, throwing her single star card in the middle before nestling the newly drawn Crown Prince beside the corresponding King and Queen. One more, and she'd have a full court.

Ira studied the tossed card, while Canary let out a little whoop. "Thank you kindly." She dragged the single star card to her side before placing her own two and three of Stars right beside it. "Count 'em. I'll take my card*sss*." She hissed with so much emphasis that Kallia snorted.

"I'd say I never pegged you as a peacock kind of player, but I'd be lying."

"Confidence is key in winning. You know that," Canary sang, taking the first three cards from the top of the main deck. When she turned them over, she gave a small, delighted noise. "But how are the other showmen peacocks you're running with? I've seen sewer rats with more stage presence."

"Exactly," Kallia said. "It's going to make things that much easier."

When it was her turn, she grabbed a card, hoping for the Crown Jewel to show itself when she flipped it: The Huntsman of Coins.

She restrained herself from throwing it back with a frustrated growl. No one watched her more closely than Canary, who added, "Still. Even if they are buffoons, be careful. Outside of these parts, we don't get many chances in this industry. If any. Not like they do."

"Think one of them is going to try and knock me out?" Kallia tossed the Huntsman onto the table's surface without care.

"I would be shocked if the majority hadn't tried already," Canary said. "Judges included. I'm not too familiar with their work, but from the looks of them, they could've never done what you pulled off. Beware the wrath of old dogs."

"They'd do better to beware of me."

It didn't take long for Kallia to have her turn at braving the deck. Most of her picks ended up being numbers and nonroyals, but she was satisfied to see the same pattern with Canary. Based on the cards thrown so far, she must've been itching to complete the Court of Stars or Coins.

"I heard there's a young judge," Ira said. "That he comes from the Patrons of Great."

"And here I thought you didn't care about Spectaculore at all." Kallia's humor died instantly at the thought of Demarco. She'd done everything she could to push him from her mind, but his eyes from the night he visited haunted her. The way they seared and searched, determined to do something she wasn't quite sure of.

"I don't care about your little show." The seamstress aimed a dirty look her way. "We've never had a Patron in town. Never had a reason for them."

"He's not a Patron, he's a performer. And young enough that he's probably staging a comeback," the flame-eater quipped, unenthused. "Though why he'd choose *this* as his platform, I'll never understand."

Kallia looked down at her hand thoughtfully, still holding out for the Crown Jewel of Flames. She deliberated like a wolf waiting to strike, but this was not a hunt she could control. Not with her curiosity piqued. "Why did he stop in the first place?"

Canary's forehead creased as she assessed her. "You mean you don't know? It was *all* over the news, years ago. What, were you exiled from civilization?"

In a sense. "Oh just tell us. Ira's clearly dying to know, as well."

"Don't group me with you, girl," Ira scoffed, though she'd pressed forward subtly.

With a sigh, Canary tossed a card out. "I don't follow magicians that much in the papers. Most are greasy pigs who just party, not very interesting. But Demarco had an angle, as a son among the Patrons. If Patrons are the law and order of magic, then performers are the chaos. Which came with a special kind of spotlight. Up until the very end."

Kallia picked a new card from the deck, instantly throwing it back when it wasn't the Crown Jewel of Flames. "You make it sound so morbid. It's not like he's dead."

"Not him." The other girl's face's fell. "In his last act, there was an accident. His assistant."

A short gasp came from Ira. Kallia's muscles seized. "What sort of accident?"

"Something to do with a broken mirror—I honestly didn't *want* to know the details." Canary shuddered. "Sad thing was, Demarco and his assistant were really close. I think that's why he stopped performing rather than simply get a new one. Sometimes you can't do magic anymore without certain people in your life. Sometimes you just . . . don't want to."

The knot in Kallia's stomach had tightened tenfold, pressing into her like a knife.

How many times had she asked him why he didn't perform?

How many times had she *taunted* him about it?

"So what, you forsake magic only to become a judge of it instead?" Always the skeptic, Ira rapped her fingers against the table. "That sounds logical."

"I don't get it, either. But that's all I know." Canary shrugged, motioning for Kallia to take her turn. "Enough about Judge Demarco. Let's play."

Kallia stretched her neck, realizing the Conquerors had dispersed from over their shoulders. The tables were a bit emptier than when she'd entered, and she suddenly wished she were no longer here with the turn this game had taken.

Without thinking, she tossed out her Crown Prince of Coins onto the unruly pile of numbers and faces.

Canary let out a victory screech.

"Yes!" She gleefully seized the Crown Prince, slamming her

cards against the table. She pumped a fist in the air. "Court of Coins!"

"Congrats. Encore," Kalla spoke drily. "You deserve it."

"Oh, don't be down. Even prima donnas have to fail at something."

"I did *not* fail." Glumly, she tossed her cards to the table. "Though I am without performers now, so excuse me for sulking."

Canary's sharp victory smile rounded in amusement. "Just because you didn't win doesn't mean you lose us. We've been dying to get back on that stage and see those judges weep."

A spike of relief went through Kallia, bubbling into a laugh. "You're obnoxious, you know that?"

"Couldn't have you going all soft on me." The girl shoved her good-naturedly in the arm before turning toward a Conqueror who'd tapped her on the shoulder. Kallia reached out to help gather the chaos of cards into order, only to find Ira pausing at the incomplete Court of Flames.

"Interesting," the seamstress muttered, drawing the last card waiting in the main deck. The Crown Jewel, of course. She pushed it in Kallia's direction to complete the set. The Court of Flames, at last.

"What?" Kallia said, unnerved by the storm of emotions flashing across the woman's face. "What do they say?"

Before she could linger on the dark crowns of the royals, the intricate black lace-work flames bordering the sides, Ira swept the entire row back into her hand. "You were looking for the hand of the Alastors. That says enough."

The master of the House watched night rise outside his window, over the Woods and past the glimmers of a cityscape that towered like blades above the forest.

Another day, another night.

For the past few days, he'd distracted himself by devising new tricks for the stage. With the wave of a finger, he conducted instruments to bend to the new, changing melodies in his head. He stole the shadows of objects and gave them new masters—a candle casting the shadow of a goblet, a stack of books showing that of a sword's. He'd destroyed the grand chandelier hanging from his ceiling again and again, only to piece it back together in one snap many times over.

All to put off creating a new headliner.

The club had gone long enough without one. The people could only be amused by simple drinks, games, and memories for so long. She wasn't returning, and there was no hope of that changing after his last visit. Her fury, the hatred with which she regarded him now. It burned all the ways she'd looked at him once, and the memory sliced at him every day since.

He'd waited long enough.

He needed a star.

An illusion.

How she would laugh, if she could see him now: designing someone to take her place, resorting to deception to keep his club afloat.

Or perhaps she would regret, if only a little.

Her joy hadn't all been pretend.

Raking a hand through his hair, he paced over the broken glass covering his room. What had been real and what hadn't no longer mattered. The one real person in his life was no longer beside him, and he knew what he had to do.

Grudgingly, the master delved deep into his memory, plucking a figure like a flower from a garden. A dancer like her, but from a long time ago. He couldn't fully remember the face or how they'd met, and that was almost more preferable. He covered the blank slate with a mask, crafted her in his mind more easily than he could've imagined. No memories or thoughts, no emotions or bonds to cloud her purpose.

It was easy to build a performer like this, nothing more than the shadow of a person.

With a snap, the illusion vanished from his mind and took shape in the center of the room, a specter at first. A faded figure slowly gaining more color, more shape. More life.

Her bare feet solidified over the floor covered in glinting shards. The sea of broken crystals from the crashed chandelier he hadn't bothered to clean up yet. And as she walked upon them, pointing and flexing her toes, she uttered no cry of pain. No blood, no skin torn to the bone. She was just as much a part of his game of destruction and creation as the chandelier was. Foolishly, fixing one thing made him believe he could fix everything.

A lie he often told himself, whenever he looked out to the gates of the city. Small and quiet in the distance, but he knew better. Each time he'd made his rare visits over the years, he couldn't leave fast enough.

The horror lying beneath that place.

The pieces he hid, to keep them there.

The master sipped from his glass as he turned from the window and avoided the sea of broken crystals. With a snap, they rose like frozen rain around him and the illusion, who wordlessly watched him, unaware of the floating glass. At his command, they lifted up to the ceiling to re-form their original shape. Piece by piece, they linked back into the chandelier it once was. Grand, glorious, and fragile as the day he'd first acquired it.

It was only a matter of time before he broke it again. With the second show night looming over his head like a storm, it would probably be sooner than he thought.

It was far too late to stop the game. From here, it couldn't touch him. A mercy of the Woods he wouldn't take for granted.

The master couldn't return now. He wouldn't.

Even if they found her, if they hadn't already.

21

Kallia wiped her dirty palms over her thighs, raking in a labored breath. She relished the satisfying burn of her muscles. Like dancing for hours until only the inevitable ache could stop her.

She hopped on the stage, waiting for the worker on the ladder reaching the elaborate proscenium of cards. The rust and wear across the shapes were hardly noticeable to the audience, but Erasmus demanded the entire stage glitter at its finest before Spectaculore returned for its next night. They only had so many labor magicians on hand, and Kallia couldn't help but pull back her sleeves and lend a hand when she'd entered the theater that morning.

When the worker rose to the top of the arch, right where cards with stars danced with flames, Kallia raised her palm. Slowly, the paint can lifted to the worker, who tipped his hat at her.

She released her hold with a satisfied exhale. Strangely enough, the sounds of hammers banging and orders shouted across the show hall brought her a comfort she couldn't quite place. It was the music of busyness, and she loved how everything could drown in its presence. She'd been hoping it could drown the earlier parts of this morning.

The fresh memory assailed her. With the next show only two days away, she'd felt the need to familiarize herself with the playing field once more before returning to it. As usual, she had risen earlier than Aaros. Earlier than the city, for how quiet the world became as she flicked her wrist toward her door. The lock of her room clicked behind her.

At that exact moment, the door across opened.

She stilled as Demarco stepped out, casually turning his key between his knuckles until the motion paused at his notice. In the quiet, her heart pounded.

You should be focusing on other things.

Trust me, I know.

The words dug under her skin. Demarco sent a short, polite nod her way before locking up behind him.

"Good morning." Kallia fiddled with her door handle, finding it rigid. She'd already locked it. Zarose, what was wrong with her? "Didn't realize anyone else would be awake this early."

Demarco pocketed his key. "I'll get out of your way, then."

At the same time, they turned down the hall. Neither looking at the other. It was awkward enough that their strides matched, side by side, all the way to the stairwell. The distance must've tripled since she last walked it, for the torture seemed to go on forever.

How many times must you apologize to me before you actually mean it?

Thank Zarose he wouldn't look at her. Not even she could tamp down the flush of embarrassment. The emotion was as rare to her as shame, which tangled in her throat as everything about his past rushed back to her. Normally she could charm her way out of anything with a smile and a wink for good measure. Neither would work with him.

"Where are you off to?" she asked, unnaturally chipper. Obliviousness would have to do.

"The library." He exhaled a noticeable breath of relief as they finally arrived at the spot where the carpet sloped down into steps. The bright foyer area of the Prima, within their reach. To spare them the pain of descending together, Demarco gestured for her to go first. Polite to the teeth, which somehow grated on her nerves more as she gave a quick nod of thanks and—

"Kallia?"

At the softened tone, she whirled around so fast, her neck almost cracked. "Yes?"

Above her, Demarco still wouldn't meet her eyes, his brow working and smoothing over again like he wanted to say something, but suddenly thought better of it. "Have a good day."

Before she could respond, he sidestepped her and hurried down as though he couldn't escape fast enough.

Her knuckles tightened at the memory as she fanned out the loose collar around her neck after lifting a toolbox. Already she'd worked up enough of a sweat to take off her coat and tie back her hair, when the doors of the show hall opened with a large, creaky echo into the room. Kallia turned at the sound of footsteps making their way into the theater.

"As you can see," Mayor Eilin said, leading the pack, "the changes are quite extensive." He gestured across the sea of red velvet seats, and the canvas-covered theater boxes along the walls. When he pointed toward the stage, he faltered at the sight of Kallia.

Behind him, a new crowd filed in, making their way around the workers and labor magicians. Judges Bouquet, Armandos, and Silu were all in tow, in their morning top hats and coats. Demarco stood impassively among them, Janette at his elbow. A few others she didn't recognize, in glossy fur coats and arms linked with Erasmus Rayne, the only face that lit up at her appearance. "Darling, what are you doing here?"

"Exactly what it looks like." Kallia wiped the dust on her hands against her pants.

The mayor gave a tight purse of his lips. "How charitable of you to offer your . . . talents. Especially so close to showtime." His dour expression brightened when he pivoted back to his guests. "Our magicians have their methods of preparing. Some choose to conserve their energy, whereas others squander it."

"Oh, I wouldn't call this squandering, Mister Mayor," she said, placing her hands on her hips. "The key to keeping your magic in shape is to never let it rest too long."

It was a lesson Jack had drilled into Kallia since she'd first started practicing with him. Though magic took its toll when overused, it was a muscle that required exercise and care.

"One girl's philosophy." Judge Armandos gave a lackadaisical stroke of his beard. The other judges chortled.

"Sure, it's one philosophy," Kallia countered with a cutting smile. "I'm certain your other magicians practice their own, putting their time to good use with wild nights at the bar—"

"Now, now, now," Erasmus interjected. "Play nicely, kittens. Don't want to scare off my guests before they've even had a look at the place."

"It would take a bit more than a little bite to scare us off," said a woman in a black fur coat that hung off her like thick molasses. She didn't seem the Glorian type, with her bright lip color and chain-strung jewels dangling in mounds around her neck. She tilted her head up at Kallia, more with intrigue than distaste. "Are you in the show, miss? A magician?"

"The *only* female magician in the competition," Erasmus boasted with far too much victory. "Do say you will stay for the next show night, my gem. You should really see her perform, she's absolutely marvelous. Like something from another world . . ."

Kallia combed her fingers over her limp hair as Erasmus continued advertising her like a prize up for auction. There could only be one reason why.

"Please join us, Kallia! I'm giving some of my old acquaintances from New Crown a tour of the Alastor Place." His grin stretched so widely, it was a wonder his cheeks didn't crack from the pressure. "They also have a . . . keen interest in the success of Spectaculore, I'm sure you understand."

Investors. They were different from the ones Kallia was used to seeing at Hellfire House, who'd drunkenly sling themselves over card tables. These people appeared refined, their sharp eyes hunting for potential.

"*We* are giving a tour," the mayor cut in. "Our young magician seems to be quite busy, so if we could—"

"Not at all. You caught me at a perfect time." Kallia jumped off the stage, landing cleanly on her feet. "I was about to take a break."

"Splendid!" Erasmus crowed, while the mayor scowled. The only one who looked more displeased was his daughter, whose frown pinched her delicate face.

"Are you sure you don't want to freshen up first?" Janette viciously inspected Kallia's appearance: a pair of black pants tucked into knee-high scarlet boots, and a baggy white shirt cinched with a black-belted sash. A little dust and sweat from hard work, but Kallia didn't mind them. Even though it seems to bother the others for some outrageous reason.

"I'm sure." Kallia brushed her fingers against one of her sweat-dampened sleeves. "Though in exploring an old abandoned manor, I fear more for your attire than I do mine."

Janette's cheeks went red. She was decked out in a long peach-colored day dress whose glossy hem peeked out from beneath a smooth tan overcoat. She quickly turned away from the group, migrating toward one of the large side doors.

They all filed through the cobwebbed hallway and deeper into the heart of the Alastor Place. The theater section of the building had been receiving the most treatment during renovations. The rest, to Kallia, remained mysterious, uncharted territory. The air smelled musty, thick as the pages of a well-worn antique book. She inhaled deeply as they walked down the dimly lit hallways, still teeming with debris and dust at the sides.

"For the ball, I want a *very*, very big space," Janette declared, clapping her hands together with relish. Her giddiness echoed off the walls. "With a large floor for dancing, room for tables and refreshments—"

"Dear, why not have it at the Ranza Estate?" The mayor sighed, treading gingerly as if the ceiling might collapse any second. "Or in the Vierra District? The slight fixes we've made there over the years make it the perfect setting to—"

"No, Father." Her stance mirrored the cadence of her voice: firm, decided. "I'm in charge of planning, and I want the Alastor Place. What point is there in renovating the show hall and not the rest? What a waste of potential space."

"Are there even any viable rooms here for that?" Judge Bouquet turned his nose up at every dusty corner and cobweb.

"I'm afraid there are," the mayor said in weary surrender. "The Alastors held their share of parties, it was told. Nobody's braved these halls in a long, long time though, nor what's left of the grand ballroom. They called it the Court of Mirrors."

Janette let out an excited squeal, dragging Demarco with her to the front of the pack. He gave a gruff cough. *"Mirrors?"*

"The room was positively covered with them. Another show hall of sorts since this place is riddled with them, but not as large as the main theater, of course." Mayor Eilin shrugged, glancing back with a snort. "Don't worry, Demarco. There are worse things to fear than shattered mirrors."

The party went silent. A silence so loud, Kallia had half a mind to leave while she still could. Mirrors were likely not the same beasts to Kallia as they were to Demarco, but she could understand his hesitation. She hated fearing something so fragile, so common.

Once they reached the grand double doors of the Court of Mirrors, it was too late to turn back. The sweeping details carved across the faded wood had dulled, the golden veneer charred along the edges like burnt toast. No doubt grand once upon a time, the doors now carried a rotted, decrepit beauty. Captivating. As though welcoming them to a ballroom of the underworld.

All too eagerly, Janette strode through. Her delighted shriek echoed immediately, and the rest filed inside curiously in stunned silence.

Kallia's jaw went slack.

The Court of Mirrors went on like a stretch of frozen sea from one end to the other. She stood at the top of a double grand staircase, mirrored on the other side with another just like it. The space between was an arena designed to fit scores of people, dancers, and entertainers alike—overrun by overturned tables, islands amount of debris and broken glass abandoned from long ago. Ransacked, from the looks of it. The frames hung crooked along the walls empty of their portraits, or so scorched and blackened their images were beyond recognition.

Kallia's eyes lingered upward at the paint-faded ceilings, where rows of broken chandeliers hung lopsided on weary chains. To imagine someone had left this whole building to ruin with age, and age with such loneliness. To think of the parties and balls, the life that must've graced these halls and lit these rooms, was to watch a candle flame die in one harsh breath. There was something tragically forgotten about it all, this place that yearned to be remembered, whispering behind walls of blackened, broken glass.

"My dear, you're shaking."

Kallia jerked when Erasmus came up next to her. She crossed her arms tightly. "I'm just . . . taking it all in."

"A beaut, isn't she?" His hand fluttered in a dramatic flourish. "If it can't be loud and flashy, be beautiful and dramatic."

"It's absolutely *perfect*!" Janette trilled, sidestepping fallen furniture and pieces of broken statues like an eager explorer bent on covering every inch. Her father trailed behind, voicing his concerns with every step until distance softened them.

Kallia was surprised not to see Demarco hanging off Janette's arm like the dutiful escort he'd entered as. Instead, he'd ambled off on his own toward a large, empty fireplace that dominated the wall like the roaring mouth of a lion. Occasionally, he'd pick up a fallen item to inspect it closer. Aimlessly wandering like Kallia, admiring and searching for something he wasn't quite sure of yet.

"The ghosts will be angry with you if you keep touching their things," she said finally.

Demarco bent toward the ground with a reaching hand, but his fingers never closed. He rose, keeping his back to her as he brushed his hands over his dark coat. For a moment she thought he might ignore her to avoid a repeat of this morning, until he said, "Tell that to the rest of our party. Though I'm sure ghosts will only excite them more."

He spared a brief look over his shoulder before continuing on to the ornate fireplace. His terse response somehow set her nerves running, and she hated it. She'd never wanted to make an enemy out of him, and she didn't want him to imagine her as one, either.

"Are we strangers now, Mister Demarco?" Kallia called after him. "Or are we just playing a rather intense game of silence and avoidance?"

Demarco's shoulders straightened into a resigned line, but he turned. "What are you talking about?"

"I think you know. Even this morning, you could hardly look at me."

"I didn't realize you wanted me to."

She didn't even try fighting the wry grin on her face. "I did not come over here to argue with you. I came here to apologize."

"*You?* Apologize?"

"I know. Between us, it's a first."

"Why?" He propped himself against the wall beside the fireplace, his head tilted. "You made your point very clear that *I'm* the one who erred, that *I* should be groveling at your feet with apologies."

His tone carried such bite that Kallia paused to reconsider him. This Daron Demarco was no longer uncertain and proper. She'd never seen him act more bold, arms crossed in disinterest. His mind, decided.

Since he believed in the power of apology so much, perhaps it would set things right between them. Maybe it would ease the heaviness that had settled in her core after Canary's story. But it was much harder coming up with the right words. It was a wonder that Demarco could do it so many times with her.

After more fraught silence, he let out a quiet laugh before shoving off the wall to walk away.

Her pulse sped. *"Wait."*

"You think I'm simply going to stand here and let you pick me apart again?"

"I'm not—will you just listen?" Kallia huffed sharply, pulling him to a stop. "I don't . . . I don't do this very often."

"And what is that, exactly? Chase after people who won't give you the time of day?"

"Apologize," she growled.

"And why do you want to make peace with me so badly?" His brows arched, his face curious and expectant and unreadable all at once. She hesitated, the full breadth of his attention on her suddenly too much.

Breathe. She chewed the inside of her lip, trusting that if she answered honestly, it would be enough. "Even for a prince, you're a man of honor. Put a plate of money and jewels in front of you, and you'd probably set off on a tireless search for the owner."

"You make me out to be some sort of saint, but I'm not." He pinched the bridge of his nose. "Nor am I a prince."

"Nevertheless, you're decent. And it was terribly presumptuous of me to accuse you of being otherwise."

"Why did you, then?" His eyes shuttered, nowhere near softening. "Were you really so desperate to turn me away?"

Jack flashed like lightning in her mind, but Kallia held her tongue. *Breathe.* "I was not myself. It was a tiring show, and took a lot out of me. And unfortunately, I lashed out at you."

Demarco merely nodded as if turning the words over in his head to find a fault with them, and failing. "Well, thank you for explaining. I accept your apology, Kallia."

The pressure started lightening in her chest, until he began walking away. The sight of his back was a slap to the face. "Wait, that's it?"

"What do you mean? You offered an apology and I accepted. That's how forgiveness goes."

"Sure, but . . ." She couldn't rein in her thoughts. But what? What else had she expected? What else had she *wanted*?

"You didn't really need to apologize to me, anyway," he said, slowing his steps. "I do appreciate the gesture, but it's for the best if we leave it at that."

A whole new level of fury trickled into her veins. "What do you mean 'it's for the best'?" she demanded. She hadn't stood there making a complete fool of herself, only to have her words thrown back at her feet. "Don't go making rules where there aren't any."

"But there *are*, Kallia. You don't see them because you walk all over them. There are rules to this competition, and restrictions to what can and cannot happen." Shoulders tense, he shoved his hands into his pockets. "You're a contestant, and I'm a judge. It's best if we remain professional and stay on our respective sides while the show goes on. Agreed?"

"What sort of boundaries would we be crossing by talking?" She gestured at the both of them. "Would this, by your definition, be perceived as unprofessional? Or would you rather turn your back every time I enter a room? Because that sounds immature."

"Not on my side of the table, it doesn't." He gave a short sideways glance at the others who occupied the far corner of the room. "Look, I'm sorry I can't show you the favor you want—"

"It's *not* favor that I want from you."

"Then what? What else could you want from someone like me? Friendship?" He let out a harsh laugh, more at himself than at her. "I'm only a name. A judge."

Kallia had thought he was her tentative ally, too, but she'd clearly been wrong about that. Demarco was so set on dismissing her that he'd forgotten he was the only reason she was here in the first place. He'd recognized her potential, given her a chance. Those weren't small acts to her.

"So what?" she said, nostrils flared. "Would it be so terrible if we *were* friends?"

"Based on our interactions thus far, I don't really think we'd make very good ones."

"We're better off as enemies, then, is that it?"

The edges of his lips quirked up, and Kallia's pulse quickened. But the light in him dimmed just as swiftly once he started off toward the center of the ballroom. "We should get back to the others," he said brusquely.

He could hide it all he wanted, but she'd seen his smile. How it had wanted to spread, if only he'd let it.

"You'll warm up to me again in time, Demarco. I'm much nicer than my thorns betray, you'll see." Kallia trailed after him with the lazy, sure click of her boots. "Maybe we could practice together sometime? Do some tricks and exercises—"

"No, I can't. *We* can't." Demarco glared at her over his shoulder. He gave a quick, suspicious look around the room, always looking at the others, though the rest of the party had long since migrated far from them. "Listen, I accepted your apology. Let's leave it at that."

At that, he left without looking back. The loneliness prickled against her skin, until it became a burn. Rising from her neck to her cheeks.

She'd apologized, admitted she was wrong. Practically begged for him to be her friend. Over the years, she'd endured much worse. Wardrobe malfunctions, midperformance. The disdainful slither of men's eyes running over her, their hollers following her everywhere.

But if this right here wasn't pure embarrassment, she didn't know what was.

Her nails dug into her palms. The scorching sensation swept through her, merciless and sure.

Separate, firecrown. Jack used to whisper in her ear when they practiced. He'd always stress the importance of the magician finding power within. Depending on anyone else bred weakness. Magic was meant to be a lonely gift.

You are your power.

Separate.

Little by little, the fury cooled from her skin.

Separate.

22

Spectator after spectator filed in, flooding the aisles of the Alastor Place to no one's surprise. The first night proved Spectaculore was what it always promised to be—the light that drew others out, a spectacle no one could miss out on.

"Did I not tell you?" Erasmus clapped his hand on the mayor's shoulder, looking out into the crowd. "Wonderful turnout. *Wonderful.*"

Daron gritted his teeth. The renovations on the show hall were finally complete, but only barely. With the majority of workers and labor magicians making headway on Janette's plans for the ballroom, he feared they wouldn't be finished with the theater in time for the second show.

But Erasmus was always one for entertaining the masses as soon as he could, and the success of it was starting to go to even the mayor's head. *The show must go on,* they each said in turn. Nothing grated Daron's senses more now than that phrase.

"Stop looking so worried, Demarco." Mayor Eilin settled into the seat beside him, fanning himself with a program. "We have audience members and a show on our hands!"

Unfortunately, Daron soon found the chair to his other side

occupied by Erasmus, donning a suit brighter than the fresh velvet of the new seats. His smile, even more glaring. "By next show, we'll have a full house. Guaranteed."

"I like the sound of that," the mayor said.

Daron couldn't have felt any more awkward than if they were clinking champagne glasses directly over his head. Both men soaked in the success. In the audience, the mayor witnessed a city coming together; the proprietor, a city of eager, new customers to entice.

"Then again, why *wouldn't* anyone want to be here?" Erasmus posed. "Everyone is positively itching to see Kallia's next act. Especially after that first night."

At that, the mayor's pleasant demeanor fell flat. "She's not the only contestant in Spectaculore. We have plenty of others who don't need to clutter their acts with a parade of circus musicians and silly dance moves."

Daron bit his tongue as the judges down the row chuckled, eavesdropping.

"You old goats wouldn't know entertainment if it danced right in front of you," Erasmus snapped. "Case in point."

"Please, it was a cheap act." The mayor gave a dismissive wave. "And what a way to cheat. We have grounds to pull her from the competition altogether! We clearly stated there were to be no other performers on the stage aside from the magician and the assistant."

"Right, *on the stage,*" Daron muttered with a hard glare. "Her musicians did not interfere. She performed each trick on her own."

"Well, when you put it like that, it was an unfair advantage to receive additional help. Another way of cheating." Judge Silu sneered, reaching into his coat. No doubt for his flask. "Don't let a pretty face fool you, young blood. It's poor form for a judge."

If all of Glorian weren't currently in the show hall watching from their seats, Daron would've decked him. Fire built in his fist, his breath. It was like magic, blazing within him, looking for a target.

Daron seethed at the irony, tuning out the bickering between

Erasmus and the mayor to focus on the closed scarlet stage curtains. His right foot twitched restlessly beneath the table, the anticipation of the show like a storm brewing inside him. He thought after he'd told Kallia his intentions in the ballroom that his discomfort would dissolve. It had only risen higher, stifling every part of him.

The theater warmed from the bodies packing in and the lit glass-encased candles adorning the walls. Fans were drawn and papers folded to wave against necks and faces. The buzz of excitement plunged into weary complaints. For the first time since he'd arrived in the coldest city he'd ever known, Daron was sweating.

Before long, he recognized one of the stage managers approaching their table, clipboard in hand. Always efficient and ready, though even the woman's cheeks appeared red from exertion.

"Is it showtime?" Erasmus asked, somehow appearing cool and collected despite the heat.

"Not exactly." She pushed her spectacles up the bridge of her nose. "There's a problem backstage—"

"Can't it wait until after?" Mayor Eilin demanded. "The audience is expecting that curtain to rise. We can't keep them or our magicians waiting any longer."

"That's the problem." The manager flipped over the papers stacked on the clipboard. "Three of the magicians haven't arrived."

"Ridiculous." The mayor scowled, gesturing for a look at the list. Daron snuck a hurried glance, finding question marks bolded beside the names Ives, Constantin, and Farris. Their faces flashed in his mind, along with glimmers of their first acts. After Kallia, these three ranked among the most solid performers. Off the stage, the most solid partiers.

With a long sigh, the mayor crossed his arms. "Are they on their way? Can't anyone fetch them?"

"I-I don't know. A couple of the contestants arrived here in a group, but no one remembers if they were among them. It's as if they've suddenly—"

"Vanished." Erasmus tapped his chin. "Out of thin air."

Daron's blood chilled at his fascinated tone.

"This is not a joke, Rayne."

Mayor Eilin dragged the list of names over for the proprietor to see, but Erasmus barely spared it a glance. As long as Kallia's name was counted among those in attendance, the man would have his show. "We simply can't stall much longer. If they left the city, I'll make sure they never find a stage again. I don't have patience for those who leave without explanation."

"Well, Mister Rayne, there is something," the stage manager said, tentatively pulling more paper from her board. "I found these, left on the chairs of their dressing rooms."

She tossed them on the table, three square-cut pieces of parchment with a brief line in the center. Three words: *Four of Flesh.*

"Oh, for Zarose sake," the mayor moaned, running a hand down his face. "Not this ridiculous nonsense agai—"

BOOM!

The entire theater shook at the roar shattering overhead. An explosion. Daron's ears popped as he covered them, screams erupting over an immense bell, ringing high from within the Alastor Place.

BOOM!

With each toll, everyone flinched.

BOOM!

The stage curtains shivered. The judges' water glasses tipped over.

"Will you *stop* that incessant ringing?!" Erasmus yelled at the mayor, whose face had gone white. The chandeliers lining the ceiling clinked and shook, threatening to fall.

"It's impossible," Mayor Eilin insisted, unblinking. "We haven't been able to get these bells to ring for—"

BOOM!

At the fourth toll, uncertain silence followed. The air had settled, chasing away all heat from the room as audience members stared wide-eyed at the judges' table.

Daron swallowed, his nerves frayed.

Whatever that was, this couldn't go on. Magicians disappearing and bell towers tolling. For the safety of everyone here, they must cancel the show before things only worsened.

Before another accident occurred.

The dark cloud blackened Daron's thoughts, taking him back to his last performance. That terrible night where something had felt off in the air, the night he'd spent years trying to push away no matter how hard grief pushed back.

No. Daron didn't want to remember her that way. The look she'd given him before they went on stage together, the mirror—

He shut his eyes tightly for a breath, before blinking open to the sight of Erasmus, shaky on his feet, climbing onto the seat of his chair and turning to the crowd.

"Ladies and gentlemen, we are *terribly,* terribly sorry about that most upsetting disruption," called out the proprietor, impressively chipper for how his knees trembled. "We're still in various stages of fully renovating the Alastor Place, so our deepest apologies to anyone distressed or alarmed."

Daron's mouth warped in alarm at the slow curve of Erasmus's smile.

"Rest be assured, what happened earlier was only an accident," the man continued gaily, looking to the other judges with blazing intensity. A brightening gleam in his eye that Daron had come to dread. "Tonight's show *will* go on!"

A tentative round of applause came from the people settling back into their front-row seats. The adrenaline mixed with the earlier terror finally hit the crowd, building back up into an excited clamor. It didn't take long for everyone to return to hooting and hollering for the spectacle to finally begin.

Daron could only glare at Erasmus. "This isn't wise, and you know it."

"Actually, I don't." He stepped down from his platform, like a king dismounting from his war horse. "Rough patches happen all the time."

"When lives could be at stake, then no. They *shouldn't.*"

"Don't be dramatic. And no need to go running to your aunt. This is show business. Just because in your last performance, your assistant—"

"Don't." Daron's voice went deathly cold. Murderous.

The rage returned, filling him in a way magic never had before.

If it weren't for the widening of Erasmus's gaze, there would've been no stopping him from throwing the man on stage and giving everyone a real show.

"Apologies, Demarco. It was a low blow." Erasmus patted him good-naturedly on the arm, his version of a genuine attempt. "But one failed night is all it takes to destroy everything, and we can't afford to delay any longer."

The man began dabbing at the sweat across his forehead with a bright handkerchief. From heat or nerves, he couldn't say. No matter what Erasmus intended, his reassurance did not ease Daron in any way.

One night.

He knew, better than anyone, the damage one night could cause.

"What the *hell* was that?" Kallia swore, slowly rising. Her entire dressing room had rippled under the force, but nothing could compare to the sound. Ominous and heavy, thundering loudly overhead again and again.

Until at last, silence.

"I think . . . it stopped." Aaros cautiously uncupped his ears. The air had grown still, the walls no longer shaking. The sudden peace seemed to unnerve him even more as he made for the door. "I'll find out what's going on and check on the Conquerors."

Kallia nearly followed, but willed herself to regain focus. She'd finally reached the right headspace for performing when the room began to shake as if the Alastor Place were careening off the surface of Glorian with every thunderous *boom*.

The force had sent a few small paintings clattering off their nails, along with the drape she'd thrown over the dressing room mirror. She waited a few beats for her heart to slow. Her pre-show ritual was a sacred time. It would take longer to achieve that concentration again. Meditate and relax. Separate.

Separate from all else, and you will conquer on your own.

Jack's words. His centering mantra that had become hers. She wanted nothing of him fixed in her mind, and yet his words were all she knew.

Nothing could ever be just a coincidence.

Furiously, she shoved the nearest portrait back into place and began setting the room to rights. Did he have to intrude upon everything she did? Ironic how fear was the last thing coursing through her blood. Only irritation.

"Jack." She sighed sharply, reaching for the drape to hang over the mirror. "What did you do this time?"

Terrible things

Kallia dropped the drape. She spun around at the voice, finding no one else with her.

The worst things imaginable, to those like us

Her blood drew cold. If the icy wind in the darkest parts of the Dire Woods could talk, it would sound just like this. A choir of voices becoming one, all-knowing and watching.

And much closer than she realized. The mirror had frosted at the edges, fogging the center until her reflection was no more than a blur the color of her gown. Kallia didn't dare touch the surface; the chill seeped through her dress, deep into her bones. She couldn't stop shivering.

"Sh-shut up," Kallia muttered, unwilling to entertain the illusion further.

She was not afraid.

Not of glass, or what lurked behind it.

Taking a deep breath, she ignored her reflection and picked up the drape again, rising to her toes to hang it over the ornate frame.

Don't

Don't let him win

You've been hidden for so long

Let us help you, Kallia

At her name, she froze, grateful the drape partly covered her face.

What if he steals you away again?

Then you'll never know

"Leave me alone." Her fingers trembled, the drape slipping between them as she tried securing it tightly. "Whatever you are, I want nothing to do with you."

Did he teach you that?

Everything in her paused. The whispered question struck her like a knife; she'd never considered it like that. Never once thought that his warnings and lessons could all be lies.

The undercurrent of anger that always seemed to linger inside spiked.

Here, you can choose

He hid from you

Lied to you

To make sure you would never find out

"Find out what?" she demanded.

No answer came. She let the drape fall, searching the mirror with abandon. But the spiky webs of frost along the edges were gone. Kallia saw only a clear reflection of herself. Her lips painted bold red, her eyes wide and stained with fear, wet at the edges. Wary to touch the surface as if it would ripple like water.

Cold traveled down her spine, an odd scent flooding her nose. Like smoke, blown from whiskey-laced mouths. The muffled cry of a trumpet rang out nearby, and when Kallia blinked, her reflection had darkened. Showing not her, but someone else.

Jack.

Kallia lurched back, but he didn't notice. He gazed right into her, fixing his bow tie without concern. His brass knuckles glinted by his collar, designed like black piano keys down his fingers. *"I don't care if anyone survived. It's not my concern anymore."*

She startled at his voice, the clear smooth tenor right in her ear. He was in conversation with someone, but she heard no response. Only knew someone had spoken from his answering snort.

"Oh they are, down there?" Jack smoothed his hair back, which appeared longer than how he usually wore it. *"They'll spend a long time waiting, then. This place will never recover. It's as good as lost to the rest of the island. Thanks to them."*

Kallia's thoughts spun, trying to place what he was saying. Who he was talking about. The image of him looked like a different Jack altogether, from a different time.

Anger flashed in his gaze. Whoever he was talking to was not giving the answer he wanted. *"I don't need to stay any longer than I already have. It's humiliating. The world of humans and mortal magicians can rot for all I care."*

A knock sounded behind Kallia, but the line repeated in the back of her head. *The world of humans and mortal magicians.*

As if he were something else, entirely.

"Knock, knock."

Aaros. His muffled reply ended with the turn of the doorknob.

Her senses snapped back, pulse racing. In the mirror, Jack listened on sternly as though he'd heard the knock as well. His shoulders straightened as he peered closer, leaning nearer.

She had to stop this. Kallia shot up, fingers wringing at her sides. He was not going away. Aaros would see.

"Yes, Sire."

Kallia froze, the name unleashing so much inside her. A flood of memories, a realization. Her chest rose and fell fast, the snugness of her dress suddenly too constricting for the need to breathe. To hide.

She snapped her fingers.

Crunch.

The glass fractured at her back just as the door opened. Her startled gasp must've come out more like a shriek from how Aaros covered his eyes. "Oh, sorry! I should've waited."

"Stop it. You . . . caught me by surprise, is all," Kallia said flatly, pressing a hand to her abdomen to quell the nausea. The fractured mirror remained lifeless. Whatever she'd seen, she wanted to forget it. That voice in her ear, Jack as her reflection. And Sire. So many questions and sensations burned at her until her teeth chattered. "Come in, tell me what's happening."

"Everyone's fine. A little shaken, though." His shoulders eased. "Some strange mishap up in the bell tower, apparently."

"What of the show?" she demanded, smoothing her hair. "Oh, would you *stop* covering your eyes?"

"Only respecting your boundaries, boss." As soon as he closed the door, he slid his hands from his face, which instantly fell. "What's wrong—are you okay?"

Kallia cursed inwardly. "I swear, you ask me that twenty times a day. I'm *fine.*"

Over the past few days, he'd been very attentive. So much so that it was starting to irritate her, though she knew it came from a place of concern.

"Fine," he repeated, approaching her quietly. Kallia stiffened as he reached behind her, across the vanity surface, and plucked what looked to be a fallen black feather. No remark about the fractured mirror, to her relief. "You just look . . ."

His pause dragged on as he casually spun the feather between his fingers.

"*Absolutely fabulous* better be your answer." Kallia strutted over to her chair, lowering into it with languid grace. "You didn't answer my first question. Is the show still on?"

Aaros watched her, gaze absent. "Yeah. You're on in five."

"*What?*" Kallia shot up, not the least bit graceful. "But . . . I'm last. I can't possibly be next."

"Well, tonight is your lucky night. A few contestants dropped out at the last minute, so Rayne insisted on your act being moved." Aaros whistled out a low breath. "You're up."

23

The theater hushed at the sharp, demanding clicks of her heels. An entry rhythm that pulled every attention in the room under her spell, while the glow of stage lights illuminated her arrival. She'd chosen her armor well that night: a velvet backless dress of midnight blue clinging to her like ink and flaring out over her legs. The plunging neckline was risqué, even outside of Glorian, but Kallia had no care. Without even a word, she already had them all in the palm of her hand.

Anticipation crackled beneath her skin at the sight of the shadowed attendees flooding the rows of the show hall. Goose bumps traveled across her flesh, but she quelled her shiver. She relished the pinch of fear as it sparked every nerve, shooting adrenaline into her body and a clarity emptying her mind of all thought, all worry.

She narrowed in on the long table before her. All judges accounted for. Even Demarco.

"Ah, finally without your helpers," the mayor declared in what he might've considered a joking tone. "What, no raucous parade tonight?"

At his resounding chuckle, Kallia gave an equally coy laugh. "Not yet."

The judges' smiles dropped, while a few hollers burst from the front row. Her behavior no longer earned full-fledged shock, but delight. Excitement. And she wasn't foolish enough to lean into that safety by delivering the same act again. She had to pull off something new, daring in a different way.

Behind the curtain at her right, Canary and the Conquerors waited with their instruments in tow to play to whatever mood the performance called for. Aaros stood at her left, ready if needed. Her best cards on her, even if they stayed at the sides. She just had to play them right, and at the right time.

Through the trapdoors of the stage emerged a small cloth-covered table at the center, and an immense cloaked object that towered behind it. A myriad of *oohs* and *ahhs* burst from the audience at the rise of the new arrivals. Her props.

"Your prompt for tonight's act is as follows . . ." Erasmus sent her a conspiratorial wink before deepening his voice. "Down in the world below, the magician could not escape. Not without mystifying the gatekeepers within."

As if by command, the cloth lifted from the small table, revealing a silver-handled tool upon it. "A dagger." He pointed behind, where the cloth descended from the clasps of the tall, looming prop. "A full-length mirror, and . . ."

Kallia tensed at the razor-sharp edges of the mirror frame, searching for the last prop. "And?"

"A member of the audience to be part of your act." It was the mayor's turn to beam. "And no, you can't choose your assistant or from the circus you're no doubt hiding backstage. That would be *cheating*."

The bite barely dug at Kallia. She'd never performed with an audience member. A dance at Hellfire House, yes, but mixing big magic tricks with a drunken patron was a liability if she ever knew one. Especially in this scenario, when nothing was planned beforehand. With all three props revealed, her mind worked to combine them as safely as possible.

No room for error, with a spectator playing a role in her act.

Thankfully, Kallia had grown used to looking out into large crowds without a drop of panic. Across the seated figures, some perked up to be chosen while others withered into their chairs to avoid notice. She nearly gave into the temptation to choose one of the judges just to see them sweat, but she needed someone who would cooperate. Someone willing, curious.

Her searching gaze slid away from the more elite attendees and landed down at the front, where she met a set of wide, unblinking eyes. The girl couldn't have been more than ten years old, decked out in a ratty sweater that hung off her like a potato sack, but she stared at that stage like she belonged on it, and it lit her up like a flame.

Kallia crooked her finger invitingly at her. "Would you like to come up and help me?"

Whispers swept across the theater, some intrigued and others confused. The girl's brow crinkled, looking around as if there must've been someone else she was addressing. The older boy to her right shook his head. "You don't want my sister. She's a shy thing," he called out, rising from his seat with his chest puffed out. "I, on the other hand, would—"

"Be more than happy to escort your sister to the stage?" Kallia finished, arms crossed. "Such a gentleman."

The boy's bravado deflated. Head hanging low, he nudged his sister roughly in the arm, all petulance as he kicked back into his seat. The girl yanked him in the ear before racing out of her row and down the aisle, eager. The sight of her approaching made Kallia smile, until the mayor stood with a huff. "Excuse me, but you cannot bring children up there. It's too dangerous for little girls to be involved."

The little girl in question threw the fiercest glare at him on her way to the stage.

"You said I could select anyone in the audience." Kallia planted both hands on her hips, daring him to refuse her. "Just be glad

I didn't choose any of you, because the temptation was certainly there."

The judges collectively pressed back, saying no more as the girl reached the stage. She faltered when she met Kallia's gaze, as if suddenly remembering herself—prey caught wandering in the hunting grounds. Scared, but she didn't want to be.

"It's all right." Kallia was surprised by the gentle encouragement in her voice. She bent her knees a bit so as not to appear so much taller. "What's your name?"

"Marjory," she said quickly. "But everyone calls me Meg."

"Well, thank you very much for joining me, Meg." Kallia walked closer to give her a proper handshake before sweeping an arm out to the crowd. "Can I please have a round of applause for my guest?"

A delightful burst of applause rang out, and Meg's cheeks bloomed red. It struck Kallia, how she'd rarely spent time around children. Hellfire House was certainly not the place for them. But in flashes, she remembered herself as a child under Sire's care, running down the halls of that large, empty home with a strange sort of freedom she'd lost the more she'd gotten to know the House. But the moment she'd tapped into her power, everything changed. Everywhere she stepped became a stage rather than a prison.

"Are you ready to see some magic?" Kallia winked.

After swallowing a belly-deep breath, Meg nodded. Kallia guided her toward the front of the stage, gesturing for Aaros to stay by the mirror. At the snap of her fingers, the musicians to the other side began playing, trying to find the heartbeat of the act—the slow curling whine of a violin, met by the soft rapping of drums beneath. A hypnotic reel made for shadows and night.

Perfect.

Kallia's mind worked better with music lifting the air. Her eyes flitted between her props and Meg, quickly formulating an act.

The crowd hushed at her back, anticipating how she would use the props in harmony. They would probably be disappointed to not receive the same fire and strident beats of the first performance, but Kallia hoped it would be enough.

She nodded at Aaros to keep moving the mirror until it stood right by them at the center of the stage. An old mirror, large and grand with the gilded frame of a magnificent portrait. Kallia imagined queens and empresses beholding themselves before this mirror, now nothing more than a prop.

It's only a prop.

"Tonight," Kallia said, and the music bowed to her voice. "You will learn to always think first before trusting your reflection."

The words fell from her lips naturally, but it bit at her to bring any of Jack's lessons onto the stage with her. She took up the dagger, tilting the blade into the light so that it gleamed like a smile. "For tonight, I will bend what the mirror shows you and give you something else."

Whispers unleashed across the audience, a few in protest and disbelief.

Illusion, not manipulation. It was the only distinction she could bear, for she would never mold minds and make them her own. Even if it were easier, when minds were so malleable.

The girl's probing gaze wandered from the dagger in Kallia's hand to the mirror, uncertain.

"It will be all right, I promise," Kallia reassured her. "All I want you to do is stand right here—with a large step between you and the mirror . . . *yes,* there you go—and when I ask, I'd like you to tell me what you see."

Meg nodded, her hesitation melting away. She stood directly in front of the mirror, the huge frame dwarfing her so parts of the audience could still see themselves reflected. Additional credibility. Kallia needed it, even for an illusion as small as this.

She moved a few paces away from Meg. Head held high, weapon in hand.

As the soft violin notes floated back into her ears, Kallia spun the dagger in the air, but it never fell. Gliding away from her, like a slow-moving arrow with the blade facedown, it traveled to the space between Meg and the mirror.

Kallia washed away the faces in front of her, shoving them out of focus as she concentrated on the object. The dagger. A small, familiar object, though that had nothing to do with the illusion. Jack had hardly taught her the trick when he'd presented it, but she'd always been quick to figure out the truth behind the magic.

The power lay not in bending what the beholder could see, but in convincing the reflection it was something else.

The blade is not a blade, she thought. *The hilt is not a hilt.*

She imagined the opposite of sharp edges and deathly points, her thoughts drifting toward green-leaved stems and soft petals wet beneath sunlight.

Her garden. Her greenhouse. It looked exactly as she'd left it, unfurling an ache inside her. Her heart, bruising sweetly at the sight.

It was a welcome visit, until the strain started to hit. Hands still raised to keep the weapon levitated, the imagery vined around it. A chant spoken again and again, to give it more power, more strength.

Not a blade. Not a hilt.

Beads of sweat slid down Kallia's neck as that voice of the wind returned, joining hers. Whether real or imagined, her temple began to throb. The act of focus and willing magic into another tugged inside her, but soon, the pressure eased. Her fingertips tingled. Her heartbeat pounded vividly in her ears as the dagger began to vibrate in the air.

The shivering was undeniable, emitting a subtle hum. The object listened, trying to obey. It would've been much easier for Kallia to turn the dagger into a flower, but who ever preferred the easier challenge?

At once, the theater burst into exclamations, a wave of chairs creaking as everyone leaned in. Kallia pushed their noises away. Focused only on the power she delivered like a prayer.

Separate from all else.

Magic thrummed through her veins.

You are your power.

The words struck inside her heart and made her stronger. She, alone and separate from the world. Powerful, because of it.

Finally she released a deep breath, jutted her chin toward Meg. "What do you see before you, in the mirror?" she asked, half with hope, half with exhaustion.

"Speak up!" someone called. A judge. "What do you see?"

"I-I see a dagger before me," the girl exclaimed, blinking. "But in the mirror, it's a rose . . . a bright, red one."

The nods of the people in the front rows confirmed the observation. Others dared to walk down the aisle for a closer look. Down at the judge's table, most of the men stood, their faces hard as stone yet unable to mock what was seen in the mirror.

"I see a rose, myself, and the audience around me," Meg confirmed with breathless wonder, before her head started to tilt. "And something else. A shadow."

Kallia blinked. The hot stage lights hitting her skin grew cold.

"A shadow, child?" Erasmus inquired, craning his head around Meg's form to see. "Of what?"

"I'm not sure," she went on. "But it's coming closer."

Kallia's blood iced. She'd conjured no shadow, had done nothing but manipulate the reflection of the dagger.

This wasn't part of her trick.

"Keep going, kid!" a spectator yelled. "Tell us what's coming. Is it the circus?"

That earned a light shower of laughter, but Meg only shrank back from her reflection. "It's the shadow of a man."

Kallia's heart raced. She thought of the voices in the mirror, of Jack looking out from it, and frost inched over her skin, down her back. Spearing through her ribs.

"He's walking closer."

The confirmation tore through her.

"And he's reaching out to—"

No.

Kallia flicked her finger and sent the dagger straight into the mirror.

She'd meant only to crack. Instead, the tip pierced the surface and it *exploded*. Screams ripped from the crowd as Kallia instinctively shielded Meg from the shards of glass, and the wave of angry black darts that flew from the empty rocking frame as if freed from their cage.

Not darts, *birds*.

Kallia's breath caught in her chest as she pushed the girl to the side, into Aaros's arms before the birds or jagged pieces could touch her. A few shards and birds raked against her back, but she barely felt them. The creatures continued pouring from the frame, swarming the ceiling overhead before violently diving through the aisles.

Cries of panic rose. Kallia's knees buckled to the stage, over mirror pieces that pierced her dress, her skin. She ignored the pain and gathered what was left of her, building everything inside—

Released, as she brought her hands together.

A bone-shuddering force ravaged the air, right through the frame and the theater—vanishing the violent, hawking birds as suddenly as they arrived, into black petals falling soft as snow. Or rain, from the pattering applause that suddenly echoed in the back of her mind.

The impact of the force sent her staggering back, unable to bow.

Her thoughts, blurry.

Blood ran down her arm as both hands met the floor in a jolt. Pain burned through her. She winced at the crushed glass digging into her palm, sprinkling over her head as the mirror groaned and teetered in place, the rest of the pieces, jagged icicles dangling along the frame.

The first one crashed by her fingers.

The screams around her went mute as she closed her eyes, tired. *So* heavy.

So exhausted.

Until light.

The warmest light surrounded her in a cloud, circling and doming around her body like mist. The glass that would've struck her fell off the sides, plinking onto the stage away from her.

She wasn't doing this. She *couldn't* be.

Wavering in and out, Kallia peered through the mist surrounding her. Someone in the audience stood with his hand outstretched toward her, light streaming from his palm.

Demarco.

The last thing she remembered. His trembling form, the panic in his eyes.

Before darkness carried her away.

P eople wouldn't stop clapping for Daron or patting him on the
  back as he passed them in the after-show party of the hotel foyer.
He cringed, each time.

Wrong. It all felt *wrong*.

As soon as the ominous mirror had arrived in full display, he had
to force himself not to run as he'd been tempted. One moment, he
was in his chair observing the act, and the next, he was on his feet.
The instant the dagger met the mirror and the shards of glass fell, one
word had roared in him: *no.*

Not again.

Not her.

It unleashed something in him, unlike anything he'd felt before.
Magic that leapt without thinking, without waiting.

"For someone who barely uses them anymore, you've got quick
hands, Demarco," Judge Silu said, a burning cigar hanging from his
lips. "The Patrons would be proud. Could've gotten gory up there."

Daron grimaced. He didn't need more praise, or the visual. Once
his protective shield had faded, Aaros had collected Kallia and

rushed her off the stage. All the while, the audience applauded with almost mindless joy, thoroughly entertained by Daron's display.

He was no hero. Not used to being treated like one, either.

Of all the protection Kallia could've conjured the moment the mirror shattered, she'd chosen her own body as a shield. The little girl came out of the performance shaken, but without a scratch. Kallia had taken those hits without so much as a cry of pain, even as the birds tore past her into the air. And even still, she continued performing magic to protect others. For a powerful magician, it was a wasteful pain. For her, it had been instinct.

Daron took a long sip from his glass, waiting for the burn to kick in. For his nerves to calm.

". . . a shocking night, indeed." Erasmus's voice rose above the crowd, tutting softly as his group made their way to the bar. "It's almost as if the show isn't over, even after the curtain's dropped."

Daron cringed at how the man could fashion a tone both solemn and garishly amused. Tonight's show had stopped after the incident—not like there needed to be any eliminations after a handful of performers hadn't even bothered to come. But when he saw the opportunity that was the chaotic end of Kallia's performance, he milked the sympathies of every attendee to cross his path.

"But that ending, that girl! And the judge!" One of his companions gasped. "Such a dramatic performance. Was it all planned?"

"Of course it was."

Mayor Eilin approached with his crew of top hats, their disdain undeniable. Thankfully, no one had yet noticed Daron cradling his drink at the bar. But even with his back to them, his hackles rose.

"Oh really?" Erasmus challenged. "And you know this how?"

"She's the talk of the night, isn't she? I've never seen a performer more determined to orchestrate the entire world around her."

"How can you believe she would orchestrate an act that would cause harm to herself?"

"Are you admitting that your dazzling star has finally dimmed?"

The mayor laughed, his group heartily accompanying him. "Good. If anything, tonight was an important lesson in the consequences of the bold. Maybe her new scars will teach her not to wear such brazen dresses."

Daron's fingers clenched around his glass at the sounds of assent and laughter. A curse crawled up his throat, wishing to shut them all up.

"For a herd of respectable judges, you spend an awful lot of time staring at her clothes."

Aaros's easy voice broke in, and Daron stole a quick glimpse over his shoulder. It was the exact war he'd been imagining: Mayor Eilin with the judges to one side, and Erasmus and his guests to the other. Enemies meeting on the battlefield. And squeezing himself into the center of it all was Aaros, rolling his eyes as if he'd never witnessed a more disappointing brawl.

The mayor sniffed. "What do you know, boy? You're an assistant."

"To the best performer in the entire damn show," Aaros finished coolly.

"Oh, *you're* that dashing boy!" a woman from Erasmus's side gushed, and the mayor's face hardened at her reaction. "Tell us, was that dangerous act all a trick?"

"Magician's secret, my lady." Aaros delivered a charming wink over his shoulder that sent everyone back into a flurry of debates and criticism.

"This won't stand," Mayor Eilin roared. "I'm penning a summons to the Patrons tonight."

"You will do *no* such thing—it's finally getting interesting!"

Daron hunched deeper into his shoulders, wishing to disappear altogether. The thought of Aunt Cata joining the fray pierced even more nausea through him.

If she saw him, she would know.

They would *all* know.

"Hiding in plain sight never works well for the prey."

Daron startled as Aaros took a seat next to him. Hailing the bartender's attention, his sly expression slid into a grim, unsmiling mask. "Why isn't the hero basking in his well-earned glory?"

"Please, don't." Daron downed the rest of his drink before tapping the rim of the empty glass to signal for a refill. "I can't bear to hear another—"

"Quit your worrying. I'm messing with you. I know you shy away from the spotlight more desperately than a bat. It's what everyone's saying back there, though."

"I wish they would stop."

"Well, you're in luck. Maybe this will give them something else to worry about." With a loud clunk on the table, Aaros presented a full leather wallet, a bejeweled folded fan, and a bulging velvet coin purse with a flourish of his fingers. "Ta-da."

Without the drink going to his head, he might've reacted with more alarm. "You stole from them?"

"You really think I would walk through that storm of gossip mongrels just for fun?" Aaros clucked his tongue, admiring his loot.

Daron had always wondered where Aaros had come from, how he'd found his way into Kallia's employment. A male assistant in stage magic was a rare sight, nearly unheard of. But he wore the distinction like a badge of honor, just as Kallia flaunted hers. Their combined mischief made them a great team. Not at all proper, and it worked all the more in their favor.

"And before you groan again, thanks truly are in order." Aaros set his half-emptied drink down with a sideways glance, a genuine smile. "Whatever happened on that stage, your trick prevented a hell of a lot more damage than was already done. My boss is very appreciative."

Daron's mind cleared. "Is that what she said?"

"No. But I'm sure she's thinking it."

What would she think if she knew the truth? About why he was here, in Glorian, in the first place?

He fixated on the rim of his glass. "Probably only thinking of how well I interfered in her act."

"That, too." The assistant nodded. "Some occasions call for a little interference, though."

An uproarious burst of laughter and clinking glasses boomed from the other side of the foyer, the party in full swing. Far more rowdy than the first show night's party, with everyone still chasing the high of tonight's exciting turn of events. No one paid mind to their quiet corner of the bar, but Daron couldn't help but glance around, lowering his voice. "So . . . none of what happened onstage was planned, was it?"

Aaros swirled his drink, letting the ice cubes roll around the amber liquor. "In truth? I don't know. Kallia could fall down three flights of stairs and claim it as an act of grace. It's how she is. She owns whatever she does."

"But surely she didn't plan on *hurting* herself? With a child in her act? Something must've gone wrong."

"The evidence stacks up to that, doesn't it?" Aaros set his drink down firmly, clearly done with the subject.

"Is she doing all right?"

The question flew from Daron before he could wrench it back, and it pulled a snort from the assistant. "She's not bleeding from the back anymore, if that's what you're wondering," he said. "What, you want my permission to go and check on her?"

"No, I was simply asking." Daron took another quick swig of his drink and consumed only air. Empty. "But after a night like this, why aren't you up there with her?"

"She insisted on no visitors. Didn't realize that included me until she kicked me out." The assistant sighed and flexed his fingers. "It was either pace around our suite until my legs gave out, or come down for a drink. I was in favor of what could take the edge off quicker."

So Kallia had shut out her assistant, too. She shut everyone out.

It was his usual reaction as well, in times of crisis. No one could perceive you as weak if they could not see you.

"When was the last time you checked on her?"

Aaros studied him, bemused. "I swear, you two act like the truest pair of ex-lovers I've ever seen. Are you *sure* you two haven't—"

Daron threw him a searing glare. "Don't start, assistant."

"Only telling you how I see it, judge." Aaros clapped him on the shoulder. "Don't you worry, it's not just you. She looks at you every time you turn away. Like clockwork."

Hearing that didn't make it any better for Daron. He pulled at his collar, his neck flushed.

Aaros gestured once more for the bartender, counting out his spoils of war from the wallet he'd snatched. "If the mayor sends for them, how fast will the Patrons come?"

As much as Daron hated being looked to as the watchdog of the Patrons, he didn't know. A letter from Aunt Cata had not reached his courier case in days, which could only mean she and her team were knee-deep in their case. Or perhaps, she'd finally given up on him.

"I don't think he will," Daron admitted, brushing the thought away. "The moment Spectaculore shuts down, so will Glorian. And Erasmus is a persuasive devil. He'd never allow it."

"What about you?" Aaros walked his fingers slowly against his glass. "You don't think this is a case for the Patrons?"

"You mean, am I going to tattle?" He stared hard at the bottom of his glass, willing it to refill by itself. "Despite what everyone thinks, I'm not a Patron. I'm not my aunt."

"No. You're not. If you were, you would've shipped Kallia off as soon as she stepped on that stage."

"I almost did." No matter how much the drink had numbed his insides, the truth of it pricked at him. How not too long ago, he would've happily sent Kallia on her way out just to preserve his own image. His own sanity.

Something in him twinged at the thought of her departure now, for had he gone through with it, then he would not be here hiding behind a glass. She would not be hurt. And tonight would never have happened.

"But you didn't . . ." Aaros mused, considering him intently, glancing around furtively. "You better not go spreading this around, judge, but I might go mad if I don't tell someone. And you're as good as any."

At that, he had Daron's undivided attention.

"Before I came down here, Kallia told me it had all been a slipup. A moment gone out of control that sent the dagger into the mirror."

"So it *was* an accident?"

"At first that's what I thought. You know, a little embarrassment. Trying to save face and all that." Aaros's fingers drummed nervously. "Until I remembered, right before her act, the mirror in her dressing room had also been broken."

A chill went up Daron's spine. "What happened?"

"Not sure, but I don't think it was any accident." Aaros lifted his drink without taking a sip. "Ever since I met her, she's been twitchy around mirrors. No clue why."

To hear they shared a fear so specific unnerved Daron. "Mirrors are not only a tool for vanity, you know."

"Clearly there's a lot I don't," the assistant admitted. "But I do know what Kallia is capable of. Do you really think she would lose her grasp on something as little as a dagger?"

"I . . . I don't know, maybe. When tackling that sort of illusion? It's hard magic to work with," Daron countered, shoving out the laughing hypocrite in him. "But I can't entertain the idea of her wanting to bring harm to an audience member when she was the first one to cover her."

"I don't think her target was the girl at all." Aaros blinked, his tone turning careful. "Remember when you told me that the last time you visited Kallia, something was off? A look of fear in her face?"

Daron nodded, wary. "And I remember quite clearly you laughing it off, saying she feared nothing."

"That was before," the assistant whispered. "Before tonight."

Kallia hiked the strap against her shoulder, panting out breaths in sharp, white clouds. Far too cold for her to be out, but there was no other option.

She'd gone over the disastrous performance a thousand times, and each time the shadow arrived, she froze. From where Kallia had stood, she couldn't see what the others viewed in the mirror, but it was in their eyes, in the air as it began walking closer. *He* began walking closer.

And yet, it was the rose that set her off.

Kallia had been rushed to her room after the show, ready to collapse and never wake. She'd never known such fatigue. Her back ached and her muscles trembled as Aaros sat her down at her vanity stool to keep her alert, waiting for the doctor to tend to her wounds. Patches of damp stickiness over her sleeves and her back marked the blood. She hissed in pain as the air bit at her cuts. Her fingers flexed and dragged over the vanity's surface, reaching for the bit of cloth she kept by the covered mirror, and stilled.

She blinked hard, waiting for her vision to clear. For her head to stop playing tricks.

But no matter how long she stared, the image remained: the rose on the cloth was dying. Petals had fallen, the frayed edges speckled in red, as if pieces of the rose had disintegrated in their descent.

It felt like a message.

Ruined and wrong, just like everything else.

Kallia took in a shuddering breath as she ducked into the streets. With every sudden movement, her back ached, still red and tender beneath the coat. After the doctor had left, giving her an ointment for her back, Aaros wouldn't leave her sight until all instructions were followed. Her tattered performance dress was tossed in favor of a simple sleeping gown, which now stuck to her like a second skin from the ointment. The blood.

It would've been worse, the doctor had said, *were it not for Demarco.*

Demarco. The mention kick-started her memory, of looming monsters and the shatter of glass—before a globe of white had surrounded her, erasing the hurt.

He'd cast something over her, unlike anything she'd ever felt before. That alone might've been more frightening than the shadow in the mirror.

He'd protected her.

And it couldn't happen again, from any of them. The faster she separated, the easier it would be.

Leave.

Now.

Before the worst escaped from the mirror, once and for all.

"Where the hell do you think you're going?"

She should've run, but the voice had her spinning around—hissing and staggering back from the pain.

"Whoa, whoa easy there." Juno steadied her gently, shooting a concerned look over her shoulder at Canary.

"I'm *fine.*" Kallia tried shaking her off. "Just going for a walk."

"Really?" Canary struck an unamused pose. "Then what's with the bag?"

Only then did Kallia remember the weight dipping against her shoulder. There wasn't even much inside, only her wrinkled handkerchief, a change of clothes, and a chunk of her earnings. The rest she left for Aaros in her scramble out of their suite.

"A couple of things I'm bringing to Ira," Kallia said. "That's all."

"This late?" Juno looked her up and down with a start. "Zarose, Kallia, you're shivering. You're dressed like you stumbled out of bed."

"Which means she needs to be *in* one," Canary snapped, reaching for the other elbow. "Let's get you back, prima donna."

Kallia flinched away, slipping the bag back up her shoulder. *"No."* Her heart pounded viciously. *Run, run, run.*

The flame-eater squared her with her usual stony expression. "Act for the crowd all you want, but you don't have to pretend with us." Understanding, deep as the first time they'd met, thrummed in her voice. "You're not alone. We all have bad shows, it's the nature of the beast."

The reassurance twisted like a knife. This beast hunted and destroyed, and he would take down anyone who got in his way.

"We don't even have to go to the Prima," Juno suggested brightly. "Come back to the tents with us. We'll patch you up right there, stay the night. No one will have to know."

More than anything, she wanted to go with them—to hole up with Conquerors, laugh and drink until the pain was a distant memory. Until the past no longer mattered. She could see it all so clearly, herself in that picture. In a picture with others.

For once, she wanted more time.

She wanted to stay.

"That's a great idea." Kallia masked the shakiness of her voice, her watering eyes. The longer she stayed, the easier that picture would break. "Once I'm done at Ira's, I'll meet you there."

Placated, Juno nodded slowly, while Canary said nothing. Once she turned her back, Kallia felt the girl's solemn stare follow her all the way into the shadows, far beyond the street where no one could see her, and no one could stop her.

The night air was chilled but warmer than usual. The next street over trickled with light laughter and chatter from those still milling about after the show.

Kallia ran.

She ran as fast as her feet could take her, until her legs were screaming and her lungs were on fire. Until the tears were too cold to fall, and there was no more feeling. Only movement and desperation and the need to run before somebody caught up to her.

The city center was a riddle of winding brick streets, but the main road to the gates intersected them all. A dark brush of gravel and cement amid the warm hues of rock that drew one deeper into Glorian. Kallia stuck to the main road, the same one she'd walked upon first entering the city.

Only one way out.

She slowed once the nightly bustle of the city fell behind her. The flickering lamplights dotting Glorian ended as it began, at the entry gates built into the austere wall circling the city.

Kallia paused when the path ended, no more than five steps to the wall. Her heart stopped, breath shallowed.

The gates were not at the end of the road.

She glanced down at her feet and up to the wall, down and up again until her vision dizzied. Along the left side, only small gatherings of trees and bushes but no gates. And along the right, the same stark stones shadowed in patches by the foliage. No gates, no anything. As if some elaborate prankster had broken down the ironwork and filled in the vast opening with cement and stone.

No. Kallia reached out to the wall. The stone was paved and cold to the touch. If anyone had messed with the wall, she would've felt the signs. Still she searched, until she began to pound and scratch and kick at the surface until her knuckles and legs throbbed with panic.

The gates were gone.

As if Glorian had swallowed them up the moment she turned her back.

As if they never existed in the first place.

Her cheeks burned, sweat trickling down her hairline when she finally surrendered. Her arms quivered from the effort, her pain sharpening as the adrenaline wore off. The chill bit at her as she stared at the wall, breathless. Unblinking.

An illusion.

It had to be.

Hooves sounded in the distance, growing nearer. Her pulse

kicked up as she stole into the shadows, wiping her face and soothing her raw knuckles. No one could see her like this, startled as a bird. Hallucinating.

Two horses approached the end of the road. The riders atop them stopped short a few paces away with deepening frowns. In the barest flicker of lamplight, Kallia detected two magicians, faint in the darkness. Robere and Eduar.

"What the—" Robere circled his horse around before he dismounted altogether. "This is the road, isn't it?"

"I thought so . . ." Eduar joined him at the base of the wall, pounding at the exterior right where Kallia had moments ago. "It's not here."

"Impossible," his companion snarled before he whirled around, searching in the dark. "You think this is *funny?* Who the hell is out there?"

Kallia pressed against the trunk of a tree, willing herself invisible even as she barely had the power for it. Not that she needed to. Their rage preoccupied them, giving her the proper cover to slip away as they returned to beating, cursing, and throwing their powers against the wall, willing it to break open.

Kallia needed a drink.

It was her sole reigning thought as she staggered through the servants' entrance of the Prima and back to her room. Her vision was already swimming in circles, but as she made it through the door, her limbs followed suit. She stumbled to her knees, waiting out the wave of dizziness. Nothing made sense.

I didn't throw you in a cage.

Everything felt numb.

You walked right inside and turned the lock.

Jack was supposed to be wrong. Everything he said was supposed to be lies.

It took all her will to hold back a sob when hands took her gently by the elbows and lifted her. She was lowered into the soft cushion of the sofa, wearing a bleary smile at the relief. Her shoes came off. Fingers pushed back her hair, traced along her temple. Her sigh drew coarsely up her throat. It burned like the rest of her, and she almost wept at the filled glass in front of her.

Water.

She downed it so fast, her insides hurt. Her body screamed for more. "Something stronger. Please."

"Are you sure that's a good idea?"

Kallia shook awake, finding Jack standing over her with his hands braced by her head. The nearness of him so dizzying, she thought she might be dreaming.

But he was there. His presence, his closeness, the furthest thing from a dream.

She shoved him off of her with a desperate glance at the windows. Their long gossamer curtains hung lifelessly, catching the moonlight outside and softening with a pearly glow. No movement or wind rustled their hems.

"Locked glass and closed curtains are nothing to me. You know that." Jack stepped back, smoothing out a wrinkle along his sleeve before grabbing the glass of water on the table. "Here, have some more." When she wouldn't take it, he sighed and snapped his fingers. "Happy?"

A dark, burgundy liquid now occupied the glass. The ease of the trick unsettled her; she could barely conjure a flame in her state. How much power would it take to banish him like last time? To banish him for good, if it were possible?

"Don't bother tiring yourself out, firecrown," he said, knowing her too well. "I'm not going anywhere."

Everything hurt more with him there. To see him see her like this, no longer strong and powerful. Nothing like the magician he'd known in the House.

"Well, I don't want you here." She curled away from him. "You've done quite enough."

"And what chaos have I wreaked this time?"

It was too much to unpack. All the disappearances and accidents, her disastrous performance, the city closing in on her—they hung from his finger, ornaments swaying before her eyes. Delicate, and at his mercy.

"Don't forget, I *did* tell you things would go awry the moment you stepped into this city. I warned you." He set down the glass on the small table before them. "You chose not to listen."

"Is this your way of punishing me, then?" she demanded. "Destroying my prospects and everything I worked for? Trapping me here so I couldn't escape it?"

Every scornful glare and taunt, she stomached. Every trick and act, she executed until her muscles burned past feeling.

All for the applause. For a moment.

All ruined, after tonight.

"What do you mean, trapping you here?"

The crease in Jack's brow only fired up her temper. "Like you don't know. The gates are gone, which means I can't leave. I saw two other magicians try to flee and they too—"

"You were trying to leave?"

Kallia didn't know what infuriated her more: the curiosity or hope in his voice. No matter how he tried to mask it, it tugged at her. "Not for you." It was unbelievable he could even entertain such an idea. "To get rid of you."

His jaw clenched. "And how might you go about doing that, I wonder?"

"Lucky for you, I guess we'll never find out."

"Oh, firecrown. You honestly think *I* had anything to do with it?" He threw his head back with a low laugh. "This city is the one you should be pointing fingers at. I didn't want you to come here in the first place."

"Why? *You* did," she demanded, breath ragged. "Don't deny it, you've been here and have returned perfectly fine. Why can't I? What exactly is your business here, Jack?"

His smile faded, as close to a flinch as she'd ever seen from him. And still, he wouldn't answer, unwilling as ever to show her even the slightest truth.

"I saw you in the mirror," she said, suddenly remembering the conversation she witnessed in her dressing room. Real or not, the way it forced him back an inch told her more than he ever would.

"During your performance?"

"That was just your shadow." She glared at him. "No, I saw you clear as day somewhere else, saying—"

The world of humans and mortal magicians can rot for all I care.

The reminder stilled her, reaffirming what she'd always thought but feared deep down. That Jack was powerful in a way other magicians weren't. Not like her, or anybody else she knew. Power like that could easily turn a house into a cage. A city into a trap, with all the strings pulled from above.

"Don't listen to the mirrors," Jack muttered, his manner terse. "You failed to heed one warning, don't make the same mistake again with another."

"What are you so afraid of me seeing? The truth?"

"No. Lies that you'll all too freely believe and follow, no matter where they take you."

"After living with you for years, I think I know the difference," she said, looking down. Dark smoke misted over the floor where his feet should've been. A man made of shadow. Not real, but for whatever reason, still here.

"It wasn't all lies, Kallia."

The searing intimacy in his tone made her shiver. A reaction he saw immediately, like the first sign of a light in the dark. "I've got an illusion running your act back at the club," he said softly.

She'd been replaced by an illusion. An odd feeling swept over her—imagining another girl descending from that chandelier—shifting from anger to confusion, leaving her hollow. "You got exactly what you wanted. A perfect puppet." She shrugged. "If you had the option all along, I don't know why you even gave me the role."

"Because it made you happy."

Her heart clenched. *Lie,* she insisted. It was all a lie. He didn't care, he never did. Though everything about him stilled, too, as if he didn't quite understand it, either. "I did a lot of things, to make you happy."

Lie. She bit the inside of her cheek, the pain stinging. "It wasn't enough."

"And any of this is?" His face blanked as he gestured his hands widely. "Seems you've gotten more than you bargained for here. And unfortunately, there's nothing I can do for you anymore."

"Good," Kallia seethed, wanting him to hurt. To make him as raw and angry as she was inside. "Leave, then. You're not really here anyway. If you were, you wouldn't hide behind—"

The table between them disappeared.

And his hand lashed out to her wrist, bringing her close to him.

Jack glared down at where he had trapped her hand—against his chest, solid to the touch. Kallia was sure he must've willed these parts of himself to become corporeal to unnerve her, and she hated how it worked.

For it felt like an embrace. A cruel one. Arms crushed her to him, bringing them close enough for her eyes to trace the hard shadows of his jaw, the slight scar over his left eyebrow.

If he could seize her so easily, why hadn't he taken her away already? Why was he so bent on remaining a voice in her ear, a shadow in the corner that took shape only when she was alone?

Kallia couldn't tell what Jack was thinking when he looked down at her, but it softened his grip. Warmth coursed through her, a betrayal. The fist she held to his chest faltered as she unfurled her fingers slowly, curiously. If he were really here, she would feel his heart, and her palm went searching for that steady beat.

Nothing. Only hard, cold muscle, with their breaths quieting in the dark.

"I wish I could've done things differently."

There was something mournful in his tone, and she almost asked what he meant. Instead, she glanced down, at her feet lightly veiled through the smoke. His legs, nowhere they were supposed to be. Just like his heart.

A noise rustled outside.

Kallia froze at the sound of feet and a muttered curse.

All at once, a new cold entered her. She mustered enough strength to push away from Jack, but he still had her in his grasp. He moved her, slipping his hand to her shoulder and turning them both in view of the door. "Ah, the weak one is back."

He thrust his arm over her shoulder, palm facing the door. The force from his hand shone across the entrance like a light, baring what lay beyond. The frame of the door, the thickness of the wall, had faded into a translucent barrier.

Kallia went still at the sight of Demarco on the other side, digging through his pockets. Noticing nothing amiss. A one-way trick.

Go, she screamed in her mind, barely breathing. *Please, just go.*

"Seems the poor fool has lost his key," Jack whispered close to her ear. Demarco had unearthed his hands in empty fists, giving a furious, futile pound to his door. A kick. And still, the slab of wood remained stubbornly shut. "But what is a closed door to a magician if not an excuse to use magic?"

Because magic was never an excuse for him. That, and he was drunk. She could tell even from here as he braced his hand against the door, steadying himself. Trying the handle, fruitlessly, again. "He's just trying to get into his room," Kallia seethed. "Why are you wasting my time with this?"

All the malice in her voice couldn't ward him off. "Curiosity."

As if he could somehow hear them, Demarco stopped. He dropped his raised fist and looked behind, at the closed door of Kallia's suite. His brow creased, gaze lost.

He began stepping closer, hesitantly.

"Stop it, Jack," she scoffed in a measured tone. "Leave him alone."

"I'm not making him do anything," he replied just as evenly. "Go on, open it. Looks like he wants to come in."

What would Jack do if she didn't? An unpredictable energy radiated from him, his smile dark as a storm. His face, cut from lightning. Expectant. Kallia glared over her shoulder as she moved, every muscle clenched. Wrestling with the question that wouldn't stop beating for Demarco. *Why are you at my door again?* She had strictly ordered no visitors, and still, he came.

Why?

Was it to turn her in? To tell her the Patrons would come for her in the morning?

Kallia slowed her movements as she watched him through the door. The way his knuckles grazed the surface, tracing the lines and indents, before he shook his head at himself. Raking one hand through his hair while sliding the other against the door frame, staying there.

She stayed, too. For once, she could study him without looking away. His eyes, an honest brown. Much softer than he betrayed. Out of focus and slightly glassy from the few drinks in him. Their haunting effects had taken hold, guiding him.

Kallia had no such excuse. She traced every inch of his face in a devouring sweep, and his was handsome. Kallia had thought so before. Now it hit her in full force, when she was close enough to see how a face so carved from stone could carry so much. Confusion, sorrow, curiosity all in one. Stone could not do that.

She almost flinched back when he raised his fist again to knock. He waited a beat, and another, before unfurling his fingers back over the door. A frustrated sigh.

What are you waiting for?

Across the plane of the door, their eyes met—the world falling away, becoming all color and the racing beat of her heart. Until a flicker of movement forced him to glance over his shoulder.

The door to his room had swung wide open to the darkness of his suite.

The sight jolted him, and he stepped back swiftly. As if her door were on fire, like he never should've been near it in the first place.

Don't leave.

An ache bloomed inside her as he turned away and disappeared into his room.

Kallia stood there, even as the entire wall of her suite returned. Solid and dark.

Surprisingly, Jack hadn't joined her. He'd barely moved from where she'd left him. "Be careful with that one," he said. "He's not as powerful and mighty as you think."

Kallia gave a harsh laugh, shaky at the ends. "You're kidding. In case you didn't see earlier, he performed magic I've never seen before. Magic to protect me."

Jack's brow rose high. "Don't be impressed so easily."

"Why are you so threatened by him?"

With a *have-it-your-way* shrug, he swished the drink in his glass. "You'll soon see, if he even makes it past the next round."

The threat pricked at her. His certainty promised disaster, and she felt even more helpless over it here than she had in the House.

"What's it going to take for you to stop?" she asked through gritted teeth, walking toward the hearth. "I can't go back. I can't even leave."

It was like the city had turned on her, becoming the place Jack had warned her about all along. None of them could leave, which only meant more people would get hurt. More accidents, more nights like this—and she could only watch, wait until the puppeteer tired of his game. "What do you *want*?"

"It's not about what *I* want," he said. "It never has been."

Her temper rose. She whirled around to demand an answer, only to find his glass abandoned on the small table. The couch empty, the room undisturbed.

No sign of Jack, anywhere at all.

The sight of him gone angered her more than anything. He didn't get to be the storm who blew through whenever he wanted, upending everything in his path. Hadn't he done enough?

A splitting pressure cracked in her chest. Her nostrils flared.

Hadn't he done *enough*?

Before she knew it, she was moving across the room to his abandoned glass, the rim still wet. Breath shuddering, she threw it as hard as she could. It shattered against the wall, the remnants of liquor dripping down like blood.

Tears seared her vision, hot and unwelcome.

Stop it.

She dragged them away with the backs of her hand.

Stop.

But one tear became more. And soon they streaked down her face without end as that rawness she'd shoved inside broke open. Finally.

The scars of the House splintered back at full force. The ghosts and illusions, the memories she'd remembered. The ones stolen. And Jack, the worst lie of all, who made sure she'd been all out of choices. Who'd given her everything, as much as he'd taken away.

Again, and again.

Even now. Even here.

Kallia sank to her knees, crossing her arms tightly about her. The pain so great, so sudden. She'd held it off thinking she could stop it. That if she buried it far enough, it would never be felt. It would never stop her if it couldn't take her.

And so she'd left the House. Gone to Glorian. Risen in the competition. After all, she was more powerful than weakness, harder than hurt. She *had* to be.

"Kallia?"

She jerked up at the door's slam, her vision swimming as a figure rushed to her in a blur. Aaros. His face cleared right before hers, and she'd never seen him looking more alarmed. "Zarose, Kallia, why are you out of bed? What *happened*?"

More tears leaked out, and this time, she let them fall. "I . . ." She filed through every excuse, the habit second-nature. "Everything hurt too much, I just needed some air."

"So you got it by smashing a glass against the wall?" He glanced at the broken remnants that stained the surface. "Tell me the truth."

"That is the—"

"You need to stop pretending and acting like everything is fine," Aaros muttered, his jaw set. "Trust me, I know what it's like to live on excuses with the hope that nobody catches on. Eventually someone does."

His dark eyes fastened on her, razor sharp. Expectant.

Filled with concern. So much. It hurt her for him to see her like this. Yet the sight darkened him as well, as if her pain twined with his the moment he entered the room.

Before she knew it, Aaros had propped her up against him on the floor and wrapped his arms around her, careful not to squeeze her wounds. "What are you doing?" she asked.

"Helping you keep everything together." He placed his chin over the top of her head, and proceeded to smooth his fingers through her hair. "You don't need to be alone to do that."

It was what she was used to. Recovering alone, processing alone. Taking on *everything* alone, because she'd rather do that than let anyone see what a mess everything was. Especially when nobody could help her.

"Let's get you to bed, now," Aaros said. "You've had . . . a night."

She didn't even have the energy to snort. "I'm too tired to move."

Too scared to be alone, to close her eyes.

They were drifting now, the darkness whispering at the corners of her vision.

"Then rest." He sighed, settling more comfortably on the floor, shifting her in his arms. "I'm not going anywhere."

"Promise?"

If he answered, the warmest sleep pulled her under before she could hear it.

26

Daron stumbled into his room sick to his stomach, berating himself over two very important points.

He shouldn't have had that last drink.

And as soon as morning hit, he should request to switch rooms.

Daron wandered, lingered, *stared* at her door each time he passed. At this point, he'd committed the fixture to memory. Every intricate carving around the frame, the slight scuffs around the doorknob. After his last visit hadn't gone well, he'd resolved never to touch it. No matter what he heard.

This time, he'd almost knocked. For no reason at all.

Daron raked both hands through his hair at a sudden *thud*. A glass smashed, or some other noise from his imagination. He ignored it. A chill settled in his bones as he strode deeper into his room, nearly stumbling in the dark were it not for the patches of moonlight haphazardly lighting his path.

Light. He needed light.

Fire. Candles.

It used to be so easy.

His common room fireplace, a pit of shadows and ash, glimmered with the dark orange flare of embers dying within. Drawn by the warmth, Daron dropped his jacket on the edge of the couch, missing his target. It landed with a soft thump on the carpet. He nearly dropped to the floor with it, dead tired. Not just from drink slowly drifting from his system, but magic.

Daron's muscles trembled.

His body so unused to the surge of adrenaline after so long without.

Tremors continued running through his wrist, alive with residual energy from the light he'd cast hours ago. Over Kallia, for the whole show hall to see.

The moment felt more like a fever dream now.

His tremors turned into a violent shiver. Glorian was cold as anything, especially at night when the air went frigid and unforgiving. Daron stared heavily at the embers darkening in the hearth, too fatigued to grab the materials on the overhanging ledge to build a flame.

Darkness. It was a better place to think, anyway. And he needed to think. This had not been part of the plan.

This . . . changed *everything*.

He closed his eyes and rubbed his hands together for warmth. They wouldn't stop shaking.

Maybe some of the rumors are true.

Daron inhaled sharply.

If there was a source of magic, a different kind, well . . . that's something worth hiding.

Eva's voice returned, but for once, he wanted it gone. The reminders and riddles she'd posed years ago had all been dead ends. Nothing had ever rung true, and he supposed that made it easier. To come up empty so he could keep searching. Always searching.

Maybe it depends on where you are.

Perhaps she had been right, after all.

Light flickered beyond his closed lids, a trickle of warmth and smoke accompanying it.

Daron's eyes shot open. His lips parted at the fire raised where dying embers had been, a fresh set of logs burning before him.

No, no, no.

Magic trailed in fresh tendrils through the bones of his fingers. Fear spiked through him. He didn't want to look at his palm, but it was impossible when the lines across his skin flared. Fire in his veins, magic in his blood where it hadn't been in years.

Not since the night everything went wrong during his last performance on stage. The night his powers deserted him.

Until tonight.

For hours, Daron sat before the roaring fire without feeling its warmth. Until the light died in the hearth, as it faded from his palms.

ACT III

ENTER THE LOVERS:

THOSE ROSES ENTWINED

AMONG TWISTED THORNS

The master watched the girl descend from the ceiling in a large birdcage forged from rose-gold bars and crystal tassels.

A new act, though not like his guests noticed the difference.

Hell, they couldn't even tell a magician from an illusion cast by one.

Once the gilded cage had lowered to the ground, the masked girl within waltzed out. Short silver-white hair, with smiling pink lips and a petite frame. By morning, she'd dissolve back into nothing and emerge only when summoned.

If only all magic could be so easy.

The master had known things would grow worse in that cursed city, and nobody had heeded the warnings. The show was not the only thing that could go wrong the longer they remained behind its gates.

The fools were trapped. Like wild game too tempted by the bait. Once you spent enough time in a city like that, it was rarely likely to let you out. Starving beasts never indulged their prey with mercy. Not until they had their fill.

There was only so much time left before they dug their claws into her.

He could feel them, even from here. Beckoning him to come, to listen and follow. Each time he visited, their calls grew louder. Not screams. Whispers to lure, saying all the right words.

He couldn't listen to them again. She'd gone to them, despite all she had here.

She'd made her choice, and now nothing could help her.

Not even him.

"What do you *mean* we can't leave the city?"

Hostility burned among the gathered group at the Alastor Place. Daron almost declined joining the emergency summons to the theater that morning. When he awoke that morning, his throat grated like sandpaper. His mind throbbed, too weighed down from every glass he'd thrown back.

His mind was not so heavy anymore.

"We'd had enough of this. Everything's been pure disaster from the start," Robere declared, rising from his seat with a prim nod. "I'm not being paid nearly enough to entertain it for another night. So I packed up. And Eduar offered to join."

Erasmus scoffed. "You both decided to take the coward's exit and jump ship?"

"A sinking ship."

"Call it what you will." The proprietor folded his hands. "But alas, your little failed escape into the night did bring to our attention our very . . . odd situation."

"*Odd?*" Judge Bouquet bellowed. "The gates have vanished. We can't bloody leave the city."

Daron focused on breathing evenly, trying to keep his head while everyone around him lost theirs. He hadn't tried leaving, as the others had done. Once they heard of the vanished gate, everyone laughed. But each contestant and judge who had approached the wall since found nothing. No gate, no way out. If they tried scaling the walls, there was nothing but the Dire Woods to take them—and nobody wanted to test the mercy of that possibility. Others could enter and exit as they pleased, for carriages still regularly roamed down the streets to and from the entry path. However, the show's players found only a cleanly paved wall. Their eyes alone, veiled with this madness.

The tension was palpable in the room, the reactions ranging from quiet alarm to violent pacing. The vastness of the Alastor Place had shrunken to a cage. And the birds within squawked loudly, nipping at every person's last word as if fighting for the last seed in the feeder.

Surprisingly, Kallia remained quiet in her seat. Just as she had when he'd left his room earlier that morning. After receiving the urgent summons, it was hardly a shock when her door opened right after his. No Aaros in tow, for it was a closed meeting. What shocked him most were the bruise-like shadows under her eyes, the puffy redness of them marked with exhaustion.

"Zarose, what happened?"

Daron wished he could take it back the instant she bristled. "Rough performance night. What's your excuse?"

The bags under his eyes took on even more weight as she grumpily pushed past him; her gait slow, measured. The magic she had exerted had taken a toll. And no matter how much Erasmus spent on miracle creams and ointments for his star, her back couldn't have healed that quickly.

It could've been worse, the proprietor had remarked all night, drunkenly patting Daron's shoulder in gratitude. *Drink up, you saved the show!*

He swallowed painfully, the knot in his throat having tripled in size since last night. Before he knew it, he was at Kallia's side, reaching for her.

"I *don't* need help." She swatted him away, tossing back her hair. "I'm fine on my own."

Her grimace said otherwise. When it was clear she couldn't shake him off, she gave a resigned huff, ignoring him as he matched her stubborn pace. If she paused to rest, he paused, his hand inches from her back. They walked side by side down the hall, down the stairs, and to the Alastor Place without care for the whispers at their backs.

Thankfully silent all the way, until she abruptly parted ways with him as they entered the show hall. Contestants on one side, judges at the other. The harsh reminder jolted him.

From his seat, Daron watched her brow furrow so deeply, lost in thought. He was grateful she didn't return his stare, for it took much longer than he wished to admit to finally look away.

"Rayne," Mayor Eilin spoke delicately. He appeared to be the calmest in the theater. Disturbingly so. "What in Zarose name did you *do*?"

"Nothing!" the other man insisted. "I like having tricks up my sleeve but this was not one of them."

Daron was inclined to believe him. If he'd had a hand in this, he would've acted far more coy and obnoxious about his part. His astonishment, while perversely amused, was genuine. "If we should be pointing fingers at anyone, Eilin, it should be you."

"Me?"

"It's *your* city walling us in. A little warning would've been nice."

"Nothing like this has ever happened before," Mayor Eilin sputtered. "Not until you arrived. No, it was that damn contract, wasn't it? You made us all sign it, and now look what's happened. What in the world did you put in it?"

"The only bit of magic infused in that contract is a locator," Erasmus reassured. "If you run from what you signed up for, it's my right to be able to find you. Easily."

Something sinister lingered on that last note.

"Then how do you explain the other magicians who've gone missing?" demanded Judge Silu. "And every other accident that's happened since?"

"Like I would ever sabotage my own show. That's just desperate." Scalding offense dripped from the proprietor's scoff. "But those cads are still in town, somewhere. I did think it rather odd when their locations remained in Glorian, but now I suppose it makes sense all things considered."

"*Nothing* about this makes a lick of sense." Mayor Eilin threw his hands up. "I don't see how you can be so cavalier about this."

"Would you rather I mope and hiss like the rest of you? Because that's productive." He smoothed back his gelled hair, looking smug when no one responded. "Honestly, it's not as if we're dead or in imminent danger, we're simply . . . stuck. Which is convenient, for we've got a show to put on."

"You can't be serious." That left the mayor's jaw hanging. "This all ends now."

"Fine, try it. But you'll be met with disappointed audience members. In your case, you'll have a whole city of them to deal with."

"Citywide disappointment," the mayor deadpanned. "How will I ever recover?"

"How about citywide ruin, will that change your tune?"

Mayor Eilin stopped short. "It's already ruined. This whole thing is completely beyond us, Rayne. It's a matter for the Patrons, *that's* the level we're approaching."

For once, no one glanced Daron's way. The relief was short-lived at the rise of Erasmus's knowing smile. "Then why haven't you corresponded with them yet? Last night—hell, the instant you heard the news this morning—why didn't you rush straight to your desk and start scribbling out a cry for help?"

The blood drained from the mayor's face, little by little.

"Because you know," Erasmus drawled on, "the moment this ends, so does everything else."

"What do you suggest we do, then?"

"What this city does best: keep itself under wraps. Raise no sign for alarm, return once the dust has settled," the proprietor advised, dancing his fingertips against each other. "No Patrons, no press. At least, not until we've got a better handle on things. That way, when we've got our bearings, we'll have the world lining up at the gates, waiting."

Daron couldn't have been more relieved this man was not a magician, for he would make a dangerous one. It was almost frightening, how he worked with nothing more than his cool, slippery nature and still enchanted a room. Moments ago the mayor looked close to knifing him, but now, his brow creased pensively down at the empty stage beneath him. "This is . . . just not how I thought any of this would play out."

"That's the best thing *about* show business. Nothing ever goes as planned. But with everyone's cooperation, we can guide this ship back on course. Correct?"

He peered out at the others with his bright snakelike eyes, and in the end, the mayor simply nodded. Decided.

Unease pricked at Daron. Wrong, this all felt so wrong.

"Demarco?"

Erasmus had stopped the mayor from pulling the trigger, but he wasn't the only one in the room with access to the gun. If only they knew he didn't want the Patrons in Glorian any more than they did. The thought of Aunt Cata breaking down the doors of the Alastor Place, asking every question imaginable until she pieced it all together, speared nausea into his gut.

Daron nodded.

Relief swept the entire room.

"That's a good chap. I'm glad we all have an understanding." Erasmus clasped his hands with vigor, pacing down the stage. "We'll continue on. Though, with a few changes in light of our current limitations and last night's interesting turn of events . . ." He tossed a sympathetic smile to Daron and Kallia. "We'll proceed to the mentor round."

Cold shot down Daron's spine. He thought he'd be long gone before this part of the game.

The mere idea of him on stage again.

Performing magic. *Teaching* it.

He would be exposed before he even stepped into the spotlight.

The image took root in his mind, tormenting him. He looked warily around to see if anyone else shared in his discomfort. Most of the judges were exchanging subtle looks with the contestants sitting in the rows across from them.

Alliances, already forged.

Figures. Daron's fist tightened over his knee. Just like that, he was back in his amateur days, an unpolished magician left to the wolves. He'd had Eva, of course, but he'd been new to the wild game of show business. He'd been branded an outsider as soon as he pulled up a chair at the judges' table, and they would only shun him more if they knew.

Glorian was having some sort of effect on him. His magic, once gone, was slowly returning. Or so he thought. His power felt nothing like it had before, just an energy he couldn't control after having gone for so long without.

He almost preferred having no magic at all.

Mayor Eilin and Erasmus began listing off pairings, each one hitting him with dread. He knew, even before they'd started, which magician he'd be matched with.

"Excuse me," Daron interjected, half-rising from his seat. "I don't think I—"

"Patience. You're next." Erasmus assessed the list with a sound of delight. "You'll, of course, be working with Kallia."

A couple of the men around him chuckled, almost with pity.

Finally, Kallia spoke, a bitter edge to her voice. "What do you mean, 'of course'?"

"Can't you just see it?" Erasmus wistfully clutched at his heart. "The hero and the damsel, joining forces—not that you're a damsel, darling. But the crowd will simply eat it up. And we need them hungry again once we're back on stage."

"Exactly." The mayor smirked. "No need to shy away from the spotlight now."

Kallia's eyes slitted, daggers sliding from their sheaths. Ready to stab.

The same resignation weighed Daron back into his seat. After last night, their names would always be thrown together. The ever-watching audience loved a good story, and of course, Erasmus would capitalize on it.

Daron ran a hand over his face as the last names were called. Through his fingers, he caught a glimpse of Kallia—already rising to leave like the others, only they had their new mentors in tow. She turned without gracing him with a look, and something twinged inside him.

Of course she didn't want to be paired with him. *He* wouldn't want to be paired with him. She would probably argue to forgo a mentor altogether, having no patience for somebody so overly apologetic, who criticized without being asked, who'd venture all the way to her door only to—

"Naturally you'd be trying to hide in plain sight."

Daron jerked in his seat, lowering his hands to find Kallia standing beside him. She wore a long, dark green coat buttoned at her waist, and tan pants tucked into boots. Today, her hair was half-pulled up by a loose tie. Usually, she kept her hair free and over her shoulders.

He hated how he suddenly knew that.

"Excuse me?" He straightened, forcing a cool expression over his face.

If Kallia thought he was flustered, she was doing a good job of holding her tongue about it. "If you wanted to hide from me, you could've at least run for the doors or even the dusty corners. I hate getting my clothes dirty."

A lie. Daron recalled her attire dusted with dirt not too long ago in the throes of the theater renovations. She had wanted to help. He hated how he suddenly knew that, too. "Noted."

"Good. Now, come on. Pick up your feet," Kallia said, already half-turning. "Or are you going to sit there all day?"

No trace of disappointment in her voice. None that he could detect, at least. "Don't you . . . don't you want to change partners?"

"It seems I'm stuck with you." She gestured around, slightly bemused. "How could everyone *not* be dying to work with me, right?"

It wasn't even ego, but honesty. Kallia was clearly the crowd favorite everyone was betting on. Except for Mayor Eilin and the other judges. For them, the game had stopped revolving around winning so much as beating Kallia, a force far scarier to them than being trapped in a city. Someone powerful, unstoppable, and nothing at all like them.

"If I didn't know better, it would seem *you* were the one looking to switch," she said, shifting her focus to her fingernails. "Am I really that impossible to be around?"

"No." *Yes. No.* He was unsure what to say. How to convince her what a mistake it would be to pair them together.

If anyone could see through him, it would be her.

Her lips dipped into a frown. "I know this throws the most awful wrench in your attempts to avoid me, but—"

"Look, I *never* said—"

"Shut up, Demarco." Kallia raised a brow, waiting until she was sure he was going to listen. The fire in her eyes, both certain and uncertain in equal measure.

"Whatever problems you have with me, they're nothing compared to what bothers the others. They always find something to say about how I act, how I dress, how I go about my day." She rolled her eyes.

"I don't care if you think I'm too difficult or too much. In all honesty, I have a feeling we'd work fairly well together."

"Why?"

"Among the top hats, you're the only one I can tolerate. And deep down, I think you tolerate me, too. When you're not too busy running from me like I'm the plague."

She thought he couldn't stand her. He'd certainly imagined she felt the same of him, back when only suspicion towered between them. But somehow, both mountains had flipped. He couldn't even define where it left them, only knew that something hot and tense coiled in his chest every time she was near, telling him he could not work with her.

"And I never got the chance to thank you."

Kallia spoke so quietly, Daron wasn't even sure it had come from her. Soft words from a sharp, red mouth, the combination derailed him. "For?"

"Last night, on the stage."

She didn't face him as she said it, not out of embarrassment. As if no one had ever done such a thing for her, which he couldn't fathom. "Kallia," he murmured. "You don't have to thank me for that."

"You didn't have to help me, either."

"Of course I did," he countered, immediately irritated at himself for owning that power, like it had been his intent. His choice. "It was nothing."

"Don't go all modest on me, it *was* something. And that's why I have to at least try." Something akin to longing lifted her voice as she cast a sad gaze to the stage. "I can give you a win. But I need a mentor, or else they won't let me perform. Those are the rules."

"Aren't you fond of breaking those?" A dumb question. If he didn't stay with her, they'd force her to forfeit. No wonder the mayor looked particularly gleeful about their pairing. No doubt relying on something to go wrong. A fight, a split, something to take her out of the game.

"I never signed up to be a mentor," he admitted. "That hadn't been part of the deal."

"You don't even have to do anything," she promised. "Join me on stage and let me do my act, that's it. I swear, I can give you a fantastic show and you can brand your name on it next to mine, it's just . . ." Her lip quivered before stiffening into a sharp bow. "If I lose, I *can't* lose this way. Not by default."

Daron studied her for a long moment. "Is this competition really so important to you?"

She threw him a withering glare. "After all this—every bad name I've been called, every accusation—how could it not be?"

"You don't need to prove anything to them, Kallia. It's . . ." He struggled to find the right words. "It's a silly competition in an old city that's lost its place on the map. Nothing more."

"Easy for you to say. You've had your years of spotlight. I'm fighting for *days*."

"Surely you know your talents would be far more appreciated in a bigger pond," he insisted. "You don't need to waste energy on a small-time show like this."

"Every step to the top counts. And please, don't patronize me." Kallia's jaw hardened. "Make no mistake, I know I don't have to prove a single thing to them. What matters most is what I prove to *myself*. Giving up would be an insult to everything I know I'm capable of. And I've already come this far."

A different light entered her eyes. Her ambition, laid bare. A flash of the armor she wore every day. Not her usual strutting around like she couldn't care less—but the truth, her wanting this more than he'd ever seen someone want anything.

"Stop looking at me like that."

Daron flushed, averting his stare. "Like what?"

Kallia crossed her arms tightly. "Come on. You're more perceptive than that. Even I've figured that out about you."

The way she said it worried him. With the kind of knowing only a friend would show, and the strangeness of it struck him. He'd lost so many friends in the past. It had been easier to shake blokes he'd partied with for years than a girl he'd known for a short time. She was one frayed tie that refused to be cut, and wanted this victory enough to put up with him.

No. From the look in her eyes, she *needed* it.

Daron blew out a tired sigh. "I won't have to dance, will I?"

The stern line of her lips twitched. "Dancing the first night was to get their attention. Parading myself around like that a second time would be overdoing it."

"But don't you like dancing?"

"Love it. Especially if I can use it to my advantage."

"Never without strategy, I'll give you that much."

"I'll take that as a compliment," she preened, moving out of his way as he exited the row. "You won't even have to lift a finger."

This was exactly what she wanted: to be given the reins of an act without much standing in her way. Daron couldn't have asked for a better scenario, yet he found himself saying, "I don't think that's going to work."

Shut up.

What are you doing?

"Really?" Kallia's shoulders sagged. "After everything, *now* you want to help?"

"Do you want another disastrous incident? Because I don't think it will win you any points." Why couldn't he be quiet? The more his thoughts warred, the more his traitorous side spoke. "You probably have some large, flashy spectacle planned that's full of risks, but I will not be content to stand there as some prop mentor who approved it all."

"So what then, Judge Demarco?" Kallia huffed. "I've never seen an unwilling mentor so eager to have his say."

"Even as a reluctant mentor, I have things I can teach you."

"What sort of tricks?" She tilted her head in interest. "Like from last night? Teach me what that was, and maybe I'll—"

"No." Daron swallowed, heart thrumming fast. "No tricks, no magic. Not from me at least."

"Then what else is there?"

For all of his hesitation, he wanted to offer her something of value. He could teach her moderation, how to dispense her energies more deliberately rather than exhausting them. There were many ways to be impressive, and they didn't all have to be charged with power. The unexpected worked just as well.

"Only one way to find out," he said.

Kallia's eyes flashed, considering. "Maybe you won't be such a prop after all."

It had to be a dream.

Kallia entered her greenhouse, sunlight beaming through the windows. She strolled among flowers she didn't recognize. Those with fire for petals, plants with slowly beating wings, leaves curling off vines that dripped with perfume. The fragrances of smoke and roses and the winter's chill, swirling her senses.

Through the thick of green and shadows, someone waited.

A stranger.

As she drew nearer, the greenhouse dimmed. The fire petals' flames turned to gray in the changing light, as the warmth from the sun overhead slid into moonlight across the leaf-strewn floor. Kallia shivered.

A muffled beat sounded, reverberating through the glass until it shook. Her ears popped at the sudden trill of trumpets and drums and lively strings joining in a wild tune. As though a club had opened its doors right outside.

Her heart beat loudly in her ears as she moved toward the figure beyond the leaves. Tall and broad-shouldered, familiar in a way she couldn't quite say. She reached out to him—

Only to find a tall, ornate mirror.

Her form, in its reflection.

There was no one else, if there ever had been. She checked all around her, knocked on the glass before her fist froze against the surface. Darkness like smoke misted her surroundings in the mirror. No fiery flowers or jewel-toned bursts. Kallia glanced over her shoulder—still the greenhouse, fragrant and full of life.

But her reflection showed another scene, another world.

The surrounding windows that scaled the walls in the dark were gilded bars in the mirror.

I didn't throw you in a cage.

The air around her tightened; the music rang louder, faster. Her pulse beat heavily as she stepped back, poised to run.

Until a cold hand burst from the mirror and pulled her by the neck.

Kallia shot up from her bed, sweating.

Her gaze tore across the room; dark, even as light filtered in through cracks in the curtains. She was all alone, and all was silent, yet she could still hear that music. A song that would never leave her.

She massaged her ears to coax it away before hugging her arms around her knees. It wasn't the first dream she'd had like it, and whenever it came, it was like dying. Each time, more violent.

Her rose cloth lay on the bedside table, next to a candle that had burned itself out in the night. She'd spent the better half staring at the design, willing it to be what it once was.

All that remained was a ruined rose, petals still falling along the fabric.

Kallia wrenched the blankets off. She made for the window, flinging open the curtains to a punishing brightness. Baring herself to the light chased the dreams away faster, and the Glorian sky was a blinding gray white in the morning. It always looked like it was close to raining—eyes a breath away from crying, though tears never came.

Kallia had grown used to it. It was no longer a marvel to see the pointed spires of buildings from her window view. But some mornings, she feared it would all be gone. That one day they would turn back into the tall, shadowy treetops of the Dire Woods. And she'd find herself in her room at the House, as if she'd been there all along. Simply waking from a dream.

Daron,

I wish you would respond, so I know these are reaching you. Mail by courier case is not exactly inexpensive, you know. I only have so much sway with the post.

My messages may be more sparse than usual. We've taken in a few magicians affected by the case on the eastern border, and think we might be on the brink of a new magical classification. That's all I can say for now.

Please write back when you can, and remember to eat something green and fresh once in a while.

—Aunt Cata

Daron liked to skim her brief letters the first time—fondly looking for the scolding note at the end—before reading slower the next. Again and again, until he had the thing memorized.

He ought to write back.

Just once.

Eva had always been better at correspondences; Daron tended to let them fall to the wayside, hopeless at keeping up with others with hardly the time to do so.

Now, he had no excuse. With all the time in the world, locked in a city where everything seemed to go wrong, he had every reason to pen a letter to his aunt. Yet . . . if he finally did send word, she would come. Be it the middle of the night or in the heat of battle, she would drop everything at the slightest indication that something was wrong.

He sipped at his coffee, glancing up from the letter once more. The chair across from him, still empty.

She was late. He'd watched guests come and go, ignored the majority of letters received just to reread his aunt's, and even pored through the *Soltair Source* for old time's sake before finally, a little while later, he heard the imperious, *"Ahem."*

Daron tilted the paper away while Kallia straightened her hair testily without the least bit of shame. "What right do you have to be so put out? You're late."

"I'm here, at least." A wooden screech sounded before she plopped down in the empty seat. He heard a clink, a sip, and a disgruntled cough. "Really?" Kallia set her coffee cup down with a loud clank. "Cold coffee? That's mature."

"It was hot when I ordered it." He casually folded the paper and smiled. "Funny how things cool down when enough time passes. Would you like another?"

"I'm fine with this, thanks." She took another sip as if in rebellion.

Daron was tempted to order a whole pot of fresh coffee anyway at her ragged appearance, the way her hands gripped her coffee cup as if clinging to whatever meager warmth she could. Still recovering from her last act, it seemed.

"Stop pouting. It's not *so* unbearably early," he reasoned. "I've seen you wake up before the crack of dawn on purpose."

"That's before a *performance*." She swished the remnants of her coffee.

Seeing her so unguardedly cranky was a far different version of Kallia than the glamorous one who strutted around him. This side of her intrigued him, and he did everything in his power not to appear so amused. "We agreed upon this time."

"*You* agreed." Kallia downed the rest of her cold coffee, impressively straight-faced. "I swear, for someone who didn't even want this, you know how to be quite insufferable about it."

"Really? And here I thought I was the only one you could tolerate."

She squared him with an even drier look. Though for all her protests, she remained. She would undoubtedly laugh at what he was about to suggest, but avoiding each other had somehow only heightened their tension. The only other solution lay in the opposite.

"This might not be a favorable hour for you, but we must use this time to our advantage." Daron pushed their empty cups to the side, leaving nothing between them. "The Conquering Circus will be performing in public for a short period. After that, there will be a party at the Alastor Place prior to the final show." Kallia perked awake at the mention. "And even with all that, there's not nearly enough time."

"For what?"

"Trust to build."

She arched her brow as if he'd grown five heads. "Pardon?"

Daron steepled his fingers beneath his chin. "I may not participate much in the handling of the act, but this is one request I must insist on. How can we even begin to work together when we don't know a thing about each other?"

She angled her head, as if she'd never considered it. "Is it *really* that important?"

"It's important for a proper partnership. And it's good that we start off on something slow, since you're still recovering."

Her expression iced. "I'm fine."

It was no surprise she wanted to hit the ground running, and he certainly understood her skepticism. Everyone had their secrets, him more than anyone. But that wasn't what this was about, and he hoped they would be able to treat it as such. For the good of the show.

"Look, I'm not asking you to bare your soul to me. I certainly won't. We simply need to find a level of comfort with each other so when it's time for our act, we don't appear like total strangers."

He'd witnessed performances where the assistants and their magicians clearly weren't getting on. Their acts suffered for it. "From my experience in stage partnership, it's always beneficial to get to know each other. Look at you and Aaros."

Kallia's eyes briefly flashed to his. "You had an assistant, too, right?"

He stiffened. Figures she'd have heard something by now. Most everyone knew, a good and bad thing. Everyone toed around the subject. He didn't even have to dodge it on his own. Until now.

Daron looked away. "Ultimately, when we go on stage, you're not alone. There's no point in separating yourself when you don't have to."

A long silence stretched between them. *She'll never go for this.* He'd worried about that possibility without any other plan to cushion the blow. He was in no shape or form a teacher, nowhere near qualified in his current state. There was nothing more she could possibly need, nothing he could give her, when she was already so powerful. All on her own.

"And what do you propose we do?"

For once, the ice in her face was not as hard a mask as she usually kept it. Both surprise and relief loosened his shoulders at the rare sight, before he offered her his elbow with a grin even he couldn't fight. "Let's start with a walk."

Their first walk was quiet. So quiet, Kallia thought she might explode. It wasn't that she was shy—she was *never* shy. Certainly not around Demarco. They'd simply never spoken without a reason to fight. The absence of one made it harder to string more than three words together.

Yet, at the end of their walk, he asked her to accompany him on another one. And another. Until one day, finally, she snapped. "How much longer will this go on? You ask me to walk with you every day, yet you rarely say anything."

Smothering a laugh, he cast a sideways glance at her. "Shocking, but you haven't been the most talkative, either."

Kallia resisted the urge to punch him. They had only a brief period before the last act, and sooner or later, it would creep up on them. "It doesn't matter whether or not we're friends, Demarco. That's not what this show is about."

"Wasn't it not too long ago you'd asked why we *couldn't* be friends?"

Her nostrils flared at the memory he'd unearthed with such smug recollection. That was when the two of them had been so wildly unsure of one another, when it was clear he was avoiding her out of some misplaced sense of propriety that felt more like an insult. Though at the moment, she would gladly take the insult over whatever was happening between them *now*.

"Don't worry, I'm not asking to be your friend. I'm trying to be your ally," he drawled. "Which, in case you haven't noticed, you don't have very many of."

Kallia drew in a hard breath. There was no use arguing; it would only prove his point more. "Fine. But let's lay out some ground rules."

"What sort of rules?"

"Respect my privacy," she said. "If I say no questions, I mean it."

"All right." He nodded. "As long as you pay me the same respect."

"Fine."

"Fine."

They glared at each other, unblinking. Both unwilling to look away, as if locked in a challenge. A very petty challenge. It was amusing, the flare of stubborn fire in Demarco; he usually exuded such a reserved and contained demeanor. Not around her.

Despite herself, Kallia felt her lips curl slightly.

So she played his game, and for the rest of the way down the sidewalks, picked his brain on all she could. His thoughts about Spectaculore, the other contestants, the judges he disliked as much as she did. In turn, she gave him her thoughts, soon realizing he was just as guarded as she was, with the things he wouldn't answer.

For him, it was his magic, his former stage life, or anyone to do with it. The areas Kallia was most curious about, to her dismay. His assistant flooded her mind—a faceless, beautiful woman Kallia had begun imagining the moment Canary had mentioned her. As much as she wanted to learn more about who she was to him, she restrained herself.

"What about your home?" Kallia posed instead. "You said you lived far from here."

"Tarcana is all the way out east." Demarco's strides were slow and relaxed. "Almost an island of its own, with how the ocean hugs our shores."

"A whole ocean?" Her mind conjured up endless stretches of water. Years ago—before true escape ever entered her mind—she'd foolishly tried venturing into the Dire Woods to reach the ocean's edge, only to lose herself in the maze of trees and shadows that built her path. One of Sire's servants had ridden on horseback to retrieve her, and after, she never entered the Woods out of curiosity again. With the mind such easy prey in that forest, it was not worth the risk.

"I take it you've never lived near the water?"

The crease in Demarco's brow drew a shrug from her. "Never seen it."

The slip revealed too much, but rather than pry, he asked, "Do you want to?"

"Why?" Something warm and nervous settled in Kallia's chest. "Are you offering me a grand mansion by the sea?"

"I'm not offering anything. But if you win, your talents could bring you all the possibilities in the world. A mansion by the sea—the sea, itself, even."

"Don't be ridiculous." His compliments were not the usual type she received; they were statements. Facts. He spoke in a way that made everything seem possible. Because he genuinely believed it. "No one can own the sea."

"I'm sure you'd find a way."

The way he said it made *her* almost believe it.

He was good at this. Too good. She couldn't stop herself from sinking into the pictures he painted of the world. How wonderful it must've been, to come into this life with the searing blaze of choice. To practice and learn magic however you wished. To go wherever your feet could take you.

It was only too easy to imagine how such a life might've changed her.

To have had the glory of choice over the promise of power.

"Careful." Kallia's lips formed a bemused line. "That almost sounded like a compliment."

"What can I say, getting to know a person can be a lot like eating bread," he said. "You have to really butter it up for it to—"

Kallia thwacked him in the chest, which rumbled with a rare show of laughter.

Idiot.

As they crossed over to the next sidewalk together, she took his arm once more.

30

Without the show, the people's attentions shifted all too easily to the dark purple circus tents. They arrived without warning, dotting the plain streets of Glorian like scattered jewels. A few children dared to poke at one, and swore an animal growled from within. Others whispered that they heard the sharpening of knives, the distinct hissing of snakes. Still, passersby couldn't help but linger near them.

"The Conquering Circus officially opens to Glorian *tonight*. About time, too," Kallia had informed him earlier as they neared the Prima. For blocks, they'd passed nothing but curious spectators hovering near the tents. "Did you ever come across them in your travels?"

"Not really. I'd heard of them, but we rarely crossed paths on the circuit. I was always onstage, they were—"

"Outside. For the general public." She snorted. "Snob."

"That's just the way things were." He gave a rueful grin. "And that's *all* I'm going to say on that."

"*You* were the one who brought up your stage days, not me," she countered, squeezing his arm. "Besides, it couldn't have been all bad."

No way was he taking the bait. "No. Questions."

Daron was sure her rule would've posed a huge barrier between them, but unsurprisingly, it became more like a game. A challenge. If anything, he discovered more about Kallia from the questions she wouldn't answer.

Where did you live before this?

Who taught you magic?

Did you work anywhere previously?

She had a past. That was easy enough to parse. She moved through each day like it was one more mile away from somewhere else. But he never pushed, and neither did she. Details might slip here and there, but his old life rarely came up. And he was grateful. Without magic, those glory days were only days. He'd made peace with it a long time ago, until Glorian. Until magic had trickled back into his system.

Yet he no longer felt that power from the night of the second performance, and didn't dare try tapping into it again. He didn't know how, so unused to power all of a sudden. Unsure how to wield it.

If this truly was the magic Eva spoke of, the uncertainty of it was torturous alone. Each day with Kallia, that same torture rose, fearing she'd soon figure it out.

"Fine, remain mysterious." Kallia casually peered down at her fingernails. "Back to the circus . . . if you're not busy tonight, would you like to meet for the grand opening?"

His insides clenched instantly. He'd always asked her to meet him. Never the other way around. "What—why?"

Kallia's face didn't so much fall as crinkle in vicious irritation.

"No, no, no," he said quickly. "Sorry, I-I didn't realize you'd want to meet outside of . . . *this.*"

This.

Mentorship, alliance. Whatever it was. He didn't know the name of it anymore.

"I know. Hard to believe when I've already filled my Demarco quota for the day." She rolled her eyes. "Look, you don't have to come. I just thought you wouldn't want to miss—"

"I'll go," he cut in, "Do you want to leave the Prima together?" His heart beat so loudly in his ears, it was a wonder she couldn't hear it.

A grin slowly caught like fire across her lips. "No, you're going to meet me there." She waved her fingers before turning toward the hotel doors without him. "You'll know where to find me."

Her words stayed with him until nightfall.

Which was how he found himself exiting the Prima—in a freshly laundered coat, his hair combed back—with the stream of hotel guests taking to the streets. The sidewalk lamps flickered, aided by the glossy silvered-fire torches interspersed between tents.

Everyone beside him was draped in thin fancy coats to those in patchy jackets and fingerless gloves. The night was brisk, but no longer frigid. As if the shared, bubbling excitement had warmed them and the sky above.

Daron looked up at the night, freckled with stars and ribbons of mist. He inhaled, catching the sweet scents wafting over from stands selling caramel-spiced popcorn and hot butterscotch rum.

It was warm enough that he no longer shivered with each step, but a jitteriness ruled his movements as he craned his neck over the heads surrounding him.

You'll know where to find me.

"Oy, judge. You lost?"

Daron turned. Aaros, leaning against the tent nearest to him, waggling his brows. "Or are you looking for somebody?"

Jaw clenched, Daron stared straight ahead. "Nope, I'm lost."

"Liar." He inspected his cuffed sleeve. "Kallia told me you'd be snooping around."

That flicked at Daron's temper. "Hold on, she *invited* me."

"You won't find her around here."

"Then where?"

"Just watch." The assistant supplied a sage smile, and waited a beat longer before abruptly knocking over the torch between the two tents beside them.

The crowd screamed and edged back as the fire met the fabric, consuming the tent from top to bottom. The flames reached the next tent, spreading until one by one, all of them were burning.

Daron cursed and moved to pull Aaros back, but the assistant stopped him with a calm hand. The air around them rapidly filled with smoke so thick, Daron could hardly see. Shrieks pierced the air—but no more than a blink later, the smoke cleared.

Silvery mist snaked around their ankles in a cold, frosty kiss. It rose around the burning tents before vanishing like a curtain drawn, nothing scorched or smoking.

In the tents' places stood burnished, dark purple platforms, bearing each member of the Conquering Circus.

Drums started a wild beat at their appearance, and the street-wide panic from earlier dissolved into wondrous applause. Surprised laughter burst from the spectators, staring up in breathless amazement as the Conquering Circus held court from their stages. Girls in sleek, gold leotards posed in impossible angles, seamlessly stretching from one position to the next. One striking woman in nothing but a short-sleeved, high-waisted outfit stood proudly, flaunting glimmering tattoos that moved across her body at the snap of her fingers. Another juggled knives high in the air, letting them fall in a perfect ring around her. Others swam, trapped in wide, clear tanks. They wore gem-bright dresses that billowed and swayed against the water. The audience gasped, in fear of them drowning, but the ladies reassured them with the graceful waves they delivered behind the glass.

He held his breath alongside everyone packed in the street, witnessing each Conqueror perform a taste of their talents from where they stood, capturing everyone easily.

"If you think *this* is amazing." Aaros laughed, nudging him by the elbow.

At the sudden burst of awe, Daron turned to the center platform, where a brush of magenta fire in the shape of a rose plumed overhead. Drawing closer to the stage, he caught sight of long, ruby hair—Canary, he remembered—in a leathery ringmaster's getup wielding a lit torch like a baton. And beside her, a familiar cascade of dark hair.

Kallia.

She wore an outfit similar to her audition getup. Only this time, the glittery dress was sleek and black, jewels embedded along the bodice like the dark heart of a spider's web. Her scarlet lips parted in a hoot as Canary poised the torch before her, blowing out another fierce wave of fire. The audience edged back with delighted gasps and claps, transfixed as Kallia reached out to still the fire. With a snap, the fire turned stormy gray. As she curled her fingers, its shape rounded into a cloud, raining sparks over eager hands reaching to touch.

From there, she transformed the fire into an endless reel of marvels: a green bottle of champagne popping open, a dark purple horse galloping into the distance, a grand golden chandelier dangling with fiery jewels. Onlookers began shouting requests—a deck of cards, a top hat, a water fountain—and she took on each challenge. Effortlessly.

"You've got a little bit of drool over there, judge."

"Shut up." He shoved Aaros in the shoulder, slowly clapping after Kallia's last trick. She bowed before giving the floor over entirely to Canary, who bent her head under the wave of applause.

"Welcome, conquests, to the real show you've all been waiting for!" she shouted over the lively beat of the drums. "However, before we allow you entry into our menagerie of madness, we have one rule: respect the Conquerors, and we'll all have ourselves a good time." Her warm grin turned sharp as a nail. "However, if you touch, grab, hurt, offend, or commit any other despicable act against us or another unwilling person while in our domain, then you deserve every awful misfortune that awaits you. One such misfortune, for example, is our very good friend, Aya."

A deep roar sawed through the silence. Every head shifted to the platform across from Canary's, boasting an enormous black-haired, growling lion who only calmed beneath the palm of the trainer standing coolly behind.

"So, any foolish beast who even dares to bite without asking, beware. Aya never says no to fresh meat." Canary cracked a laugh, laced with an undeniable threat that had everyone nodding immediately. Half in excitement, half in fear.

At the raise of her hands, the drums started up again, accompanied by trumpets and pipes breathing life into the night. "Without further ado, on with the show!"

Right on cue, light burst high into the sky. It crackled and sparked before exploding into spirals of colors. Again and again, lights shot from Canary's stage, until it looked as though all the stars had taken on different shades and faces, falling like wishes granted.

All heads tipped back and gaped in pure delight. From the way even Aaros looked up, Daron was certain the people of Glorian had never seen so much color in all their lives. In the sky, in their streets, surrounding them entirely in the most impossible ways.

As each burst skyrocketed, Daron watched Kallia standing behind Canary. Her hands twisted outward, fingers beckoning at the colors to soar. She drew no attention to herself, her movements so subtle, one would have to tear their gaze from the sky to even notice the magic wasn't appearing out of thin air.

Daron noticed.

He noticed the strain in her jaw, and the smile that stayed. The slight quiver of her fingers, and the strength of their hold. He noticed the cheers rising louder around him, the spectacle no doubt growing more fantastical by the second, but he was fixed on her alone, unable to bring himself to look back to the sky.

Kallia stumbled down the stage, laughing all the way. Exhilarating performances always exhausted her until everything seemed a little funny. The rickety squeaks of the stairs, how high her heels were, how off-balance she was.

"Careful there, prima donna."

At the last step, Canary all but broke her almost-fall, propping them both up. "You need a hand back to the hotel?"

"I'll be *fine*." Kallia steadied as the crowd's maddening applause faded behind them. "Just need a second and I'll be back on my feet soon enough."

Canary righted her and steered them both toward the only tent stationed between two of the backmost platforms. "Good. Because Conquerors don't sleep on the first night."

"Are you saying I'm a Conqueror?"

"Glad you stuck around, now, aren't you?"

Neither of them had spoken about that night of the second act. Kallia had seen them plenty of times since then to practice for tonight's opening and make well on her promise to the Conquerors. No questions asked, no explanations necessary. As if they knew it was a night worth moving on from. Kallia couldn't be more grateful when Canary tossed back her red hair now, as if forgetting she'd even said a word about it. "Enjoy it while it lasts."

Kallia most certainly would. It was the most herself she'd felt in ages, the adrenaline running through her veins. Her heart wildly beating from the high of a spectacular set. She entered the tent with her chin raised high, steps surer—taken aback by the round of hoots that met her. Camilla, who'd been sharpening her green-edged knives, clinked them loudly together. Juno, sending them a salute as she bent toward the vanity. The Starling twins, slouching on a large, jewel-orange couch, immediately perked up as Canary and Kallia passed through, tossing two small packs in their direction.

Canary caught them without turning. "Thanks, Cass."

"What's this?" Kallia began untying the string that clasped the velvet pouch closed.

"Essentials, to keep your energy up," the acrobat stated blithely. "Chocolate bombs, cherry-rum candies, and sugared ginger. We collect sweets from each town we pass through."

"They've got buckets of it hidden under their beds, it's disgusting," Canary whispered, before a cherry-rum candy smacked against her temple from across the room. The other Conquerors laughed as the ringmaster picked up the fallen candy and triumphantly crunched it between her teeth.

Kallia popped a sugared ginger in her mouth, the spiciness invigorating. A warmth rushed through her that had nothing to do with magic. It was everyone around her. It was smiling and relaxing and laughing so much, her teeth hurt. Her eyes watered. Her throat rasped until she could hardly catch her breath when Juno impersonated Erasmus's possible over-the-top reactions at not being the one to deliver the circus's welcome speech.

"Do someone else," the Starling twins crowed. "Try the mayor!"

"That's easy." Juno's tattoos shifted into a grumpy rouge against her face as she raised a stern finger. *"Ah Kallia, bane of my existence. I don't know much about what's going on, so obviously that means I need to yell at you for no reason."*

Everyone howled. Kallia almost choked on her candy from laughing so hard. She was about halfway through the small bag, feeling much more revived, when a small bell dinged outside the tent.

"Is it next shift already?" The knife-thrower began reaching for her weapons until Aaros suddenly popped his head through the entry flap, withdrawing in an instant.

"Shit, sorry, I didn't—I saw nothing!"

"Keep poking in here unannounced, and we'll make sure of it," Canary called out.

"Sorry about him." Kallia shrugged, rising from the couch. "We still need to work on personal boundaries."

"I heard that," he grumbled from the other side. "May we come in?"

At the ladies' assent, Aaros waltzed in to no fanfare. But when Demarco entered, Kallia immediately swallowed the lump of chocolate she'd been chewing. His presence shouldn't have startled her—she'd invited him to meet her, for Zarose sake. Still, it was strange seeing him here. She knew him against the backdrop of the Alastor Place and the streets of Glorian, but not in the tight, cozy confines of the Conquerors' tent. Each step he took inside, the room seemed to shrink around her.

The Starling twins both blushed. Juno *hmphed*, a bit too smugly. And Canary bent low in a mocking, regal bow. "Your Highness. Welcome to our humble abode."

Demarco threw a dead-eyed stare of blame at Kallia.

"Are you truly a Patron of Great?" one of the Starling sisters blurted, as the other exclaimed, "You're the Daring Demarco!" She, out of all of them, regarded him with the most awe, and Kallia almost laughed at his confused expression.

"No, I'm not. And yes, I used to be." He spared them a tight smile before burying his hands inside his pockets. "You can just call me Demarco, though."

"What do *you* call him, Kallia?" Juno whispered at her ear teasingly, and Canary snorted. Unamused, Kallia elbowed both of them as she strode forward.

"All right, two men in a women's dressing tent is two men too many." She took both of their arms, and saluted the Conquerors on her way out. "Ladies—thanks for the night. Cheers to many more."

"To many, many more!" the others howled back. They continued laughing over another shared joke too muffled for Kallia's ears as they strode out of earshot.

"Popular among wolves?" Demarco said. "Why am I not surprised?"

Kallia shook her head with a smile as they stepped into the cool night air. With a shriek of delight, Aaros latched onto her hand still cradling the Starlings' pouch. "Oh Zarose, is this *candy*?"

"*Mine.*" She tugged back.

"If you give it to me, I promise I'll leave you two alone for the night."

"But I didn't ask—"

Aaros snatched the bag and gleefully ducked into the crowd.

They spent a solid moment watching him disappear, before finally turning to each other with a laugh. "Is he always like that?"

"Unfortunately." Goose bumps spiked over her skin. When she rubbed at her arms, he began unbuttoning his coat. She wrinkled her nose as he draped it over her shoulders unannounced. "What's this?"

"It's night. You might get cold."

"Trying to cover me up?" she asked dryly. "It's warm enough to go without, nowadays."

"Fine. Give it back."

It smelled too good, though. A hint of fresh smoke, the dark spice of some cologne. Or from the gel taming his messy hair, which she hadn't noticed until now. Staring straight ahead, she tightened the black coat over her shoulders. Biting the edge of his lip, Demarco held back his comments, gesturing forward to the stream of spectators milling about. She hadn't planned to go on a walk with him again, but what else had she expected when she told him to come?

Zarose, why had she even asked him in the first place?

"You put on a good show tonight."

Kallia snapped a sideways glance at him. "Was that *praise*?"

"I could also give you criticism, if you'd really like some."

He had to be joking. Tonight had gone flawlessly, and she'd felt it in the air, in the sea of faces still looking up in wonderment at the performers.

"I thought we were still getting to know each other, Demarco. Let's save the business talk for later."

"Fine by me," he said. "Lead the way."

The pair wove past bodies moving in a slow procession, observing each performer standing on display, proud as art. The Starling twins had taken their places on two pedestals directly across from each other, connected by only the thinnest tightrope that made them appear as if they were walking on air. Rova, the animal tamer, strolled between the platforms with Aya, for whom everyone parted a wide, cautious path. Laughter rang into the air, accompanied by disbelieving gasps and quick inhales. The lively percussion and the sharp strings joining in song.

"All shows should be like this," she mused, looping her arm tighter within Demarco's. Warm and content. "Loud and unpredictable, always moving. If Spectaculore were more like this, Glorian would be saved in a heartbeat."

"Or ruined, according to them." He nodded up ahead at a dour group standing amid the chaos. In the center, Mayor Eilin crossed his arms, refusing to look up as if there were nothing to see.

Kallia and Demarco smirked knowingly at each other. Jokes rarely slipped through the stern line of his lips, but when they did, it gratified her every time. "Regardless, tonight was a success," she said. "If only every performance night were this exciting."

"Yes, but there's more to life than performing." Demarco angled his head at her. "What do you enjoy doing when you're off the stage? That is, if you have other hobbies."

"Of course I do. I'm not completely obsessed." Kallia bit her tongue in thought. Naturally the moment she needed a quick answer, they abandoned her. "I love to dance."

"Also performance-related."

"*Fine.*" Kallia gritted her teeth. She hadn't realized how much her life revolved around performing until now, how little a life she had outside of it. "I used to tend to my own greenhouse."

Demarco's brow lifted a little. She'd never told anyone, not even Aaros. It was a piece of home to keep tucked away. Her life at the House, fading at the edges bit by bit. Still, the greenhouse had been the one thing she wished she could bring, the one place that remained so clear in her mind.

"It was always the place I loved most, aside from the stage," she murmured. "Every morning, I'd walk through, just to water the flowers or sit on the rooftop. There was something about being alone there, it was—"

"Quiet," he finished softly. "Which flower was your favorite?"

"Can't tell you all my secrets, can I? Besides, it's my turn."

The abrupt look of dread on Demarco's face was laughable. She paused, tapping a deliberating finger against her lip. "Your family comes from the Patrons. The most honorable group of magicians, and yet you never talk about them . . . why?"

It had been on her mind. She just assumed everyone else knew more about Demarco than her, so no one felt the need to ask. Still, for someone with so great a family behind him, it was like he had none at all from the way he carried himself. The way his face fell, now. "I don't really keep in much contact with them."

"Really?" Kallia wondered who penned all those letters she found him reading most mornings. "Why would you not want to talk to your family?"

A breath. Sharp, yet not unexpected. "No questions."

"Seriously?"

"We agreed."

"Yes but . . ."

"Think of it this way—would *you* answer it, if the question were turned on you?"

He knew what she'd say. What she wouldn't, more precisely. "Fine. No family talk. Clearly it's not a subject either of us enjoys delving into."

Demarco gave a discernible sigh of relief. An irritating sound. It was the first shut door he presented that she was tempted enough to crack open just to see how far she could go.

It itched at her, how much she wanted to know.

How much she wanted to know him.

As if she couldn't be bothered, she pulled his jacket close around her and led them deeper into the wilds of the circus where there was no more space for talking. No more questions about the world outside of this.

31

There was only so much stalling Daron could get away with before they had to start practicing. All the other pairings had already staked out the spaces closest to the hotel and performance area. The Alastor Place, the Fravardi Mansion, the Vierra District. All corners of the city occupied, except for the one farthest from the Alastor Place. A ruin in and of itself, just like much of Glorian.

"The Ranza Estate?" Kallia's nose scrunched up. They approached a wide, crumbling building of sun-kissed brick hugged by dried vines and roots. A quieter area than the others, at the edge of the community. There was a peace to the way this part of Glorian existed behind the pack.

"It was the only space I could reserve for us." Daron scratched the back of his neck. Sweat gathered against the collar of his shirt.

"What about the circus tents?" Kallia suggested. "They did say they didn't mind us using their space when—"

"We're not using the tents." Not where there were people, watching. "We need a place where no one will bother us."

His excuses sounded weak to his ears. Soon enough, it would all unravel. Already, he felt the threads pulling loose from his fingers, unsure how much longer it would take for her to see.

Realization flickered in Kallia's eyes. He braced himself, but she merely threw her head back and scoffed. "Embarrassed to be seen with me, Demarco?"

"What?" He blinked. "Of course not."

Tell her. His pulse pounded out the words, again and again.

Tell her.

"Good." With a pleased nod, she skipped up the stone steps to the front door as though entering a still grand, dazzling mansion. If anything, she seemed more drawn to the structure's ruinous state. What appealed to Daron was its solitude. He welcomed it, all too eager to escape Glorian's scrutiny each time he and Kallia embarked on their walks, journeying up to their rooms together—never mind that they were neighbors, to which Kallia only replied, "There's no use in convincing a crowd what to believe. Let them think what they will."

He wished he had her armor. Years of performing steeled him when it was only his name to look out for. Now, the rumors cut harsher. Were he paired with any other magician, no one would think anything of it. The rumors would not be as fast-taking as fire, and it rankled him, how they targeted her. How the eyes that followed saw something that wasn't there. That *couldn't* be.

Kallia pushed through the front doors, a heavy, rusty groan emanating as they swung forward. Without looking back, she took off.

"Would you . . . *careful*!" Daron called after her silhouette, which bounded through the archways and into the open courtyard. While the estate could do with a grand renovation like the Alastor Place, it had withered with all the remaining beauty of an aging rose. Petals ashy gray, the stem brittle and dry, yet from a first glance, it had bloomed beautifully once upon a time.

Kallia's shadowed form found light as she walked briskly to the center of the small courtyard opening. Statues of dancing figures surrounded her like a band of guardians, framed by marble archways gray with age.

"Look at these statues—this fountain," she remarked, taking in the splendor. "This must've been a wading or wishing pool of some sort, once."

"Then get out of it." Daron leaned against one of the columns while she continued strutting proudly in the middle of the bare courtyard.

"It's not a pool *now*. It probably hasn't seen water for quite some time." She stepped out from the ring of statues with a graceful twirl. "This could make a good practice space, don't you think?"

The wind ruffled her hair while she spun, stopping gradually in a grand ringmaster's stance. Her laugh breathless, eyes alight.

Daron's throat clenched.

Stop. His heart skipped a heavy beat, running faster than it should. Even as time slowed.

Thunder crackled in the skies above, as if answering the lightning flash of Kallia's smile. Unfurling her hands like flower petals opening to the sun, her palms raised to catch the drops beginning to fall. At first they sprinkled the dry stone around her, before the drops thickened, spotting her dress and her hair.

Only when the rain intensified to a harsh chorus did Daron gesture pointedly. "Unless you can somehow control the weather, too, come inside. You'll be soaked."

"You think I dance under the rain to stay dry?"

She looked up at him then, gathering the ends of hair that had stuck to her neck. It truly didn't bother her—not as much as it was bothering him. The scowl on his face must've appeared most unamused, for Kallia relented and ducked under the cover with him.

With a shiver, a chuckle, she said, "Is there any other sound quite like it?"

He tried not to focus too much on the smell of her, mixed with the rain that hit his cheek as she tossed back her hair. "What?"

"It sounds different here." She half-shrugged and squeezed the ends dry. "I know rain as it hits the trees, how it trickles over roof-tops and down windows. That's all I knew of the sound of rain."

Daron said nothing. He didn't want to frighten this rare piece of her away by releasing so much as a breath. He wanted to know more, as much as she would give him. As much as she would trust him with.

"What does it sound like now?" he whispered. Her face was still slick with water, and the clench in his throat returned, pressing harder when she met his stare.

"Here, with you," she said, showing a small hint of teeth. "Sounds like applause."

Ruin and all, Kallia adored the Ranza Estate. There was something undeniably warm and open about its shape and air, even as they sat huddled inside away from the rain. Even better, their cursory check for any wild strays that managed to crawl their way in, had also turned up with no mirrors. Demarco relaxed at the observation, a happy coincidence for them both.

For once, the silence was as it should be. The stillness, unbroken and true.

Kallia shivered. Her clothes clung, still wet. Hardly drying, even as Demarco fed more wood into the fireplace. It felt too warm in Glorian for a fire anymore, as if the city had somehow begun to thaw around them. A changing of seasons. Even so, as they ducked inside to escape the rain, there was no hiding Kallia's shivering.

"We're here to practice magic, and you tell me not to use it on myself?" she demanded against the chattering of teeth. She could be dry in a matter of moments. "What sort of mentor are you?"

"Just because you can use it doesn't mean you need it for every-thing."

"So says the monk magician."

He stopped pacing by the fireplace. "What?"

"It's what your fellow judges called you once. You refrain from using your magic whenever you can, like how a holy man resists all vices." Kallia wrapped her arms around herself. "Seems I know who they poke fun at when I'm not around."

She was also freely ridiculed right to her face, but it didn't bother her. Those words were not daggers. They were boorish tosses with sloppy aims, hardly ever sticking.

Yet when thrown at Demarco, somehow *that* annoyed Kallia. Even Jack had gotten his jabs in. *Weak magician.* She was sure Demarco had heard worse. His cool shrug was probably a tool of survival.

"They think there's only power in power," he stated, more a fact than a defense. "The moment I grew too reliant on magic simply to keep me here, present, the more I always felt like a performer wherever I went. Like I never got off the stage."

"You make it sound so serious." Kallia shook out her hair. "There's no harm in dividing magic between performances and how you go about your day."

"Clearly." Amused, he looked her up and down. "Did you do that to spite me?"

She raised a hand to her face, her hair . . . realizing both were dry and warm. Her clothes were still a bit damp, but the chill must've triggered the reflex. "Oh come *on*, it was cold. You expect me to freeze to death?"

He chuckled, turning back to the fireplace. No magic had gone into the fire he'd built, and already it was ablaze. One of the first tricks Kallia had learned was raising fires—with the snap of her fingers, in the heart of her palm, the element came to her naturally. But as she sat on the dusty floor in front of the hearth, she didn't know if she'd ever seen a fire brighter or felt such heat. A fire born of true labor.

"Your method is easy to follow when you're retired." She tried to resist drying the last damp patches of clothing that chafed against her skin. "I was taught to exercise well, and often. Treat magic like a muscle, not a time capsule."

"Not all magic is the same. But I think we can agree that nothing thrives under excess and waste."

Days wallowing in bed, exhausted to the bone, flashed across her mind. "If not all magic is the same, why are you trying to force your ways onto mine?"

Pensive, Demarco picked at a stray piece of wood he'd ripped from a block, shredding it splinter by splinter. "I'm not forcing anything. Not trying to, at least. I'm only hoping to show you another way, something different." He threw the long splinters into the fire, holding one between them. "Don't be like this wood."

Kallia snorted. "Flammable?"

The shadows and light of the flames played across his face as he took one strip of wood, guiding the tip into the fire until it sparked. "See how quick it is to dance along the length, before it tires and dies?"

The flame had burnt itself out no more than halfway down the stick, leaving a blackened strip in its wake. Kallia bristled. "So you don't like my style. Not the first time you've said so."

"That's not what this is about." He threw the rest of the stick into the fire. "But even I'm sure you'd love to be able to finish a performance without feeling like collapsing."

Her simmering silence said it all. She didn't want to change her way, but at least trying could benefit her. Perhaps it could even rid Jack's words from her head, those bars forged around her each time she slept. If she could break them, it would all be worth it.

"I'm not changing for you," she stated. "It's my choice and my performance, so if I don't like whatever mold you're trying to fit me in—"

"You don't need to be changed or molded, Kallia. I want you as you are." His throat bobbed under a swallow, yet he didn't turn away. "The crowd certainly agrees."

"Is that so?" Even as she raised a brow, her face went hot. She blamed the fire, alive and roaring before them with no hint of dying. "Show me what you've got, then."

32

When they were younger, Daron and Eva would play in the old manors abandoned on the seashore of Tarcana. They'd pretend to be on Patron missions assigned by Aunt Cata, create routines like the magicians who'd grace the theaters all over Soltair. Old houses were like empty stages, and the Ranza Estate was no different. Only it was far more decrepit than the buildings they used to frequent, a project in Daron's eyes more than a place for pretend.

"What kind of practice is this?" Kallia had demanded earlier in the week. "You want us to clean up as an exercise? Like I would do this for free."

Lies. No matter how she tried to hide it, she examined every corner of the room too eagerly, as if picturing the potential beauty beneath. Other competing magicians would've sneered, but Kallia appeared more excited than ever. Especially when Daron said she could use magic.

"I won't use any myself," he said, uncuffing his sleeves, "but it's good to vary your abilities, to try practical use as well as performative. However you wish to use it. Your power, your call."

"However I wish?"

The mischief in her voice worried him.

He left the hotel early that morning, without Kallia, for time to gather his thoughts before she blew through the door like a storm. But even as he walked through the halls of the Ranza Estate, he found himself wishing the storm would arrive. At least then the building wouldn't feel so still.

In some areas, the mayor had attempted renovation, but clearly abandoned the project to tend to the more established areas of Glorian. So he wouldn't mind if they simply picked up where he'd left off. Probably wouldn't notice, with all the work under way for the final show and Janette's ball.

Sighing, Daron shoved Glorian society from his mind, continuing down the hall of the estate's left wing. Darkness cloaked the area, with only bare slivers of morning light streaming through, and a pair of doors tall as pillars standing at the end.

Daron hadn't fully explored this part of the house yet. The doors blended in so well with the shadows, he'd somehow missed it in their first quick search. Normally, he would've been hesitant, but the impulse reared through him as he pushed open the doors.

Light poured in from everywhere. The air, humid with a smell he couldn't quite place—caught halfway between fresh and old, a fragrant rot. The room stretched surprisingly tall and wide, with walls and ceilings of dirty glass, housing a collection of empty pots and dead plants sprawled all over.

A greenhouse. Abandoned, but well-loved once. Daron had one like it back home, in his library. So different, but just the sight reminded him of all the colors and life rampant in his greenhouse. Unlike here. Brown-dry pots littered the floor, with flowers and leaves shriveled and shrunken within their containers. The trees connected by vines around the room had whitened like bone. With each step, his shoes crunched upon dried petals scattered in his path.

His mind was already whirring when he heard the muffled crash of a door beyond.

"Judge, I've got a delivery!" Aaros shouted. "She's loud, complex, a bit curvy—" A slap rang out, followed by a string of pained curses. "Obviously I mean the violin."

Violin? Daron immediately retreated, securing the greenhouse doors behind him. Down the hall, Aaros occupied the entryway, dragging in oddly shaped cases. Kallia traipsed in with a few more, nodding to Daron.

Aaros blew out a whistle while taking in his surroundings. "So this is your new love nest?"

Kallia delivered another slap to the back of his head before Daron could even scowl. "Pretty, strong boys should be seen, not heard," she hissed. "And be careful. Canary will murder me if these do not return to her safely."

"Would she breathe fire in your face or go a more discreet route?"

"I'm not as fascinated as you are to find out." Deadpan, she gestured firmly toward the common area.

"Bossy, boss." Aaros was quick to understand, gathering up the cases. Not before shooting a look of pity at Daron. "I don't envy you today. Or your poor feet."

Grimacing, Daron turned to Kallia. "What's this?"

"Aren't you proud?" She called over her shoulder, lugging cases in the direction her assistant had gone. "Didn't even have to use magic. Pick up the last, will you?"

The dread piled higher in Daron as he took the case by its handle. It could've been any old container, but its weight gave up the secret: a solid, wooden instrument.

"I said no dancing."

"You never said *I* couldn't." She laughed from the other room. "Relax, Demarco. I just like having a bit of music playing in the background while I work. It'll make this place feel a little less grim, don't you think?"

Aaros unlatched the last of the cases. "Don't be fooled." He capped Daron on the shoulder, leaning in on a whisper. "At first, it's a little mood music. Before you know it, she'll have you flying across the floor with her."

The idea could not have sounded more unappealing. "Don't count on it."

"Stop scaring him with your exaggerations." Kallia continued gently positioning each instrument on the floor. "And leave while I'm still too blissfully distracted to wring your neck."

"Love you, too, boss." He winked at them on his way out. "Behave, children."

The soft click of the doors closing set Daron on edge. Kallia had not budged, fixated on the array of instruments laid out before her. "You'll be using them right now?"

"Don't worry about magic. They're charmed," she answered readily. "Any beholder can play them, any magician can manipulate them. Cheaper that way, but they still hold a tune. Apparently these beauties can absorb each song that's been played and play it back at the snap of—"

Daron snapped his fingers and jerked back as the instruments erupted in harsh, discordant howling.

"How dare you snap first!" Kallia shouted over the clamor bleeding into the air.

"*Seriously?*" He cringed sheepishly. "I wouldn't exactly call this music."

With an exasperated curse, she snapped her fingers twice.

The hellish chorus ceased.

"That's because these instruments were born to different masters, passed down to all kinds of musicians. They sing their own songs first until slowly coming together," she said, a little too defensively. "You know, it *would* be easier if I infused them with my memories."

"*Easier?*" Memory magic was no simple feat, but she spoke of it as easily as brushing hair. And she thought *he* was a harsh mentor. Her teacher before must've been stricter than a war general in the field.

"Memories take a lot of mind power. You sure you want to squander it for a few songs?"

He might as well have told her to never eat food again from how she balked. "I swear, it'll be fine. In fact, I haven't used it in days! Not to the extent I used to, anyway."

That, Daron could believe. She moved differently, lighter on her feet. Sometimes she'd even twirl from one room to the next when she thought he wasn't looking. He couldn't deny he'd enjoyed the same lightness after he retired. Without magic, his mind had grown less clouded, the life in him less restless. His sleep deeper without the endless worry of what impossible things he could achieve next.

In all honesty, it hadn't been too terrible of a life to ease into, having the world at your fingertips one second, and all too soon, nothing. The opposite proved far more difficult: the world shoved back in your hands without warning, the fear that it could happen at any moment. Power driving into him like a knife he couldn't control.

Daron shoved the thought away. "Okay, okay," he said, raising his hands up in defense. "I trust you."

Something strange flickered in Kallia's grin. "Good," she said, bending to the last heavy case, left unopened.

"The whole band you brought wasn't enough?" Daron stared on in dread. "What's that, costumes?"

Out of spite, Kallia snapped her fingers and let the awful music roll over his words. But when he snapped back, the instruments changed their sound. Snap after snap between the two, the harsh music flooding the Ranza Estate changed from discordant scratches to sounds slowly folding into one stream. Like a pack of wild wolves who'd been separated, finally realizing they'd walked together before. The melody mellowed, the instruments remembered.

As Daron prepared to snap again, Kallia effectively silenced them. "But they were finally getting along!"

"They'll survive." Her lips bunched, holding in a laugh, as she popped open a trunk. "Don't forget why we're here, Demarco."

Not costumes, to Daron's chagrin. Nothing colorful or with any flair. He had to reach in for the slim handle of the feather-topped object to believe his eyes. "A duster?"

"You wanted this place cleaned up." With the proud lift of her chin, she removed the rest of the supplies. "Struck a deal with the hotel maids to look the other way while I raided their closet."

"What kind of deal?"

"Front-row seats to the next show. We have more admirers than we realized." She snatched the duster right out of his hands. "Now, pick up a broom and a dustpan, and get to work."

They cleaned without speaking in their respective corners of the room. The instruments had regained their collective rhythm, weaving songs softly in the background while they worked.

Kallia used the end of her duster to scrape out a thick gathering of cobwebs, while Demarco began lifting large pieces of overturned furniture, righting them. Sometime in between, he'd shed his coat, revealing a casual white shirt with the sleeves pushed up to his forearms. His shirt had begun to plaster to his back with sweat when, perceptive as a hawk, he glanced behind with a scrunched brow. "What is it?"

Her pulse jumped. "You missed a spot."

She returned back to dusting with a fury. It was the music pushing at her nerves. Not that it wasn't beautiful and lively. But her soul preferred edgier rhythms, the kind of songs made of night that soaked into her body and escaped in the drumming of her fingers, the need to move.

To her surprise, Demarco was not as averse to it as he'd implied. She'd amused herself the whole way to the Ranza Estate thinking about how he'd react, but he treated it as a welcome addition. As long as it stayed background music. Nothing else.

Darting a glance at Demarco, she sent a whisper of a song that had been weighing in her mind, and speared the memory of it into the hearts of the instruments. The change was abrupt—the upbeat jumps of the violin slid into its new notes like a knife spearing smoothly, deeply, into flesh. Another violin harmonized, just as the guitar went from strumming to plucking a crisp, melodic undercurrent. The cutting edges to all the smooth lines.

Kallia didn't even wait before she let her hair fall loose, unbuttoning her light jacket while kicking off her boots to her socks.

"Wh—" The shift in Demarco's shoulders was instant. "What are you doing?"

"What does it look like?" She tossed her belongings to a newly cleaned corner before spinning back around, letting the movement ripple from her leg to her hip. "You don't have to turn away, Demarco. It's not like I'm naked, I'm only going to—"

"I know what you're doing." Stubbornly, he kept his back to her. "And if you think I'm joining you, you're out of your mind."

"I'll keep to myself," she promised sweetly, arching her hands in the air, lifting her leg high. Warming up. It had been too long since she last felt she could move so freely.

She swayed over to the trunk of cleaning supplies for a broom. Its bristles slid into corners as she hummed the song behind her lips, lost in it. She imagined herself at the House, dancing until her body was on fire, leaving trails of sweat from her dripping hair behind her. She'd wipe the floors with the instruments still playing, preferring the show to go on even if it was all in her head.

It didn't feel like that anymore, with Demarco's eyes on her.

"You're staring," she said before kicking a bucket of water across the floor.

"You're distracting," he shot back, watching the soapy liquid spread. "You'll slip if you're not careful."

"I've danced over worse."

Barefooted over fiery sparks, heeled over sheens of ice. Dangling from the rim of a chandelier. No audience was ever content with seeing the same act for too long. They wanted constant excitement. A thrill wrapped in marvel and disaster.

"So you were a showgirl?"

Kallia hesitated. He should've known better than to ask such questions, but the charade of it seemed so trivial, all of a sudden. Their secrets, their rules. She didn't want to play that game anymore. She hadn't for a while.

"What, think it's beneath you?" She slapped the mop over the water. "Everyone else does."

It was a relief Demarco was not from these parts; there was no chance he would've frequented Hellfire House. Not that anyone from Glorian would've recognized her. Any patron who would've graced the club saw her as much a bird as Jack did. A small creature with no other tricks but to stay in her cage, and never fly away.

"When I was on the circuit, I crossed paths with many showgirls and stage performers and assistants," Demarco said, after a long, solemn pause. "They're some of the hardest-working people I've ever met. Even when so much of their work goes thankless and unrecognized."

The way he watched her made Kallia want to turn away now. He could pin her in place with a word, a look. A laugh, a smile, even the raise of a brow. She didn't like the way it came out of nowhere, the impact of even the littlest movements.

"I wish I could've seen you perform," she confessed under her breath, rolling out the tension from her wrist. "I wish you'd never stopped."

His shoulders tensed. "Why?"

She didn't care if he turned her down, if it sounded silly. Perhaps by putting it out into the world, it could happen. "So we could really perform together one day."

More and more, she'd begun to imagine it. Performing with him, seeing how their powers played together—if they clashed discordantly, or found harmony. Magic was so intimate, in that way. Kallia

never felt more alive, more in tune with herself, than on stage performing. Or learning tricks with Jack. There was a closeness to it
she hadn't expected, an understanding. She would never forget that
familiarity they shared, no matter how hard she tried.

All at once, the air turned cold. The music had fallen silent without
Kallia's influence, her focus on Demarco as he turned away. "That
won't happen."

She bit the inside of her lip. "But why—"

"No questions. Please." He pinched the bridge of his nose, and
tossed his rag to the ground. His posture rigid. Unyielding as rock,
as if they'd landed back to her first audition. Strangers.

"You asked first, and I answered." Unable to help herself, she
reached out for his elbow. "Look, I don't want to fight with you."

Demarco moved out from under her hand, shaking his head.
"This . . . this was a mistake."

Her hand still hovered, outstretched at his retreating footsteps.
"What do you mean?"

"I shouldn't be your mentor."

He didn't mean that. Every muscle in her drew tight as she stalked
off after him. *"What?"*

He just kept walking away. Ignoring her. Without her heels, he
didn't hear her coming up behind him, or see her before she planted
her back against the door, stopping him in his tracks. Their faces
close, chests nearly touching. His eyes fell to her mouth, blinking
with awareness before he shuffled back abruptly.

Kallia's heart fluttered, her thoughts awry. "Forget what I said.
I'm sorry." She'd vow never to pry, to never ask him about performance life, if it wiped the resigned look off his face.

"I'm sorry, too, Kallia."

She didn't like the way he said her name. Like something close
to an end. "Tell me, what did I do?" she demanded. "What *can* I do?"

"Move from the door, please."

He was really going to leave. No explanation, nothing.

"Make me." Her skin hummed, her muscles vibrating in a pull of strength that would keep the door shut. "Let's settle this the old-fashioned way."

"I'm not dueling you." A grimness set within his jaw. He turned on his heel, marching back the other way for an exit. With the disrepair of the estate, he could probably crawl through a hole in the wall or the rickety windows if he was desperate enough to escape.

Kallia couldn't tell if the sight enraged or annoyed her more. "You think it wouldn't be a fair fight?"

"No," he muttered, haunted. "Let's not bring magic into this."

"I think it's about damn time we did." She crooked a finger that sent a chair from the other room sailing at his feet.

Demarco went rigid. "Really?"

"You started it."

"And you're making it worse." He sidestepped the chair, but it followed. Effectively keeping him in place. "I'm not going to play this game."

"Seems like *you're* the one playing games." Kallia circled him, keeping her finger raised like a maestro orchestrating the screeches and scratches of the chair's legs. "Tell me, what exactly did I do to make you so frantic to leave?"

Tell me, so I can fix it.

So I can get you to stay.

The thoughts clawed against her throat, but she shoved them away. She already looked desperate enough chasing after him. The last thing he needed was to see more of her frayed edges.

"You didn't do anything." Demarco exhaled. "It's me. I thought I could do this, but it's . . . I should've ended this long ago. It's not right."

"What are you *talking* about?" she demanded, and still, he refused to look at her. Except for quick glances to see she was still there. Shocked to find she was.

That enflamed her. What reason did he have to doubt her? Every walk, she'd accompanied him. Every talk, she'd brought questions. Even this cleaning of the Ranza Estate was one she'd readily brought supplies to.

Kallia had been nothing if not committed to making it work so she could win.

So *they* could win.

"If you thought this was such a bad idea, why entertain it?" She wanted so badly to punch him in the back. Get him to turn around. "Why work with me, make me believe I can win, only to run off for no bloody reason?"

"You *can* win. And you will," he said. "But not with me."

"Don't tell me you don't want to win this as much as I do. You'd be lying."

"Perhaps you don't know me as well as you think, Kallia."

Something snapped inside her. Whether it was his assumption, or his dismissal, everything in his tone, Kallia finally pushed back.

It was like hitting at a boulder, but his muscles practically jumped under his skin. "Did you just . . . *push* me?"

"I'd slap you if I could, but you won't even look at me." Her hand vibrated at the contact. Shaking, yet the trembling would not reach her voice. "I know you better than you think, and it's all your fault."

With the next push, her fingertips sparked with a small shock. Harmless, yet helpfully annoying as they met his back, exhibiting a grunt from him.

"*Stop* that!"

"Make me," she seethed. "Tell me, what's wrong?"

Like prey under the predator's gaze, he didn't move, stayed frustratingly quiet. Rather than push him like before, she raked her fingers down his back, sending a light current that jolted his spine straight.

"*Kallia,*" he growled through his teeth, not at all in pain. She was playing with him, and he was letting her.

"Ah. I know why you're worried," she mused, dancing her fingers by his neck. "And I don't think it has anything to do with being an unfit teacher at all. Don't be shy. It's me, isn't it?"

"No."

"Liar." She traced a finger from one of his tense shoulders to the other. "Afraid I'll overshadow you and your great reputation? Wouldn't be the first magician who'd think so."

He swallowed hard.

"Or do you fear me in a different way?" Her whisper went low. "An improper way? Afraid they all might see, or that I might even—"

Demarco twisted around, grabbing both of her wrists before they could tease some more—and for a moment, Kallia forgot how to yield magic, how to even blink, as he gripped her.

As soon as their hands met, light shone between them. A burning white, like a spark to the smaller shocks she'd delivered to him, that showed the sweat at his temples, the shadows beneath his panicked eyes.

Everything before Kallia began dissolving at the edges.

Her vision, her thoughts, muddling against the light.

Her knees buckled forward as a shout came over her.

N*o, no, no.*

Daron caught Kallia before she fell. Her head lolled to the side, breaths shuddered. Still awake, still alive.

Still crumpled in his arms.

His heart was racing. Just like that, he was back on that stage. Every fear, every taste of panic when he saw only himself reflected in the broken pieces of mirror.

Do *something.* Do *anything.*

"No." Shaking, Daron cupped her face, pressing below her jaw for a pulse. "Wake up. *Please* wake up."

This couldn't be happening.

Not with her.

Bells began ringing from afar, but it was as though they were clanging in his ears. They softened when her eyes fluttered— *movement.* And Daron swore his heart ruptured from relief. His grip on her tightened, unsure whether to pull her closer or to run.

Kallia gave him no choice, grasping at him. "See . . . that's why you're here. Why you're my mentor," she slurred, a loose smile on her face.

"I'm sorry." There were no other words. "I'm sorry. I'm *so* sorry."

"I'm not. I baited the beast. Didn't know such power was hiding inside." She deliriously clawed at his arms and shoulders, pressing at the muscle. Each touch set off a whole other mess of alarms in his head he couldn't stop. Why wasn't she afraid?

Hell, *he* was afraid.

"I have to get you to a doctor," Daron muttered, straightening her.

"No!" Her voice went hoarse, her body jolting upright. "We're not going out there. Not like this."

He frowned at the frantic turn of her breaths. "Kallia, we have to . . . you're not well."

"I'll be fine in a bit, it's nothing. *Please,*" she hissed. "Don't bring me outside. Don't give them another reason to laugh at me." Her mouth screwed in an angry grimace as if to wrench back what she'd said.

Without thinking, he brushed the hair back from her face, behind her ear before laying her back down. His hands still buzzed with energy, but no longer held any light.

Safe. For now.

Releasing a heavy sigh, he shifted her closer to the fire, grabbing the coat he'd tossed over a table and balling it up as a pillow for her head. The tension fell from her face when she turned to it with a deep inhale. "Smells like you."

His voice grew thick, insides knotted. "Are you sure you're well?"

"Of course. A surge of power is sometimes followed by a bout of delirium. Haven't you seen me after my performances? Even I'm not immune," she said, studying him. "Are you saying you feel nothing at all?"

"With the exception of panic, no."

The smile continued to curve lazily over her face as her fingers brushed his on the floor, trailing to his wrist. "Figures. You go weeks, months, without using magic, and come out of this with barely a sway in your step. And look at me. I wonder what you must think." She laughed bitterly, the haze drifting from her eyes as she clasped her hands together and stared at the ceiling. "What am *I* without magic?"

More. He didn't know where it had come from, but deep inside, a voice yelled. It had learned that even without magic, you still had worth. You weren't only a performer on stage or a walking hat full of tricks. Only in times without did you truly learn what you were made of, and he wished she could see that, too. He wished he could take her hand again.

You are so much more.

"Is that a fact?"

He didn't even care that he'd said it aloud or how tired she looked as she smirked. She had to know she was more. With or without her power. It had taken him losing everything to figure out as much about himself.

Perhaps she could understand him.

"There's something I must tell you." The way she looked at him like he was a marvel, a Great like Zarose, turned his insides. How fast would it take for those brown eyes to turn cold, distrustful. "I—"

With a *slam*, the main door flew wide open.

"Kallia! Judge!"

Aaros burst in, running, panting. His footsteps frantic, nearing. "Kallia, are you . . . *oh* . . ."

The assistant stumbled through the archway, breathless. He took in the scene—the two of them on the ground—and his mouth only dropped farther.

"No jokes," Daron barked. "I mean it, this isn't—"

"I know, I know." Aaros knelt to the ground, placing a hand on Kallia's shoulder. "Is she okay?"

"Yes, she is." Equally agitated, Kallia pushed herself up. Still fatigued, but clear of delirium. "I'm a magician, not a one-winged butterfly."

"Happy to hear it, boss," he said. "I'm not even going to pry into how you got on the floor with Demarco. My imagination can run wild with that one."

Daron took as much interest in the floor as Kallia did peering into the fireplace.

"But I had to make sure." The assistant broke off, his jaw working. "Something's happened. Two magicians, and a circus performer . . ."

Kallia's gaze shot to him, as she asked, "Who?" right as Daron said, "What? Have more gone missing?"

"No." Aaros shook his head grimly. "Not exactly."

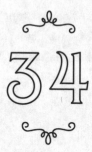

34

Three bodies lay in the beds, eyes closed, breaths slow.

Two magicians, and one Conqueror.

Juno.

Kallia neared her hospital bed, her head pounding even harder. The girl's face tattoos—metallic feathers dusting across her cheek— had stilled and lost their luster over pale skin. The magicians, Kallia remembered their names briefly. Soloce and Lamarre. A bespectacled woman had been hovering by their beds, taking notes when Kallia, Demarco, and Aaros arrived. Her shrewd stare latched on Kallia, with a marveling sort of recognition that disappeared as Demarco demanded details of what happened.

The magicians had all been with their mentors in the Alastor Place, enjoying a few drinks on stage, when the contestants just dropped to the floor. Around the same time a circus performer collapsed in her tent.

Not dead; unresponsive.

"Was it poison?" Daron murmured.

"That was the first suspicion, given their recent activities," the doctor supplied, her voice gruff and hair wild and in her face as if she'd spent the day running to and from chaos. She lifted one of the men's hands, watching it fall limply before making a note. "But how do we explain the other victim? And how are the other fellows who'd been passing the same bottle around still on their feet?"

"Magic gone awry?" Aaros suggested.

"Didn't seem like these gents were practicing any tricks." The doctor pushed up the thick, tinted spectacles that took up half her face. "Obviously competition brings out the beasts in most people, but something strange is at work here. Each of them had this clutched in their hands."

She showed them a crumpled piece of paper, bearing a single line of words:

Three of Mind

"Can you make anything of it?"

Kallia wrung her fingers into a tangled clump. Aaros and Demarco appeared just as perplexed. They were dots with no connection, and only she could see a possible link between them. A line marked in blood.

Jack. The stabbing beat of her heart knew he was behind this.

Kallia stilled her fingers, opening her palms as if in offering. "Do you mind if I try?"

The doctor lifted her brow. "To do what, exactly?"

"Reach inside and see if I can wake them. Or at least find out what's wrong?"

Invasive magic, bordering on manipulation. Every instinct in her recoiled at the suggestion. But what choice was there, other than to watch these three rest until they withered away?

As the doctor pondered, probably debating the ethics of it, Kallia felt a nudge at her elbow. "You're sure you want to?" Demarco whispered. "After today?"

It was clear the doctor heard, from the curious cock of her head. Aaros, too. Kallia's cheeks heated as she recalled it in flashes. A force of light, falling into his arms before being laid on the ground. A surge of magic, unlike anything she'd ever felt. Remembering it, the weariness returned. A heaviness that still hadn't left her bones entirely.

"What use is power if you don't use it to help others?" Kallia pressed forward, ignoring his disapproving silence. Magic of the mind was not easy. The kind she'd performed on the second show night had been much more difficult without direct contact to the audience's minds. With touch, however, it became all too simple to open doors.

When the doctor didn't stop her—merely scribbling notes behind the shield of the clipboard as if for plausible deniability—Kallia neared Juno's bed. She flexed out her hands, crowning them against the girl's temples. Skin still warm, but not entirely alive. An unnatural texture hovering between life and death.

Seeking connection was the trick. It was how Jack reached inside her mind, her memories, while she could never get a clear read on him. She had been too trusting, not guarded in the way she needed to be with him.

Juno's guards were down, as well.

As soon as Kallia's fingertips pressed, the room around her vanished. Blackened.

Iced.

A dark expanse surrounded her, running jagged with light and rapid like a flickering flame across the walls. The images blurry, the sensations cold as her first step into Glorian. Unforgivable. Like how a curse would feel, if one could touch it.

Every part of her shivered as the light settled ahead in the darkness, to a line of silhouettes in the distance.

A group of shadows, walking toward her. Their pace was languid, slow.

Almost.

Almost.

Almost.

The voice slithered. It pierced her with a familiarity she suddenly couldn't recall. In vain, she tried to run from it, to sever the connection. But there was nowhere to run in the dark, nowhere to hide. A sickness filled her as they loomed ever closer, terrors faceless and formless as the expanse surrounding them. The darkness, spilling.

It was like drowning and screaming underwater, where no one could see or hear you. Where no one could—

"What do you think you're doing?"

Kallia gasped, the breath thrown back into her. The light of the room nearly blinded her as she edged back from the hospital bed, bumping into another, Aaros behind her, grasping at her elbows.

When her vision cleared enough to peer over his shoulders, she saw the mayor with a few other judges in tow, looking every bit as disgruntled about her presence. Only this time, they weren't the least bit surprised.

"Move away," Mayor Eilin ordered. "Not even you can hide her sabotage."

"What are you talking about? She's done nothing except try to help," Demarco gritted out. "Which is a lot more than you pointing fingers."

As they squabbled, Kallia's heart raced in every direction, as if fighting for a way out of the very confines of her chest. Her skin flushed, but icy sweat dripped down the back of her neck. There was no unseeing what she'd found in Juno's head. For a moment, she had felt, tasted, *lived* something truly terrible.

"What happened?" Aaros whispered, but she couldn't answer. She inhaled and closed her eyes, letting her mind stitch its ripped edges back together.

You are not allowed to break. Kallia clenched and unclenched her fists, repeating it like a prayer. The only one she knew. *Not for them.*

Her insides still tremored when she raised her head, her expression one of cooled grace. "You gentlemen are determined to make me stand trial, even in a hospital wing." She stepped out of Aaros's hold, grasped at Demarco's shoulder to bring herself forward. These were her wolves to fight. "Have some respect."

"Don't pretend you're innocent," the mayor fumed. "We go off to inspect what's going on with that ruddy bell tower, and *this* is what we come back to? What were you even doing, standing over them like that?"

"I was trying to help them. But sure, blame me," she said through her teeth. "This has nothing whatsoever to do with your incompetence."

Mayor Eilin's face reddened. "And where exactly were you when these contestants fell?"

Her blood boiled as her chin tilted toward the third bed. "It wasn't only contestants."

"Irrelevant."

Before Kallia launched herself at him, someone stayed a hand against her back. Demarco, just as irritated, said, "She was with me."

A snort erupted from the judges. "Doing what, I imagine?"

At that, Kallia's fingers curled into talons at her side, while Demarco's hand fell from her back. Without a word, he neared Judge Bouquet, calmly and sure-footed, as though he were walking up to shake his hand. The judge barely had enough time to wipe his sneer off before Demarco's fist cracked against the old man's jaw, sending him to the floor.

"This town, I swear." Demarco sounded like cold murder itself. He regarded the others, who instinctively backed away. "There's clearly something wrong happening here. How about you worry about *that*, before someone else gets hurt."

"Someone else? There are more?" The doctor watched with keen interest, blatantly ignoring Judge Bouquet's wails as he cupped his face.

At the interruption, the mayor's furious scowl deepened. "And just who are *you*, miss?"

"Zarose, you're all useless. She's the doctor." Aaros scoffed, just as Demarco, shaking out his knuckles, suddenly stilled.

"No," he whispered, realization creeping into his voice. Horror dawning. "She isn't."

Unease prickled the air as Kallia turned to the woman. Everything about her seemed to have transformed in a second. The professional air and the stress lines across her brow vanished, easy as a mask thrown off. Her posture straightened, adding a few inches to her frame. With a short hum, she pulled back her hair and pocketed the glasses that hid pert cheekbones and eyes lined to the ends like wings.

"For the record, I never said I was the doctor. Though I'm flattered you assumed," she said, her voice a much lighter drawl. The way she held out her hand was more of a mockery than a courtesy. "Lottie de la Rosa, from the *Soltair Source*."

Demarco's face lost even more blood, if it were possible. The warm hue of his skin, somewhat sickly now.

"Excuse me?" The mayor's mouth dropped at the woman's declaration. Desperately, he began snapping for the pair of guards by the door, and the woman laughed as they approached her.

"You don't want to tangle with me, boys. I've got immunity, thanks to your ringleader." After scribbling down an errant thought, she blew the ink dry on the page with a satisfied sigh. "And I'm an old friend of the young judge."

"You *know* this woman?" Mayor Eilin shrieked, but Demarco remained speechless. Kallia could see the razor blade of tension working in his jaw, the sharp bob of his throat. As if he'd seen a ghost, or something far worse.

"Oh, we go years back." With a smug, fox-like smile, the woman flipped through the papers on her clipboard to land on a fresh page before settling her gaze on the magician across from her. "Hello, Daron. Long time no see."

35

This was a disaster.

Daron never thought he'd live to see the day when he agreed with the mayor of Glorian, joining the furious mob of magicians trailing behind him to the Alastor Place. They'd prodded him relentlessly for more information on the way, and his mind had all but blanked.

Lottie de la Rosa.

They'd asked who she was to him, but there were no words to properly describe her or how upside down the world felt now.

"RAYNE!" Mayor Eilin roared, frothing at the mouth as he stormed through the show hall doors. "What exactly have you brought upon us?"

His bulging gaze latched onto the proprietor's figure casually sitting in the empty second row, feet propped up against the first. "Calm down, Eilin. You make it sound as if I've summoned some sort of demon."

"Close enough. Demarco was practically catatonic at the sight of her," Mayor Eilin muttered sharply. "Spending her time masquerading as a doctor, and Zarose knows what else!"

"All part of the job, mayor. She didn't become known as the Poison of the Press from primly sitting at a desk, you know."

Mayor Eilin grimaced even more. "We all agreed: *no* press under any circumstances."

"No, we agreed on no press until the right time."

"We just lost a couple more players. That is not something to tout around for the rest of Soltair to see."

"We may not be the picture of success, but we are riding on the wave of a juicy story. Can't you see it?" That troublesome gleam returned to the proprietor's eyes as he gestured grandly at some imaginary horizon. "Magicians go missing on performance night, accidents strike between acts, and three mysteriously fall cold?"

The relish with which he said it sickened Daron. "You certainly sound excited about it."

"We can use this to our advantage—imagine the headlines!" Rayne exclaimed. "Think of it this way, which events are remembered most in history? The well-to-do ships that make it home safely, or the ones that sail into dangerous waters and live to tell the tale?"

"We're sinking hard, Rayne." Mayor Eilin's nostrils flared. "The last thing we need is a damn spotlight."

"Trust me, mayor, I've seen worse ships go down. It may not be too thrilling for those on board, but the ones witnessing it from afar will never look away. And since we're all stuck here, I invited dear Lottie to help us reach the outside world."

The logic to his madness was a fearsome thing to behold. Daron had waded through his share of tabloids and papers, journalists who dug and found what others might not. They gloried in the scandalous. And unfortunately, Spectaculore was rife with exciting material for someone with a pen and the ear of society.

That it had to be *her* was an additional punishment. She'd certainly gloried in Daron's shock, a predator's joy right before the kill. After refusing all her interview requests, visits, and letters, he should've anticipated this sooner.

He could almost hear Eva chuckling in his ears.

"No one will come here if we're painted as a bleak tragedy," Mayor Eilin said.

"Don't underestimate her way with words. Though I'm sure you all know to be on your guard with what you say in her presence. Lottie de la Rosa always was the prettiest snake I ever met." Erasmus sighed fondly. "Even when we were married, she never let me forget it."

The mayor choked. "You two were *together*?"

"Briefly. It was an explosive marriage, as you can imagine."

"This is insanity." Mayor Eilin looked close to ripping his own hair out. "Mark my words, Rayne. The Patrons will catch wind of this and it'll be over before you can say, '*showtime.*'"

"Then we better act fast." He smirked before nodding to Daron. "Besides, from what Demarco said, I doubt tabloid gossip will have them running from wherever they're stationed."

It didn't matter; his aunt would come the instant she heard he was among the roster of judges. He could already feel the weight of a letter in his courier case. Lottie, he might be able to avoid for long enough. But his aunt, as well?

He'd be lucky if he came out of that collision of forces alive.

"They won't." Reflexively, he glanced back at Kallia. No matter how well she hid it, she'd had a lost look about her ever since she touched the head of the fallen Conqueror, and there was no knowing what she'd seen. Everyone else had apparently forgotten all about the incident, so fixated on the show. The damned, stupid show.

"Ah, see, there we go. A cooperative chap."

At the jovial pat on his arm, Daron bristled. "Just because they won't come immediately doesn't mean they won't come at all."

"But by then, it'll be too late to shut us down. You know as well as I that in this industry, these things do happen—and what a waste it would be if only our small corner of the island knew about it," the man said. "I thought it best to keep it that way for a bit, but circumstances change. Luckily Lottie arrived just in time to see the plot thicken, and she has the contacts and clout to make us heard. More coverage means more business, isn't that what you wanted?"

"Not like this." The mayor's face lost its color. "Not with all these threats to people's lives."

"The threats will *make* the show," Erasmus promised. "Don't you worry. We're hitting two birds with one stone because nothing gets past Lottie when she's on a story. In due time, we'll know who to point fingers at. The only way to unearth dark secrets is total exposure. A spotlight that will bare all."

Daron swallowed hard, and out of the corner of his eye, he thought he saw Kallia flinch, too.

The countdown to the final show ticked on, with the circus leading
each night by storm.

Kallia had yet to explore the entire spectacle coiling around the
city. She was glad for the brief interim—it gave her time to take in the
grand sights the Conquering Circus had to offer—but the absence of
Juno still weighed heavily on her. Though grand, the show around
her was fragile as a kingdom of cards a breath away from falling. The
audience hardly noticed beyond the dazzling constancy of each night,
with each performer holding the circus together without fail.

The Starling twins tiptoeing over wires and flying from one
building top to the next.

The Cygna sisters, dancing gracefully underwater in glass cases,
without fear of drowning.

And those daring folk who played with flames for fun.

Kallia would never forget the first time she'd seen Canary perform. She now knew how her own audience felt—wide-eyed and
waiting. After ingesting the fire on her baton, Canary sent Kallia a
wink before dropping to her knees, covering her mouth with a wide,
frantic stare. Choking. The crowd circling her gasped, even Kallia's

stomach plummeted. Until Canary opened her hands, freeing the flames inside in an immense fiery kiss to those around her.

Despite being down one performer, the Conquerors never showed it. Whenever possible, Kallia lent a hand to their acts if they needed it, accompanied them as they visited Juno. They were a plague of loud laughter and chatter upon the hospital wing. The Starlings filled the bedside table with a messy assortment of candies and trinkets. The Cygna sisters brushed Juno's hair, braiding it into different styles each day. Even Rova attempted to join them with Aya, but the doctor drew a firm line against permitting entry to an enormous, black-eyed lioness.

They joked and cackled as they would in their tents, but nothing woke Juno or the other magicians. Not noise, or hunger. Not even family.

Canary fell more silent with each passing visit, Kallia noticed; too worried to pretend as time crept on. But at night, she would throw on her costume without complaint, and perform. No stops, no breaks. No tears or fuss. And no one was the wiser as they watched their entertainment.

Kallia wove through the stalls and tents with Aaros, waving to friends she'd made and performers she knew in passing. They stopped at the dagger thrower's tent, a show of heart-stopping thrills and near-misses timed to the music gloriously pumping into the air. Other acts soothed, like the aerial performers who glided on ribbon-rippling fabrics cascading from the ceilings of the taller tents. Kallia adored it so much, she wondered if she could beg for a lesson and possibly incorporate them into her final act.

Demarco would never go for it.

She turned as if his disapproving frown were aimed at her now. Rayne had stayed true to his word—after the arrival of Lottie and her ever-present pen, people from outside flooded the city with their invitations and maps to navigate the Woods. A dangerous journey, but apparently worth the risk for a taste of Spectaculore. And with their arrival, Demarco had all but disappeared, avoiding the fray. Avoiding her.

They hadn't practiced in days, barely spoken at all. Kallia already dreaded the imminent headlines, when they'd all find out she and Demarco would no longer be performing together.

"Hey." Aaros looped his elbow with hers. "Want to turn in for the night?"

At least she had Aaros. Even he could tell something haunted her. When she couldn't focus, couldn't sleep. Without even prompting him, he'd somehow maneuvered both of their beds into the common room of her suite. She'd simply returned one day to find him casually lounging on his mattress no more than a foot away from hers as though nothing about the room had changed.

"I was bored." He'd shrugged, and it had taken everything in her not to jump on his bed and tackle him in a hug. Such gestures were his way of helping when she didn't have the words to tell him what was wrong. With Jack, with Demarco. Everything. He didn't have to know to be her friend. He was just there to be there, and for that, he'd become her truest friend.

Together, they navigated the Conquering Circus, learning its secrets and sampling every delight it had to offer. The crowd provided enough cover to get them through undetected for the most part. But with Lottie's arrival, it was best not to chance staying longer than they needed to. Demarco avoided the circus altogether nowadays, not keen on becoming the next story of the Poison of the Press. Or so he claimed, in those fleeting moments with him before he fled.

Heat rushed to Kallia's cheeks. His silence affected her more than she'd dare admit. He hadn't mentioned dropping from the competition since their last practice, but he'd never taken it back, either. She had no idea where his head was at, had never felt further from a person.

"Enjoying the show?"

Kallia had barely been watching the street act when the voice snapped her attention to Lottie de la Rosa, smiling as if she'd found herself a prize. "Even in a city as small as this, you're a hard woman to track down, Kallia . . ." She lingered as if to say a last name, and found the lack of one more interesting. "Mind having a quick word?"

Aaros had already begun tugging her away, but Lottie only followed more fervently. "Honestly, what's the harm in a little conversation?"

"I don't like my words twisted and used against me." Slowing to a stop, Kallia's gaze drifted to the notepad held by a red-polished set of fingers.

"Aw, did Demarco warn you about me already?"

"He didn't have to." His efforts to avoid her at all costs told Kallia enough. Nobody earned a name like The Poison of the Press without having killed a few roots in her path.

Lottie's head cocked, as if battling the instinct to scrawl out more words—before surprisingly, drawing the notepad back into her pocket. "Fine. Let's speak frankly." Her sleek lined eyes eased their aim. "The mayor, the judges, and the remaining contestants have all given me accounts that have painted you in *their* truth. And it's not the most flattering."

Kallia couldn't care less what they thought of her, though a small part of her ought to. A bad name gave you infamy, extra press, and attention, but the outside world might be a different story. Eventually she would have to find a new act, and if she were truly honest with herself, nothing terrified her more than free-falling into that uncertainty, blindfolded.

She shoved the thought away. "As if I care."

"Good. You shouldn't," Lottie said. "I didn't come here to give a spotlight to Soltair's most insecure men. I didn't even come here to solve Rayne's mystery. Not really."

Kallia's brow crinkled. "Then why travel all the way here?"

"To see you," she said, as though it were obvious. "A brilliant and powerful female magician who's stealing the show? It's not something you see every day."

"Is that all?"

"You probably wouldn't believe me if I told you."

She was baiting her, the wry twist of her smirk wrapped around a secret.

In the barest slivers he'd revealed of his old life, Demarco had told her how reporters used to hound him. The way they clawed for a moment and made it something entirely different, how they dug into lives for sport and a headline. It all felt like a warning for now.

And yet, Kallia was curious about the woman before her. More than she'd dare admit.

"Aaros, I'll meet you back at the room." Kallia shot him a look. After a hesitant blink, he nodded, knowing she could fend off the wolves herself.

As soon as he disappeared, Kallia resumed her sharp, waiting stare.

"You know, I adore your spirit. You're not the least bit shy, nor afraid," Lottie said, her features now grim. "I think that's why you've lasted longer than the rest."

"Who?"

"Why, your fellow female stage magicians. You may have noticed, there aren't very many. If any," she muttered. "But there are many who would like to keep it that way."

Kallia's frown deepened. She thought back to the scorn of the mayor and the judges, the way Jack had always spoken of female magicians living quietly across Soltair because that's the only way society would have them. The only truth he ever told her, the most disappointing one of all.

"Magician or not, we've always lived in a series of clubs we're not allowed to enter," the journalist went on. "We're told we're simply lucky to be in the room, as long as we stay quiet. Make even a little murmur, and it's like we've disturbed the order of life itself."

"Trust me, I know," Kallia said curtly. "Since arriving, I've been constantly reminded."

"That's because they're scared. If you can't stay small in the box they've built around you, they will make you feel small until you fit right back in it."

"That won't happen."

"It better not. If even a little harm comes to you here, this place will wish it stayed quiet."

A sudden outburst of *oohs* erupted from an act nearby, but it dulled to the unflinching ferocity in Lottie's voice, the fierceness in her eyes that belonged to a friend. Not someone she'd only met days before and avoided every day since. It almost made Kallia choke up. "But . . . you don't even know me."

Lottie paused, inhaling deeply. "Have you ever heard of Enita Son?"

Kallia shook her head. Lottie nodded in understanding. "Gone a week after opening a show at the New Crown Amphitheater when the first magician backed out. Almost a decade ago, and never heard from again," she said. "What about Adeline Andradas?"

The shake of Kallia's head grew slower.

"Known in Deque for her card tricks—from close-up guessing games to shuffles in the air where the cards danced in formation. She'd perform on the streets for sport, until one day, some gent offered her a wealthy sum to perform at a major private function. According to witnesses, she never showed, and was never seen again, performing or otherwise." Lottie paused with a haunted expression. "By now, you've heard about Eva—"

"All right, enough. I don't want to hear any more."

"He never told you?"

"*Who?*" Kallia exhaled sharply, her temple throbbing. All the names paired with silent ends, and she hadn't even heard that many yet. Only enough to know there were so many more, and so much she didn't know about magicians like herself. Why none had ever risen past clubs and tricks in the streets.

Lottie observed her, eyes troubled. "You . . . really have no idea, do you?"

Her tone wasn't out to hunt, but Kallia chose her words carefully. "I never had much access to current news before this. And everyone in this town barely talks about what happens outside of it."

"Yes, it's quite disturbing," Lottie grumbled. "Though it's not only Glorian when it comes to the stories of female magicians. As a whole, people in Soltair prefer plugging their ears and pretending everything is fine."

"Why?"

"People are ignorant. Or they simply choose to be when threatened." She sniffed. "I heard a theory that female magicians were once regarded as the most powerful in ability and skill. Back when the Soltair cities warred with one another, before the Patrons stepped in, it was said female magicians were chosen for the forefront. Throughout the years, it's been shaken off as rumor, which is rather convenient for those currently dominating the stage."

In all her studies, Kallia had never touched upon such a fact, not that it would have mattered. She knew her strength, how her power felt in the grips of a trick. And Jack had never once made her feel lesser. But it was all too easy for a fact like that to become a small secret, tucked into the corners of time. Lost, until it was nothing more than a lie. The people of Glorian who regarded her with scorn would rather see her weak than dare admit she was stronger than them. Even with the evidence right in their faces.

"You're suggesting history and public opinion have been manipulated," Kallia deadpanned. "That's ironic coming from someone called the Poison of the Press."

"I never lie for my own benefit." Lottie tossed back her hair. "I don't frame facts I don't like as silly myths meant to amuse my readers."

"Then I hope they're ready. Because I'm a far cry from some silly, little myth. And I'm not going anywhere."

The woman's face brushed with a hint of sadness. "That's what I'm hoping," she said. "When I heard about Spectaculore, I thought for a small town removed from society, an experimental show couldn't hurt. That was until Raz told me about you, and the accidents. The disappearances."

"You think they're connected? Those were male magicians."

"The show isn't over yet, Kallia."

Cold seeped into her blood as a round of applause scattered freely into the night. Usually the sound comforted her, but each clap pricked at her hard enough to draw blood. Just like everything this woman said, everything she was implying. "Miss de la Rosa, no matter how many people want me gone, I'm not going to just disappear. I'm not exactly defenseless."

"Oh, I've heard about your power. But even shields can double as targets."

Resentment flared through Kallia. "How could you even understand? You're not a magician." A hot wave of embarrassment trickled beneath her skin when she remembered the notepad hidden from view. "You're only out to catch your next big story."

"How soulless of me, for doing my job. But I chase stories based on facts that don't add up, and I've been following this one for years." Lottie's lips pursed. "And I might understand you better than you think. You're not the first magician I've tried to warn, and at the rate you and this show are going, you probably won't be the last."

37

The sounds of the circus sank through the walls of the Ranza Estate, dulled from a distance. Trumpets blaring, drums booming, laughter and gleeful shrieks piercing the air.

A splatter hit Daron's shoe. Wet seeping in. Jerking back, he tipped up the rusted watering can, aiming it toward the line of pots again. Normally, maintaining the greenhouse calmed his nerves, the last few days of orders and preparation keeping him busy. The final shipment of plants arrived just this morning, the last piece to the picture he'd envisioned the moment he first saw this room.

There were times when he thought about asking for Aaros's opinion, and even more times where he knew he'd regret it from the potential jokes alone.

More than ever, he wished he could ask Eva. She wouldn't even have to see the room. She'd take one look at his face and know exactly what to say.

Just show her, Dare.

Just tell her.

Except he hadn't talked to Kallia in days, didn't trust himself the more his mind replayed her falling to the ground, his palms burning.

That hopelessness in his veins came back raw even now. He'd hurt her, and he'd never loathed his magic more.

A hard thump sounded outside, snapping Daron to attention. He set the watering can down and rushed out. Only he ever stayed at the building this late. And with the circus going on every night, there were certainly far better things for outsiders to do than break into an old manor.

Daron hurried over the dust-ridden floors, past cobwebs laced between the rusted, round lamps dotting the walls, faltering when he recognized her. Unsure if he were dreaming. "What are you doing here?"

Kallia absently traced the table propped against the wall. "I could be asking you the same thing." Her finger resurfaced with a mound of dust. "Nice work you've been doing."

He scratched behind his ear. "I just cleaned that the other day."

A lie. He wasn't sure how long he'd been keeping a slower pace, enjoying the sight of the halls ever-riddled with cobwebs and stretches of paint-dotted canvas they'd forgotten to put away. They were reminders of work still to be done. It meant there was still time.

"Dust never goes away." Kallia pulled her hair back, winding it around her finger. "No matter how often you wipe it clean, it always comes back."

He stared at the finger that kept twirling her hair, taking in her face. Hardened and cool as always, but some sadness glimmered beneath. "Are you all right?"

Her brows drew, as though insulted. "I'm fine. Question is, are you?"

"What do you mean?"

"I haven't seen you in days, Demarco."

If he didn't know better, he thought he detected a trace of frustration. But perhaps he was seeking it. Seeking *something*. He rubbed grains of soil between his fingertips. "I've had a lot to think about."

"Like our little accident?" she posed, casting her gaze to her feet. "You didn't hurt me, just so you know. It was wrong of me to bait you into using magic. I know you prefer not to."

He swallowed hard. The way she said it, uncomfortable but apologetic, made his insides turn and tear.

I'm no magician.

I'm nothing.

He should tell her now. Everything.

"Were you still thinking about dropping from the show?" She grew quiet, watching him. Wary. "Have you changed your mind?"

Daron didn't give himself a chance to be lured by that lilt of hope. He shook his head. "I can't, Kallia."

"Why?"

Say it. Say it. The words were there, but he couldn't let them go. Couldn't let them make him into nothing before her. "It just . . . won't work."

"Why *not*?" she fired back. "I thought you believed in me."

"I do—"

"No, if you did, you wouldn't be doing this. You wouldn't be hiding away in this house, thinking no one would notice and hoping the show goes on without you."

"This show doesn't need me, but it does need you."

"Don't you see? I can't compete without you." Kallia's lips pressed into a thin line. "According to the rules."

Daron raked his fingers through his hair. "I'll talk to Erasmus and the mayor."

"I don't want you to talk to them. I want you to talk to *me*."

Her eyes had never looked so defenseless, reaching. Like she knew there was something just within her grasp, if she kept at it. Kept at him.

"I don't even know why you come here, if you don't want to do this anymore." Kallia gestured around at the Ranza Estate, scowling. "What *are* you even still doing here?"

Daron took an instinctive step back in the direction he'd come. "Nothing."

"You expect me to believe you sat here for days, doing nothing?" she asked sharply, before giving a curious tilt of her head. "What's in that section of the house?"

If only she could've stayed angry. He took another step back. "It's just a room I started working on."

Kallia glanced at the unkempt, dust-ridden corners. "You're lying."

"I am not."

"Are, too." She chuckled, advancing to the door. When he attempted to block her path, Kallia sidestepped and ran behind him. Triumphant.

He didn't even try stopping her. Not like he could. The plan he'd crafted carefully in his head would shatter the moment she pulled those doors open.

It wasn't supposed to be like this.

And yet Daron just stood back and watched her walk through, mesmerized as her movements slowed entirely.

As she looked up.

And fell completely silent in her own world.

It was a wonderland of sights and smells, glowing lights and glimmers in the dark.

Glass walls rose high into a crystal domed ceiling, letting the night in. Almost too dark, except for a soft luminescence flooding the room, swirling along vines. Were it not for the glow of petals and the veins of leaves, Kallia would not have been able to tell they were flowers. Some glimmered at a soft constant, while others flickered gently in the way fireflies did in the forest.

The air hit her, warm and humid with a sweetness she knew all too well.

A greenhouse.

Kallia could hardly breathe as she moved from one row to the next, fingers grazing the flowers in full bloom. Her chest tightened, almost painful. "You . . . you did all of this?"

Demarco leaned against the archway of the door, so shadowed that she couldn't read his expression. "You're not the only one with an affinity for this," he said. "It's like another type of magic, growing something from the ground up. Watching it thrive."

Of course he'd see this as one of his practical magic indulgences. Yet whenever she'd spoken of her greenhouse, he rarely reacted. "But . . ." she stammered, unable to stop. "But you never said anything."

"I didn't think you'd care, all things considered." With an infuriatingly casual shrug, he pushed off the wall to step farther in. "I was going to add some lights, maybe a few hanging lamps or . . ." He drifted off, looking away. "Most of them aren't even opened or in full—"

"Those are my favorite." Her fingers were poised around a sparkling lily nearing bloom, the delicate stem holding a closed, firm head with a glow about its petals. "The best flowers are the ones just about to bloom. They are untapped potential. A possibility, about to become."

And this room was filled with so many beautiful possibilities. So many inevitabilities.

"It's for you."

The soft lull in Kallia's head cleared. "What?"

"All of this." Demarco came up beside her. "It was supposed to be for when you won. I didn't know what else I could give you, until I stumbled upon this broken greenhouse one day."

She was suddenly unable to hear what he was saying, or anything at all. Her skin prickled as she watched him glance across the room. The dim lighting of the greenhouse obscured half of his face, but she'd know it anywhere even without light. Darkly curious eyes, intent with their aim. Nose prominent, jaw sharp. Tawny skin that warmed under any bit of light.

Her chest tensed. Her heart, pounding out of control. Lifting out of place.

Stop, she whispered to it. *Stop, stop, stop.*

"Dance with me."

After the longest pause imaginable, Demarco lifted a brow. *"Now?"*

Kallia nodded. The world spun around her, moving in too many directions all at once. The greenhouse, Demarco, the furious beat of her heart, Demarco. The chaotic smells of too many flowers, the circus noises muffled by glass. Demarco.

Everything whirled faster, until she couldn't see straight. Dancing always made the world stand still.

"We have to practice for the ball." With her heel, she edged aside a few small pots and empty watering cans. "It would be a shame if you embarrassed me on the dance floor all night."

"But there's no music."

She tilted her head at the windows, the faintest melody thrumming through the glass. A slower beat, transitioning from the high energy of the start of the night to the gradual, inevitable end. The hum of violin strings glided over low, smooth piano chords. A song to savor, a song to dance to.

He bore an expression that bordered on pleading. It was almost enough to make her forget all about it, until he dragged a resigned hand down his face.

In surrender, he extended his right hand.

An invitation.

She fought the triumph from bursting on her face. It felt more like a gift than a battle won. She treated it as such when she gingerly took his hand, about to ease him into the proper position—

Suddenly, all the air in her chest *whooshed* out as she was spun sharp as a top.

Strong arms caught her in a binding low dip that pressed them chest to chest.

The world froze.

Her jaw snapped shut. "I-I thought you didn't dance."

"Never said I couldn't." Demarco's eyes hovered over hers, crinkling at the edges. He led her into the next position, seamless as muscle memory. "I used to attend galas and balls on a weekly basis. Being a decent dance partner was practically a method of survival."

The shock wore away at the amusing thought, imagining him moving from party to party, dancing with guest after guest. "See? It does have its uses. But you've been holding out on me."

"Don't act like you wouldn't have used it against me. Besides, I've seen you dance alone. You're . . ." He trailed off, lost in a thought cut short as he cleared his throat. "You don't need a partner."

"Still feels good to have one," she admitted, still warmed by the surprise. Demarco wasn't an expert dancer by any means—a little rusty in his movements, like clothes he hadn't tried on in a while—but as they adjusted, he *led* her. With a confidence in his grasp, enough to catch her off guard.

So she simply followed.

It was the first time she'd danced like this with someone who wasn't Jack. Sometimes she'd choose a guest at Hellfire House to join her on stage, but there was safety when it was all for show. Masks and distance and drink to keep it from being real.

She could feel the distinctions beneath her fingertips. In their slowing movements, forgetting the song. Their hold, no longer proper as they leaned into each other. No space between them, Kallia pressed the side of her face to his chest, hearing his heart pound. His breaths, uneven.

A light flickered in the corner of her sight.

His palm, against hers, faintly glowing.

Suddenly, he tensed against her, about to pull away. "Don't," she mumbled against his shirt. "Please."

Her limbs had grown warm and tired and heavy, her heartbeat slow and her eyes so tempted to close in sleep. She needed him to keep holding her so she wouldn't, for them to keep dancing long after the music had quieted.

"What does it mean," Kallia began, smiling up at him sleepily, "when a magician who's sworn off power to the world shows his magic to someone?"

His troubled gaze locked on their joined hands. "I don't know," he said, before finally turning to her. Everything in his face softened. "Guess it depends on who—"

The sudden ringing outside cut through the glass, distant but clear.

The light vanished from their palms. Warmth washed over by ice at the realization.

The Alastor bells, far away, ringing twice like a warning.

38

The bells' echoes haunted the streets as they neared the center of Glorian.

"Everyone, stand back!"

Daron tried peering above the heads of the crowd, but he saw nothing. Could only taste the cold panic in the warm air, a razor blade cutting the night short.

Kallia squeezed through the cluster of people by sheer force of will. Her eyes straight ahead, hand in his. Finally, they caught sight of Mayor Eilin standing at the hub of it all on a street corner, flanked by a few people in uniform who gestured onlookers aside to clear the space. "Check the Alastor Place!" he snarled, even though the bells had fallen still. "And get these men out of here."

He hailed over a pair of medics who stretched two gurneys out next to two sprawled-out figures, moaning in pain. *Alive*, Daron thought with relief. One was a judge, the other a magician. Judge Bouquet and Robere.

Daron gripped Kallia's hand tight, but she just looked blankly at the scene, mesmerized by the horror. Lost in it.

"Their eyes," she said, softly. "They're . . ."

A shiver ran through him. He caught glimpses of the figures being transferred onto the gurneys. Bloody strips of cloth lay where both victims' eyes should've been, and Daron's insides wrenched.

A hand clapped over his shoulder. An imposing man in uniform looked over their heads to where the mayor stood surrounded by contestants and judges, sternly waving them over.

"Just follow and cooperate," the man said gruffly. "And we won't have to use force."

Kallia and Daron shared a glance as their escort pushed them through the crowd. A few faces turned in their direction, and Daron's whole body began to sweat.

"This has gone far enough," Mayor Eilin whispered furiously once they reached him. He towered over Kallia so his citizens could not hear. "You're going to put a stop to this whole sick charade."

No one appeared more unamused than Kallia. "This *wasn't* me. I don't even know what's happened."

"Oh, how convenient. What a bloody coincidence that when two magicians are found with their eyes pulled straight from their sockets, you only now just waltz through in the aftermath."

A stillness entered her, as if she were holding herself back. "We did because the bells started ringing."

"And I wonder why that is," he seethed, shifting to Daron. "I'm not letting this go any further. As a precaution, I'm afraid I have to make cuts to the show. I will not have any more accidents plaguing my town and my magicians."

The ice surrounding Daron's bones cracked. "You're forgetting that *she* is one of your magicians, too."

"She's trouble, that's what she is. I knew it as soon as I saw her."

Before Daron had a chance to raise a fist, Kallia stepped forward. "I won't play guilty for you just because you're looking for someone to blame. *You're* the mayor of this city. Take ownership of it, for once in your life."

Angry, red splotches speared across the man's cheeks, especially when he finally noticed the lingering group of stragglers watching on. Even the other contestants and judges remained, observing without sneers for once. Only fear. Fear for whatever was hunting, and if it would be coming for them next.

After a tightly drawn breath, the mayor said, "As the leader of this city, I aim to do best by my home. You're out, Kallia."

On the outside, she appeared every bit composed. But the small cracks of her armor veined the surface. The small twitch of her brow, a slight quiver of her lip. "Kicking me out won't solve anything. Why not cancel the whole show altogether?"

"And risk being stuck here for the rest of your days?"

Lottie emerged as if out of nowhere, notepad in hand. Erasmus trailed behind her with an expression of fascinated concern, like how someone would look upon the carcass of an animal in the street. While he at least bared a morsel of regret, Lottie showed none. Only knowingness, edged with certainty.

"What are you going on about?" Judge Armandos demanded.

"A theory of mine," she said. "You all can't leave this place because of a game you signed up for. And I doubt the game will let you go simply because you want to stop it."

"You speak as though we're cursed."

"Maybe you are. Maybe this city is. No one knows what's going on, so would you really want to risk angering whatever force is keeping you here?"

"We are not cursed." Mayor Eilin raked a hand through his hair. "We made a bad deal. You can't go back on a deal around here."

"Oh?" Lottie scrawled in her notepad. "And why is that?"

Mayor Eilin blinked rapidly, wordless for a moment, before the veins of his neck bulged at her movement. "What are you writing down? You . . . you can't publish any of this." The more she wrote, the more flustered he appeared. "*Rayne,* she'll ruin us—stop her!"

"I can't stop her any more than I can stop a storm with my bare hands," the man said with affection. His arms crossed in casual defiance.

"I can't risk more accidents, or more magicians going missing."

"Magicians go missing all the time. I wonder why you're only noticing now," the journalist muttered in mock astonishment. "If you look closer, Mister Mayor, there's a pattern to the misfortunes that have befallen your show. Four go missing, three have yet to wake, and two . . ." She trailed off with a quick shudder. "The hunter who works like that—with a system in mind—won't react well when surprised. You either play this person's game, or they widen the game board to more victims."

"Are you suggesting we just stay here, like sitting ducks?"

"You're already sitting ducks," she said bluntly. "But if you cut everything this far into the game, you'll be left with nothing more than a horde of dissatisfied customers, an empty show hall, and a ballroom you've spent a fortune trying to renovate."

The mayor's jaw clenched. "Of course you'd say so. You're only here to fill your gossip rag, after all."

"*Gossip rag?* You wound me," Lottie said with razor-edged relish. "Before you doubt me, Mister Mayor, you missed something." She thrust a piece of paper in his face. "You went straight to pointing fingers and didn't even check the scene of the crime properly."

Mayor Eilin's eyes narrowed on the paper, before his entire face blanched.

"*Two of Sight,*" the journalist read sharply. "You've gotten these before, haven't you? When those other contestants *mysteriously* vanished? And the other three *magically* fell unconscious?"

Everyone regarded each other warily, confusion edging into suspicion. When Daron glanced at Kallia, even her gaze was turned to the ground.

"There's nothing magical or mysterious about it. If you're going to point fingers, point them at this." Lottie flicked the paper in the air, leaving the mayor to struggle to grab it. "Find whoever's leaving these, and you'll find your saboteur."

39

Kallia had never liked Judge Bouquet and Robere, but their pained moans drifted in and out of her ears long after the streets cleared and everyone dispersed for the night.

She fidgeted and wrung her fingers as she and Demarco walked back to their rooms in silence, the tension in the air taut as ever. The mayor hadn't mentioned throwing her out again, and she wondered if that made Lottie her biggest ally, or the one person who had all the tools to expose her and everyone else in this show.

"You want to talk about it?"

Demarco slowed to keep at her side. New shadows seemed to have formed under his eyes in the last hour. She felt her own carving into her skin, weighing her down. "It's been a long night. I think we've all had enough."

She wished for nothing more than to walk into her room and sink into bed, but the loneliness of that image hollowed her. Even Demarco paused, simply looking toward his door. "How freeing would it be to leave all this behind and not look back?"

A laugh pulled from her. "Is this you inviting me to run away with you?"

"Would you say yes?"

What an idea, when they had no choice. "Where would we go?"

"Anywhere." He turned his room key between his fingers. "It doesn't matter to me. I've pretty much toured all of Soltair already, so you get to pick the first city."

"What if I don't want to go to a city?" she challenged, a step closer. "What if I want to be out on the water?"

"Then we'll get ourselves a boat, and see how far it takes us."

Kallia's stomach coiled tight again. The warmth, overwhelming. It rushed back to her from the greenhouse, the feel of him around her. Of music through glass and the beat of his heart against her ear. Of swaying so slowly, it was hardly a dance anymore.

"The greenhouse," she began, sensing the memories playing behind his eyes as well. The coil inside her wrung tighter. "How long did that all take you?"

"Just a few special orders and some maneuvering of shipments. Nothing, really." He scratched the back of his head, looking down at his feet. "It wasn't quite finished. You found it much earlier than planned."

Her heart started. "What was the plan?"

"It doesn't matter anymore."

"It matters." She swallowed, all of it too much. "Humor me."

Weeks ago, he would've turned right to his door with a terse goodnight. Now, he blew out a sigh, before rolling back his shoulders as if he had nothing to lose. "You'd win the show first," he stated. "Despite the other judges' attempts to low score your act, the audience loves you. You'd win by a landslide. Everyone would reconvene at the Prima to celebrate. Champagne and flowers, and the fakest of smiles from everyone who doubted you. You'd have fun rubbing it in their faces for a smug amount of time." He snorted and went on, "Next, you, me, and Aaros would duck into the Conquerors' tents for a far better party. Better music, to be sure. I'd eventually invent some excuse for us to visit the Ranza Estate, one last time. Then I'd—"

Kallia kissed him, then. A soft, brief press.

Thank you.

It yanked apart everything inside her. Her skin over his, the warmth of him pressed to her, chest against chest.

She pulled back before he could respond.

"I'm sorry." Her cheeks flushed, everything inside her on fire. Demarco said nothing. His face, stone once more.

"I didn't . . ." She swallowed, feeling stupid—*so* stupid. "I shouldn't have done that."

He just stared. In agreement. In shock. Kallia couldn't tell, only waited for him to step back and pretend it hadn't happened. Only it had, and her heart had never thrashed so violently in her chest with hunger. This strange thing with claws, it had been pricking at her day by day. Wanting this, for much longer than she even realized.

"Sorry," she whispered, and the word cracked right between her ribs. She felt foolish, felt too much. "I'm—"

"Stop saying that."

Kallia's brow furrowed at his gruff tone, the way he caught her face between his hands.

He took a moment to look at her. Just look. And she caught something in the dark of his eyes—the softest certainty—before he finally pulled her to him, and kissed her.

She froze. Her mind, blank. But the slowness melted as she breathed into another kiss. Then another, and another, following the rhythm he set. The music between them.

Nothing in the kiss tasted of regret.

As his fingers slid through her hair, his lips urging hers to open, she tasted want. *Need.* It answered hers in such a wave, that she locked her hands behind his neck to steady herself.

This can't be happening, this can't be happening.

This can't be happening.

Her pulse hammered as he kept going. Pressing impatient kisses to her skin, running hands down her back, memorizing her. A noise rumbled deep within his chest as he kissed down her neck, every inch of her searing. A smile cut across her face, and she was relieved how distracted he was to see it. "I thought it was only me."

"Should I have gotten you something bigger than a greenhouse?"

Her whole body shook under a laugh as she watched the way her arms twined around his neck. The impossibility of it. "I just . . . I wasn't sure."

"I haven't been sure about anything in a while." Demarco's eyes finally met hers, heavy and half-lidded, as though he were dreaming. "You've been in my head since the moment you first walked on stage."

She remembered that day well. She'd barely noticed he was even there until he spoke. He would've vanished from her periphery altogether had he not become such a thorn, always catching at her. Pulling on the thread between them day by day, slow and gradual.

"I can't believe this." Slowly, he drew back, scanning her face. Kallia almost laughed at his hair, a wreck. His eyes, ruined. "Should we talk or . . . ?"

Already, he wanted to analyze this. This thing she hadn't even wanted, until it showed itself in the dark.

In answer, Kallia pulled him to her. Breath held, lips barely meeting—before the lights around them dimmed for a brief, sharp pause.

It lasted barely a second, but it was enough to wring her cold. She jerked away, hitting the back of her head against the wall. Demarco edged forward instinctively, before searching the hallway—empty. "What's wrong?"

"Someone might see us."

It struck her, how out in the open they were. *Stupid.* He stiffened at the realization, but one hand remained at her side. "Can I . . ." He nodded at her door. "Can I come in?"

Usually Kallia was skilled at composing herself, but that warranted a look. Enough to fluster him. "Oh no, sorry—only to talk, about what just . . . I think we need to . . ."

He ran a hand over his face before knotting his fingers in front of him. She marveled at how she once believed him to be made of stone, and how little it took to soften him into such a mess of nerves and uncertainties. There was honesty in it. Gently, she stilled his fingers under her palm, untangling them one by one. Brushing each knuckle, each fingertip.

So easily breakable, if the wrong hands found them.

And so she said nothing, but he read her silence. "Tomorrow?"

"Tomorrow." Kallia nodded, tempted to take it back as he played with a thick strand of her hair, touching her so easily. As if he'd been doing it for years.

They glanced down the hall, waiting for signs of movement, before Demarco took her face back in his hands. Kallia should've turned away, but instead arched her neck up. Eyes closed in waiting. First, a light brush, deepening as she wound her arms around him. Her nails scratched behind his neck, a surprisingly vulnerable place from the sound he made, and she wondered if she'd ever get used to it.

When he pulled back, he tilted his head at her with a lazy smile, pressing it once to the grin forming on her face.

"Good night, Kallia," he said, and backed toward his room. Un-hurried.

Tomorrow. She would see him tomorrow.

Kallia closed her door behind her with a soft click, the fluttering in her heart quieting as the darkness swept over her. Silent, save for the nightly wind rattling against the windowpanes above her and Aaros's beds.

"It's bad luck to keep dying flowers."

Everything blackened in an instant. Gone was the sun. In here, came the night. Waiting, Jack towered by her vanity, looking curiously at the covered mirror before assessing the old cloth she always kept by it.

"It's just a piece of fabric," she snapped, hoping he wouldn't touch it.

"It used to look different." A long pause, contemplative. "Years back. Like a rosebud, blooming. Now, it's . . ."

For once, he didn't sound bitter. Only sad, which riled her up more. He was at the heart of this darkness, after all. A player in this game. The master of it.

"It's changed ever since things started going wrong here." Kallia's nostrils flared. How dare he stand there as though he didn't enjoy every moment of tonight. "What are you doing here?"

"That's where you're mistaken," he said, absent. "Things have *always* been wrong here."

"You didn't answer my question."

His entire face sharpened, the restraint apparent in the lines of his jaw. He looked up from the vanity, and turned. "You need to stay away from him."

Her cheeks flamed. Panic pulsed through her, at what he must've seen outside her door. What she must've looked like now. Still, there was no anger to him. His quiet unnerved her more than any rage he could've released.

"Is that all you came here to say?" she bit out. "Of everything that's happening, you fixate on *that*?"

"He's made you weak," he said, tone clipped. "And it'll only get worse. You can't even see that he's lying to you."

Kallia didn't want to listen. Everything he said was a poison entering the air. "You're one to talk. This story sounds all too familiar."

His jaw clenched. "Then you should be wise enough to listen. You don't know what you're up against."

"Enlighten me, then," she said. "Because all I see in my way is you."

"That's all you want to see." He stepped closer, cutting through the shadows. "It's easier to hate me, blame me for everything that goes wrong. Every missing magician *must* be my doing. Every terrible accident is *undeniably* by my hand."

The words were grossly familiar to the ones she'd spat in the mayor's face earlier, and she hated the sound of them being thrown back at her. She circled a table to let it divide them, refusing to be cornered.

"Why? Because I'm the only monster you've ever known," he continued, undeterred. "What you fail to realize is there are other monsters in this world. Outside of the House, I'm hardly the worst of them."

"Then who? If not you, who would be so cruel as to do all of this to one little city?"

A beat of silence passed between them, before a shadow swept across the floor. A spill of darkness, rising swiftly before her. She'd steeled herself when Jack took shape, her muscles seizing.

"Would you even believe me, if I told you?"

Kallia didn't know. To humor him felt like giving an inch. To believe him, a forgiveness.

He gave her no choice as he took her hand. His grip, tight and cold. She struggled and pulled back. "Don't *touch* me."

"I'm trying to show you," he said, cautious. "You can never tell who's listening."

Kallia's skin prickled. "There's no one else here."

"Not that you know of." Jack raised a hand to her head, threading his fingers through her hair. His fingertips pressed at her skull, and her mind fell still.

At first, darkness.

Then, shadows.

They rose, monstrous dolls come to life—darkened figures, walking toward her, just like the ones from Juno's mind.

Kallia.

Kallia.

Kallia.

They spoke in one voice, familiar as a dream. Her breath broke as she slammed her palms onto his chest to push him away, nearly falling when her fingers met mist. Jack didn't glory in the illusion this time. Form fading, he calmly stepped back.

"Believe me or don't, that's your choice. But don't pretend like I haven't spent all these years trying to keep us both away from this," he said, as if beginning a sad story. The end, already foretold. "I've only ever tried to let it sleep. By coming here, you woke it up."

A sudden rustle in the room sent a jolt through her. Jack's gaze ran beyond her shoulder, and he sighed. "I have to go."

"Wait." Her voice went ragged. She grasped at his arms, but there was nothing. Just an outline of his body, beginning to fade. He looked down at her grip trying to keep him in place, brows drawn at the sight.

"Whatever happens, remember what I said. He will only put you in harm's way, and soon, you will not be able to protect yourself," he said hurriedly. "You must be careful."

In an instant, he was gone. The room lightened in his absence, the flickering candles regaining brightness and the flames in the hearth crackling heartily amongst the logs. Whatever Jack had seen was enough to startle him away.

Heart beating fast, she took in the room.

There was no change, nor anyone else around as she'd feared.

Only the vanity, standing proud. And the mirror uncovered once more.

40

aron stood at the foot of the Prima's grand staircase, looking up so often his neck began to creak. He waited for that familiar flash of dark hair or colorful burst of a dress among the passing flood of strangers who eyed him in confusion. He nodded at them in awkward greeting, drumming his fingers along the rail.

Kallia hadn't knocked at his door last night. Not that he'd expected her to. It was better that she hadn't, for how his thoughts ran in restless circles all night, processing it all. What had happened in the hallway, what it meant. If it changed nothing at all, or everything. One thing he knew for certain: he needed to see her again. Almost every day, he'd seen her, though this time was different. Uncharted.

When he'd swept his fingers through his hair this morning and left his room to find her, someone already stood outside her door.

A uniformed guard, arms clasped behind him and feet planted solid.

"Is . . . is everything all right?" Daron sobered instantly. "Has something happened?"

"Everything is perfectly fine, Judge Demarco. Only a safety precaution," the man said, looking straight ahead. "If you wish to see her, I will be escorting her downstairs when she's ready."

Daron cocked a brow. "Does *she* know this?"

The guard said nothing more. A dismissal.

Which was how Daron found himself at the foot of the stairs, watching one hotel guest after another pass him. Once contestants began trickling down the steps, accompanied by their own guards—at the mayor's command, no doubt—he was more at ease.

Until he noticed the lingering looks.

Hushed laughs and whispers, weaving through his ears.

The notice sent a prickle down his spine. True, he looked every bit a fool waiting at the stairs, but that didn't seem scandalous enough for how everyone observed him. One girl had been whispering furtively to a friend when she stumbled at the foot of the stairs, dropping her purse and—

Spectaculore Speculation:
Players Entrapped in a Wild Game

The headline glared at him from the ground. The most recent issue of the *Soltair Source*.

His stomach dropped. He'd been avoiding the paper ever since Lottie rolled into town, dreading her coverage. Her commentary. He'd managed to avoid her spotlight for this long, he worried what words the Poison of the Press would spin about him now.

"Can I borrow this?" Daron asked as he handed the girl back her purse, gripping the paper.

"Keep it." Her cheeks went pink as she and her friend departed in a burst of hushed laughter. Daron swallowed and flipped through the contents. Lottie's style always read more like a story than a news account, adding edge and dramatics where she liked. *Honesty with flair*, Eva called it, endlessly amused. Daron, not so much. The piece chronicled the incidents of Spectaculore so vividly, he might've thought it all a hoax were he not in the thick of the madness. A thrilling tale to any reader, no doubt.

His eyes latched onto the section detailing the contestants and judges, and immediately regretted it.

> ... old, notable names of the stage, these judges come from "a long line of tradition amongst magicians," Mayor Eilin states. A tradition the aforementioned contestants seem all too eager to carry on.

> In contrast, nontraditional does not even begin to describe the pairing of Judge Demarco, the infamous Daring Demarco who's emerged out of retirement—and the current crowd favorite, a notorious dark horse in her own right, Kallia. The two have reportedly been "inseparable" and "mad over each other" from the start; and sources say since teaming up, the partners have kept busy perfecting their final performance in private. Others, however, speculate with a question all of Glorian is really hungry for an answer to:

> Amidst a dangerous, thorny garden, can a partnership bloom into something more?

> For even in the darkest show business, the heart still beats. And if this show has taught its viewers any lesson, it's that anything can happen behind closed doors.

> Both parties refused to give any further comment—

"Judge Demarco! What a surprise."

Daron suppressed the frustrated sigh firing up his throat for a morsel of enthusiasm. "Hello, Janette—"

He froze at the sight of the mayor's daughter, eagerly smiling in a long, dusky-pink coat, arm in arm with a beaming Lottie de la Rosa. "Yes, Dare. Quite a surprise."

She all but dangled his name in front of him, as casually as she'd raked it in the news. By the end of the piece, he'd been tempted to rip the paper to shreds but restrained himself by closing it, stone-faced. "Good morning."

"How are you faring, after last night, Mister Demarco? It was quite a scare, what happened to those . . ." Janette's face paled, a glimmer of remembrance before she shook her head. "I swear, this show has brought nothing but trouble."

"At least it's attracted some business." Lottie assessed the crowded state of the Prima lobby, before honing in on the paper locked between his fingers. "And I see you've read the latest." Her eyes gleamed. "Raz was right. I didn't even have to do much of anything. It's a wild ride all on its own. My kind of story."

For Janette's prior aversion to the press, she sure took quite an interest in silently staring at her feet at that moment.

"We're not characters for you to play around with," Daron bit out. "Our lives aren't for you to sensationalize."

"Don't act put out because you don't appreciate the angle I chose for you." Lottie inspected her nails, shrugging. "You refused to chat with me, so I did the best I could with what I had. No lies, just deduction. And the readers obviously agree."

She knew that last bit would stir a reaction in him, and he hated how much it had. He shouldn't give a damn what people thought, but such gossip wouldn't do him or Kallia any favors moving forward. False or not, rumors always consumed the truth. Not that Lottie cared which side won out.

Janette primly coughed, switching the subject. "If your schedule isn't too filled, Lottie and I were going to have some tea. Would you care to join?" Her eyes trailed to his waiting palm on the bannister. "Or are you about to go up?"

His simmering anger deflated in a blink. "No, I'm waiting—just standing . . . here." He seized his hand back. "I'm waiting."

The journalist's face subtly lit up. "For *who*?"

Janette sighed, as if the last thing she wanted was to hear the answer. "Tea and cakes are *far* more preferable to standing around alone. We were about to discuss the upcoming ball. Lottie graciously offered to cover the whole event."

Daron masked his shock. No way could they entertain the idea of having the event after all that had happened. "The ball is still . . . ?"

"Of course! If the show must go on, so must the party." Janette, oblivious, barreled on. "Father was a little concerned, too. But eventually, we both agreed that we've put far too much effort and money into renovating the Alastor Place to change plans now."

It was an effort for Daron to keep his mouth shut. He couldn't imagine the rest of the competition going smoothly, much less a lavish party. Too many accidents. Too many risks. Nothing was more damning than pretending that it couldn't possibly get any worse.

"Lottie's keen to spotlight the night as the event of the year in all of Soltair! Can you believe it?" Pride shone so brightly in the girl's eyes, Daron couldn't hold it against her. "And we were also talking about how of all the judges, she hasn't had a chance to profile you yet. Which is absurd, since you're apparently old friends. It's such a funny coincidence."

"Yes," Lottie chimed in. "So funny."

Daron was sweating. Unaware, Janette's smiling gaze widened. "You should absolutely join us! We won't take no for an—"

"I'm afraid he can't."

Relief set in as he turned to find Kallia standing with the same guard from before, her head tilted and hip cocked in that expectant manner of hers. She wore a simple outfit—a purple buttoned shirt pale as lilac cinched by a long, black skirt. The only pops of color, her lips red as the rose barrette clipped by her ear.

His mind blanked entirely. Seeing her in the morning light, that scowling red mouth of hers. He knew what it felt like, pressed against his.

"We have an appointment," Kallia reminded firmly.

"Yes. Yes, we do." He turned back to the ladies with a small, apologetic smile. "We have some show matters to take care of. Must've slipped my mind." Too eager. He forced his movements to slow when he faced Kallia. "Shall we?"

Her stare lingered on the journalist before dropping to his offered elbow. Without preamble, she brushed past it. "Yes, let's get on with it."

It was a smack in the face. She was so distant, he wondered if he'd simply imagined last night. He recovered quickly, following after her, same as the guard who gave no sign of recognition. Only a nasty smirk of amusement.

"Keep up, Judge Demarco," Kallia called over her shoulder, letting him lag behind. "We've got a lot of work to do."

She regarded him like an annoyance. Or worse, a stranger. "I'm not the one who came down late," he muttered. "I've been waiting all morning for you." As soon as he said it, he swore the edges of her lips quirked up.

The moment Kallia stepped onto the bustling street, people started sneaking looks and whispering. Without a care, she continued walking as if nothing were amiss. As if everything from last night was not even worth a second thought to her.

Daron reached for her. "Kallia—"

"Wait," she snarled, her strides becoming more determined through the clusters of pedestrians. He didn't know what made it more impossible to follow, her or the crowd rapidly filtering in. A wave crashing, over and around them. Even the guard trailing behind appeared concerned by the influx, sweat trickling down his face at the constant bump of shoulders that pushed him farther and farther away.

The breath knocked out of Daron at the grip on his arm.

"Do you know how annoying it is, to wake up to an old man outside your door who won't leave you alone?" Kallia huffed, eyes alight. Just as his pulse regained normalcy, it picked right up again, especially when she took his hand in hers with a squeeze. Every so often she shot a look behind her, powering them through the street. "This way, or we'll never lose him."

———

Kallia had never been so relieved to lock the doors of the Ranza Estate behind her. No guards. No looks and whispers following them, more than usual it seemed.

"I'm honestly astounded Mayor Eilin remembered me." She let her head rest back against the door. "This would've been the perfect opportunity to leave me in the dust, completely defenseless."

"You, defenseless?" Chuckling, he smoothed back his dampened hair from his forehead. One side of his lips curled, and it was all she could focus on.

The press of them against her neck, her jaw.

Her skin flushed, remembering it all. Their shoulders barely touched against the door. Yet the slightest brush made even the walls feel as if they were shifting closer. His eyes found hers. The comforting shade of brown darkened.

In one sure movement, he turned, surrounding her so entirely, and Kallia's breath caught. A sliver of distance lingered between them, questioning, before he took her hand and dropped his head by hers. "Good morning," he whispered, and she could hear his smile. "How did you sleep last night?"

Not well. The worst, most restless night of sleep she'd ever had. But as his jaw scraped against her cheek, she'd never been more awake. More aware. His knee knocked right by hers, his hand spreading her fingers against the door. Last night he'd been bolder, but today, he was patient. Waiting for her to turn her chin up and meet him halfway.

Remember what I said.

She flinched right as her hand found Demarco's waist, fisting the warm shirt fabric, all of a sudden cold.

"What's the matter?"

Kallia forced her face away from his. No more distractions, no more pretending everything was all right. If she looked, she'd forget what she came here to do. And she couldn't, this time. No matter the consequence, she *needed* to get him away. Away from Jack.

He wasn't safe.

"Kallia."

Jack's voice whispered its way into her thoughts while Demarco's was at her ear.

Her eyes shut.

"You were right. Before." Her voice droned heavily, in line with the script in her head. "When you said you were a judge and I was a contestant."

Little by little, his face fell. "What do you mean?"

"Technically, you're my mentor. How would it look if . . ." They already had the answer to that question. Her insides gripped tightly with each new breath, and she broke. "I don't want that. Don't want any of this."

"Wait."

Demarco grasped at her elbow, enough to stop her from pulling open the door.

"Is this about the paper?"

Her brow furrowed. "What?"

"About us, the article from the paper . . ." When she gave no sign of recognition, even more disbelief carved into his expression. He stepped back, spearing a hand into his hair. "Then where is this coming from?"

"From you."

"Before. That was *before*—" His lips flattened into a hard line. "What I said before . . . things have changed."

"*Nothing* has changed. We're still in one big game, playing different parts. This will never work if we want to win."

"Why not?" Doubt crossed his face in shadows. "I thought last night . . . you felt it, too, didn't you?"

Kallia bit the inside of her cheek, the sharp pain masking the knife in her chest. She didn't think this would hurt so much. She'd withheld information from him before, about her past. About Jack. But she'd never lied like this. To hurt him.

"We've been working closely together for some time. A lot has been building between us. It happens a lot in show business."

"Oh, I know, Kallia. And trust me." His jaw worked. "*This* doesn't feel like show business."

Steady, she told herself. *Breathe.*

Remember what I said.

"Maybe for you." She coolly tossed back her hair over her shoulder. "If I felt the same, maybe this would be different. But I can't afford to lose focus. If I drop my guard for one minute, I may be the next to go."

Demarco shook his head in disbelief. Refusal. She meant in the competition, but an accident could be headed her way all the same. At this point, no one was safe. Jack was right about that. She'd need all of her wits about her if the worst came to collect, and Demarco could not stand in that crossfire.

"Regardless, I know what I've always wanted," she added quietly. "And what I want is to win. *That's* what I came here for."

They were farther apart now. Kallia had moved from the door without realizing, backing away from him. Far enough to see the silence wedging deeper between them, turning distance into a feeling. A wall.

On the other side, everything in Demarco changed. His stance straightened, face closed. Like her, he could wear a mask well and at will. "If that's the way you feel."

Without another word, he turned and exited without a good-bye. Kallia's chest squeezed at the sight: his back, before the door shut behind him. The hike in his shoulders, the quickness of his steps.

A burning prickled at the backs of her eyes, almost causing her to laugh in disbelief.

Don't.

Even when she was alone, she wouldn't allow herself to cry. It wasn't a side of herself she indulged in, and she wouldn't start now.

Don't.

Kallia walked aimlessly through the Ranza Estate, the emptiest it had ever felt.

Don't.

Somehow it worked, for the tears were gone.

41

Daron took to the sidewalks of Glorian, walking nowhere in particular. Good thing, too. If his feet hadn't made the decision to leave, he would probably still be standing before Kallia like a statue.

I thought it was only me.

He replayed the past few moments in his head, again and again. When they'd shut the doors behind them, he'd been so ready to pull her to him. So drunk on memory and sensation—her heartbeat against his, his hands in her hair—that to meet the opposite made him question if any of it had been real.

I thought it was only me.

Her words. Her dismissal.

Something wasn't right. Kallia carried herself with a viciousness, not a cruelty. Then again, her ambition defined her. Guided her. And she'd made it quite clear he was not in the cards. Only a brief infatuation.

Same as her, she hadn't come here for that. The opposite, in fact. He loathed himself for the stark reminder. For forgetting.

If anything, Kallia woke him up. The overwhelming need for red dandelion tea had struck him as soon as he'd left. Eva would always brew a pot to clear their heads and the storms they weathered.

With the press, the shows, their family. They'd share in silence, sipping cup after cup, until the first person to finish it off would start a new pot.

His hands began shaking. She was the one he should have been focusing on.

Nothing shamed him more.

A breeze whispered around his neck as he drifted toward the mayor's house. A large, stark building right in the middle of the Fravardi Fold. It had been a while since he'd looked at the public records, useless as they might've been. Perhaps he had overlooked a detail, missed something.

Eva was still out there, somewhere.

He couldn't afford to waste any more time.

When Daron arrived, the doorman waved him through in recognition. His ears were ringing, head still heavy, but he'd never been more prepared to fall into the solitude of research. The smell of warm wood and worn books, even the dust in the air, soothed him. Only the rustle of paper and the wooden screech of a chair interrupted the silence. Usually the scholar overseeing the meager records collection could be found sleeping soundly at his desk, but no snores met his ears as he entered the main room. Only the testy tick of a tongue, right by the papers stacked over the main table.

Lottie de la Rosa.

For once, she was without a notepad, and he tensed even more at the absence. He edged back and turned as softly as he could, taking each step with care.

"If you're going to run away, at least make it fast."

His jaw snapped shut. Lottie had not even looked up as she turned a page. "Fleeing slowly only drags out the torture more."

Muscles frozen, he genuinely thought about making a run for it, but felt ridiculous enough already. With a sigh, he pivoted back calmly. "You always did have good senses."

"No, you just have bad feet." She finally lifted her chin up as he took a seat across from her. An edge of triumph in her eyes. "You never were the graceful one on stage."

His pulse started up, like a gear kicked into place. "What are you doing here, Lottie?"

"Ah, countering a question with a question. Good tactic." She grinned. "There are many answers. Obviously, I'm in Glorian to cover a show. But right now, in this poor excuse of a library, I'm here to learn. Best way to get my hands dirty is to know what they're touching. It's time to see if any of the rumors of the lost city in the woods are real."

"Trust me, you won't find much of anything in here."

"So you've been here already?" She didn't even sound surprised. "Looking for what?"

Her way of asking was always more for confirmation than answer, for she always knew. Just as he knew. Fury still lingered beneath her shiny, dagger-sharp veneer.

He reckoned he'd have to meet it someday.

"Silent as always, Daron. I suppose you also won't say where your partner has gone off to? I thought you'd only just left with her." Lottie pushed her glasses back up the bridge of her nose. "Trouble in paradise?"

She'd barely gotten a glimpse of his face, and already could see the broken pieces of his partnership. It was her job, after all. To find the loud in the quiet, unearth the chaos in the peace.

"What, so you can write another story about it?"

"And crush the dreams of my readers rooting for you two?" There was a mischievous twinkle in her eye. "Join me. It's the least you could do since you've returned all my letters *rudely* unread over the years. If anyone in this room has the right to be agitated, it should be me."

Daron scratched the back of his neck. "Can you blame me, Lottie? I needed time."

"I needed time, too, but I didn't go dark on the world to get it," she said.

"No, you chose to spin stories for your own gain, for the people. As you always do."

She barely flinched, staring hard. "That's my job, Daron. And it's what Eva would've wanted—"

"Don't." He shook at the scalding rise in his blood. "You don't know what she would've wanted. She'd never want to be headline news like that."

"Clearly it's what you wanted, too, since you didn't fight me on it. You didn't do anything."

Do something. Do anything.

Blame. Fresh and sharp as it had been that night, when she'd thrown it in his face.

"Despite what you think of me, I'm looking for answers. I'm *still* looking for them." Lottie slammed her book shut. "I don't know what you've been doing since she's been gone, but I thought maybe you'd be looking, too. Especially when I heard that, of all places, you ended up here."

He crossed his arms. "What I'm doing here is none of your concern."

"It is if it concerns *her.*" She took off her glasses, as if to ensure every dagger she glared his way aimed true. "I'm not oblivious. Why else would you go out of your way to judge a small circus show like this? In Glorian, of all places, which we know—"

"Is only a dead end," he finished. "There's nothing here of interest to you. You should go, while you still can."

"You can't be serious. Dead end or not, there's something not right about this city, and you know it." She gave a slight shudder. "It's too quiet."

"What did you expect from a town that's been reclusive for decades? It's no New Crown."

"Certainly not." Lottie huffed, setting her books aside. "You mean you don't find it strange, how the people here act like there is no past—how they know nothing about what goes on beyond their gates? How their buildings are modeled after symbols of families no one really talks about?" she posed, before gesturing roughly at the small library. "How *this* is all the history they preserved for a city that's stood just as long as all the other cities in Soltair?"

It was Daron's turn to shudder. He'd allowed himself to forget the strangeness, living here long enough to accept unanswered questions as one of Glorian's quirks.

Or perhaps he'd forgotten to question altogether. So distracted, so selfish. Lost in a dream he'd only just woken from.

"What are you suggesting?" Daron asked. "Another conspiracy theory to add to the pile?"

"For Zarose sake, you and the others can't even *leave* the city. Nothing is too unbelievable to be true . . . at this point." She paused, tracing her fingernail up and down the wrinkled spine of a book. "It would be easier if we worked together."

He kept quiet. If the written word was Lottie's weapon, silence was his.

"We need closure. We wouldn't both be here if we didn't," she insisted. "Tell me what you know, your side of the story, and we could piece everything together. It's what she would've—"

"*Don't* use her to manipulate me," he bit out. "I won't give you more material for your next piece."

"That's not what this is about," she whispered. "She was my friend."

"Yes, and just like then, I still can't trust you."

Her nostrils flared. Her fingers tapped along the surface, by her pen, as if fighting the urge to write. "Fine. But I'm not the only one in the wrong here. You are just as much to blame for how things unfolded, and if it comes to it, I'll fill in the pieces on my own."

Daron's face grew hot. "What are you talking about?"

"You didn't leave the business simply because of good ol' loss and heartache, did you?"

Everything in him stopped cold.

Her gaze contained more than curiosity. There was certainty.

"People who leave always have something to hide," she said, donning her glasses to return to her reading. "And before those secrets start to slip through the cracks, at the very least, your partner deserves to know."

Show no reaction, no emotion. No matter how well she poked and prodded. No matter how much it hurt. "You talked to Kallia?"

"Yes, some nights ago," she supplied rather drily. "I thought surely she must think the world of you, to be able to ignore your background. But imagine my utter astonishment when clearly she knew *nothing* of what happened before. Of Eva, your career. The accident."

"And you didn't seize the opportunity to stir the pot? How unlike you."

A muscle ticked in her cheek. "She wouldn't have believed me anyway. Only you."

His chest tightened under a new, unfamiliar weight.

"Then again," she said, slowing rapping her fingers against the table's edge. "*A Most Dark and Daring Past* has a nice, timely ring to it. I'm sure this city would like a refresher."

How could Eva have possibly been friends with someone like this?

Glaring, Daron shot up from his seat and stalked away, the rage rushing in his veins so forcefully, almost like magic. And fear, slowly stopping him short of the exit. "Why are you doing this?"

"Because when something is broken, you need to tell the truth. And I'd hate to do that for you, because Kallia's your partner. Which means she'll find out, one way or another," Lottie shouted at his back, as he resumed his departure. Away from her, away from everything. "The truth *always* comes out, in due time. Out of you, and this city."

To the master's displeasure, the morning papers spoke of nothing but the show.

Spectaculore Speculation:
Players Entrapped in a Wild Game

MISSING PERSONS
and Comatose Contestants

Magicians Mentoring Magicians
for Magnificent Finale

Each headline ran with a ridiculous note, the images and stories accompanying them even more so. And yet the master read them whenever the news crossed his table. Wading through the scandalous phrasing intended solely to seize readers' attentions, he saw the underlying truth. The danger beneath the gossip that turned everything into a farce, until they truly believed it was all just a game.

Such thoughtless moths, following the spotlight.

Feeding it.

The master crumpled the paper before throwing it aside. He'd ignored the mirror long enough, the summons from Sire to put an end to all of this, like he should've done long ago.

He could've waltzed into that city, and wiped the whole game board clean once more. Even if she tried to stop him, even if *they* sensed him on their grounds, at least he'd have done his duty. Served his only purpose on this worthless land.

And now he was too late. Everything was too far beyond his control, and the countdown had begun.

Four magicians missing. Three unresponsive.

Two more hospitalized.

And then one.

Almost

Almost

Almost

Their whispers ticked in the back of his head as surely as a clock, waiting.

ACT IV

ENTER THE SHADOWS:
THE TRICKS OF LIGHT, THE TRUTH FROM LIES

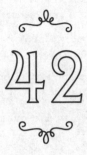

42

The bleak morning trickled through the windows above as Kallia strode down the aisle of hospital beds. Two magicians, Soloce and Lamarre, remained comatose, their bodies turned by the staff every so often to bring movement to their muscles in hopes of waking them. Only Robere's bed stood empty. He'd been discharged early in the morning so no one could see the wraps across his face. Similarly bandaged, Judge Bouquet slept soundly in his bunk, mostly due to the nearly empty bottle of heavy tonic consistently replenished at his bedside.

The bitter stench of coffee stirred no reaction from the bedridden men as she walked past, carrying a tray with a freshly filled pot and two cups. Seated by Juno's bed at the end of the row, Canary perked up. "Bless you, prima donna. I'm in need."

"Thought you would be." Kallia set the tray on one of the side tables. "Last night went late, yet here you are."

Ever since the first night of the circus's opening, Kallia had freely offered her talents to the Conquerors. Special effects, extra assistance, adding flair wherever it was needed. Even more so now, ever since Juno and the magicians fell. After nights of watching the

Conquerors take their stages with Juno missing from hers, it was all Kallia could do.

The girl appeared just as sickly as the other magicians lying near. Her brown hair, tied back and dulled. Her tattoos, last fashioned as long-stemmed feathers pluming against her hands, neck, and face, had faded considerably to a gray tinge. Her eyelids, fluttering every so often. Asleep, though not entirely at peace.

"If she wakes up and no one is around, we'll never hear the end of it." The flame-eater knocked back a hearty gulp from her cup, shuddering afterward. "Also, you're one to talk. You don't look any better than me."

"Thanks."

"I mean that as kindly as possible. Something isn't right." Canary spoke into a yawn, observing her. "Everything about you seems . . . smaller, somehow."

"I'm fine." Kallia concentrated on the black liquid steaming the edges of her cup. The first few nights, she'd stayed up with the Conquerors as they wound down with a few drinks and some music around a silver bonfire. Of late, she returned to her hotel room, too exhausted to even change before hitting the mattress, escaping into dreams to rid this heaviness hanging over her.

Every trick was a trial, and nothing was worse than someone noticing.

"You want to know why I really dropped out of the academy?" Canary stared pensively into her cup, letting the steam swirl against her face. "I actually thought I could do it all on my own, and I'm not even that skilled a magician."

Her voice was not the same as it usually was amongst the Conquerors. Loud, boisterous, on the edge of laughter. A leader's gaiety, to lift any low spirits. But this softness struck Kallia all the more, the rareness of it. "You made it, though, right?" she supplied. "You run the Conquerors."

"I run *with* the Conquerors," she corrected. "Nothing can be done alone. Nothing worthwhile, anyway."

"But what if you want to make it alone? To prove something to yourself?"

"And what exactly are you proving?" Canary countered. "You don't often find good people in this business, but when you do, it's precious. Nearly impossible."

Impossible. She'd been lucky then, to find them as she did. When she first walked through the gates of Glorian, nothing had felt right until she met Aaros. Her nights had been empty, until she found Canary and the Conquerors.

And Demarco.

Her heart gripped. For so long she'd envisioned only herself on the stage, an image that always kept her going: basking in the spotlight, hearing her name and cheers over everything else.

Strange how applause was just noise, when you were all alone.

"Boss?"

At the sudden snap of fingers, Kallia blinked awake. In the Prima. It took her a moment to place herself sometimes. Glorian often felt like a blur now, of firelight and endless cheers, to hospital visits and circus tents deadened under daylight. Before it was Canary, but now Aaros sipped at his coffee across from her, his eyes piercing her over the rim.

"I can't take this anymore." He set his cup down with a clatter. "It's only been a few days and it feels like the parents are fighting."

She blinked wearily. "We're not fighting."

"No, you're not talking." His frown deepened. "You're not trying to do *anything*."

If only he knew. As a friend, Aaros was relatively safe. Jack hadn't brought him up as a threat in any way. And selfishly, she was not ready to give him up. To lose anyone else.

Even though he could still annoy the guts out of her.

"Sure, take *his* side," Kallia snarled.

"Listen, we're all on the same team. It's not like Demarco's doing anything, either." He sighed, frustrated. "He's been just as much of a shut-in, doesn't even go to the Ranza Estate anymore."

Her breath quieted when she thought of the greenhouse. How long would it take for flowers like that to die? There was no way she could go back. It would be too hard.

"So boring, really," Aaros continued. "He spends most of his time going to this town's shoddy post office when he's not in his room."

Kallia shot him a look. "You've been following him?"

"I *knew* you'd be curious."

She scoffed, though the tight coil in her chest relaxed. He wouldn't leave Glorian, even if he could. He had more dignity than to let her coldness defeat him. The same could not be said for her. She cringed, remembering the things she'd said to him.

Her finger traced her lips, remembering that, too.

It had worked all too well. Jack hadn't appeared in her room or showed hints of his presence in the dark. No accidents, no one missing or turned up injured. Whether or not his silence marked his approval, it was a temporary peace.

Aaros abruptly kicked at her seat. "Look alive, boss."

Her brow drew at the shadow falling over the small table from behind her. She inhaled stiffly, catching that fresh clean smell edged with a spice she couldn't name. She hated these little pieces of him she'd collected, that her memory would not let go.

"Sorry to interrupt," Demarco said, looking between them.

"Not interrupting at all." Aaros rose. "I was about to use the restroom."

Kallia glared daggers across the table. "Funny, I was about to do the same."

"No, you were going to order me another cup." He threw her an impish grin before tipping his hat. "Nature calls." He all but skipped away from the table, in the opposite direction of the public facilities.

"Does he know he's going the wrong way?"

"Taking the long route, is all." She rapped her fingernails slowly against the table's surface. "I was actually about to pick up the check, so I don't—"

"Let me get it," he murmured, gesturing at the nearest waiter before Kallia could. He thanked the man, scribbling his room number and signature on the bill. It was such a normal scene, them at a café table, and she almost wished she could play along. With him next to her, the act only grew more difficult. The air between them, infinitely tighter.

Damn it.

"What do you want?" she blurted out.

Never one to act oblivious, Demarco exhaled. "If you humor me, this won't take long."

There was something removed in his gaze, the straight line of his mouth. Like looking at a stranger, and it tore a hole in Kallia worse than any lie.

Just say it. Just leave.

"Will you come with me to my room?"

Kallia lightly braced herself against the table. "E-excuse me?"

Normally, he'd be stumbling over his words, citing decorum and polite intent. Here, he was calm as ever. "I want to show you something." His brow hardened. "I *have* to."

Panic quietly flared through her. "Why can't you do it down here?"

"It's . . . private."

"You don't need to tell me everything, Demarco. If it's something better unsaid, it might be best to leave it that way."

"I'm guessing it won't stay that way for long," he said, lips flattening. "Regardless, it's something you should know. Something I want you to know, from me."

That seized her attention. This answer held weight, the kind he'd never give on their walks. No questions, until now.

"Please." The cracks in his calm and composed mask gave way in the trickle of sweat at his temple. His breath, deliberately slow.

He was nervous.

So was she. So nervous, that a rational part of her mind objected. She was better off leaving him, closing the door altogether. Locking it.

It's precious. Nearly impossible.

Her muscles tensed, heart squeezed.

"Make it quick, Demarco," Kallia heard herself say as she rose. Her heart blared in refusal, but her mouth kept running. "Lead the way."

Daron had no idea what he was doing. And still, Kallia followed.

There was no going back, after this. It was a wonder the other judges hadn't raised his issues before, though they'd probably spoken at length behind his back. Men caught up in scandals and tragedies so often walked from them unscathed.

And he was one of them. So lost in his search of Eva, that he hadn't noticed he'd come out of it with barely a scratch.

How foolish, to think it would never rise back to the surface.

As they reached the first floor, it struck him how easy it had been to turn back into strangers. Too easy. Their laughter gone, light manners replaced with impeccable posture and footsteps matching the other's almost too perfectly.

He gripped his room key in his pocket, the metal teeth biting at his palm as they veered toward his door. Daron had always thought his room far too big for one person, but as Kallia entered and strode right into the common area, everything fit. The large fireplace was not so menacing. The windows, not as towering. The couch, once too big, now just right when she sat on one end. "Demarco?"

So often, he'd imagined her there with him. The reality was far more intimidating. He blinked. "Sorry."

"You don't . . . seem well." She sounded wary. "Maybe it's best if I—"

"No, I'm fine." *Get it together.* Daron inhaled, already stepping toward the dining table he'd pushed against the wall. "Over here."

Every inch of him tensed at the entire surface covered in ripped brown packaging envelopes on one side, and newspaper spreads on the other. Kallia's gaze immediately fell to them, widening at the large-lettered headlines dancing across each stack.

"Demarco Dares Once More," she read slowly, her finger pausing over the black-and-white inked picture of a young magician bowing on a stage. "This is you."

"Just a few years ago, when I was the Daring Demarco." He smiled sadly at the images splashed across the table that showcased him as the centerpiece of the act. If one went by the images alone, you'd think he'd accomplished every spectacle by himself.

Foolish are the ones who believe anything great can be done alone.

"Weather storms onstage, floating sword fights, saving a burning boarding school?" She traced every headline, finally looking up. "You used your magic like that?"

He shrugged, though the school incident was one of his prouder moments. He traced the crisp papery surfaces, not old enough to yellow, but faded. It was a miracle Gastav had been able to send them from Tarcana so quickly. Even the manager at the post office long ago stopped dragging strange looks his way with his visits. No shipments of strange plants to fill an empty greenhouse this time, but a collection of his glory days immortalized in print. He'd never bothered to read them, barely recognized himself between the words.

Dread gusted through him as she reached the end of the table.

The last of the issues.

Daron hadn't been able to look, immediately facing it down. His shoulders bunched at the sound of paper crinkling before she flipped it over. He forced himself to look at it from over her shoulder. The mirror he could never fully avoid.

A photograph dominated the center, of a closed coffin lined with flowers.

"Daring Deed Ends in Tragic Last Act." No more than a shaky whisper as she read on in silence. It tormented him, watching her. Remembering the first time he'd read Lottie's words, how the walls closed in on him like a prison.

Outside of Glorian, it was a story that followed him relentlessly. A promising young performer and his charming assistant, a talented pair who never failed to light up a show together. A true stage match, with a tragic end.

"You loved her, didn't you?"

Kallia didn't look up from the paper, studying every word. Daron fought back the hardness working up his throat. Not once did the papers ever name her, not even in this one.

It's what she always wanted, Lottie insisted, and it only made Daron hate her more. Even the last story written about Eva had painted her as a lie.

"My sister." A burning began at the back of his eyes. "Eva."

He hadn't spoken her name out loud to anyone in so long. No one would understand, no one would believe.

A hand came to rest softly on his back, circling slowly.

"I had no idea," she whispered. "I'm so sorry, Daron."

He looked up at the ceiling, fighting the urge to pull her to him. To bring those hands around his neck, to feel something more than darkness.

Would she believe him?

He squeezed the bridge of his nose, hoping to siphon the pressure racing to his skull. "It's not true, Kallia."

"What's not?"

"Eva. She isn't dead," he said, swallowing hard. "She disappeared."

Grief did funny things to people, Kallia knew, even if she'd never properly felt it. The death of Sire hadn't fazed her. The loss of Mari came close, but realizing someone wasn't real couldn't be the same as losing someone who was. However many times Kallia mourned a friend, she might never know; Jack swept her grief away so diligently.

A small mercy, perhaps. But there was no puppeteer reigning over Demarco's mind, no one to wipe the pain away before it festered into something worse.

"What do you mean?" Kallia did her best to keep her voice even. She glanced furtively toward the papers to make sure she hadn't misread. The picture of the coffin adorned with flowers remained, framed with words and phrases in bold. *Tragic. Fallen. Vanishment. Last act. Funeral.*

"You don't believe me."

Something in Demarco's expression fractured as he walked out from under her grasp to the other end of the table. Kallia's hand hovered a moment too long before she let it fall to her side. "If you don't explain fully, how can I?"

From the other end of the table, he shot her a look. Uncertain, dubious. She hated how someone had put that in his eyes—many people, it seemed.

Yet he must've caught something in her eyes, too, for he relented with a sigh. Exhaled, as if breathing for the first time in a while. "Eva's my older sister by two years. Same as me, she's a born magician. Always had a sharp eye for the stage, a brilliant mind to entertain an audience." He spoke slowly, with care. "But women were not allowed to perform when we first started. It was . . . just the way things were."

Kallia's brow arched. *"Were?"*

He had the decency to look chagrined. "There's still a long, long way to go," he amended. "But you, having a top spot in a competition like this? That would've been unheard of when we first started the show circuit. We found out the hard way when venues turned away our act for months. Nobody wanted the Daring Duo. And our aunt certainly wasn't keen on Eva wasting her talents on the stage when she could one day lead the Patrons."

"Girls can't take the stage, but it's fine if they take over the magicians' vanguard?"

"The Patrons don't exactly parade themselves across Soltair like performers do," he explained. "It's a respectable position, but not the loudest. One that comes with a lot of responsibilities Eva didn't want to tie herself to for the rest of her life."

"Why didn't you take over, then?" It seemed a natural fit. One that allowed him to use his power with purpose, favor the shadows over the spotlight. That he'd led such a notable performing career had been the biggest surprise of all to her when she'd first met him.

"Eva was the better magician," he admitted without shame. "Aunt Cata wanted her to inherit the Patrons, but Eva didn't want to be the next Aunt Cata. Our aunt wasn't the biggest supporter of the path Eva wanted, and neither were the venues. It was suggested we take on an assistant to incorporate more elaborate acts so no one could refuse. But Eva and I didn't trust anyone else on the stage with us." His brown eyes shadowed. "So she took on the role herself. Disguised herself, so no one would know."

Kallia frowned. "To get you through the door?"

"For a chance to be on stage," he said, digging his hands into his pockets. "She'd always say that even if everyone came for the Daring Demarco, the applause was for her. Even behind masks and costumes, she made her mark clear. She designed the shows, supplemented the magic, helped me brainstorm every trick to be better than the last."

"She sounds brilliant." Kallia smiled, a little in awe. To hear of another magician like this—like her—made her feel that much more seen. As if she'd been alone, screaming into a void, only to realize others had been there with her all along. "I almost wish she'd left you in the dust and gone solo."

Demarco let out a quiet laugh. "You two would get along famously."

The way he talked about his sister, it was as if she might walk through the door at any moment. "What happened in your last act?"

His knuckles whitened over the edge of the table. "The props for our newest set hadn't been ready in time, so we decided to fall back on a popular trick from our early days. *The Vanishment.*" He uttered it like a ghost's name. "All you need are twin mirrors—of the same make, from the same maker. Most theaters keep their mirrors uniform, so it was easy to cobble the act together when needed."

A chill ran down Kallia's spine. "How does the act go?"

"Have you ever walked through walls before?" At this, she shook her head. "It's the same concept, but it's tough magic that requires transfiguring your entire body. I was always shit at it so I didn't even try, but when Eva encountered difficult magic, she took on the challenge until she could do it in her sleep. She spent over a year trying to walk through concrete and brick and all manner of stone—all to make gliding through material thin as glass seem easy as breathing.

"So for the act, I would unveil a mirror. Floor-length, front and center. I'd knock against the glass like a door, confirm with the audience that it was indeed only a mirror," he said. "And when the mood of the room lightened with laughter, I'd push Eva in."

Kallia tensed, envisioning the act.

The dramatic silence, the alarmed gasps.

"She was supposed to cross out of the other mirror, waiting in our dressing room, and walk out. People would cry out in shock, applause would sound." Demarco blinked slowly. As if coming to after years asleep, the nightmare still clinging to him. "But something went wrong. This mirror was different."

"Different how?"

"It fractured as soon as she passed through, and she never re-emerged." The moment weighed on him as he spoke, as if it never stopped. "No matter how long we waited, no matter how long I sat across from the other mirror, she . . . never returned."

A heaviness sank inside Kallia as if an anchor had dropped in her chest. "So they ruled it a death, and you stopped performing," she murmured. "And you think she's still out there?"

"I'm her brother, I'd know if she was truly gone." Demarco bristled, arms crossed. "The question is: *where?* I've been searching for years, and never had a clear lead until this show was announced."

"Glorian? What does Glorian have to do with anything?"

"Eva was eternally curious, and I thought there was something to that. *The city lost in the woods,* she called it, always dreaming about it. Collecting rumors wherever she could—the more ridiculous, the better." His small chuckle was a hollow sound. "She thought something existed here that didn't want to be found. She had her own theories, convinced there was magic here. Spectaculore was my only chance in, so I took it to explore."

"But . . . there *is* magic here." Kallia treaded cautiously. "There's magic everywhere."

"No, a different kind. Something worth hiding. The kind that could cross time and defy all reason. Power that could"—his jaw clenched—"bring someone back from anything—death or else-where."

Fighting back a shiver, Kallia shook her head. Jack never said it wasn't possible, but he'd always dissuaded her from asking. There were some problems too unsolvable for magic. Or maybe that's what they wanted everyone to think, to keep them from asking such questions in the first place.

"Well, it can certainly explain how a city with a way in suddenly has no way out."

His gaze flickered to her face in disbelief. "You . . . you don't think it's complete nonsense?"

"I'm the last person to judge what is and isn't nonsense." Kallia shrugged, considering him. "Question is, have you found anything that makes you feel like it's not?"

He looked down at the table, at his life laid out before him. So badly, she wanted to wipe the darkness from his face, to take the hurt away from the memory.

She wondered if that's why Jack did it, if he'd cared too much to let loss swallow her whole. Not that it justified the act, but Kallia could understand why she might do it. If she could rip the grief away, the ropes that bound him to this hurt, she would do it in a heartbeat. Even if he hated her afterward.

"Yes, and it has to do with something else," he said. "Something I haven't told you."

Nothing shook Kallia inside more than his tone. All the times Demarco said nothing, never answered her, stretched raw across his face. "I'm not who you think I am. I haven't been, in years."

The world shrank. "What do you mean?"

He was all edges. He ran a hand down his face, his knuckles curling into a fist. "After Eva disappeared, so did my magic."

The silence was stifling. Kallia lost hold of her breath, her heart racing in her ears. Somewhere in it, she heard Jack. Laughing.

"What?"

No denial. Only pain.

"That's impossible." It didn't make sense. She didn't want to believe it, *couldn't.* "You're . . . you're a born magician."

"I know."

"Wait a second, you—" She pressed at her temple, the sudden throbbing. "You performed magic, I've *seen* it. Felt it."

The night of the second performance. That day at the Ranza Estate. Those hadn't been imagined. Her bones still vibrated with that power from Demarco. The light between them, that force, had been real.

"No, I-I don't know . . . it comes and goes in bursts, but nothing I can control or take credit for. Not really." Demarco's voice grew hoarse, heavy. "My magic has been gone since that last act, until I came to Glorian. Until I met you."

She shut her eyes. Looking at him was suddenly too difficult. "So you've been lying to everyone, this entire time?"

The pieces fell and fit before her in ways that hadn't made sense before. The questions he avoided, the answers he withheld. His method of abstaining that others mocked. The way he'd agreed to mentor her, before cutting ties entirely.

Weak, Jack had always called him.

This was why.

This.

"How could you not tell me?" Tears simmered beneath her eyelids. She feared if she opened them, they would fall. "Me. Your partner. How could you lie to *me*?"

"I'm sorry," he said roughly, and all she heard was his pain. Raw, and truthful. "I-I wanted to . . . I was selfish. I didn't know what I was doing. What I was thinking. I thought if I told you, you would see that I have nothing. I *am* nothing."

Her heart twisted. "What?"

"I'm not powerful." He looked away, his breath hitching. "I'm not the magician I used to be. My name means nothing."

She should've pitied the shame pouring from him. But nothing made her more furious. Like a lit match, catching across her skin.

"I don't care about your name, Demarco. I never did." Kallia snapped. "I don't care if you were a god or a king before any of this. *None* of that has ever mattered to me."

The tension in his face dropped. "It didn't?"

The hope she found there stirred something inside her. Memories, shaken loose. Jack, opening a door with only the jut of his chin. Him, adjusting the lights of the club to her routine with the wave of his palm. Him, waiting in her dressing room with another pouch of seeds to grow, and a bouquet of wildflowers still blooming and un-furling before her. Power, forever at his fingertips, had always been something to give, to glory in and share.

And her first flower from Demarco: a broken rose he'd caught that had fallen from her hand. Not even the greenhouse, but that limp stem, petals falling off. It had even died, shortly after.

It took her by surprise, how every flower she'd ever known paled in comparison.

To keep steady, standing, Kallia gripped the edge of the table until her fingers went stiff. "Why are you telling me this, now?" She nodded down at the papers. "Why show me all of this?"

Silence stretched between them, before he stepped forward. "You would've heard my story from someone else eventually. I wanted you to hear it from me."

"Why?"

A lump formed in her throat the closer he drew.

"Because even if you didn't believe me, I knew you would listen."

Kallia pressed a hand to his chest, stopping him.

"Because I wanted to give you something true. For once."

"Please." Kallia said it more to herself, not realizing how much her hands had been shaking until his wrapped around hers, stilling them. She never thought he would get this close to her again, never realized how much the distance ate at her.

His voice went thick. "Do you want me to stop?"

He would, if she told him. He would pull away without another word, because he listened.

Wordlessly, she lifted his hand to the side of her neck, watching his expression. Uncertain, but patient. Burning, as he touched only where she guided his hands—one at her hip, while the other at her neck rose to her jaw. His fingers tangled into her hair, the pins she'd speared through starting to snag back, undone.

"What do you want, Kallia?"

Even in doubt she knew. And without another thought, she pressed her lips to his.

She wanted him to stop watching her like a stranger. She wanted him to stop looking at her like she would disappear. She wanted him safe. She wanted his hands on her. His laughter in her ears. She wanted them for more than a moment. She wanted more time.

He kissed her back readily, relief slamming through them both. Warming her eyes, catching in their breaths.

He held tighter as she gripped the back of his neck, pulling him close. As close as possible. The backs of her thighs met the corner of the table in a light hiss of pain that startled her, yet she didn't break away. With a heated curse, Demarco lifted her by the waist and set her on the edge.

Her thoughts swam as he kissed her jaw. "Wait, the newspapers . . ."

Demarco gave a gruff hum against her skin as he dragged her to him with one hand, before his other swept behind her to the crash of papery stacks hitting the floor.

Every nerve under Kallia's skin lit on fire. She wanted to do away with her coat, her boots, every article of clothing so she could breathe.

Every breath was torture, not enough air.

Not enough.

She began unbuttoning his coat instead. He shouldered it off as she went to work on the collar of his shirt while his palms rubbed along her thighs—

"Hold on." He stopped short, panting. "We should talk first."

Kallia's gaze fell back on his reddened mouth. "We have been talking."

"And it was a lot. I just want to be sure."

"You're so honorable, it makes me sick sometimes."

His smile curled deeper, changing his face entirely. The most relaxed and patient she'd ever seen it. Like he didn't want to waste a single moment, staring at her just like this.

"I only want to know where your thoughts are. If they're in the same place as mine." He placed a small kiss on her mouth. "Because tomorrow morning . . . ." Another kiss. "I don't want you to shut me out like last time." He paused, before drifting his lips beneath her jaw. "And I don't think you do, either."

Need rolled inside Kallia so fiercely that she wrapped her legs around his, bringing him closer. He groaned. "Stop that."

"You're the one who put me here." Kallia leaned back invitingly, her spine touching the table. "There's enough room for two."

"Nice try," he bit out through a tortured grin. "How about you sit up so we can—"

A crash sounded.

The shatter of glass.

They broke apart instantly and searched the room. The walls. Ice settled in Kallia's chest as she observed the frame knocked facedown over a golden velour blanket, pieces of glass covering the carpet like silver rain.

Mirror shards.

"Holy *shit*. Did you feel the room shake or anything?" Demarco assessed the rest of the room, his jaw ticking. "Perhaps the nails broke off."

Kallia couldn't rely on perhaps. She saw only the blanket, pooling beneath the shattered mirror frame. A shield secured over the mirror, like hers always were.

Unless some other force knocked it off.

Kallia slid off the table, discovering her legs were far more wobbly than she'd anticipated. "I-I'm sorry, I have to go."

Demarco's face lost that glimmer of mirth. "Go where?"

She fixed herself up, hurrying across the floor without stepping on the fallen newspapers. So fixated on her path, she didn't realize Demarco was already there, stopping her by the elbows.

"What happened? Did I do something?" he asked, peering at her face. Concern shadowed across his eyes. "Kallia, you look . . ."

Remember what I said.

The trembling had returned. Not even she could hide it now. "Let me go."

"Stay." He spoke against her temple, pressing reassurances against her skin. "I can't help unless you tell me."

"No one can help me."

"Let me try." His voice grew heavy. "Please, let me *try.*"

Tears gathered again, and she cursed them. She couldn't put him closer to the line of fire than he already was. The thought of him injured, or disappeared altogether, made her want to retch.

"Not here," Kallia whispered, clutching him. There was no use in pretending anymore, no protection in it. "Come with me."

44

The Ranza Estate came into view ahead, its proud tiled roofs and sun-kissed stone exterior a sight so familiar, they might as well have declared this section of the city as their own. A home.

"Why are we here?"

Demarco had been quiet the entire way, keeping up with her pace without question. Even though he clearly had many burning inside. It didn't seem fair, after he'd told her so much.

"It's the only place where I've never felt watched."

"By who?" he asked, shutting the door behind them.

She didn't know how to begin. How to say anything, when she always carried that sinking feeling of Jack looking over her shoulder. Always watching, listening.

She gripped his shoulders, unable to stop herself from glancing around the room. She couldn't be certain of anything, not even a house without mirrors.

"Have you ever felt like you were trapped?" She gritted her teeth to keep them from chattering. "Like you have all this power, but in the end, you're still . . . *powerless*?"

The sharp edge of Demarco's mouth softened. "Yes."

Of course he knew. Better than anyone. That didn't make it any easier, but she wanted him to know. A truth, for all the ones he'd given her.

"Before all of this, I had an old friend who taught me a lot . . ." Every word traveled on one strained breath. They were so foreign, heavy. "He's a very powerful magician."

"Would I know of him?"

She winced at the laugh that shuddered from her. "No, he keeps to himself, mostly. Very private—"

"Did he hurt you?"

Her eyes flashed up at him. "Why would you ask that?"

He studied her. "Ever since I met you, it seemed like you were running away from something. Someone. No one runs unless it's from somewhere bad." His jaw ticked when she didn't deny it. "So it's true?"

The way he looked at her just then, she couldn't define it. Softness but also anger, simmering underneath in a promise. A certainly. A question, there in his eyes, seeking a way out. To her.

She had to look away.

"Not the kind of hurt you're thinking of." It was wrong to justify what sort of hurt mattered and what didn't. Anything that left scars came from hurt. Only now was she realizing the scars she bore and had trained herself not to see.

"I'd stayed," she stated, owning her choice. "Only because I didn't know all that was out here. What I'd been in." The shadow of the monster from her dreams returned, and the cold silhouettes of dark trees surrounding her. Images that would follow in the back of her mind forever.

"But sometimes," she continued, "it feels like he's still everywhere around me, watching. Waiting for me to . . ."

"To go back to him?" A harsh noise erupted from the back of his throat. "When you win, you'll have no time to look back."

"And if I don't?"

Ever since she'd arrived in Glorian, everything had always been a *when*. An *eventually*. Never *if*. Confidence came with armor. She wore it the night she left Hellfire House, the day she seized the audition, and every moment on stage after, never taking it off. To never doubt meant she had nothing to fear. There was only one option: win.

She couldn't afford to give doubt a voice.

Didn't mean it never whispered.

"Win now. The rest will come later," Demarco stressed. "Focus on what you do best, better than anyone else in this competition, and things will fall into place. Whatever happens after, we'll figure it out." Her eyes widened slightly as his shut tight. "You. I meant *you . . .*"

"You said *we*." Her pulse raced.

With a groan, he looked up at the ceiling. "Unless you were thinking of leaving me in the dust after this town."

He said it half-jokingly, his smile unsure. As if, for once, he couldn't get a solid read on what was to come after.

After.

It was difficult to imagine a clear after for herself, but she knew this much: the prospect of one without Demarco already filled her with loneliness. In Glorian, they'd become many things to each other, but the friend she found in him surprised her most of all. Whatever this was, she couldn't see herself leaving the city without it.

"This . . ." Kallia swallowed, her hand gliding up his arm. "For now, this stays between us."

Demarco tilted his head at her touch. "Embarrassed to be seen with me?"

It wasn't too long ago she'd scoffed those exact words at him, and she gave his shoulder a playful shove. "It's good like this, when it's just you and me."

"Trust me, so many others saw this coming way before we did. We've honestly got nothing to—"

"*Please.*" Her breath wavered. "Only until the show's over. Letting this go public would make everything that much harder, and you know it."

A brief frown creased his features. As if he didn't entirely believe her. But it disappeared in a smile, and she wondered if she'd imagined it as he curled her knuckles to his lips. "All right, no one will know." He kissed her inner wrist. "For now."

"Does this mean you'll be my partner again?" she asked, suddenly still. "Be on stage with me?"

He dropped her wrist between them. "I don't have magic, though. Not in the way I should, I'm not—"

"Don't you dare finish that sentence." Her temper flared. "It doesn't matter. You're my partner, which means I can't do this without you."

And I don't want to.

It was strange to no longer feel those thorns of lies, coursing through her with excuses. Freer, lighter. Even he appeared just as struck by it, though it was far from the first honest conversation they'd ever had. Just the first without those last walls. The tallest, most impenetrable ones that were never built to fall, but had done so anyway.

"What do you have in mind?"

Her face shifted from sweet to sly as she leaned forward, sliding his hand to her waist in a familiar position. "Just follow my lead."

With a snap of her fingers, the instruments lifted from the cases they'd lain in for too long, and began to play.

The night of the ball loomed nearer every day, the final performance of the show not too far behind. Daron ought to feel more
flustered at how little time was left, but he couldn't afford to slow
down. Neither of them could.

"Again," he said at the end of the song, swiping the sweat off his
neck, the dampness reaching down his spine. He would've taken his
shirt off, but they'd barely gotten through the routine the last time he
did. There would be no props for their final act, no rules except that
the contestants deliver one hell of a performance.

Naturally, Kallia chose a dance.

A complicated collection of movements on the sort of stage no
other would dare cross.

Even in his performance days, Daron had never pushed himself
so hard to hit every move right, nor had he ever been so distracted.
Behind the doors of the Ranza Estate, even more so when they were
in public. Everyone watched them with eager eyes, renewed interest
at the sight of them together again. He could hardly believe it himself.

"We should take a break," Kallia suggested, stretching out her feet and legs. She sounded weary, but would never admit it. Neither would he.

Practice. It was a word drilled into his head the moment Kallia had devised her act, and Daron long ago made his peace with the whole theatricality of it, throwing all of his focus into playing the perfect part. He couldn't give her power, but he would be her partner every step of the way.

And by some miracle, that was enough.

"Again," Daron repeated, smoothing back the damp ends of his hair.

"And I thought *I* was hard on myself," Kallia said from the ground, her breaths finally evening. "You've got the steps down fine."

He stretched an arm out to her. "I don't want to let you down."

"Who's the mentor here, again?" She took his arm, lifting herself up before looping her arms around his neck. "We're due for a break."

His focus cracked. Before he could lean in, pulling her by the hips, she spun away. "A *real* break," she tutted. "Let's get something to eat. If I'm hungry, I'm guessing you are, too?"

He shook his head but couldn't stop smiling, grabbing his coat with a shrug of defeat as she buttoned up hers. Like clockwork, before leaving, they overlooked each other's appearances—rubbing away lipstick smudges, smoothing back messy hair, straightening collars from disarray. She clucked her tongue at him when he reached for her hand, which she shoved in her pocket.

He almost grabbed it back anyway, to pull her from the door. To remain as they were inside. But as much as he wanted to slide back onto the floor with her, he wanted more. He wanted days and nights. He wanted all that time would give.

Until he heard the telltale click of his courier case.

A letter.

It had been a while since his aunt had written, and the weight of a newly arrived piece of paper filled him with dread.

After arriving back at the hotel, Kallia went up to her room to freshen up, and most likely kick Aaros awake before he slept well into the day. Daron nursed a cup of tea at the Prima café. He flicked the seal off and unfolded the letter, filled with far fewer words than he was used to seeing.

Daron,

I've read the papers. They can be so useless, littered with false alarms, but I saw your name. I saw the headlines.

Is it all true? Or just some publicity stunt?

Let me know that you're all right, or if I need to come. Please.

—Aunt Cata

It wasn't a long letter, but his tea had gone cold from how many times he reread it.

Please.

He could almost hear her saying it.

"Bad news?"

The chair across from him scraped backward, by none other than Lottie in a serpent-green jacket and skirt that clung primly to her form. He should've caught sight of her right away, so out of place amongst the soft golds and pastels embroidering the café.

Too late, Daron swallowed and quickly folded away the correspondence. "No, just family business."

"Same difference." She rapped her nails along the table. "How is good, ol' Cataline anyway? I've heard things are not looking too good out east."

He didn't know what that was supposed to mean, only that he wanted to end whatever this was immediately. "What do you want, Lottie?"

"Breakfast." The journalist tried to hail a waiter, only to find them all occupied. "And a chat."

"We chatted the other day. I thought I made myself clear—"

"That you want nothing to do with me? Yes, that was obvious. And rude, by the way." She gave up and clasped her empty hands together. "Though I don't think you'll maintain that stance once you hear what I've found out about this place."

"How?" He shook his head. "You've not even been here two weeks."

"I'm good at my job. And not as easily . . . how would you say it?" She danced her fingertips against each other. *"Distractible."*

His face heated. "You could be lying."

"I don't need to lie to get what I want." The coyness slipped from her voice. "And even so, Daron, why would I lie about this?"

It was impossible to meet her eyes, to see more than the steeled, searching gaze of someone digging for secrets. Anything softer would convince him she cared. About Eva, about him. About the truth.

"I can be ruthless, but I'm not a monster. I want to get to the bottom of Eva's disappearance as much as you do."

"You believe she disappeared?" He bit back a hard laugh, recalling all the headlines and write-ups after his last act. *Daring Deed Ends in Tragic Last Act. Demarco Deals in Death on Stage. When Fatal Accident Meets Assistant.* All alliterative nonsense, all hooks Lottie could not resist. "The woman who blew all the whistles about her death?"

"Death is a faster story to accept. No one listens to disappearances. I know that all too well." Something new reared up in her voice, a bitterness so sharp it bled. "And I think you know, too, otherwise you wouldn't be here."

Everything she was saying was exactly what he'd wanted to hear—someone who believed him, believed in *this*—which was the trouble of it. It was a long, deep inhale after having no air for years. Eva had trusted Lottie far too quickly, and it had led to lies about her in the papers. An end to her story, when there was far more to it.

Suddenly, he imagined what would've happened had Lottie published the truth instead. The assistant of the Daring Demarco walks through a mirror, leading her Zarose knows where, only to never return. A story like that would result in either dead silence or utter chaos. The papers would hound him, Aunt Cata and the Patrons would descend. The world would watch.

Surprisingly, Lottie chose the story with less questions.

Death, the most believable ending.

Daron lifted his cup and sipped at the last, cold remnants. "So what did you find?"

Pleased, she leaned back comfortably in her chair. "I spoke with the mayor the other day. The man seems to be in the weirdest daze of resignation—not that I blame him. The mess Raz has unleashed is worse than any he's ever left behind, that's for sure.

"But there's something curious he said that went beyond stress," she continued, her finger dragging in small circles on the table. "He's very adamant about not talking about the city's history, always looking forward. Except when I asked him a simple question—how long he's been mayor of this city—he couldn't remember."

Daron paused. "That's it?"

"What do you mean, *that's it*? Surely if you're the leader of anything, and as prideful about it as he is, the least you could do is remember basic facts," Lottie said pointedly. "I even asked who his predecessor was, and he gave no answer. He just up and *left*."

"Because he's hiding something?"

"No, I know the look of a person who's hiding something." She stole a quick glance at him before returning to straightening the silverware beside her. "Mayor Eilin looked like he had absolutely nothing to hide, nothing to say. Not even a lie to cover the nothing, *that* I would've at least expected." Lottie bit her lip. "It was the same when I asked a few other locals. They *all* had the same look, the same nothingness."

A chill ran through him. "What do you think happened here?"

"You tell me. Eva always thought this place held a strange sort of power," she said. "It makes sense. People are disappearing, accidents keep happening, locals remember nothing, and you lot can't leave for whatever reason. I can only wonder what else is wrong—or what else *could* go wrong."

As the café quieted around them, a waiter approached to clear Daron's empty cup. Lottie didn't even look up as he whisked away, not even to ask for the coffee she'd wanted.

"I haven't had a chance to ask the others," she began, "but has your magic been feeling . . . different, lately?"

He stared down at his palm, the words racing up his throat like they couldn't get out fast enough. He swallowed them down.

"I know you don't perform anymore, but I heard you cast some protective magic over Kallia during the second night. Stopped the show altogether," she continued. "I'm assuming you two patched things up since you're looking to be in much better spirits."

At the sudden hunger and intrigue in her voice, his guard shot up. It was a wonder how little it had taken for it to lower. "We're not here to talk about her or me."

"Sorry, bad habit." Her smile lingered, her writing hand restless against the table. "I just thought maybe the strangeness of this place couldn't be all bad. Maybe it could've offered some key to finding Eva."

It was what he'd hoped, too, but whatever magic had seeped back into him changed nothing. It only made him more unpredictable, more dangerous. "Maybe the key is still here."

"If it is, then someone sure spent a lot of effort to make everyone forget about it."

46

"Look at you, a vision in . . ." Aaros trailed off, circling Kallia after she stepped out of the dressing room. "Red."

Kallia smirked. "It's not too much?"

"Oh, it definitely is." Canary waltzed around with a greasy paper bag of day-old caramel spiced popcorn. "Those top hats will be reduced to nothing but a pile of scandalized tears. Can't wait to see it."

"You can't eat in here!" Ira marched back in with her pincushion. Canary bared her teeth, exposing the kernels stuck in between like bone and flesh. The seamstress grimaced. She'd seen what Canary could do with a fire-lit baton between her teeth. It was quite a sight, Ira intimidated by anybody that wasn't her own reflection.

The seamstress stood beside Kallia, her cool demeanor returning as she scanned the fit of her dress in the mirror. "You will be turning heads, that's for certain."

"Was that a compliment?" Kallia teased. "Have I finally worn you down?"

"Keep fishing and I'll take it back." The seamstress inched away, hand pressed to her temple, her frown deepening.

"What's the matter?"

When Aaros tried to support her, she swatted him away. "Nothing. I . . . I haven't been sleeping well, is all."

"Anything we can help with?"

"Stop trying to be heroes, children. It doesn't suit you," she grumbled. "It's only the old memory box giving me a kick, so get a move on before you make it worse. I'll ring you up."

They watched the old woman hobble away to the front of the store before Aaros broke the silence. "So, what'll Demarco be wearing?"

"How should I know?"

Aaros and Canary shared a look. They'd been sharing a lot of those anytime Demarco was mentioned. They, and the rest of Glorian. Kallia was sure she could trust them, but there was something about keeping this only for her, and him.

It made everything uncertain feel a little safer.

"Fine. Be coy." Canary munched on another rebellious handful of popcorn. "And be smart. These sorts of things don't typically survive beyond the stage."

Kallia's eyes narrowed slightly, but Aaros interjected first. "Oh great, you've just doomed it."

"What? I'm being honest," the flame-eater said, licking her fingers. "Everything is heightened during a show. Like a dream. You can't really be sure if what you're feeling is real. It's what I tell all the Conquerors if they find someone on one of our stops. Warnings prevent the heartbreak, at least a little."

"You must make for a bleak, blunt confidant, canary bird."

"Careful, pretty boy." She growled. "I carry matches with me everywhere."

"I will not be overcharged from damages because of you two." Kallia crossed her arms imperiously. "Out."

"Yes, Mother." Aaros's head hung as he ambled out of the dressing area with Canary crunching and following behind.

Alone at last, she spared a quick glance at herself in the trifold mirrors, at how the silky red material wrapped around her body like a second skin, the long skirt cut artfully by two high slits that gave her legs the mobility she needed. The entire dress was made of sleek red, but underneath, black velvet. The open neckline draped off her shoulders, leaving room for jewelry to drip down her neck if she wanted.

Usually putting on a fabulous gown brightened her entire aura. Any bold costume she wore gifted her with a boldness in return. But Canary's words rang in the back of her head, chipping away at her.

Truth was, it was hard to believe something like this could last. Everything was still so new. So good.

And Zarose, she wanted to keep it that way.

A blink later, the lights began to dim. Shivering, Kallia rubbed her worn eyes. They were playing tricks on her. She'd woken up tired more days than she could count. The price of practice and performance.

As much as she'd love to waste the day away with Demarco, she'd drop cold on her feet if she didn't sneak in a few more hours of rest.

An amused smile tugged at her lips. She wondered what he'd think of the dress when she walked down that grand staircase of the ballroom. How he'd go still. How his jaw would drop.

Stunning.

Beautiful.

Otherworldly.

Kallia grinned at the praise wrapping around her, before finally turning away. A chill brushed over her as she descended off the car-peted pedestal, her back to her reflection—when the feel of cold fingers wrapped around her arm.

Only when she looked down, there was nothing.

No one near her, at all.

She forced herself to still. In the corner of her vision, she detected movement, a presence before it grew more solid. A chest at her back, when there was nothing behind her. The trail of fingers down to her elbow, the breath at her ear.

It took her longer than she was proud of to finally turn.

In the reflection, Jack stood right behind her, both hands at her shoulders. The pressure of his touch so real, existing only in the mirror. "Look at you . . ." There was a haunted quality to his voice. As if he didn't like what he saw, but couldn't look away. "Exhausted."

She swallowed back a scream. It was the first time he'd visited her in daylight, in public. Anyone could walk in, and she feared what would happen. What they would see, what he would do.

But despite his confidence, he'd come through a mirror.

Only an illusion.

Illusions, she could banish.

Kallia no longer avoided his gaze in her reflection—she met it head-on. A new fire edged around her eyes. After all, his touch was real only within the frame and a deception outside of it. His words floated back to her, the trick of illusions. They were made more real by every emotion latched onto it. Fear, desire, anger, anything, like water and sunlight to a flower. And with the unpredictability of a mirror, she had to do more than deprive.

Kallia cleared her mind, meditating the way she did before a show.

No more.

No more fear, no more anger.

No more of the yearning that lingered, regardless.

After everything, that emotion shocked her most of all. She wanted it gone.

Sweat ran down her face as her eyes blinked open, snapping her back into the room. Her ears thundered, head throbbing sharply from the effort. Magic never came easy. Even if she could fool hundreds in the audience to think it effortless, it was difficult. That was the only way she knew it was working.

Jack steadied her. "You can't force me out of here."

Kallia growled out a pant. "Watch me."

"Don't squander your energy when you're already running on so little, firecrown. Not even I'm worth it." He glanced toward the exit, the still curtains leading out. "Where's your magician to save you?"

Give nothing away.

"You can't hide it, Kallia. From everyone else, from me." His voice dropped lower than a whisper, strained. "It could never work between you two."

The silence within her burned, until she could no longer contain it. "Because he's not you?"

"Because he has no power."

He said it like he'd dropped an explosive in the room. One that would shake her world and destroy everything within it. Kallia lifted her chin higher. "I know."

His brow tensed, he hadn't expected that. "You know everything he's done? What he's been—"

"I *know*." Her nostrils flared. "And I don't care."

That shadow of a mask he so often wore cracked for barely a second before it smoothed over once more. "Then you're a fool," he muttered. "If you perform with him, hell, if you even go to the ball, terrible things will happen."

It sounded suspiciously like a promise.

Her focus cleared on a deep breath. "You're not here," she intoned, hollow but strong. "You're not here, you're not here, you're not here . . ."

"Remember what I said about mirrors, firecrown?"

Shut up. She did not want him to teach her. She did not want his lessons or his tricks any longer.

"It's much harder to stop what you see in the mirror when it's like a world unto itself, a world so much like yours."

"You're *not* here." Kallia began sweating once more, working through the ringing against her temple. "You're not here."

"Focus harder. Concentrate. You can try cutting me off all you'd like, but when do you stop believing it's real?" he asked, that familiar challenge. Always pushing. "How can you honestly look into that mirror and not realize—"

Crack.

A split ran across the surfaces. It cut over her reflected body in a clean, thin line, the flaw providing a soothing reminder. The rest of the glass, showing her alone across all three mirrors.

"Quick thinking, Kallia."

The whisper of wind danced across her shoulders, by her ear. She didn't dare turn around, refusing to give him the satisfaction.

"But be prepared to be surprised, tomorrow. If you don't heed any of my warnings, heed that one at least."

Before she could spit a curse his way, the air around her loosened, as if freed from a poison. The whisper, the touch at her back—gone.

In the mirror, she found herself alone in the center, broken by the crack in the surface that spanned across her body.

When the master of the house slammed his palm against the wall, the House shuddered.

There was no way they would leave her be tomorrow. Not in *that* house, at night, at a party so much like the ones they used to throw.

It made him sick, the way history circled itself. The farther he thought he'd gone, the closer he was.

Inevitable.

That's what Sire always told him, with the way he ran the city of mortals. How he ran this House by day, and the club at night.

Memories.

His specialty, and his mercy.

His mistake. No matter how much he took, it always came back, a story far too ugly to be retold and remembered. One he thought could die if no one spoke of it again.

He was wrong.

And she was in trouble.

The master clenched his fist against the wall, running his thumb against the black brass over his fingers. Perhaps it was always meant to happen—this unavoidable game, one that began long before she stepped into that damned city. It would come alive like a risen hell and swallow her whole, back in a cage without even the grace of a lock and key. Only bars.

He couldn't bear the thought.

Beyond his fear, he feared for her more.

That night, the candles of the House went dark. He laid to rest his loyal illusions, destroyed the path that led to his club as best as he could. There was no longer a need for it. No need for guests or their business or secrets. No more masks, no more hiding.

No more.

The master said his good-byes to the kingdom he'd built, and prepared to return to the one he'd once served.

47

The Alastor Place was a force of splendor against the night. No longer the shadowy towering structure of ruin Daron remembered upon first seeing it. No longer the stranger on the street you wanted nothing to do with, but the one across the room who intrigued you.

The ornate exterior held its same dark hold against the dusky sky, but inside, it burst with light. Life and laughter bubbled from the main entrance like champagne fizzing into sparkling flutes. Not unlike the audiences that flowed through the building before, but Janette had purposefully ordered the show hall to remain locked. Tomorrow, the last performance would begin.

Tonight was all about celebration.

Of what, Daron didn't know anymore. All the accidents culminating into this, all the participants missing an event meant for them, only added to the mounting wrongness of tonight.

At the first set of doors, a servant stopped him to pin a bright rosebud on his lapel, a token every attendee bore. Daron joined the sea of red roses, just as floored as those exploring the Alastor Place for the first time, all gaping mouths and eyes tilted up to devour every inch of lushly painted ceiling. Small chandeliers hung like sparkling bushes of crystal flowers, gradually increasing in size down the trail to the opened double doors leading into the Court of Mirrors.

Immediately, two bodies flanked him.

"Demarco, you're looking sharp." Erasmus patted him swiftly across the shoulder while they descended the grand staircase. "Not escorting anyone tonight, are you?"

Figures he would aim straight for that. "Didn't realize I needed to."

"Of course not," Lottie chimed in. "We both came alone, but do you think either of us is leaving the same?" Once they reached the bottom, she straightened the rose latched to her ex-husband's breast pocket before laying a hand on his chest. If Daron didn't feel like he belonged in this conversation before, he definitely didn't feel so now.

"Where's my star magician?" The proprietor eagerly lifted a flute off a passing tray. "I thought surely she would've arrived with you."

A knowingness laced his tone that prickled at Daron. He had nothing to hide with Kallia. In times like this, though, he was relieved that as much as people assumed, they controlled the truth. At least it was theirs.

"I'm her mentor," Daron scoffed. "Not her keeper."

"Fine, fine. Absolutely *nothing* is going on with you two down in the Ranza Estate." Erasmus winked. "So dedicated, practicing at every free moment. Hope you're ready to dazzle us with a spectacular act when the time comes."

They'd been practicing far more than any other pair, from what Daron could gather. But what they had up their sleeves couldn't compare to what he had with Kallia. A true partnership. The act was hers, but the stage would be theirs.

But after that, what then?

"We're ready, don't you worry."

Erasmus let out a noise of delight as he gulped down the last of his champagne. Lottie's remained untouched, her fingernails tapping slowly against its shape. "Speak of the devils."

The atmosphere of the room shifted in a blink. Heads tilting up and the chatter softening into hushed murmurs. A sudden stop, to which Daron looked up.

She stood at the top of the grand stairs, Aaros and the Conquering Circus at her side in all their finery. An absolute explosion of color, the lot of them. Like the bursts she sent into the sky when the circus first opened, spiraling across a dark canvas.

For once, Kallia didn't even seem to notice the attention. Beaming, she took in the whole of the party the way a sailor looks at the sea—a wistful expression, edged with a quiet excitement of coming home to something familiar. Even she wasn't impartial to the grandeur, nudging Aaros to look at the rows of chandeliers lining the ceiling, pointing at the vases of blooming flowers that reigned at every corner.

Their eyes met across the crowd. There was no change in her expression, except the slightest curve of a smile. Not once did her gaze leave his as she gave a brief farewell nod to her escorts before descending the steps in a slow saunter. Wordlessly, he excused himself from Lottie and Erasmus to meet her halfway, his focus thrown by every step she took, mouth growing dry. The sleek red fabric of her dress rippled against her legs, revealing whispers of skin, down to her black heels.

He didn't even try to stop staring. It was impossible when she traveled as if a spotlight followed her everywhere, especially in that dress. So different from the full-skirted gowns the other guests wore, the color of crushed rubies spearing through the clouds of neutral colors most people sported in their attire tonight.

And yet, Kallia looked like she belonged in this world—a life of parties and ballrooms, of shows and magic dipped in extravagance.

"Perfect," she said, once she made it down the stairs.

Daron's heart stuttered out of beat. "What is?"

"Your face. I've been imagining what it would look like once you finally saw me in this dress." She toyed with the rosebud pinned to her bodice, a teasing smile tucked in the corner of her lips.

It took everything in him not to pull her in, breathe into the crook of her neck and stay there. For all to see and whisper about, he didn't care what they said. This was not a game anymore. It stopped being one for him a long time ago.

The closest he could get to her was offering his hand. "Dance with me?"

Kallia arched a brow, as if she couldn't decide whether to laugh or not.

"Come on." He flourished his fingers, waiting. "I've been taking dance lessons from a fine teacher. Might as well try out the moves in a setting that calls for it."

"Stop it." She threw him a stern look, begrudgingly taking his hand.

"Stop what?" He let his thumb rub across her fingers, leading her to the floor where other couples had already started spinning to the swell of music.

"Flirting. Everyone can see."

"Let them," he said as he bowed. "We're dancing, not committing a crime."

With a reprimanding sigh, Kallia rose from her curtsy. She, who'd thrown fire in the faces of the judges, scandalized dinner parties without batting an eyelash, stolen the stage again and again. And yet Daron had never seen her look so rattled before.

"Now *you* stop it," he parroted back.

"What?"

"Looking nervous. It doesn't suit you."

She attempted to iron out the bemusement from her expression, but the littlest cracks emerged. Her masks, paper thin when it was just them.

"One dance," he spoke as they came together. Hand in hand, one to her waist while hers met his shoulder. "Then I'll ignore you for the rest of the evening."

"Well I don't want *that*, either."

He pulled her closer, whittling their distance to just a sliver.

One dance. One dance was polite, expected of them from those watching around the floor. Normally he never cared what other guests thought, but he was glad for the excuse.

"Demarco," Kallia said warningly. "You look entirely too happy."

"I can't help it." He stole glimpses over his shoulder. "This is new."

"You *like* people watching you?"

"I like being here, like *this*, around everyone." He pulled her to him, just a little closer. "It almost feels like . . ."

Daron couldn't finish the thought, it felt too big for words. Too big to fit in just one sentence. His temple dropped to hers and his mind clouded entirely, unwilling to give a definition. Something nameless and vast, sitting heavily in his chest.

This, it said.

If they could stay just like this, that would be enough.

She drifted her fingers across the back of his neck. Not at all the proper hold, but she never missed a step. "I know."

They stared at each other as they followed the rest of the steps in silence. It could never be just a dance between them. The song would soon end and the floor would clear, becoming just another moment of the night. After tonight, tomorrow, he wasn't sure when else they would have another one like this.

He would've let his nose brush hers, their lips touch, if it weren't for the showering applause. The music, slowly drawing to a close. No one noticed as he kept his hand at her back, both turning their attention to the latest arrival: the mayor, overlooking the party like a king from atop the stairs.

"People of Glorian, visitors from afar, generous donors, and contestants—it is truly a pleasure to see such a remarkable turnout for our city," Mayor Eilin proclaimed, beaming at his audience below. "We are immensely thankful that Glorian is no longer a city to whisper about, but one with a much louder voice. And flashy headlines, I might add."

Laughter echoed across the room in a light, airy current that filled Daron with the oddest dread.

"Spectaculore has been nothing short of wildly unpredictable, as you all know." With a coy grin, the mayor continued, "As is typical in this business, but we aim to end on a high note. For tonight, we have a surprise in store for you." He made an exaggerated display of peering over his guests. "Everyone has their roses, yes?"

Daron instinctively touched the rose that had been pinned at his lapel, as people began whispering curiously amongst themselves.

"Good, because every voter needs a token. And you'll all have a chance to cast yours for the one magician who will emerge from the world below. For tonight, we finish the story . . ."

All at once, Daron stiffened.

"Satisfied as the gatekeepers were of the magician's feat, they demanded one more spectacle. One last test."

He reached for Kallia's hand, and it was just as cold as his.

"Welcome, all." Mayor Eilin had already begun clapping, exposing a teeth-baring grin. "To our final performance of the show."

B e prepared to be surprised.
　　Jack had said as much, and yet shock slammed into her.

Amid the applause, a high-pitched shriek erupted from above. Mostly everyone had returned to the ball, barely paying mind to Janette as she dragged her father down the stairs to the bannister and away from the revelry. Kallia could still glimpse her pristine face, fury-red, in the shadows.

"Father!" she cried, as the other contestants and judges inched closer to their area. "What is the meaning of this?"

"Sorry for the quick change in plans, darling. Surely you understand." The mayor absently gestured for the others to join, despite his daughter's outburst. "We didn't want to trouble you with more show talk. I know how tired you've grown of it."

"Yes, because it's *all* that's ever talked about. And I'll be damned if you let it ruin tonight."

"Janette, please contain your—"

"I will not." She crossed her arms, practically heaving. "You put me in charge of this event, and I will not see it derailed for yet another bloody performance."

Her rage was palpable, especially in the face of naive party guests who tittered at the prospect of tonight's events. The grandeur of the ballroom, forgotten in light of the upcoming entertainment. Kallia felt a trickle of sympathy for her. The night she'd spent ages planning, envisioning, executing—in a few words, was no longer hers, but her father's.

"Did you know about this?"

Demarco stood at the outskirts with her, grim-faced as he watched the father and daughter bicker on while servants unveiled a row of three large, empty, crystal bowls glinting against the fireplace. Kallia couldn't quite place his expression, but it wasn't fury. An uneasiness had settled across his brow.

"No, I didn't." Not completely a lie. "But I'm assuming the others did."

She glanced over to where the remaining contestants stood, donning top hats like their mentors. They shared smirks and whispers over the rims of their short glasses, as if this chaos was something they themselves had made from scratch.

"I'm so sorry." Demarco exhaled, following her line of vision. "I-I should've known. Done . . . *something*."

"Stop. It's not your fault." Kallia gently pressed her fingers into his wrist. "They're the ones who should be scared."

The challenge called to her. To the part of her that wanted to win, made her hungrier for it the more unpredictable the path.

The fools thought they could treat her like a flower—take away her sunlight and water so she would shrivel up and die. But she was more the stubborn plant, the kind that thrived anywhere if that's what it took to live. Their first mistake was in thinking obstacles gave them an upper hand. Little did they know, she would always find a way to grow through cracks in the stone.

"Are you sure you want to do this?" he asked as she led them both to the gathering of contestants. She kept her chin raised while his jaw worked the whole way over. "This is unfair. We have no proper stage, no time to fully prepare for—"

"The world is our stage, Demarco. And we've practiced far more than any of them, and they know it." She chuckled at the expression on his face. "Don't panic. You know our act. All the tricks are on me, you're simply there to look pretty." She winked, squeezing his hand firmly. "Now, we *win*."

The word felt good on her lips. She could taste the victory, so close. None of the other contestants reverberated with quite as much energy when they finally reached the group.

"Quite a night this has turned into," one of the few remaining contestants said with a nasty leer. "Are you nervous?"

Kallia beamed. "For you."

His face went ashen, but the bravado remained thick in the air in the small circle of magicians. The guests of the party looked on from a short distance, whispering restlessly amongst themselves as they waited for the performance to begin.

Erasmus entered the ring, his face alight with trickery.

"Apologies for the sudden turn of events," he said. "Have to keep everyone on their toes as much as the participants, no matter what."

"Oh yes, I'm sure *all* the participants were treated equally and knew *nothing* until this very moment." Lottie appeared beside him, her viper stare aimed at every top hat in the circle. "Isn't that right, Mister Mayor?"

"Miss de la Rosa, who said you could drop in on a private meeting?" Mayor Eilin sniffed. "And I don't know what you're getting at."

"Sure you do. I heard it all in our last interview regarding the treatment of the contestants. You said, and I quote, *'Boys will be boys, and we stick together.'*" She grimaced. "Guess that applies to cheating as well."

His face reddened even more, eyes turning murderous. Though not as murderous as Erasmus as he regarded the mayor. "You told everyone?"

"Not *everyone*," Demarco chimed in pointedly.

"Surprise, surprise." The proprietor threw up his hands. "Those who rig the game are the weakest players of them all, you know."

"This is not solely your game, Rayne. You may have bound us all here in that contract of yours, but you don't make all the rules. What does it matter, whether things were fair or not? That's life," the mayor declared, snapping a triumphant finger. "No, that's *show business*. And if any contestant is too rattled to perform, well, I'm afraid they're not cut out for it."

"You should be afraid," Kallia interjected, hands on her hips. "Because I'm ready."

You're not ready.

Jack's words from long ago kicked back in her mind, the ones she hadn't wanted to hear. The ones she hated.

She inhaled deeply.

You're wrong.

She was ready, and she always had been.

The mayor stammered in irritation before spinning back to the crowd. The faces of contestants and judges throughout the circle turned frustrated, while others grinned. Demarco, surprisingly, not one of them. Kallia didn't know what to make of that, but the flutter of unease dissolved as the guests quieted, save for the servants clearing away stragglers from the center of the floor.

"Rather than move everyone into the main theater," the mayor resumed his announcement, all tight smiles for the party, "we thought the ballroom would make a worthy arena for our final performance. The Court of Mirrors, after all, used to be quite a showroom itself, back in the day. With a stage already beneath our feet." He raised a gloved hand, crooking two fingers upward. "Gentlemen?"

Kallia jerked at the harsh, rusty groans, one after the other. Across the floor, where she and Demarco had danced, the surface shifted. Servants in elegant black suits pulled floor panels up from the ground, raising them to their full height and forming a wide ring within the dance floor. The six raised panels encircled the center like petals unfurling, surrounding a spacious expanse right beneath the largest chandelier of the ballroom. The guests clapped in awe at the beautiful display it formed, the way the lights hit the reflection with an otherworldly glow. A stage like a bright cage for all to peer into.

Made entirely of mirrors.

Kallia blanched. The surfaces gleamed dangerously like well-sharpened knives raised over a chopping board. Before she could grab Demarco's hand—to pull him aside or make a run for it altogether, she didn't know—the mayor gestured invitingly to her.

"And since our lovely Kallia is *dying* for her time onstage," he said, a little too gleeful, "it's only fair to give her the privilege of going first!"

Daron wanted to break something.

This couldn't possibly go on. And yet he moved closer to the newly raised stage with Kallia, who seemed just as dazed when, only moments ago, she was determined to tear this show to the ground.

"I-I need a quick word, with Aaros about the music. I'll be right . . ." Kallia didn't even finish, rushing to meet her assistant at the edge of the mirrors. Even in the frenzy, her expression was shrewd, focus pushing through. Never one to let a twist knife at her, unlike him.

As soon as those mirrors were raised, it took everything to tamp down the urge to run.

"You really think this is a good idea, Daron?" Lottie sidled beside him. The last person he needed to see, when he needed to remain calm.

"What do you mean?"

"I think you know."

Eva.

"It's a very different act," he bit out. "This isn't the same."

It wouldn't be. They wouldn't even be going near the mirrors. The proximity to them would set him on edge, so he would focus on Kallia. Just Kallia.

And she would win. There was never any doubt in his mind about that.

"That's not what I meant."

A new, quiet panic entered him as Lottie pulled at him, her expression blazing as he'd never before: desperate, haunted. "Don't perform, Daron. Nothing good will come of tonight."

His breath hitched at the cold certainty in her voice. With how little he had to do in the act, he honestly couldn't see how. Until all at once, he remembered those moments when power had burst through him without warning, out of pure reaction. Instinct.

There was no way she could've known that. "What are you talking about?"

Lottie was never speechless. It was the first thing he'd noticed about her when Eva had first invited her to join them for a post-show dinner, like bringing a wily stray cat home who had refused to be ignored. Daron never thought it a wise friendship, but Eva never cared. She preferred the company of those who were clever with their words, magician or not, and Lottie had an endless supply. Arguing, persuading, criticizing—each play of words, her specialty.

But now she didn't know what to say. And as much as he wanted to wait for it, Aaros frantically waved him over to the stage area.

"I need to go." Daron shook out of Lottie's grip, his heart thundering.

"Dare." A low growl of warning. "If you do this, I'll—"

"Write a thousand stories about me for all I care, Lottie," he said, backing away. "I'm not leaving her alone in this. I'm not going to do that to her."

She did not try to stop him this time, instead grabbing the nearest flute of alcohol and drowning it in one swallow. A bolstering vote of confidence. Whatever it was, he couldn't let her panic bleed into his.

He concentrated entirely on Kallia as she conversed with the musicians arranging themselves around the stage of mirrors. Aaros lingered behind, beckoning Daron to the side.

"How does she seem?"

Aaros looked troubled. "Fine."

That wasn't a good sign.

"Take care, judge," he continued, digging into his coat pocket before passing off an item. "If anything has shaken her even a little, something bad must be in the air tonight."

Daron didn't want to think that way. Ominous thoughts only led to ominous things. The assistant departed, leaving him with Kallia. Once the musicians took their places, her arms crossed, fingers running over a small scrap of cloth, a hint of bloody petals along its edge.

"Everything is going to be all right," he promised, reaching for her. "Those fools wouldn't dare mess with the act in front of all these people. It will go just as we rehearsed."

Kallia nodded slowly, tucking the cloth back into a hidden fold of her dress. Her fingers tensed at the absence. "And if it doesn't?"

"Then no one would fault you for having a bumbling oaf of a mentor."

That drew a snort from her. When she looked up at him, *truly* looked at him, his whole world narrowed.

"You'll be here, at the end of all this, right?"

Doubt. It was strange to hear it in her voice, and he wanted it gone. "I'm not going anywhere." He ran his hands up and down her arms, warming her. "We're doing this together, remember?"

Kallia nodded, less shakily. "Yes."

She looked at his mouth right as Daron looked to hers, his eyes grazing to her neck where he could almost feel her straining pulse beating beyond its limits. He laced their fingers together, not caring what others would think. What rumors would spread, what stories would be written. Before he lost his nerve, he led her through the open space between two mirrors so they could take their place on stage.

As the welcoming applause washed over them, Daron avoided looking at his reflection. Just like Kallia they focused on each other instead. And for a small, quiet moment in the din of the cheers, it was as though it were only them. Like a practice, at the Ranza Estate.

At her wink, the weight lifted off him. He made quick work of his jacket before throwing it to the ground, pulling out the scrap of fabric Aaros had passed to him once the room hushed.

"Tonight, we have prepared a *very* interesting dance for you," Kallia declared to the audience. Bold, without a trace of worry in her voice. He both feared and admired the masks she could so easily don. "One that could turn deadly, if we take even one wrong step."

With that, she thrust her hand out, letting her fingers beckon toward the ground at their feet. A flame sprouted like a flower, before it grew and spread around the mirrors as if oil drenched the floors. The fire built into a blaze, surrounding the floor inch by inch, teasing nearer and nearer to them until there was no way out without burning.

Given Glorian's aversion to fire, the gasps and shrieks in the crowd were unsurprising.

"To those who've danced over flames before," she added, lifting the black fabric over her head for all to see. "Have you tried it, wearing a blindfold?"

Kallia made sure to run her fingers over the fabric to confirm there were no slits cut, that it was not sheer enough to peek through. Confirmation and credibility.

After Daron tied the fabric over her eyes, he guided her into position only breaths away from him. The fire licked near their legs. Sweat began to drip from his temple. There were only a few times during their practices when Daron had nearly gotten burned, but Kallia never allowed it. Even blindfolded, she could anticipate her mistakes before they happened, and would pull him back before the fire could so much as graze him.

One more dance among the flames.

The lights of the ballroom dimmed, before blacking out entirely, the sea of fire the only illumination over the floor.

And all of a sudden, Daron became like the dark, transported by shadow at the first low swell of a song rising in the air.

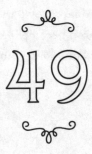

49

Kallia was grateful for the blindfold. She could sink more easily into the music, into the movements that came more from muscle memory than sight.

Blacking out the rest of the lights around the ballroom was an effective touch, bringing in a reel of gasps from the guests. There was nowhere else to look but them, and though she wished to rip off her mask for the chance to see, it was a relief that she couldn't.

Behind the blindfold, there were no mirrors.

Only Demarco. Only fire.

Each step they took was the only area untouched by flames, but they had to keep moving. Fire may part, but it was never content to stay back.

The low, sultry rise of strings reached into the air, tightening every touch. She hooked her arms around Demarco's neck, leverage for when he lowered her in an agonizingly slow split. The usual burn ran up her thighs as he lifted her back to facing position, when she summoned a handful of flames from the floor and unleashed them into the air. Their heat teased around her—around them both—while he spun her out of harm's way. One sharp turn after the other, to avoid this added obstacle.

Like her audition, she thought, wishing she could see the judges now. Their audience. Each time a swirling orb of fire grazed around her a little too quickly, startled gasps of both fear and delight sounded. Whenever a lean or a lift led them out of the fire's path, relieved breaths and clapping trickled in over the heady beat.

Demarco was letting her lead more tonight, his movements less sure. She would never hold his nerves against him, when there was so little warning. If anyone had more reason to fear when it came to mirrors, it was him. The fact that he chose to stay by her, in spite of it all, meant everything.

So she gladly seized the lead. Relieved to be in control, when all else felt out of her grasp.

Her chest heaved slightly as they reached the next phase of the act. She squeezed Demarco's shoulders to signal the lift. He took her by the waist, holding her up as she raised her arms high above, the music dropping with the boom of a drum.

She sliced her arms downward, feeling the orbs of fire falling back to the floor in bursts around them.

The audience roared. Triumph shot through her veins, on top of exhaustion. Her legs trembled from the effort as he lowered her, but his grip was looser. Familiar, from all the practice.

He had initially hesitated over a fiery dance floor. One drop, and she could fall into the blaze, despite her confidence in her quick reflexes. Still, each time they reached this point in the dance, he'd grip her tighter. A reminder. *I've got you. I will never let you fall.*

She leaned into his hold, the way his fingers spanned her waist teasingly, pressing her against him. His panting in her ear, against her skin.

Heat coiled in her belly as she arched her back out, her head tipped back and hair falling down her spine. There was only sensation, and she gloried in it. Flying over the fire, sweat trailing down her skin, applause ringing in her ears.

Kallia

Her name played on their lips like a song. She'd had no name at Hellfire House, but here, she was known. Here, she would be remembered and spoken of for longer than a night.

Kallia

Kallia

Kallia

Cheers burst loud as screams, piercing enough to make Kallia stiffen. She'd introduced no tricks, no moves to raise such a reaction.

"What's happening?" she whispered into his neck.

"KALLIA!"

She straightened at the voice echoing from the crowd.

Impossible.

It sounded like Demarco, screaming her name beyond the stage.

The cold shattered inside her. Kallia pushed at the hands around her, tearing off the blindfold. As soon as she broke her hold on the act, the fires around them died into smoke, thin as veils. Gasps erupted at the sudden end, while others clapped on.

Her eyes watered from the smoke, widening when she saw Demarco before her, a confused expression on his face. His hand, raised to the chandelier.

The grand fixture had been lightless before, but he sent colorful bursts straight from his palms into each dangling gem, transforming the entire ballroom so it looked like glimmering jewels chasing across the walls.

Magic.

It couldn't be.

"How are you . . ." Kallia looked up, mouth parted. Still hearing Demarco shouting from a distance, feeling him hold her against him. "What are you doing?"

"Distracting them."

The lights remained playing against the chandelier as he grasped her by the waist, suddenly tugging her toward him, away from the center—

"Kallia!"

Her ears perked. The same desperate shout. She turned, and in the space between two mirrors, she saw Demarco pushing himself past guests in his path, panting and grasping the frames of the mirror to lunge forward.

Two Demarcos.

Exactly the same. Same height, same clothes, same expression of shock.

One pulling her off stage, and another entering.

Even louder hoots and whistles rang throughout the room, but blood roared in Kallia's ears. She stilled before the man pulling her could take her any farther, staring in horror between the two of them.

She finally faced the mirrors.

Through the smoke, she saw herself, but it was not Demarco reflected in the mirror with her. A different figure, different height. Another man.

Jack.

"Get away from her!" the Demarco entering the cage snarled.

She ripped herself away and shifted back from them both, shuddering off the feel of Jack wearing the skin of another. He couldn't hide himself from the mirrors, his true reflection showing all across the cage.

He was here.

Shaking, Kallia nearly screamed when her back collided with another chest, but warm fingers gripped her elbow, steadying her. "It's me," he whispered, pleading. "I don't know what's happening, but I *swear*, it's me."

She should've known sooner. All the touches that seemed different, the parts of the dance that were off. Yet she'd ignored them, falling right into Jack's hands. And now he was here, looking at her with Demarco's face, and a smile that was pure Jack.

"Look at you, going to her like a guard dog." He blew out an amused whistle. "You couldn't even protect yourself when I swooped in."

Demarco glared, unblinking. "Who are you?"

Jack chuckled, and bile crept up Kallia's throat. She didn't want the memory of Jack as Demarco, of his body and face and voice used like this. "Kallia's not quite fond of talking about me to others. Isn't that right, firecrown?"

With the quick wave of his hands, the lights over their heads dissolved, and with it, the rest of his disguise. "I guess you could call me an old friend."

Still shaking, she looked away as he transformed. The sudden murmurs of bewilderment rippling across the room were enough to know he was here.

Jack, in Glorian.

Here, at last.

"Excuse me, sir, but *who* do you think you are?" the mayor bellowed, furiously making his way through the guests. "We've bent the rules quite enough for this contestant, and it clearly states the final act can only be performed with—"

"Ah, the toad who's been giving her so much trouble," Jack muttered by way of greeting. "What I would give if they'd just take you."

Kallia knew his tone, the murder it promised. "Jack, please."

"They're still looking for one more." He shrugged dispassionately. "If he's their pick, I won't stop them."

Mayor Eilin scoffed, unafraid. "Who are you?"

In one blink, Jack was at the center of the mirrors—and the next, right in front of the mayor. He raised his knuckles out to the old man, the first time Kallia had ever seen them stripped of their rings in all the time she'd known him. "Go on, take a closer look."

Black symbols branded Jack's fingers, ones he'd kept hidden all this time. She'd never once imagined anything lay beneath, but there they were in a menacing row.

Black triangles, inked across his knuckles.

The man's righteous anger died. "No . . ." He shook his head, panicked. "No, it *can't* be. The Alastors—they're gone. Long gone."

"You think so, Mister Mayor?"

The booming toll of bells began, each chime more thunderous than the last. Every familiar toll shook in Kallia's bones with their promise.

Darkness.

Chaos.

"My mercy was wasted on you and this place," Jack said over the ominous bells, sneering. "You brought this upon yourselves."

A crack sounded as he punched the old man square in the face. At the sickening thud to the ground, a high-pitched scream pierced the air. Janette scrambled over and knelt by her father, desperately checking his neck for a pulse. A heartbeat.

"You all wanted a show?" Jack stepped away from the body, already forgotten. "Looks like you've got it."

The lights dimmed. Kallia caught a flicker of movement before facing the mirror nearest to her. Black fog flooded all the frames, swarms of smoke and cloud pressing out from the other side of the glass.

In the distance, dark figures emerged in little specks.

Walking closer, growing larger.

Kallia swallowed hard, shivering as she remembered. The figures she'd seen in Juno's head. The ones Jack had shown her. Shadows she didn't even know the names of, coming for this world.

"What are those?" Demarco's mouth hung in horror.

"I don't know," she whispered, her breath cold. "But whatever happens, we can't let them come through those mirrors."

Kallia was relieved she didn't have to explain. Demarco knew all too well the sinister nature of mirrors, the doors they could be. With a swift nod, he took off for the frame across from them, using his elbow to fracture the surface.

Five more.

They stumbled as Jack reappeared between them with a force that quaked into the ground. Two of the mirrors toppled over from the impact, shattering instantly. Rather than glass, a flock of black birds surged through the empty frame. Their screeches feral, flapping wings violent.

Same as those that had plagued the theater from her disastrous second act.

Screams filled the room as the birds flew above the guests, pecking and diving their beaks into fabric and flesh. A blur of gowns and tables overturned, people rushing for cover. Kallia spotted a wave of fire burning the birds from below—Canary, warding the creatures off with her flames. In various spaces of the ballroom, other Conquerors and contestants conjured the elements they could to fight back. Even Aaros fought nearby, on a table swinging the broken leg of a chair at the birds alongside the Starling twins.

A hand wrapped around her wrist.

"We don't have much time." Jack pulled at her, unfazed by the chaos. "Come with me."

Kallia was acutely aware of his feet crunching over broken glass, no longer trails of smoke. His touch was solid and whole. Desperate. "Let go of me." She shook him off. "I'm not leaving."

"It's not safe here, Kallia," he murmured. "This city is going to destroy itself, we must go *now*."

In earnest, he reached for her and managed to half-vanish into nothing—before ripping out a frustrated snarl as he materialized a second later, again and again. Realizing she wouldn't follow. She *couldn't*.

"It looks like this magic is beyond even yours, Jack. I'm bound here." For once, it was a relief. "You can't just take me away."

Whether it was fear for her or the inability of his own magic to get him what he wanted, dread ravaged his face. "I'm not leaving without you. Not here. Not with—"

A bolt of light flew over Kallia's shoulder, knocking Jack back into a mirror. Turning, Kallia spotted Demarco on the ground, propped up on one hand. His other hand, outstretched and scarred, glowing toward them as he bore the most rage she'd ever seen.

The mirror crashed back, emptying the frame instantly. Releasing a wave of birds in its wake.

Kallia's heart gripped painfully, and she staggered to her knees.

What was happening?

Her pulse raced in her ears, her vision dimmed.

"You feel it, now?" Jack faltered onto one knee beside her, jaw clenched. "You finally see?"

She ignored him. He would never stop trying to trick her. On an angry breath, Kallia used his back as leverage to push herself up and force him back down to the ground.

Only two mirrors left. The darkened figures behind them were already pressing their shadowy fingers against the surface.

"Stay with him, Kallia, and he will destroy you and everything you could be," Jack seethed. "That weakness, blooming inside you— you know where that came from, don't you? Who started it?"

Lies

Truths

Come to us

We'll show you the difference

"*Shut up!*" Kallia screamed, the voices swirling around her. Her vision, purpling at the edges. "What . . . what did you do to me?"

"I would never steal magic from you. Not like him."

The screams of the ballroom fell to silence. No hint of trickery on Jack's face, only pity. A whisper of it.

Her thoughts blurred, chest tightening with each pained pant. "No." Her voice broke. "No, you're wrong. You're *lying*."

He must be.

He *had* to be.

Tears burned in her eyes as Demarco shouted her name, and she could no longer make sense of anything. Only the exhaustion, sweeping through her so suddenly she found herself sliding against the empty mirror frame to the floor.

"Kallia!"

She barely touched the ground, pulled quickly against a chest, a familiar scent. Demarco's arm was riddled in scars, bleeding lightly, but he held out his hand protectively before them. A bright light emanated from his open palm, aimed at Jack.

Jack.

"Wait." Kallia didn't know what she was saying, as she tried pulling Demarco's arm away. *Do not prove him right. Please.* "No, *stop*—"

The light flew from his palm and Jack ducked away from its collision with the mirror.

At the shattering impact, Kallia cried out.

A breathless scream, locked in her throat.

Pain, eating her heart from the inside.

Pain she'd sensed time and again, only to realize it now, stripping her away.

"What's wrong?" Demarco whispered, fear bending to rage. "What did you *do* to her?"

Kallia edged back, cradling herself tightly. His brow crinkled in hurt as he went to her—only to find he could no longer move.

Steps ahead, Jack kept his hand lifted. "Ask yourself the same question, magician. You've done quite enough. You gave her a chance in this inane competition, had the nerve to pose as a mentor . . ." Through a grimace, he kept Demarco in place. "When you're nothing more than a fraud."

Demarco faltered as the words struck him. Arrows stabbing their targets. She didn't want to look at his face, watch the truth ripple across him as it burned away inside her.

She'd known.

She'd known that he'd had no magic, until he came to Glorian. Until he'd met her.

"No." Kallia's mouth trembled. The same man she'd seen every day since she got here. A stranger now, like he once was. "Your magic, and mine . . ."

Demarco continued pushing against the force staying him, but he blinked long and hard in confusion as if he didn't know.

What if he didn't? a voice teased, from the mirror shards or simply from the back of her mind. She could not tell anymore, but it didn't matter.

The damage was done.

She felt it deep inside her, the parts of her that hadn't been the same in a long time. Her petals growing bitter and dry, falling little by little, day by day.

"It's not gone forever."

Jack had a way of knowing the questions that bit at her from a glance. "Around magicians like him, it might be," he said, helping her to her feet. "But if you come back with me, it may not be too late. We can escape this."

Two choices.

Both came with the promise of ruin, already in motion. Destruction reigned in the Court of Mirrors, crashing down all around her. People in tattered gowns and suits sprinted for the doors, birds wreaking havoc over their heads. Screams and hysterical crying in endless reels, the bursts of fire and collapsing chandeliers. And still, the creatures attacked. No end in sight.

A third choice.

"How can I stop this?"

His dark eyes flashed. "This only ends by giving them what they want, and that's out of the question. You leave while you still can, that's how you survive it."

Something of a memory creeped over his face, killing the cowardice of the words. He ruled by necessity; survival from what, she didn't know. "Tell me." Her breath shook. "Because I'm not leaving. I *can't*."

"I'll figure something out. Just let me . . ." He raked a hand through his hair, glowering at Demarco. At the mayhem all around them. "You deserve more than this, firecrown. More than him, more than this place and its people."

She laughed, bitterly. Even when she could barely stand, he still managed to uphold her as someone with power, worthy of more. "You can always leave," she said. "You don't even have to watch if you don't want to."

"You don't have to save them." His scowl deepened at her suggestion. "Save yourself first, Kallia. That's the only way out."

And the loneliest. All too sharply, she remembered how alone she felt the night she left Hellfire House. When she'd had nothing to lose, nothing real of her own—the choice had been so easy. She'd needed no one else but herself, her power. Like she was always taught.

Then the others came.

Aaros and Canary.

The Conquering Circus and Ira.

Demarco.

Turning slowly, she glanced at him. It hurt to look at him now, at any of them. All trapped here, same as she was, but she knew cages. She'd grown up behind bars all her life, and had escaped one before.

She could escape again, with more power this time.

"No." She spun around, facing Jack. No more running, no more hiding. "It's not."

Kallia clasped her hands against his jaw, bending his face so he could see her. He startled at her touch. It brought out something soft in him, the storm in his eyes quieting, trying to understand. He almost looked the way he did before, when it was just them. Before Glorian or the competition. Back when she trusted him, when a chandelier at night was all she had.

More.

There was so much more now.

With an apology on her breath, Kallia pushed him through the mirror.

Locked in his embrace, she fell with him into the dark.

Daron's hoarse cry was drowned by the mirror's shatter. No birds emerged from the frame. Those ravaging the ballroom had vanished altogether. And the tolling bells, silent as well. As if they had never rung. As if it had all been a trick.

One moment, both of them stood there.

Now, there was only shattered glass and an empty frame.

Impossible. He staggered over to the last broken fixture, taking in the frame. Fallen rosebuds and shards crunched beneath his shoes, but no spots of blood betrayed a pair of magicians crashing through its surface.

As if they'd simply disappeared together.

Vanished.

"No." His heart stopped. He couldn't move or see past the frame, the entire world around him gone still. "No, no, no."

She couldn't be gone, just like that.

Not like *this*.

"What happened to her?" Aaros had landed next to him, his hair a wreck and face a mess of small scars and cuts. He began digging through the scraps of mirror with his bare hands. "Where is she?"

"I . . ." It was the question his first therapist had asked after Eva disappeared, humoring him. It crushed him, the truth. "I don't know."

"You don't *know*?" Aaros grabbed him by the collar. "You were right here."

"They went through the mirror." His voice faded to his own ears, so hollow it was as though someone else were talking for him. "They could be anywhere."

"Then find her—work your magic and bring her back!"

Do *something*. Do *anything*.

Daron's throat tightened under his unrelenting grip. Aaros didn't know. Nobody could've overheard Kallia's teacher, with the chaos that had overtaken the ballroom. And yet the guests of the party emerged, gathering around the empty mirror frames. All shaken, yet watching Daron as if he had something to answer for.

"Demarco!" Aaros shook him roughly. "Don't just stand there, do something—"

"He can't."

Lottie stepped right through an empty frame, looking every bit as disheveled as the other guests. Her eyes were set on Daron, steely with quiet fury. Remembrance. "Isn't that right?"

She'd known.

The truth was not as painful to his ears as he'd thought. Distantly he heard a wave of protests fly to his rescue—citing his career, his power, knocking out mirrors moments before from luminous blasts out of his hands.

His eyes fell to his palms, now absent of light, still warm from the power that came at him like a stranger. The magic, gone.

Kallia, gone.

Where are you?

Numbed to the pain, the shouting all around him, his gaze drew to the ground, so heavy he could barely lift it anymore. But his heart thumped a beat back to life, for in the scattered glass and rose petals, a note had been left among them.

One of Soul

EPILOGUE

The stage was empty, abandoned.

The perfect place for a meeting, the powerless magician reasoned, as he sat along the cold, wooden edge, overlooking the entire theater. Darkened as the day he first walked in. Empty seats and aisles, lights dead as the grief that clouded the whole city.

Along with a small spark of intrigue. A new sort of curiosity unfolded over the city, bringing many more visitors. All taken in by the tale of unfortunate accidents and injuries. In a way, the theatrical was still running. People came for front-row seats, and stayed for the next act. The next tragedy. And the mystery of the contestant who'd gone missing without a trace.

Still missing.

Sometimes he thought he could hear her in the silence, see her in reflections. Just within reach, until he blinked and found nothing there.

Only an illusion. A trick.

The powerless magician couldn't tell them apart anymore, only knew that somehow, whatever it took, he had to find her.

The doors opened.

The others had arrived. An assistant who had the quick look of the streets about him, and a scowling circus entertainer whose ruby-red hair dominated the bleak air of the building.

"Why did you call us here, judge?" the assistant sighed.

"Seriously," the entertainer snarled, stomping closer. Within punching distance. "Give me one good reason why I shouldn't go back to my tent and return with our lion. She hasn't devoured a liar in a while."

A month ago, he would've flinched. He would've skipped town to avoid any accusation. The truth. He'd been running from it for so long, he didn't know what was true anymore. Only the lies spun over time into a far worse creature he could no longer live with.

"I know I have a lot to explain and even more to apologize for," he confessed, wringing his hands to keep them from shaking. "I will do that. I will tell you everything."

"And?" The assistant attempted to hide his disinterest. Failing. "What's the catch?"

The entertainer's jaw worked. "And why do you think we'd want to hear what you have to say?"

"Because the poor boy needs your help."

The sharp-tongued journalist, the last to round them out, shut the doors behind her. Waltzing in, she took her pen down from her bound hair and wielded it like a blade, brandishing her notepad. "Please don't say you've started without me," she said. "How rude."

The magician waited a moment, expecting the assistant and the entertainer to leave at her arrival. They didn't have to help, they didn't owe him anything. They could've left town just as easily, the moment the show was over.

Something rooted them all in place, regardless.

The journalist took it upon herself to occupy the first red velvet seat in the front row. She unfolded her spectacles, crossed her legs to prop her notepad by her knee. "No detail is too small, no theory too ridiculous—"

"*This* is ridiculous," the entertainer spat. "We don't need a head-line, we need help."

"You can't solve anything unless you have all the details first. But if you have any other bright ideas, please. I'm *all* ears," the journalist fired back, just as vicious. Neither the girl nor the assistant supplied anything more, quietly taking their seats without further complaint.

The magician had overseen theaters packed with hundreds, crowds of thousands, and yet nothing intimidated him more than this audience of three. Most of whom couldn't stand the sight of him, all things considered.

"Now, before we get started, first things first." The journalist rose from her seat, pulling a curious item from her pocket. All they could see were the smooth white edges peeking out from her hand before she placed it on the empty stage.

A mask.

"Does the name Hellfire House mean anything to you?"

The assistant nodded. The entertainer raised her brow. And the magician wordlessly reached for the mask, tracing his fingers over the white, pearlescent exterior before turning it over.

The other side was lined not in pearl, but in mirrored glass. Flashes of his face caught in the dips and bends of the mask's shape. Bloodshot eyes, disheveled hair, a hollowed gaze that cleared the instant he met it.

He would not turn away. Not anymore.

As the others talked over him, the magician stared at his frag-mented reflection without fearing it for once.

Without knowing that, on the other side of the mirror, another magician stared back.

ACKNOWLEDGMENTS

One fact about me is that I love reading the acknowledgments of a book first. I love seeing how many people stood behind one storyteller, how many names went into the creation of this book aside from the one along the spine. To see such gratitude and happiness for reaching this stage from the help of many is why I always turn to the acknowledgments.

It's an honor to now be writing my own.

To my brilliant agent, Thao Le, who is truly the best in the business. We've seen as many publishing lows as highs together ever since you plucked me out of the slush pile, and even when I doubted everything, not once did you give up on me. This is not our first book together even though it's the first we've published, and I'm happy it won't be the last, either. You've made me a better writer in more ways than I can count. I always feel so lucky to have you in my corner, along with the rest of the fabulous SDLA team who all together form the fantastic literary agency I'm proud to be represented by.

To my spectacular editor, Vicki Lame, who gave this author and book their wings and believed in us so much, even when the story felt like nothing more than a glimmer of a song. You heard what it could be, and took a chance on me. I'll always be grateful you did, as well as grateful for your enthusiasm and incredible editorial insights that helped strengthen the book so beautifully. Kallia, Demarco, Jack, and I would be lost without you, the one who got us all through the door and kept us sane during this wild journey.

Endless thanks to my remarkable publishing team at Wednesday Books—including Jennie Conway, DJ DeSmyter, Jessica Preeg, Meghan Harrington, Kerri Resnick, Anna Gorovoy, NaNá V. Stoelzle, Elizabeth R. Curione, Micaela Alcaino, Alexis Neuville, Natalie Tsay, Kim Ludlam, Tom Thompson, Michael Criscitelli, Dylan Helstein, Lance Ehlers, Rhys Davies, and all the people who've worked on this book in any way. I'm lucky to be working with *you*. You have infused so much life into this book and ushered it out in the world with a spotlight. It's wild to think that just years ago, Kallia was still dancing alone in my head; thanks to your excitement and hard work, she now has an audience and a much bigger, grander stage to tell her story.

To my incredible writing cult, my support group of amazingly talented writers, it would be cheesy to call you my found family but it's the truth. We found each other on the internet, which, as we all know, is always the best place to make friends. Thank you, Akshaya Raman and Maddy Colis, my bat signal pals from the beginning, even when my writing was just simile soup—look at us now. To Katy Rose Pool (publishing twin!!), Ashley Burdin, Alexis Castellanos, Kat Cho, Mara Fitzgerald (salt and Shrek buddy!), Amanda Foody, Christine Lynn Herman, Tara Sim, Claribel Ortega, Melody Simpson, Ella Dyson, and Meg Kohlmann (my first writing friend/CP EVER). To Axie Oh, beloved James to my Jessie, there is no one I'd rather dominate the writing world with than you. To Amanda Haas, for your invaluable pep talks and just for being the light that you are. And to Erin Bay, my one and only CO-G and fellow Phan, you've been excited about this book as soon as I threw the idea out into the world. Thank you, for always cheering this book and me on, and for knowing without hesitation it was something special. Your friendship and encouragement truly helped make this story take flight. You're emoji-sploding right now, aren't you?

To Sara Raasch, Susan Dennard, Roshani Chokshi, Patrice Caldwell, and Julie Dao—thank you for being such guiding lights over the years to this baby writer, you're all absolute legends. To Emily Duncan and Claire Legrand, thank you so much for the kind words and kindness over the years. Big thanks to writer pals Andrea Tang, Ashley Schumacher, Hannah Reynolds, and Ellie Moreton. Thank you to Sami Thomason, Joy Preble, Allison Senecal, Kalie Young, Kiersten Frost, Alexa (@alexalovesbooks), and Brittney (@reverieandink), for bolstering this book from the very beginning. And in general, to all book bloggers, booksellers, influencers, librarians, and those in the book community who have supported my book and me—thank you, for everything, especially for the important work you do that certainly kept *this* reader reading ever since she was younger. To the fanfiction community, for helping me get my start in writing and changing my life forever. And a shout-out to my CWP family, especially the Contracts and Rights crew, for all the support as I straddle both sides of the industry table.

And now, the moment *they've* all been waiting for: my family.

Just kidding. This is the section I've been looking forward to most, because none of what I do as a storyteller would be possible without my pillars of a family. You might not have always known I was a writer (remember when I used to be quiet and shared nothing with you guys?), but once you did, you believed in me fiercely.

To Papa, thank you, for all of our talks and drives, and for always encouraging me in my writing—even when it seemed like I was going nowhere, and even if it *is* just to get an island out of it. To Mama, thank you, for never once doubting that I could achieve this dream, and for indulging me on my amoeba days. I love you muy muy. Thank you both, for being there and for giving me the time, the space, and the love to create without judgment. You two are my favorite love story—and I like to think that's how the storytelling bug bit me in the first place.

To Lia, for guiding me toward books and writing. It all started with me stealing your Greek mythology picture book (which I still have). To Michael, once, you said you would invest in my first gloriously bad book which is not really how it works, but I've appreciated your support ever since. To Luke ("Master Skywalker"), Little Michael, and Sophia, you can't read this right now (Luke, never), but I love you monsters. To Chino, for your unwavering support and kindness, and for always asking how I'm doing. To Joseph, thank you, for knowing just what to say when I need to hear it, especially on my down days. And to Nina, both Mr. Tchaikovsky and daydreamer, you always knew this was going to happen, even when I didn't— thank you, for being there whenever I need you, and for believing in me as much as I believe in you. The heart of every friendship I write about always leads back to you.

There's no better family than Team Angeles (reporting for duty), but I also have to shout-out the Gochans, the Felixes, the Salases, and the Stamoulis—cousins, aunts, uncles, in-laws alike. Also Loli, with whom I'm proud to share a love of reading and stories. To Lolopops, who definitely knew I was writing and not doing homework; and especially to Lola, who listened to the fragments of my first book and inspired me to do everything differently. As a matter of fact, you all inspire me in so many ways. Family is everything to me, and I love you all *so*, so much.

And lastly, thank *you*, dear reader. For picking up this book, for wanting to read it, for reading all of these acknowledgments. I've wanted this more than I've ever wanted anything in my life, and I'm glad I get to be able to share this dream with you. If you've finished the story and ended up here, thank you so much for reading. If you're the same kind of reader as me who looked at these acknowledgments first, you're my kind of person. And I hope you enjoy the show.

Turn the page for a sneak peek at
Janella Angeles's new novel

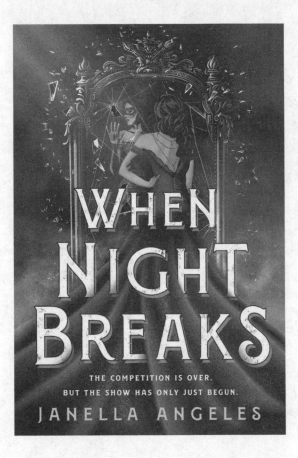

Available Summer 2021

The Dire Woods flashed by Daron's window like a nightmare he knew well. Blurs of black trees and branches jagged as thorns, bumps riddled along their path as though they were driving over scattered bones.

On Daron's first trip out here to reach Glorian, he'd tried not to pay much attention to any of it. His aunt had always warned him and Eva of the woods no one dared enter, and that first carriage ride through it had only been a taste of why. Even in the safe confines of a coach, the atmosphere tugged at him with a shadow weight, seeping through the walls in tendrils of unease.

When Daron had first seen a map of Soltair, he'd thought the Dire Woods were just the black stain of an ink spill. Aunt Cata hardly corrected him. To get lost in a darkness like that meant worse than certain death. It meant something slow, something suffering.

At this point, Daron had driven through these woods so often, he was numb even to the shadows reaching for him through the trees. Their touch had dulled, the woods no more than a horror story. Only one thing drove him back to them every day—the one thing that seemed intent on driving him mad.

Hellfire House was nowhere to be found, as if it didn't want to be. As if it never existed in the first place.

Daron shook the thought away. *No.* He couldn't entertain the idea of it. Their one lead had to lead somewhere.

He stared hard at the words glaring at him across the seat, a bolded headline bracketed between the reader's polished, sharp nails holding the paper out before her.

SPECTACULAR SCANDAL:
A DOOMED DUO, DEMARCO DISGRACED

No one can say for certain what truly happened in Glorian during the last night of Spectaculore. Conflicting stories have cropped up from all over, ranging from one outrageous tale to the next. The facts are few, but the questions remain:
How does a star disappear into thin air?
And how may it relate to a magician's fall from grace—

Daron abruptly turned back toward the window, cleared the harsh knot forming in his throat. "Do you really have to read *that*, right now?"

Lottie's serpentine eyes peeked over the top of the creased issue. "What? I'm reading quietly."

The headline taunted him even louder. "You couldn't have picked a book?"

"On carriage rides as long as yours, one can't help but catch up," she snapped, shaking out her paper in an attempt to smooth out the crinkles. "As much as it pains me to read a word of the *New Crown Post*, it's better to know what the world is reading. What stories they're spreading."

Judging by the stack of papers tucked inside Lottie's emerald briefcase, there were quite a lot of stories already being told.

"How do they even know?" Daron ran a hand down his face. "I

thought you and Erasmus arranged a deal. You've been the only eyes on the ground."

Lottie let out an incredulous snort. "Doesn't mean others will respect it, especially now. I swear, for someone who was once in the thick of show business, you really overestimate the morality of others," she said, almost with disgust. "I might be the only pen here at present, but probably not for long. People talk. Letters find their way to the right and wrong people. Your case is probably close to bursting."

Daron wouldn't know. He hadn't opened it in a while, shoved the damn thing under his bed when the soft telltale clicks of new letters began feeling more like attacks than arrivals. Just like when he'd first stopped performing, the stream of letters kept coming.

Luckily he had no time to wade through correspondences from hungry reporters and inquiring minds.

He trained his gaze back outside, searching through the dark outlines for a glimmer of something. For the flash of a rooftop or hint of a building to make itself known between the trees. He stared, unblinking, as though he could will them into being. It was a miracle he hadn't begun hallucinating from sheer determination.

For a moment, he closed his eyes.

And he saw her in the dark.

You'll be here . . .

The whisper in his ear pulled at him. Her voice, from memory. Or perhaps from the woods.

. . . at the end of this, right?

A restlessness gnawed in the pit of Daron's stomach with the itch to get out of the carriage. Breathe in some fresh air and walk a bit. Hours spent cooped up in the carriage sometimes passed in a blink, or dragged on like a slow death. Yet that was how he spent his days. Every day.

Most times he'd go by himself on horseback, but today was a coach day when Lottie volunteered to accompany him. Thankfully she was able to secure them a ride easily. Like much of Glorian, even the coachmen scowled at Daron each time he approached. But in the end, they took their payment with gruff silence for their service. Coin was coin no matter who gave it.

Not that it mattered much. Daron preferred being ignored. Far better to be alone than in the company of those who despised him.

He squeezed the bridge of his nose hard until he was sure it would bruise. "I'll drop you back off," he said, raising the heel of his palm to the roof. "I don't know why you even came with me this time."

"A long drive is good for the mind every now and then." Lottie gave a half-hearted shrug at their surroundings. "And I was curious."

Curious. The word she'd always used like a weapon for her own devices sounded strange just now. It bore an odd quiet between them. Even though Daron enjoyed the quiet, Lottie's silence was loud. Piercing.

"You're not going to find her out here."

Her voice came out small, but the wind rustling the trees outside stopped.

Daron's fist paused. Clenched.

You'll be here . . .

His heart strained. The whisper, the pain, lingered before he shoved it out of mind, his eyes steeling over as he repeated, "I'll drop you off."

"Come on, Daron." Lottie set the newspaper aside, crossing her arms as she leaned back. "You know this is a dead end. You've combed these woods for days and—"

"Sorry if it's not more exciting work. You're more than welcome to stay back with the others." Daron held back a scoff of a laugh. It came as no surprise, how easily they'd fractured not too long after they'd banded together. The first to drop from the group was Canary, who had all but screamed in Daron's face for she had no patience for hours-long rides through the endless cursed woods. No patience for him either, which Daron suspected was the root of it. The fire-eater had never much liked him when they'd begun working together, whereas Aaros at least somewhat tolerated him. Out of sheer necessity, they'd joined together, but they lasted about the length of time it took for a dinner candle to burn down to the nub. Aaros carried on his own work in the city, and Canary decided to go her own way when this was all they had: a nightclub in the cursed woods that had vanished.

If it had even existed.

"If you haven't found anything by this point, then you must move on," Lottie pressed. "You can't hope to go anywhere if you're just going in circles."

"These woods aren't normal." Daron's nostrils flared. "They're known to lie and play tricks on those who enter without safeguards." It was only a matter of time before they happened upon it. He clasped his hands tightly over his knees. "You're the one who suggested it. You of all people should have an interest in seeing this one through."

"And I know when to step back once a lead loses fire," she said. "It was an interesting lead, but it's led nowhere. We're just riding the same old path at this point."

Daron wanted nothing more than to escape this coach, but he knew his odds of walking on foot in the Dire Woods. "If that's what you think."

"I could *shake* you, I swear," Lottie huffed, clenching her fists tightly. A feat, considering the length of her nails. "When will you realize you don't have to do this alone, and that I'm on your side? We're all on your side—the *same* side."

A snort of a breath erupted from him as he gestured at the empty space around them. "Quite a team we have on our side," he said before crossing his arms. "Why are you even here?"

His voice sounded like venom to his ears. It was the ice, seizing him from the inside. Any time he felt even the slightest crack, it drew out the cold in him. In his blood, in his voice. Ice was the only thing keeping him from breaking entirely, holding him together. And no one brought it out in him more than Lottie.

He still hadn't forgotten what she'd done, all those years ago. It was as if his body were primed for attack, in waiting in case she did it all over again. The Poison of the Press, living up to her name. Spinning the story to sell her papers. Miraculously she'd stayed her pen against him for this long, but he couldn't trust in that forever.

"Despite what you think, I do have a heart." Lottie sighed. "And I know what yours is going through. *Again.*"

Daron braced himself against the seat, unable to look at her. Unable to escape any of this.

"I went through it, too. And you don't have to be alone for it this time," she continued. "Eva wouldn't have wanted—"

"*Don't.*" Daron's heart stilled for a hard moment.

The ice returned, the shadows overtaking him.

Even with every bump and jerk of the carriage, they were still. Lottie, a damn near statue. "We have to talk about her sometime," she snapped. "It's been long enough. You can't avoid it forever."

Eva. Even if they hadn't spoken about her, his sister remained between them in every room, every conversation. A whisper, a ghost. Lottie had made her one to the world years ago when her story had gone to press, even though they'd once been friends. She'd covered the tragic accident of his stage assistant as she would any news hot enough to sell to a crowd. Eva was gone, and a glamorous stage tragedy filled her shoes instead.

"Is that why you're here, why you've hung around all this time?" he asked stiffly. "To finally corner me? Get some new angle?"

"You've got to be joking," she countered, so cold that the ice in him faltered. "Is this your new front—you can't bear to confront what's wrong now so you keep digging up the past?"

"It's no front, it's the truth," he spat out. "I don't trust you."

He must've been out of his mind to think this time would be any different. From the moment she'd stepped into Glorian and spotted him, she'd been hungry for blood. No one changed hearts that quickly.

There was so much in her heavy glare, the twist of her mouth. All of which diffused under a humorless laugh. "You just *love* making me out to be the bad guy, don't you? It's so easy," she drawled out, "when really, you think *you're* any better? You're not. And I'm done hiding it."

"Excuse me?"

The passing shadows of the trees outside flickered over her face, but her eyes remained lit. Livid. "I've tried patience with you, especially now. But if you're determined to just sit in coaches for hours and days, thinking *that's* the best course of action for all of this, then let me at least give you something entertaining to listen to. It might finally wake you up," Lottie said, nostrils flaring. "I've covered your ass from social ruin long enough, Demarco. Had my suspicions even longer. And not once did I air them out, because Eva hadn't done so herself." The corner of her lip turned slightly down in disgust. "Clearly in protection of you."

"What the hell are you talking about?" The way she spoke Eva's name was no longer gentle or hesitant. It was as though she were wielding a sword, a lit match held over a trail of oil. Daron couldn't even summon a hint of anger when confusion drowned out even his temper. "All of my secrets *have* been aired out."

In front of an audience, in glimmers scattered in the newspapers across Soltair. For how outlandish the stories may be, they got one thing right.

Daron was a fraud with no power to his name. Not true magic, at least. Once it had flowed through him before, he was certain. But what was a magician if his powers had abandoned him? For years, he'd felt nothing stir in his blood, until he came to Glorian.

If he wanted to hide, he'd be long gone from Glorian by now.

"*Not* all of them," Lottie corrected sharply. "The world is calling you powerless. But that's not all, is it?"

"Enlighten me, then," Daron seethed, stopping cold in an instant. A flash of Kallia's face before she vanished returned to memory: the pain, creasing over her features as she fell against the floor drenched in mirror shards.

While he rose, power bottled in the palm of his hand.

On his rides through the Dire Woods, and all the sleepless nights before, he'd replayed those last moments a million times in his head. Again and again, like a melody that wouldn't leave. Not until he knew every note, every sound, every piece of the music.

And his part in making it.

"I . . . I thought it had to be Glorian." Eva had always talked about it, had wondered endlessly. The city lost in the cursed woods. Something wasn't right about it, or any of its alleged mysteries, that much they all knew without a doubt.

"You thought." She raised a dubious brow. "Ever thought there could be something more to it?"

Daron touched his temple and closed his eyes, begging his thoughts to quiet. They were spinning up a storm, raking their claws against his skull. Within his chest.

Guilt. It speared through him like lightning, every time he saw Kallia's face in the back of his mind, remembered her last word. Her last look.

He knew he hadn't felt the same since he arrived in Glorian. Since he'd met—

He couldn't even say her name out loud; it tangled in his breath. Even more so, when a bitter laugh sounded across from him.

"This began *long* before you came to this city, before any of this. No surprise you're only taking notice now—those in the spotlight hardly see what's actually around them," Lottie muttered on a shrug. "You really think, as the Daring Demarco, you were running the show?"

"Of course not," he bit out. "Eva and I always worked—"

"Together? Is that why you're here, and she's not?"

Cold blood thundered in his ears until they were ringing. Endlessly.

It ripped away the numbness, the deadness, like a curtain being drawn back. He didn't know what exactly she was implying, and yet he did. Deep down, he'd known something was wrong.

Every time he took final bows at his past shows, he grabbed Eva's hand so she could join him. And her fingers trembled. *Always* trembled in his hold.

The shadows under Kallia's eyes—he'd seen shadows like that before. Seen similar exhaustion such as that, after every performance.

Only to feel none himself.

Your magic, and mine . . .

Kallia's last words to him. Her last look, broken and confused. He hadn't understood what they'd meant, how they connected.

All this time, it had been so clear.

"I didn't . . ." Daron couldn't move. Couldn't breathe. "I didn't know—"

That wasn't how the world worked. Magic couldn't just abandon the magician and latch onto another, prey on another.

"No, you didn't. Eva never even told me outright, but I'm good at surmising. She showed up at my apartment late one night, practically halfway to death, while you were off at a post-performance party with your fellow gents." Lottie scoffed. "She didn't *want* you to know, didn't want your name tarnished because that's just who she is. But the clues were all there, as they all are now. You just weren't looking close enough. No one ever does."

The ringing in Daron's head intensified. With each knife of a word, she sliced truth at him until the picture she painted was all he could see. Until the details of every memory of performing with Eva finally fit into place.

Those moments of irritation. Those days she did not wish to practice with him, feigning all the excuses of brutal hangovers or nights of insomnia catching up to her.

That last performance night, she had not smiled. Not until she hit the stage, where it was easier to smile when you were also wearing a mask.

Somehow, time had passed, and his mind had parted with these moments. As if grief only wanted to hold onto the good, the happy, and never anything else.

"Don't worry, Demarco, I'm not a complete bitch. I have no plans to add more fuel to the fire you're already in," Lottie said, inspecting her fingernails. "Lucky for you, however powerful gossip is, it never lasts. You'll be fine not being Soltair's golden boy for the time being. You'll survive people hating you, losing whatever Patron privilege came with your name for a time before everyone forgets—"

"Do you think *any* of that matters to me?" Daron didn't realize how his voice had raised until it seemed even the winds outside had fallen still.

So still.

Like time had stopped, along with the world.

Daron stared hard at his palms. Nausea roiled in his stomach like acid, threatening to spill. Shame, burning inside him as he looked at his hands. *These* hands, that had stolen so much. Careless. Thoughtless.

And he'd known. Deep down, he'd felt something was wrong. Why else hide away from the world, from his aunt, in the years that he'd become nothing?

Not nothing. There had always been something sinister, lingering beneath his palms.

He just couldn't bear to face it.

Daron suddenly wanted out of the carriage. He didn't care what the woods would bring him when his feet touched the earth; he needed to stop. To breathe. To scream so loud, the Dire Woods would bend.

"Why?" he whispered, shakily. "You knew . . . why say nothing, all this time?"

Not to the world. Not even to Aaros and Canary, in the brief times they'd met. Not even to hold over his head as a threat for his years of silence. It made no sense, when there had always been that fury so clear in her eyes. Clear even now, beneath the strangest shadow of calm.

"I couldn't be sure until I met Kallia, but she wouldn't have believed me. Nothing I said could change her opinion of you. Or keep her away, for that matter," she said. "But aside from that, what good would that do to hang you out to dry?"

He felt fairly wrung dry already. "You could've turned me in to the Patrons, gotten your answers."

A snort of a laugh. "What answers? I've been shouting about magician disappearances for years and it's gotten me nowhere. The *one* time I covered one as a death, they actually cared enough to show up to the 'funeral,'" she said in stiff quotation marks. "Now that the papers are all churning out the strangest shit I've ever seen, maybe they'll finally take notice. Though I'd rather see this to the end ourselves while we have another shot."

Daron's brow creased. "Another shot?"

Lottie's thumb twitched, as if itching for a pen that was no longer there. "To do things differently." At that, her gaze locked on him. "Searching in our own corners before did not bring us any closer to anything. And now—"

There was nothing more out of character for Lottie than to stop her words and filter them. Somehow, Daron already knew without needing to hear, and his heart raced at the possibility. "You think Eva's still out there, too?"

She and Kallia had both vanished through mirrors, so reason stood that they might've landed somewhere similar.

Lottie didn't appear nearly as hopeful at the prospect. Blinking rapidly, she said, "I don't know. We can't assume. We have to be mindful of time in the case of a missing person. For Kallia, it's been a couple weeks. For Eva . . ."

Years.

Of nothing, of silence.

The stretch of time weighed heavily, as though each day brought them farther apart when they were already far enough.

"The good news is, we *do* have a recent lead with Kallia that is strong. So let's take it and focus there." Lottie nodded firmly. "It might bring us more answers, it might not. We need to be prepared for any ending, even if neither of us are ready for it. We just need to try."

"With what?" Daron shook his head. "Without that club, there's nothing else."

It was what led him to the woods for hours every day, away from the city that glared at him from every corner and street. Circling the same old trees and the same old shadows, hoping to find something different in them.

"Just because Hellfire House was a dead end doesn't mean there's nothing. Impossible, with a story as juicy as this. And we can start figuring it out by going back," she said, clearly fighting back a smile behind pursed lips as she pounded at the ceiling above. "And getting out of this—"

Daron almost flew out of his seat as their carriage slammed to a stop. Lottie cursed when she buckled forward, the piles of papers sliding to the floor after her.

"What the hell," Lottie growled, gripping the velvet seat to push herself back up, "was *that*?"

Absently, Daron helped her up by the elbow, his head still ringing from the sudden jerk. No more rocky movement or shadows passing over their faces.

Stillness.

And distant shouting, outside their window. From the hoarse cursing, their coachman was not pleased with whoever they crossed paths with.

Odd. He'd never encountered other travelers in the woods on any of his rides before. Besides himself, no one ever dared to.

Daron opened the carriage door, shaky on his feet as he leaned out slightly. "Is everything all right?"

The hulking coachman whipped his head around with a grunt. "Ask the white gloves. The little bloody caravan won't get out of my way until I tell them what my business was out here."

White gloves.

Daron's gut twisted. "What did you tell them?"

"The truth," he spat. "I'm just the reins, minding my own business and driving some sad fool through these horrid woods day after day because I guess that's what folks with coin to waste do."

Lottie's soft snicker sounded from within the carriage. Half of Daron wanted to throw them both out, and the other half—the dominant one—had turned ice cold.

White gloves.

Daron's pulse leaped as he stepped out of the carriage. He didn't know why or what possessed him. Hardly heard Lottie's shrill protests behind him, dulled the moment his foot touched the ground.

The Dire Woods.

Never walk through it. That's what he'd always been taught, though he didn't see the harm in walking a few paces to the glossy white coach standing right in their path.

Those shadows that had been pressing at him through the windows, their tendrils reached for him now.

Your magic, and mine . . .

He swallowed hard at the echo of Kallia's voice, surrounding him in the wind slicing through the trees.

For a moment, he thought he imagined her sitting atop one of the branches, peering at him like how a bird peers at a worm in the ground.

For a moment, he thought he imagined the person stepping out of one of the three compact white carriages gathered before him.

He stilled his next step, waiting for whatever terrible magic permeated the air to loosen its grip on him. These woods were strange, and deadly. They played games on those who entered on foot, showed one what wasn't truly there.

She came out white-gloved, palms out, ready to engage in a fight if prompted—before they dropped, as if unsure as well.

Even from afar, he took in each detail. Her hair was as dark as his, swirling with silver, wrapped in an unforgiving bun that sat atop her head. Her angular spectacles framed sharply over slitted, observant eyes, just as he remembered. Flaring, now, with disbelief. "Daron?"

Blood thundered in his ears at the sound of her voice. It had been so long since he'd heard it. "Aunt Cata."

Mei Lin Barral

JANELLA ANGELES is the Filipino American bestselling author of *Where Dreams Descend*. She got her start in writing through consuming glorious amounts of fan fiction at a young age—which eventually led to creating original stories of her own. She currently resides in Massachusetts where she works in the business of publishing books on top of writing them, and is most likely to be found listening to musicals on repeat while daydreaming too much for her own good.